Before You

Before You

Kathryn Freeman

Where heroes are like chocolate – irresistible!

Published 2017 by Choc Lit Limited
Penrose House, Crawley Drive, Camberley, Surrey GU15 2AB, UK
www.choc-lit.com

A CIP catalogue record for this book is available
from the British Library

ISBN 978-1-78189-393-7

Printed and bound by Clays Ltd

To my very own motorsport fans – my husband and sons.

*And to my mum, who isn't a fan of motorsport,
but is my biggest fan.*

Acknowledgements

To friends and family who continue to support me, who send me encouraging messages, put up with me banging on and on about the next book – thank you. Without you, I wouldn't have got this far.

In particular thanks to: Mum and Dad 2, David, Jayne, Laura B, Auntie Audrey Auntie Shirley, Uncle Harold, Uncle Bob, Kim, Shelley, Kath, Karley, Kirsty, Hayley, Charlotte, Sonia, Gill, Neve, Jane, Emma, Tara, Anissa, Bee, Janet, Sue, Phil, Kaye, Mr H, Priti, Sheyline, Laura, Michele, Cherylee, Yonca, Helen and Fiona.

A huge thank you to my editor, who is a dream to work with. Her clever suggestions have ensured this book is far better now than when I first wrote it.

To all my fellow authors, both in Choc Lit and outside, thank you for your kindness.

Book bloggers are amazing people. Their enthusiasm for reading and their support of writers is humbling. Thank you for taking the time to help this author.

Finally, a huge thank you to my publisher, Choc Lit and their Tasting Panel (particularly Heidi, Karen M, Catherine L, Linda Sp., Sigi, Julie T., Isabel, Lizzy D., Cindy, Alison B. and Zeynep who said 'yes' to the manuscript) for believing in this book, and in me.

Chapter One

Aiden sucked in a deep breath, plastered the required smile onto his face and strode into the press room. Flashes went off as he took his seat, all eyes in the packed room aimed his way, but his smile didn't waver. He knew racing drivers were no longer simply men who drove fast around a track. They were a commodity, a brand with an image that had to be maintained, no matter how they were feeling inside.

Today the press assembled in the Delta HQ wanted to meet Aiden Foster, the new Delta driver. So that's what he'd give them.

'So, Aiden, the start of a new racing season. Is this the year you're finally going to follow in your father's footsteps and win a World Championship?'

'I wondered when that question was going to rear its head.' He glanced down at the sleek, expensive watch on his wrist. 'Hey, and its only two minutes into the press conference. Must be a record.'

There was collective laughter. 'Come on, you can't blame us for making the comparisons,' the journo protested. 'It's not often a son follows his father into the world of motor racing. Especially when that father was such a legend in the sport.'

'My father was a brilliant driver,' Aiden agreed amiably. 'The day he died was a sad one for the sport. However, I'm not my father.'

'Well, no, by my reckoning by the time he was your age he'd already won three of his five world championships.'

The jibe hit its target and Aiden imperceptibly flinched though his lips remained fixed in a polite smile. 'Actually,

I was thinking more along the lines of me being taller and better looking than him, but hey, you've got a point, too.'

Again there was laughter; all part of the game he played with the press. He was the laid-back playboy; the joker and charmer. It was what the public wanted him to be. What *he* wanted to be. And some days he was. It's just some days he was also a screw up.

'Does it feel strange, racing for the same team as your father?'

Strange? It's bloody terrifying, he wanted to shout, but of course that didn't fit his image. 'Strange isn't the right word. I feel honoured to be racing for the team that brought my father such immense success. If I can emulate just a fifth of that success, I'll be very happy.' One World Championship. It was all he asked.

'Any regrets about your move from Arrows to Delta?'

Grateful for the shift in focus away from his father, he flashed the reporter a more genuine smile. 'Delta are a fantastic team to work for. I loved my time at Arrows, but now I have the chance to race in *the* fastest car in motorsport, so no. No regrets.' He rested back on his seat and gave the room a glimpse of the devilish grin he was famous for. 'But be sure to ask me again at the end of the season.'

'Is that before or after you lift the World Championship trophy?'

He turned to the female voice asking the question. Cute, blonde and with a glitter in her eye that suggested she might be hitting on him. 'Better ask me before. Leave it till after and I'll be too drunk on champagne to be coherent.'

'Is that a promise then, Aiden?' asked the balding man to her left. 'You're actually going to win this year?'

Aiden resisted the impulse to roll his eyes. As if there were any guarantees in this game. Even if he was in the fastest car, driving the fastest lap, he could still end up mangled against the wall. Like his father.

'The only promise I can make is that I'll be trying my hardest. I've got the backing of a great team and I'll be driving the best car. With a few dollops of luck, this could be my year.'

He smiled again, hoping it came across as gracious and confident though inside his gut squirmed like a bag of snakes. This *had* to be his year. He'd been racing in this, the highest level of motorsport, for six years now and had yet to secure a title. Joining Delta wasn't only the best chance he'd ever get to win the championship, it would likely be his last. At twenty-eight he wasn't a veteran – but he wasn't going to get any better. This was the year he could finally put the past behind him. Stop people talking about Aiden Foster, son of Sebastian Foster, former five times World Champion, and get them talking instead about Aiden Foster, current World Champion.

Shit, just the thought sent shivers up his spine.

The conference wrapped up and as Aiden stepped away from the microphones he found himself face to face with the cute blonde.

'Hi. I just wanted to introduce myself.' She stuck out a slim, well-manicured hand. 'I'm Devon, from *Just for Ladies*.'

Laughing, he shook the offered hand. 'Sorry, that's not a publication I've heard of.'

She giggled coyly, capturing her bottom lip with her teeth; a flash of white against the vivid pink of her lipstick. 'No, I don't suppose you have. We're a woman's magazine, targeted towards the yummy mummy set. We don't usually follow racing but I've been asked to write an article on glamour, sex and the world of motorsport and … well …' she licked her dewy lips '… I thought maybe I could start with you?'

He smiled, wondering again whether she was coming on to him. For some reason – the money, the danger? – women were attracted to racing car drivers. It was a side benefit he'd enjoyed over the years, though lately he found himself becoming … he hardly dared admit it, but a bit *bored* by the whole thing. Mind you, Devon did have an ID badge around her neck, so perhaps there really was an article and it wasn't her letting him know she wanted to have sex with him.

'Where, exactly, were you thinking we might … err, *start*?' he asked with a smile.

She lowered her lashes a fraction. 'Maybe we could set up a time when you're less busy? I'm happy to interview you at home, if you'd prefer. You know, somewhere more relaxing. More private.'

Aiden did know. And though sex delivered on a plate, no matter how attractively dished up, was starting to lose its appeal, she *was* cute. 'Have you got a pen?'

Quick as a flash he was offered a sparkly pink biro.

Feeling faintly ridiculous, he scrawled his mobile number across her ID badge. 'Give me a call and we'll sort something out.'

With a broad smile and a coquettish little wave, she thanked him and left the room, swinging her hips in a way he couldn't help but notice.

'Don't tell me. She works for some mindless women's mag and she wants to interview you somewhere private.'

Aiden turned to find Melanie Hunt, one of the Delta press officers, giving him one of her looks. Since joining Delta a month ago he'd learnt that Melanie could convey a world of messages through just one glare from her pretty hazel eyes. Today's message was *did you really just give that woman your phone number*?

He grinned, ignoring the mixture of disgust and incredulity that spread across her pleasantly attractive face. She was more girl-next-door than beach babe, though both had their merits. 'I thought you were all about me raising my profile, making sure everyone knows which team I'm on now?'

'As long as your *profile* is the only thing you'll be raising when she lures you into her satin pink boudoir.'

A laugh erupted out of him. With her casual, no nonsense clothes, make-up free face and wickedly sharp sense of humour, Melanie was a long way removed from the highly polished, pushy, ultra confident press officers he was used to. Thank the Lord.

She gave him a brief smile, her dimpled cheeks magnifying the wholesome, fresh-faced, farmer's daughter image. Then her attention dropped to her phone – the essential press officer's equipment. She had that in common with the others, at least.

'So tell me,' she asked eventually, having finished whatever vital phone business she'd been conducting. 'What insightful, thought-provoking article is your bunny boiler planning on writing?'

'What makes you think she's a bunny boiler?'

'What makes *you* think she isn't?'

He shrugged. 'Maybe I like my women a bit crazy.'

'Maybe you just like women,' Melanie murmured. 'So, the title of the piece?'

Aiden tried to stifle a smile. 'Sex in motorsport. Or something along those lines. I can't quite remember the full title, though I do remember the sex and motorsport bit.'

Mel found her stomach flipping as she watched amusement

flare in Aiden's clear grey eyes. She'd like to bet the bunny boiler had every intention of finding out about the subject of sex in motorsport by doing her own personal, in-depth analysis.

'It's good to know women's magazines aren't dumbing down the sport, or their readers, in any way.'

He quirked an eyebrow. 'Touchy.'

Realising he was right, she sighed. 'A little, sorry. But sometimes ... doesn't it piss you off, the assumption that you're stupid enough to fall for every pneumatic bosomed, bleached blonde with laser enhanced white teeth that pouts in your direction?'

'Err ...'

'And that the sport seems to think the only place for women is smiling emptily behind the sponsor's logo, dressed in a skimpy skirt and low plunging top?'

'Personally I don't have any objections to women wearing a skimpy skirt and low plunging top.'

His flashing grin told her he was teasing. At least she thought he was, though she found Aiden pretty hard to read.

'Sorry, you've caught me on a bad day. I usually try to keep off the soapbox during daylight hours. So, this cutting edge interview that's going to get to the very heart of motor racing. Do you *want* to do it?'

'You mean do I want to have sex with a cute blonde in a pink boudoir? Or do I want to get embroiled in a fight to the death with a bunny boiler?'

A laugh bubbled out of her. Aiden in full flow, like he had been earlier in front of the press, was sharp and funny. 'I mean, do you want to give up a few hours of your valuable time to help produce an article that bored housewives in the southern counties will spill their lattes over?'

He regarded her quizzically. 'I'm getting the sense you don't want me to do it.'

'Put it this way, there are far better, more serious, professional platforms we can, and will, use to raise your profile in Delta. So the only reason for you to do this article ...'

'Is if I fancy the sometime bunny boiler.'

'And even then, I'm pretty sure you can get what you want out of the meeting, without actually having to open your mouth.'

Once again he chuckled and, just as she had earlier, Mel found she daren't look at him. If she did her tongue might hang out and she'd lose any professional respect she might have earned in the month since he'd joined Delta. But because she was still a woman first, and a press officer second, she allowed her eyes to briefly rest on the grooves at the side of his wide, laughing mouth. To flicker over the straight white teeth and up to his brilliant silver grey eyes. Then she forced her attention back to her phone.

'Actually,' he said as she pretended to check her messages, 'I think you'll find that in order to get the absolute most out of any such meeting, I really do need to open my mouth.'

Shocked, she snapped her head up and nearly drowned in his glittering, highly amused eyes. 'Point taken.' She coughed to ease her suddenly tight throat. 'I've got a schedule of far more suitable opportunities I could do with running by you when you've got a free moment.'

'Sure, I'm happy to meet up, though I'm not really fussed who I talk to.'

She noticed his attention drift away from her then and onto that of his teammate, Stefano, who'd just entered the room. Mumbling something about duty calling, Aiden gave her a quick smile of apology and strode over to join him.

Mel couldn't help but watch his retreating back. A tall, lean figure dressed in jeans and a dark navy jacket, dark hair curling slightly over his jacket collar. He had an easy stride, one that exuded authority and self-confidence. His whole body language screamed yes, he was incredibly rich and good-looking. And yes, he was aware that people watched him wherever he went.

'You wouldn't be admiring our new driver's backside, would you?'

She swung round to find Frank, race engineer for Aiden, grinning at her.

'A woman's got to get her kicks where she can find them.'

He shook his head in mock disapproval, though she couldn't mistake the hint of seriousness in his next words. 'I advise caution with that one.'

'Do you really think you need to tell me that?' Mel looked askance at the man who'd become a surrogate father to her since she'd joined the Delta team six years ago. 'I mean, apart from the very obvious fact that he wouldn't look twice at me, anyway.'

Frank furrowed his brow, deepening the lines that fifty-five years of living had already put there. 'Why not? You're very nicely put together.'

A sound very much like a snort fled her mouth and Mel glanced down at her sensible flat loafers, comfortable chino trousers and efficient cotton blouse complete with Delta team logo. 'That's exactly what someone like Aiden is looking for in a woman, isn't it? Someone *nicely put together*? Not a blonde bombshell, or a sexy hot bird?'

A slight flush crept over Frank's weathered face. 'There are some men who don't like the obvious. Who appreciate the more natural.'

Realising she'd embarrassed him, Mel threaded an arm

through his and gave it a quick squeeze. 'Then that's the type of man I'll need to find. And it clearly isn't Aiden Foster.'

Together they walked past the slick reception area of the Delta HQ, buried deep inside the Surrey countryside, and out into the sunlight.

'Out of interest, why the warning about Aiden? Are you two not getting on?'

Frank halted, his eyes squinting slightly. 'I wouldn't put it as strongly as that. Obviously it's early days and we're still tiptoeing round each other.'

She sensed the race engineer's hesitation. 'But?'

Chuckling, he ran a hand over his thinning grey hair. 'Okay, yes, there is a but. He has all the right attributes for a brilliant driver; great reflexes, mentally quick, physically strong and in fantastic shape. Plus he has an understanding of the aerodynamics and engine capabilities that, frankly, sometimes puts mine to shame. But,' he added, smiling at the emphasis, 'he's, I don't know, I think *tense* is the word for it. Sure he can act cool and laid-back in front of the cameras, but when he's in the garage or on the track ...'

'He turns into a wrench throwing monster?'

'No, not that bad, though he doesn't mind shouting to put his point across. A keen desire to win is a fundamental attribute for any driver, but it's almost as though he wants it too much.'

'Maybe he's just finding his feet. He'll calm down once he feels more settled.'

'I'm not sure that's the answer. I really don't think being calm is what he needs. When he's behind the wheel, I actually think he needs to let go more.'

'I guess watching your father die after slamming into a wall makes it hard to do that.'

Frank turned to look at her, his sharp blue eyes missing nothing. 'Something tells me you're no longer thinking about Sebastian Foster's crash any more.'

Mel smiled sadly. 'You're right. I'm thinking about Mum and Dad's. At least I didn't have to watch them die.'

Frank took her hand in his large, reassuring one. 'Come on, sweetie. How about I give you a lift home? Or even better, why not come and have dinner with us? It would make Nancy's day. Plus it might put me back in her good books. I've been late home the last few nights. If we'd had a dog, he'd be three pounds heavier now.'

Mel giggled, grateful for the turn of conversation. 'So, let me get this right. I help smooth out the relationship between you and your wife *and* I get a delicious meal. How can I say no?'

Chapter Two

Aiden stared regretfully at Devon. It had been a while since he'd been stupid enough to let his libido rule his head but after the press conference he'd felt out of sorts, thanks to all that talk about his father. Not wanting to spend yet another evening at home with his own thoughts he'd accepted the dimpled blonde's invitation.

This morning he regretted it. Devon was talking about meeting up again, when all he wanted to do was push her out and get on with his day. He had a plane to catch. The first race of the season was just over a week away, in Melbourne, and he really, really needed to get his head into the right place.

'Look, Devon, we've been through this. What we had last night was great sex. Please don't start thinking it was anything more.'

'But you enjoyed it, didn't you?'

Her lips came together in what he guessed was meant to be a sexy pout, though to be honest she reminded him a little of a hungry goldfish.

'Of course I did, but I enjoy lots of things, like white water rafting and surfing. It doesn't mean I want to do them every day.'

He tried to soften his words by kissing her on the cheek but she lurched away from him, her eyes flashing with temper. Thankfully whatever outburst she was about to have was curtailed by the sound of his intercom.

With a shrug of apology, he went to answer it. 'Hello?'

'Aiden, it's Melanie. We have an eleven o'clock?'

Bugger. He'd totally forgotten. 'Sure, come right up.' At least now he had an excuse to get rid of Devon.

He turned to find the blonde putting on her strappy stilettoes with tight, jerky movements. 'Devon, I'm sorry, but I've got a meeting with the Delta press officer now, so I need you to go.'

'And that's it, is it?' she asked, standing so she could glare at him eyeball to eyeball. 'I was just a cheap shag?'

The remark was so close to the bone, Aiden winced. She had a right to be angry with him. Sure he'd made no promises, but a woman was entitled to think a man who took her to bed was at least interested enough to see her again.

Clasping her hand in his, he twined his fingers around hers. 'No, you weren't a cheap shag. You were a beautiful way to spend an evening. If you get to one of the races, maybe I can buy you a drink.'

'I'll be in Melbourne,' she admitted.

'Your magazine is sending you all the way to Australia?' he asked in disbelief, certain she was winding him up. 'There'll be plenty of other races far closer to home.'

'I know, but we're running a series of articles on young Australian fashion designers so I'm mainly going for that.' She looked up at him hopefully, smiling as if he'd just promised her a dream holiday instead of the shallow offer of a drink. 'So, can we meet up?'

He felt a rush of shame. This was the absolute last time he was sleeping with a woman he had no intention of seeing again. 'Look, I'm going to be a bit busy, it being the first race of the season. I can't make any promises.'

A sharp knock on his door indicated the press officer's arrival and, with great relief, Aiden went to let her in.

'Hi, sorry I'm a bit late, the traffic getting into London was hellish and ...' Melanie trailed off as she caught sight of Devon. 'It looks like my being late was a blessing in disguise.'

12

Awkwardly Aiden made the introductions. 'Devon writes for the *Ladies Only* magazine—'

'*Just for Ladies*,' Devon interjected, rolling her eyes at him.

Melanie gave the blonde a guarded smile. 'Hello, I'm Melanie, one of the Delta press officers. I take it you've just interviewed Aiden for a piece in your magazine?'

As the women shook hands, Aiden squirmed silently, wondering what the heck Melanie was up to. She knew damn well Devon hadn't spent the night interviewing him.

Devon let out a flustered sounding laugh. 'To be honest, we haven't got round to the interview yet.'

'But we'll try and catch up in Melbourne,' Aiden finished firmly, desperate to take control before the whole fiasco blew up in his face. 'Thanks for coming by Devon.' He gave her a chaste kiss on the cheek. 'I'll see you around.'

Ignoring her miffed expression, he all but pushed her out of the door.

Behind him, Melanie coughed. 'I take it you got what you wanted out of that particular interview?'

He turned to find her staring at him, pretty hazel eyes filled with an emotion that looked a lot like disappointment. As he wasn't particularly pleased with his own behaviour, he really didn't need the sharp edge of her disapproval. 'Yes, thanks,' he replied tersely.

For a second she looked wounded, and instantly he regretted taking his self-disgust out on her. Fixing a smile on his face he motioned over to his large cream sofa. 'Please, take a seat.'

She nodded coolly – he didn't blame her for the attitude – and he studied her as she went to sit down. Again she was wearing a pair of nondescript trousers and utilitarian blouse – he couldn't remember ever seeing her in anything else. If he had to guess he'd say they probably hid a really neat figure, which made it all the more confusing why she chose to downplay her looks. Either she was an absolute sex bomb outside work, or she was … what? Too scared to put herself out there?

'Can I get you something to drink?' He glanced at his watch. 'Eat?'

A small smile hovered around lips that were full and pink but unadorned with lipstick. 'Well, if you're offering, a lightly whipped omelette with salad garnish would go down a treat.'

Relieved she wasn't going to give him a hard time over his shitty behaviour, he relaxed enough to laugh. 'Ah, you have me there. I can boil a kettle to make you a cup of instant coffee, or crack open a pack of chocolate biscuits. The omelette is outside my skillset, I'm afraid, whipped or not.'

She cocked her head to one side and seemed to consider him. 'How about a cup of tea and a chocolate digestive?'

'That, I can manage.'

Mel was relieved when Aiden disappeared into his kitchen. It gave her a chance to get her head around what she'd just seen. She thought they'd been joking when they'd talked about him seeing the blonde journalist, so it was one heck of a shock to find he'd done exactly what they'd laughed about – had a meaningless one night stand with a woman who'd come on to him at a press conference. She felt oddly let down. She'd been hoping to find there was more to the man than the flip persona he presented to the press.

Sighing at her foolishness, she placed her bag on the floor by her feet and sank back into the expensive leather sofa. It was hard for women not to like Aiden Foster. Even she – used to being around racing drivers so much she was supposedly unfazed by them – had to admit when it came to Aiden, she was no different to the rest. How could she be when the man had film star looks, charisma, a dry, playful, sense of humour and a swagger just the right side of arrogant?

So, yes, like millions of women round the globe she, too, had a crush on him. It was the reason she was now sitting here feeling so desperately disappointed. Aiden Foster was exactly the playboy the media purported him to be.

'One cup of tea.' He sauntered back in and planted a snazzy black and white mug directly onto the glass coffee table. 'Plus biscuits.' With a flourish he produced a white china plate containing several chocolate biscuits of various types, all neatly laid out.

He went to sit on the opposite sofa, casually crossing one barefooted, jean clad leg over the other and Mel found she couldn't stop looking at his feet. Long and narrow, they were actually pretty sexy ...

'So, you're here to discuss my image, huh?'

She dragged her gaze from his feet, past his slightly crumpled white shirt and up to his face with its flashing cheekbones and mesmerising grey eyes. It certainly was quite an image. Taking a gulp of tea she pushed her brain out of fan mode and into professional press officer. 'It's not your image I wanted to talk about. Delta have no issue with it and it would seem you have no problem living up to it,' she couldn't resist adding.

There was a subtle stiffening in his body language. 'I presume that's a veiled reference to finding Devon here when you arrived?'

'It was and you're right to glare at me. It's none of my business.'

'True, so why do I get the feeling you're annoyed with me?'

'I'm not annoyed,' she corrected him. 'Not really. I guess, I just … I know it sounds silly, but I was hoping you'd be one of the good guys. A racing driver who's more than just a walking penis.'

His sharp, startled laugh filled the quiet room. 'Did you really just say penis?'

'Why, should I have used another word instead?'

'No, please. Penis is fine.' He laughed again, softer this time. 'Now there's a sentence I never thought I'd say. So, tell me, is that all you think I am? A man who likes to drive fast cars and have sex?'

'I'm sure there are a lot more strings to your bow. I mean, you made me a cup of tea, so there's one, for a start.'

'And now you're just trying to avoid the question.'

He was right, and though she spent a lot of her working life advising people how to skate round a difficult question, it didn't seem fair to avoid this one. Not when she'd been the one to bring it up.

'Truthfully, I don't know you, so I can't comment, but I think that's part of the problem. You don't allow anyone to know you, so we're left to speculate. Draw obvious conclusions from what we *can* see, like the fact that we rarely see you with the same woman twice. You're very good at giving interviews, always smooth and charming, but your answers don't actually say anything about *you*. The man behind the sexy driver.'

'So now I've got a penis and I'm sexy,' he drawled. 'It's getting better.'

She began to laugh, but halted when she realised what he was doing. 'That's exactly what I'm talking about. Once again you cleverly tried to divert the conversation with a quip, a line. Anything that means you don't have to talk about you.'

'Maybe that's the way I prefer it.'

'Which is fine, but unfortunately that attitude doesn't help when you're working with the media. If they're left with a lot of gaps, they tend to fill them in their own way. Hence my comment about the walking penis. It might sound like a joke, but that's how some of the press refer to you. From what I've seen from archived interviews, your father had a very different style. He tended to wear his heart on his sleeve—'

'I'm not my father,' he cut in, his cool grey eyes now glacial. 'Don't compare me to him. Please.'

So she hadn't just imagined it at the last press conference. It seemed he did have a huge chip on his shoulder with his father's name engraved on it.

'I guess you get pretty fed up with people doing that, don't you?' she asked softly.

A muscle twitched in his jaw. 'Yes.'

'Did the pair of you get on?'

His lids lowered over those stunning eyes. 'My father was a risk-taker, a hellraiser and the best driver of his generation. What's not to get on with?'

Frustration coiled in her belly at his obvious fob off but there were times to push and times to stop. This was the latter.

'Okay, have it your way, but you're going to have to get used to a lot of questions about him.'

'You think that's a change from the normal?' He threw her a casual smile though the gesture was ruined by the clenched muscle in his jawline.

'I'm well aware you're used to fielding questions about your father, but now you've joined his old team, the interest in that relationship is only going to escalate. I've been bombarded with interview requests since the announcement was made.'

'You must be really cursing my arrival then, huh?'

An image flashed through her mind of her and Sally, the other press officer, jigging up and down with glee when they'd been told of Aiden's signing. 'Not at all. It actually makes my job easier when people come to me wanting interviews rather than the other way around.' Reaching into her folder, she passed him a sheet of neatly typed paper. 'And that's what I came here to discuss with you. I've drawn up a list of interviews scheduled for the next few months. They'll take place mainly after test sessions or practice sessions. I know it's a bit of a bind—'

'It's fine,' he cut in, not even glancing at the piece of paper.

Because he still appeared tense, she tried to lighten the mood. 'I can't guarantee all the journalists will be hot-looking blondes, but I'll do my best.'

Instantly he was on his feet, swiping a hand through his hair. It sprang back, making him look rumpled and more sexy than she wanted him to be. 'Look, Devon was a mistake, I admit it. Despite what you're thinking, I don't make a habit of hooking up with women in that way.' His chest rose and fell as he sighed. 'At least I don't any more.'

She sensed the anger was directed at himself rather than her but still, annoying their star driver wasn't going to help her do her job. 'I'm sure you don't make a habit of it,' she placated. 'Even if you did, as I've already said, it really is none of my business so please, just ignore me. You'd be amazed how many people find that's pretty easy to do.'

Melanie gave him a small smile and Aiden calmed down enough to study her. She did look quiet, like he imagined a librarian might look if he'd ever ventured inside such a place. Appearances could be deceptive though, and he had a strong feeling this press officer would be impossible to ignore. She seemed to have a way of seeing past the facade and right into the core of a person. Heck, she'd already worked out he hadn't got on with his father. Nobody else had ever made that connection.

It made him wish even more he hadn't invited Devon over last night. Bad enough disappointing himself, but for some reason he found disappointing his fresh-faced press officer even harder to stomach.

'Anyway, back to the interviews.' Her eyes flitted away from his gaze and down to her notes, allowing Aiden to continue his study. Her hair was a deep chocolate brown with curls that struggled to be contained in the haphazard ponytail she usually shoved it into. What with that and her make-up free face, Aiden reckoned she must have spent all of two minutes getting dressed this morning.

'Your first interview is scheduled to take place after the Malaysian Grand Prix,' she told him, following her statement with an apologetic smile. 'It's with a guy from *Motorsport* magazine who was insistent that he wanted to explore what it was like for you following in your father's footsteps and coming to Delta. Consider yourself duly warned.'

He covered his unease with a wry smile. 'Duly noted.'

She smiled back and he realised he liked making her smile, enjoying the way her brown eyes warmed and her dimples winked. All too quickly her eyes focused back on her notepad. He tried to pretend that he cared as she talked through the rest of her list.

'Well, that's all I have for now.' She closed her notepad and tucked it into her oversized brown handbag.

Small animals, maybe even small children, could

probably live in there quite happily without ever needing to see the light of day.

The thought must have made him grin because she halted in the process of heaving the bag onto her shoulder and eyed him suspiciously. 'What are you smiling at?'

His lips twitched. 'Nothing.'

Her glance turned into a glare. 'It might have been only a month since you joined the team, but I know you, Aiden Foster. You reserve most of your smiles for when you're in front of the cameras, so to be smiling now you must have found something really funny.'

That successfully wiped the smirk off his face. 'What do you mean by that?'

She chewed on her bottom lip. 'You mean the bit about what you found funny, or ...'

'The bit about me being a grumpy git?'

Her cheeks reddened slightly. 'Sorry, I didn't mean to be rude. I have a tendency to speak what's on my mind without filtering it first, which probably isn't an ideal trait for someone in my role.' Her fingers fiddled with the straps of her bag which she still hadn't put on her shoulder. 'It's been an observation of mine that ... well ... maybe Aiden Foster the racing driver and Aiden Foster the man aren't quite the same person.'

He stilled, surprised ... no, more than that, shocked. 'How do they differ?'

She was still finding it hard to meet his eyes. 'Well, I guess Aiden Foster the driver is charming, funny, laid-back and a bit of a womaniser.'

He could live with all of those. 'And the man?'

Shaking her head, she finally looked at him. 'I don't know. He keeps himself very hidden, but I think he's much more serious.'

Her ability to see through him made the hairs on the back of his neck start to prickle. 'So you don't think I can be funny and charming without a camera lens being poked into my face?' He raised his eyes in mock despair. 'And there was me thinking you liked me.'

'I think both of you can be charming, and, yes, even though I'm sure it doesn't matter to you, I do actually like you.'

Having dropped her bombshells she hoisted her bag onto her shoulder and made her way towards the door. For a few seconds he remained rooted to the spot, trying to assimilate everything she'd just said. It was only when her struggles with the door resulted in a muted curse that he was finally knocked out of his trance sufficiently to open it for her.

She gave him the full dose of her pretty eyes. 'Thank you. You know I actually think I'd prefer the real Aiden Foster, if he ever dares to come out and show himself.'

With that she slipped out. He was left staring at her small, retreating figure as it walked towards the lift, his mouth slightly agape, probably resembling a ruddy carp.

At least he hadn't had to tell her he'd been laughing at her handbag, he mused as he finally shut the door. Mind you, considering the psychoanalysis she'd subjected him to instead, that might have been a blessing.

Chapter Three

It wasn't hard to understand why motorsport was often compared to a circus. With so many races in the season a good number of those who worked in the sport, or religiously followed it, spent a considerable amount of time on the road, travelling from circuit to circuit. Like a circus, the motor racing teams also had to transport all their equipment, plus the cars, from venue to venue, which was a logistical headache Mel was only too pleased not to be involved in. Thanks to the team's army of very efficient admin staff, all she had to do was read her itinerary and make sure she was at the airport at the right time. After that she was herded from airport to hotel and then hotel to race circuit. Sometimes it was hard to remember where in the world you were when you woke up in the morning.

But this morning Mel knew exactly which circuit she was at. The sky was a vivid blue and the sun glinted off Albert Park Lake, shimmering like a billion diamonds. Melbourne, one of the most picturesque Grand Prix circuits in the racing calendar.

She turned to Sally, her fellow press officer and very good friend. 'You know there's something pretty special about seeing cars racing against a backdrop of towering skyscrapers and a glittering blue lake.'

Sally raised her eyes heavenwards. 'Anyone would think this was your first trip to Melbourne, rather than your ... what? Fourth?'

Mel laughed and counted on her fingers. 'Heck, I think it's my fifth trip.'

'And still you're like an overly excited three-year-old on her first visit to Santa.'

'Hey, come on you old grump, don't you get that tingle up your spine when you hear the scream of the cars as they streak full throttle down the straight?'

'It's not much of a scream these days with the engine changes,' Sally countered. 'More of a loud shout.'

Mel looked at her askance. 'Come on, what other sport gives you that combination of fierce power and flashing speed?' She paused a moment as she remembered watching races with her father. The smell of the rubber, screeching throb of the engines, the thrill of the chase. Happy, happy days.

'I tell you, Sally, if the sport doesn't get your heart pumping any more it's time to call it a day and give in to what you know your gorgeous husband wants. Start a family.'

Sally sighed. 'Maybe you're right. I'm not sure this thirty-six-year-old gets the same buzz from travelling the circuits as you do.' She glanced sideways at Mel, a mischievous look in her eyes. 'And considering you've grabbed the job of looking after the drivers, it might make that decision easier. Motherhood, or continue to twiddle around working with sponsors and updating websites, like I am now.'

Mel shoved at her, hard. 'Not fair. It's how you wanted it, so that eventually when you did have a family and want to work part-time—'

'I might be able to work from HQ and not have to spend a third of my life on the road. Yes, I know.' She shot Mel a teasing smile. 'So how are you getting on with Stefano and, more importantly, Aiden?'

'Stefano is a joy, as always. For an Italian male he's surprisingly easy to work with and since he's been going steady with Francesca, it's all been very smooth.'

'And the new kid on the block?' Sally wriggled her eyebrows suggestively.

'Hardly a kid, as he's only two years younger than me.'

'Umm, interesting that you've already okayed the age difference in your mind.'

Mel opened her mouth to complain that actually, she was only talking facts, but then shut it when she realised Sally was right. Not that Aiden would ever look at her, and not that she was interested in him that way, but still. Two years was nothing at their age, right?

'Aiden is very nice,' she managed.

Sally exploded with laughter. 'Flipping heck, Mel. Of all the adjectives you could have chosen, I bet he's never been described as nice before. I should tell him.'

'Don't you dare!' As the words shot out of her, Sally giggled even more.

'Melanie Hunt, you really have got a crush on our new driver, haven't you?'

And, yes, Sally was her closest friend, but did she really have to tell her the truth – the whole truth? 'I haven't, not really. Not in the *I want to go out with him sense*, anyway. It's more that I appreciate his good looks from afar, which is how I'm happy for it to stay.'

'Why?'

She stared at her in disbelief. 'You know perfectly well why. Even if he did lower his *I only go out with women that look like lingerie wear models* standards, anything between us wouldn't last. Before I'd mastered his phone number, he'd be onto the next woman and I'd be left nursing another broken heart. Not to mention a hugely damaged ego.'

'Carlos was a slick bastard who didn't deserve you,' Sally replied bluntly.

Mel squeezed her friend's arm, appreciating her loyalty. 'True. He was also the first and last racing driver I'm ever going to date.'

Mel had long forgiven the driver who was now with a rival team, Viper. How was a twenty-something man supposed to keep turning down the stunning models who paraded around every circuit, promoting both their sponsors and themselves? What she hadn't, and couldn't do, was forgive herself for being stupid enough to fall for a man that shallow.

Shaking off thoughts from the past, Mel rummaged in her handbag for her phone. One day she'd get organised and buy one of those neat little bags that had a slot for her mobile, keys and purse. Plus the Kindle, toothbrush and notepad because she couldn't type on those stupid touch screens. Then there were the three pens, one to use and two spare, the torch because you never know when you might need one ... maybe the slick little bag was out of the question.

'Right,' she announced, at last clutching her phone and glancing at her diary. 'I need to track down a few people. I'll catch you later?'

'Sure, yes, but Mel?' Sally lightly touched her arm.

'Umm?'

'If you do like Aiden.' Mel started to protest, but Sally put a hand over her mouth, silencing her. 'I'm just saying, *if*, okay? If you do like him, and an opportunity presents itself, don't be too afraid of getting hurt to grab it. Being alone is okay, but having experienced both, I can assure you that being in a relationship is miles, miles better.'

'So says a woman who's bagged the one decent male on the planet.'

Sally waved her away. 'Don't be ridiculous. There are lots of them around, you just have to look a bit harder.'

Practice sessions are held traditionally on the Friday (two

sessions) and Saturday morning of every Grand Prix. They're a chance for drivers to familiarise themselves with the track but, even more importantly, are a vital part of getting the cars ready for qualifying, and ultimately for the actual race. Different set-ups are tried and tested to get the absolute best out of the car. Of course it's also the first time a driver really has a sense of how well his car is going to perform on that track.

Or not.

Aiden stormed through the pit garage after the morning practice session and into the technical briefing room on the first storey of the Delta motorhome. Frank, his chief engineer, thirty years older and many kilos heavier, shuffled along in his wake.

'I thought this car was meant to be the fastest on the grid this season? With this set up it's got about as much speed as my first Corsa,' he told Frank through gritted teeth when the older man finally shut the door.

'Must have been one hell of a first car then,' Frank replied calmly, plonking himself down on the leather sofa with all the grace of a hippopotamus with piles.

Aiden didn't feel like smiling. He actually felt like shoving his fist through the wall of the blasted motorhome but a smile was what Frank expected, so that's what he gave him. 'You're right. She was a pretty exceptional Corsa. Now, before you start talking to me about fiddling with the front wing or whatever other scheme you've got up your sleeve to put some pace in the thing, I need a drink. Do you want one?'

Frank nodded. 'Iced tea, thanks.'

Aiden turned full circle and headed back downstairs towards the dining area, where a cheery waiter furnished him with two tall glasses of iced tea, complete with a slice of lemon. His eyes scanned the polished wood floor, glossy black tables and gleaming bar area but he didn't really take any of it in. After six years of competing at this level of motorsport he no longer stood and gawked at how the equivalent of a two star Michelin restaurant, a media centre and a meeting hub was conjured from a couple of motorhomes.

Bounding back up the stairs, he was about to head back into the briefing room when he heard the voices of a couple of the engineers talking to Frank.

'Come on, Frank, you've watched them both. What have we got in Aiden? A chip off the old block, or a watered down version of the motorsport legend?'

Aiden froze, the muscles of his arm pulled taut as he gripped the cold glasses. He heard Frank cough. Imagined him shifting uncomfortably as he tried to think of a diplomatic answer. He didn't know the guy very well yet, but already he had a sense of a man serious about his job. Not interested in the politics and gossip that went along with it.

'Watered down is a bit strong.' The words were delivered in Frank's usual steady, unruffled voice.

'Is it? Tell me, would Seb Foster have managed to squeeze a bit more pace out of the car today? Shaved a smidgen or two off the laps?'

Automatically Aiden's grip on the glasses tightened. Sucking in a breath, he willed himself to relax.

'Look, comparisons between the two drivers are meaningless. Seb drove in a totally different era.' Frank was obviously trying his best not to get involved.

Aiden knew he should go in. At least clear his throat to make it clear he was listening. Instead he remained where he was.

'Sure it was different back then, but you must still have a sense of the driver's styles,' one of the guys needled. 'Old Seb was lightning fast. He drove every race as if he loved the speed, enjoyed taking risks, lived and breathed the feeling of rubber burning on tarmac. His son on the other hand is too much of a smooth operator. He hasn't got his father's drive, his—'

Unable to take any more, Aiden flung the door open. As it rattled on its hinges, the three men swung round, two warily, one with a sigh of resignation. 'Please, carry on. I'm dying to know what else my father had that I apparently don't.'

The two engineers glanced awkwardly at each other and then at the floor.

'I think it's time you two were somewhere else,' Frank remarked.

With an embarrassed glance at Aiden, they slipped out and shut the door.

'I'm sorry you had to hear that.'

It took all Aiden had in him to give his shoulders a casual shrug. 'It's not the first time I've heard that stuff, and it sure as hell won't be the last.'

Frank narrowed his eyes, as if trying to work something out. 'What do *you* think, Aiden? Was your father a better driver?'

Startled by the direct question, Aiden found it was now his turn to take a sudden interest in the flooring. 'How the heck would I know? I was eight when he won his last world championship. Ten when he died. I was hardly in a position to judge his driving ability.'

'But you must have reviewed his races since then. What does the twenty-eight-year-old man think now?'

Shit. Aiden felt his stomach clench. He didn't want to talk about this. Even if he'd just blasted round the track as the fastest in practice, he wouldn't have wanted the discussion. He especially didn't want it now he'd found out his bloody car was nowhere near as fast as the paltry allowable pre-season testing had indicated.

'I think it's time we talked about how to get that ruddy car round the track quicker,' he replied tersely.

During the next practice session they made adjustments to the suspension, aerodynamics, tyres and engine settings. When Aiden finally climbed out a few hours later the balance was better, but they weren't there yet.

Feeling as if he'd gone twenty rounds with Mike Tyson, he wearily peeled off his helmet and safety collar. It was a fact few outside the sport were aware of – driving a racing car was both mentally and physically knackering. Of course he stayed in shape, running long distances to keep up his stamina and spending time in the gym to build his strength, but being stuck inside the heat of a cockpit while being thrown around a racetrack at high speed was pretty demanding on even the most conditioned body.

'Are you okay to do the press briefing now?'

He turned to find Melanie, dressed in a crisp white team shirt, tailored trousers and sensible loafers.

'Give me a moment to towel down?' Sweat was dripping off his face and, call him vain, he hated facing the media looking like he'd been dunked in a bucket of water. Plus his head wasn't in the right place yet to field a bunch of questions on his car's performance.

'Sure.'

She moved away to give him some privacy and he almost smiled. Most of the women he came into contact with were only too keen to do the opposite. Stare at him.

'How did the practice go?' she asked, her eyes looking everywhere but at him.

'It went.' He peeled down his overalls, struggling to get his mood into a better place. Melanie might have figured his press persona was different from his real one, and after his latest outburst Frank probably had, too, but the media hadn't. He wanted to keep it that way.

Mel tried not to watch as Aiden wiped his face with his towel and secured his sponsor hat on top of his damp hair. Tried and failed. Tired and sweaty from driving, he was still better looking than most film stars on a good day. It was so hard not to simply ogle him. Really, really hard.

'Are you okay?' she asked finally when he looked set to go.

'Sure.' To prove it, he grinned and even though it was a dynamite smile, complete with gleaming white teeth and sexy grooves, she knew it wasn't real. His grey eyes might have crinkled, but deep inside there was no sparkle.

She sighed. 'Look, I know you're not okay, but if you don't want to talk about it, forget it. I understand.'

She started to walk towards the waiting press but he put out a hand to stop her. 'Sorry, I'm not used to being so transparent. To be honest, your ability to read me scares the shit out of me.'

It was probably the first truly honest thing she'd heard him say and Mel had to smile. 'Well, you shouldn't worry. I don't actually have a clue what you're thinking. Only that you're not as one-dimensional as you like to appear.'

'Okay,' he drawled. 'But for now can we put this one-dimensional version in front of the cameras?'

True to his word, he did. He smiled for them, joked about his apparent lack of pace, reassured them it was early days and he didn't expect to have a perfect car on day one. Then deflected all questions about his father like a true pro.

Mel hung back, admiring his easy confidence. Admired it all the more now she knew that underneath the man he was pretending to be was somebody quite different. A man who she suspected was utterly disillusioned that his car wasn't as fast as he'd hoped.

Just as Mel started to warm to him though, Aiden proved that his public persona was indeed partly accurate.

With mounting incredulity she watched Devon, bunny boiler and so-called journalist, sidle up to Aiden when the press began to dissipate. Mel held her breath, willing him to shake his head and walk away. Instead he put his arm around her, kissed her cheek and smiled into her eyes.

With a sense of crushing disappointment, Mel spun away and headed in the opposite direction.

Chapter Four

Saturday night. The night before his first race for Delta, and what was Aiden doing? Trying to extricate himself from the clinging arms of a blonde he knew damn well he shouldn't have slept with again last night.

His excuses? The lamest, but sadly also the most truthful, was that she'd been there. The right place, the right time, coming up to him when his defences were low and smiling at him like she was so happy to see him. Yesterday had been a bitch of a day. First his car proving to be more tortoise than cheetah round the five kilometre track, then the veiled references from his own team that he wasn't up to the job.

None of it gave him the right to use her though, and in sleeping with Devon again last night, he'd done just that. Gone and made the same mistake twice when he was old enough to know better. He had to stop using sex as an outlet for his anger and frustration.

Devon tripped up the steps to the hotel and let out an alcohol-fuelled giggle. 'Oops. Are we going back to your room, Mr Hot Rod?'

He looked into her glassy blue eyes and shame did more than prickle down his back. It slammed into him.

'No, Devon.' Carefully he removed his arm from hers, but when she started to teeter he cursed and supported her again. 'I'm afraid this is where we have to call it a night. Big race tomorrow, remember?'

'Oh.' Her bottom lip came out in a slightly comic pout. 'Are you turning me down?'

Jesus, he didn't have time for this. Why had he hooked

up with her again tonight? He'd been ducking out of the sponsor dinner, heading for an early night, when she'd launched herself at him, dragging him into a waiting taxi. From there they'd somehow ended up in an intimate restaurant, her getting more and more drunk, him wondering why he preferred being fawned over by a ditzy blonde to being stuck alone in his hotel room.

'I'm telling you I need to get some sleep,' he replied sharply, finally letting his frustration show.

She seemed to realise he wasn't in the mood for games any more because she tried to straighten up. 'Well, how about one more kiss before you go?'

Figuring it might be the quickest way out, he bent his head and prepared to have his mouth sucked off.

Dimly, while Devon was trying to tangle her tongue around his tonsils, he was aware of the sound of voices laughing behind him. Two males and a female. The female sounded very much like …

'He doesn't look like a man who wants to be interrupted right now.'

He dragged his head up, aware his lips must look like they'd been stung by a hive of bees, and, yes, just his bloody luck. There was Melanie, standing with Frank and, oh joy of joys, Hugh, the team principal, aka the boss. All of them wearing expressions of disbelief.

Devon chose that moment to stagger again, forcing him to wrap his arms around her to steady her. 'Silly me,' she gushed. 'I think you plied me with too much wine, you naughty boy.'

Aiden bit down on the retort *you kept reaching for the bottle, you silly cow*. The three stooges were still glaring at him as if he'd committed a cardinal sin. As if he'd been drinking, too, which of course he hadn't. He might be stupid when it came to blondes with come-to-bed eyes, but he wasn't *that* stupid.

He managed to half carry Devon over to one of the lobby chairs. 'Wait here. I'll call you a cab.' When he turned back to the reception area, the three disapproving faces had disappeared.

Sighing, he yanked down his tie and undid his top few buttons. If he didn't perform in tomorrow's race, he'd have hell to pay.

The next time Mel saw Aiden was in the paddock, before the drivers' parade. He'd just come out of a pre-race briefing and looked tightly wound, his handsome face set in hard, tense lines. Or maybe it was just tiredness, due to too much nocturnal activity.

The moment he saw her, he headed in her direction.

'Melanie, I'm glad I've caught up with you. About last night.'

'It's none of my business,' she replied coolly, a bad night's sleep and a morning run having failed to dispel her anger towards him.

'I know, but still, I want to explain.'

'There's nothing to explain.'

He dragged out a long, frustrated sigh. 'So that's it? You're just going to condemn me without hearing all the facts?'

That took her off guard. 'Why do you assume I'm condemning you? And more importantly, why do you care?'

He ran a hand through the dark hair that had fallen onto his forehead. 'I know you're condemning me, because last time we chatted you told me you wanted me to be one of the good guys. If you thought I wasn't one then, after last night's performance you've probably got me pegged as Satan, the Devil and Darth Vader all rolled into one.'

Despite her frustration with him, a smile tugged at her lips. 'As I told you, it really doesn't matter what I think. You should be more concerned by what Frank, and especially Hugh, think.' She moved to walk away but he blocked her path, leaving her staring at the bright red Delta logo on the chest of his sparkling white overalls.

'I can already work out what they think. I was kind of hoping …' He paused and tried again, 'I was hoping you might cut me more of a break.'

Surprised, she stared up at him. 'Why would I do that?'

He shifted, his eyes no longer on hers but fixed at some point in the distance. 'Because you already know I'm not really this perfect, calm, easy-going person at all. That instead I'm …' he broke off to curse under his breath '… I make mistakes, damn it. I made one with Devon.'

'I seem to recall you said that last time.' It was hard to remain angry with him when he was looking at her so earnestly. When he was trying to be so honest.

'Maybe I'm a slow learner?' A spark of self-mockery lit his eyes.

'Where I come from, the saying goes once a mistake, twice a habit.'

He nodded. 'I've also heard once a mistake, twice stupidity. I can own up to that.'

He looked so sincere and so utterly … sad. It made her heart melt and she had to turn away before he could see how stupid *she* was, wanting to hug him and banish the troubled look from his eyes.

'Well, good luck in the race. I'll catch you later.' She marched away before he could stop her again. She had to, for her own sanity. When she'd told Sally she didn't fancy Aiden in an *I want to date him kind of way*, it seems she'd been lying.

And that was despite knowing he was a too handsome millionaire racing driver and she was an average looking, average earning press officer. Despite knowing that last night she'd seen him draped around a ridiculous blonde when he should have been getting a good night's sleep. And despite knowing, with absolute certainty, that though he seemed remorseful now, when the opportunity presented itself again, she'd find him draped over some other attractive blonde. Or maybe even the same one again.

The cars were lined up on the grid, Aiden in fifth position, one behind his teammate. Eyes focused ahead, he tried to clear his mind of everything but the race. There was still a chance for a podium finish and for his first race with a new team, he'd grab onto that with both hands.

The lights turned to green, indicating the start of the warm up lap and Aiden began the process of weaving back and forth across the track, trying to get heat into his brakes and tyres. His pulse started to accelerate, as it always did at this point. By the time the race itself had begun, his heart rate would be nearing 200 beats a minute.

'Start a series of burnouts,' Frank instructed through his headset. His was the only voice he would hear for the next hour and a half.

As he made his way around the track, Aiden performed a series of sharp accelerations to warm the tyres and set the clutch bite point.

Then he was back in position, eyes fixed on the starting light gantry, waiting for the five red lights to go out. Waiting for the race to begin.

He got off to a howler. From fifth to seventh in the blink of an eye at the first corner. As he jostled to defend even that position, Aiden cursed the image that flashed through his mind. That of the team back at the pits, shaking their heads, muttering to themselves that Seb Foster would have done better.

He gripped the wheel tighter and refocused his energy into the job.

Forty-nine laps into the fifty-eight lap race he'd punched his way up to fourth. His left thigh was aching like blazes from the braking, each push on the pedal the equivalent of 60 kilos of pressure on his gluteus. The rest of him wasn't fairing so well, either, which just went to prove no matter how much hard work he did in the gym, the only thing that really simulated the stresses and strains of driving, was driving.

'You're consistently lapping faster than Bauer,' came Frank's voice. 'Tyre degradation is fine and there is no issue with fuel.'

Aiden read between the lines. He had a chance of catching the German. If he did, he'd get a podium finish, alongside his teammate Stefano, who was now comfortably in second.

Two laps later, the German edged slightly wide at turn three and Aiden saw his opportunity. Steeling himself, he edged his car up the inside as they flew into the right hander.

Moments later he was spinning out of control off the track and coming to a halt on the gravel run off area.

'What the fuck?'

Dazed, angry and really, really disgusted with himself, he rested his helmet on the steering wheel and shut his eyes.

Post-race interviews were tortuous at the best of times. When you'd just made a complete arse of yourself, they were off the scale.

When he finally made it past the media and into the pit garage, his team were noticeable by their silence. They held the obligatory post-race analysis, though it didn't exactly require the genius of Einstein to work out what had gone wrong. Aiden held up his hand, apologised for the umpteenth time, and that was pretty much that. After a few more nerve twanging minutes, during which nobody looked him in the eye, they all trailed out. Including Frank, who probably went to find somewhere private to bang his head against a wall.

Aiden couldn't even blame them. They'd done their bit, managing to conjure up a car capable of achieving a respectable third place. He was the one who'd failed to play his part.

Exhausted and emotionally wrung out, too tired to even find a lift back to the hotel, Aiden slunk into the drivers' room in the motorhome. Thankfully it was empty, Stefano no doubt off somewhere celebrating his second place. Slumping onto the couch he leant forward, hung his head in his hands and wished for the impossible. That he could do that overtake again, only this time without clipping his front wing on the car in front.

The door squeaked and the couch shifted slightly as someone sat down next to him. Someone with shoes remarkably like those of the Delta press officer. Barely glancing up, he let out a rueful grimace. 'You drew the short straw, huh? Everyone else too scared to come and rattle my cage?'

'Too upset. Too disappointed.'

Though she said the words without malice, it made him want to hang his head even further. 'Yeah, well, that makes all of us.'

'They put a lot of effort into getting that car ready today.'

Slowly he raised his head. 'Are you saying I didn't put any effort in out there?' Try telling that to his exhausted, bruised, dehydrated body.

Melanie being Melanie, she didn't flinch from his stare. 'I'm saying that from this side, it doesn't look like you cared enough. You didn't exactly spend the evening mentally preparing yourself and getting an early night.'

Immediately his spine stiffened. 'As you said before, how I spend my damn evenings are nobody's business but mine.'

'It's everyone's business when the results of it spill over into the next day.'

'You seriously think I wasn't trying my damn hardest out there? That I was too knackered from some sort of sexual marathon, and hey, yes, why not, too hung-over as well, that I couldn't perform to my absolute best?' He leapt to his feet, more hurt than he'd ever admit. 'As I told you in the quote for your press release, I lost because I cocked-up. I made a stupid mistake. It happens sometimes when you're haring round a track at two hundred miles an hour. So, yes, dismiss me as a fucking useless driver if you want. I'm sure others will.' He swallowed at the ball of emotion lodged painfully in his throat. 'But don't tell me I don't care enough.'

Angrily he grabbed at the door, his head thumping so much it was threatening to split in two. He was halfway through it when she spoke again.

'I'm sorry.'

One glance at her lovely brown eyes, now brimming with tears, and the angst that had bloomed hot and vicious in his chest deflated, leaving him hollow and empty. With a sigh he stepped back into the room and shut the door.

'I didn't mean to insult you,' she continued, delving into her monster handbag. After a lot of huffing she found a tissue and used it to wipe her eyes and blow her nose. 'God, I can't even begin to understand how you can drive one of those machines on the straight, never mind hurtle round corners and pass within inches of other cars. I guess my emotions are running too high. We're all just so disappointed—'

'In me. Yeah, I hear that loud and clear.' More shaken than he wanted to let on he leant back against the wall, feigning nonchalance. 'As I tried to explain earlier, what you saw in the hotel lobby was me trying to remove myself from Devon's clutches, not encourage her. About two minutes after you'd gone she was in a taxi and I was in my room. Sober, I might add.'

She gave him a weak smile. 'Okay, yes, I can believe that. I guess I put two and two together and made what I thought was a pretty obvious four.'

'After what you'd seen back at my apartment, it would be hard for me to fault your maths.'

Her smile was wider this time and Aiden was once again struck by how pretty she was.

'Still, I'm sorry for making the leap.' She stood and walked towards the door, turning to give him a small smile as she opened it. 'And for the record, I think you're a brilliant driver. Not a, what did you say? *A fucking useless driver?*'

He watched the door swing closed behind her and shook his head, laughing for the first time that day.

Chapter Five

A week later the team were in Kuala Lumpur for the Malaysian Grand Prix. The two Friday practice sessions had gone surprisingly well and Aiden was pretty confident the car set up they had now was more competitive. The weather though, was another roll of the dice. Blazing hot one minute, with track temperatures at a whopping sixty degrees centigrade, the next they were coping with tropical downpours. It certainly added a bit of spice to the occasion. Not that throwing his car around the track with twenty odd other drivers, all wanting to be the one in front, needed the extra ingredient.

Aiden was in the briefing room, wading through all the telemetry results with the team. They'd have another shot at trying out further combinations of suspension and aerodynamic settings at the Saturday morning practice, but the huddled group were pretty certain of the race strategy now.

'Okay, gentlemen. I think that's all we need for today,' Frank announced. Before Aiden had time to blink, the others shot off, leaving the two of them alone.

Frank cleared his throat. 'Did Hugh catch up with you?'

Hugh might carry the title of team principal but as far as Aiden and Frank were concerned, he was God. Of course there were other top men, like the operational director, managing director, probably a director of wiping arses, too, for all he knew, but Hugh was it for them.

'Yes.' He hoped Frank understood the wealth of meaning conveyed in his simple answer, because he sure didn't fancy rehashing the conversation. Yes, he and Hugh had talked. Yes, he'd been taken to task for being seen snogging an inebriated female when he should have been safely tucked up in bed. Yes, even though Hugh assured him he knew that had nothing to do with his overtake balls-up the next day, others would see it differently and judge him for it.

'Good.'

Aiden waited for Frank's follow up question, but it didn't come. Relieved, he gathered together his essentials from the seat next to him – wallet, key card, water bottle – ready to hightail it out for some much needed down time. A shower would be good. Some time in the gym, maybe, though not necessarily in that order. He'd started to ease away from the table when he realised Frank was watching him.

Reluctantly Aiden released his grip on his belongings, letting them slide back onto the chair. Frank was probably right. Now was an opportunity to bond, to go beyond the professional politeness they seemed to have stuck at.

He shuffled his bum back on the seat. 'How many years have you been with Delta, Frank?'

Frank grunted. 'More years than you've been on this planet. I joined as an engineer in the factory straight out of college. Probably getting on for thirty-five years now.'

A chill settled over Aiden and he silently cursed. Of all the questions he could have asked, he had to choose one that left him with no option but to ask the obvious follow-up question. Why the hell hadn't he asked the guy his favourite meal/colour/film instead? 'So, I guess you were here when my father was, then?'

'I was.'

'What was he like?' When Frank looked at him quizzically Aiden added hastily, 'I mean, what was he like to work with, you know, as a driver.'

'Well, when he first joined, he was pretty green. Of course, I wasn't his race engineer. Then.'

A thick cloak of dread settled on Aiden's shoulders. He had a feeling he already knew the answer to his next question. 'You were his race engineer later?'

Slowly Frank nodded his head. 'Yes, I did have that honour. I took him through the last of his two World Championships.'

'But ...' Aiden wracked his brain, trying to remember the coverage of his father's crash. He was pretty certain he couldn't recall Frank's name in any of the articles.

'That final season we had a swop round and my counterpart, Ed, became Seb's engineer,' Frank filled in for him.

'Right.' Aiden was still trying to get his head around the fact that the man who sat in front of him – the owner of the only voice he heard while he was lapping round the circuit, his eyes and ears outside the cockpit who advised him of when to push on and when to pit, his right-hand man – had done all that for his father, too. How on earth had that piece of information not come to light before now? 'How many years *were* you his race engineer?'

'Four.'

Plenty of time to really get to know both the man and the driver then. 'Well ... I mean, wow. I hadn't realised. Nobody said when I joined. I knew there was a chance some people would still be here who worked with him, but sharing the same race engineer ... Jeez.' There were other words he could have used. One began with f and ended with k.

'Is it going to be a problem?'

Too bloody right it was ... but Aiden couldn't say that. He couldn't admit to the absolute terror he felt on discovering that the one man who would have a real sense of the comparative abilities of him and his father, was the one looking at him now. The same man he desperately, desperately needed to believe in him. His stomach churned, threatening to spew up its contents, but Aiden swallowed hard and slapped on a smile. 'No problems on my side.'

'Good, because it'll be a great tale to tell my grandchildren sometime. How I was race engineer for two World Champions. Sebastian and Aiden Foster. Father and son.'

The words were really no more than platitudes, but the tone of Frank's voice made Aiden look up and stare at the older man. Though his eyes were slightly amused, his face was deadly serious.

'You really think we can do this?' he blurted unthinkingly.

'Of course.' Frank's stare was quiet and steady. 'Don't you?'

Stupid, stupid question. 'Well, yeah, I wouldn't be here if I didn't, but somehow, I didn't think … I wasn't sure …'

'You didn't think *I* thought you were capable of it?'

'I'm a very different driver to my father,' he countered, at the same time kicking himself for sounding so defensive.

'That you are.'

'It doesn't make me any less good.'

Frank let out the smallest glimmer of a smile. 'No, it doesn't.'

'He was much more … chilled. Relaxed behind the wheel.' Crickey, why couldn't he stop blabbering? 'I envy him that.'

'Why?'

'Because he made it seem so easy. In the clips I've seen, he looked to be enjoying himself. Having the time of his life. Sometimes …' Hastily Aiden slammed his mouth shut. He'd said far too much already.

'It's easy to enjoy yourself when you haven't got the weight of expectation bearing down on you,' Frank replied quietly, his eyes full of understanding. 'If you want some advice from an old man, which you probably don't, but I'll give it to you anyway. Your natural driving style isn't so very different from that of your father's.'

Aiden started to shake his head, ready to disagree, but Frank lifted his hand. 'No, hear me out. Having worked with your father, I took an obvious interest in your career. In the early days, when you were coming through the motor racing ranks, you drove with that same ... I'm not sure what to call it. Abandon, I think. It wasn't reckless, but it was carefree. It's only over the last few years, since the media have started to become more interested, that you've tightened up a bit. Now your driving is far more controlled, which I'm not saying is wrong. In fact it's something your father never had.' He paused and looked Aiden in the eye. 'Were you at the track when he crashed?'

Aiden tensed automatically. 'You think that's my problem? I'm scared?'

Frank shook his head. 'No. It's understandable you'd want to learn from his mistakes though. Be more cautious.'

Stiffly Aiden got to his feet and walked towards the door. 'I'm not scared of crashing into a wall, Frank.'

He nodded his goodbye and left the room before he blurted out the truth. That he was waking up in the night drenched in sweat scared of never living up to his father's legacy. Of not being good enough.

From her vantage point at the back of the garage by the telemetry consoles, Mel watched the last of the three qualifying sessions on the TV screens with more nerves than usual. She always got into the race, willing her drivers to do well, but today she felt an extra surge of adrenaline. The way her eyes remained fixed on any mention of Foster on the timing screen was a pretty clear indication of why. The crucial last fifteen seconds seemed to go slower than ever today but finally the laps were done and Aiden and Stefano managed third and fourth, respectively. Not great, but good enough for her to exhale a sigh of relief.

At the obligatory press conference for the top three qualifiers Aiden looked slightly happier than he had after leaving Melbourne. She wondered if he'd seen any of the media reports from the last race. Hopefully not. They'd been pretty cutting, drawing the inevitable, damning comparisons with his father. She knew she had to find a way of defusing the whole Foster angle, partly because it detracted from Aiden and his own integrity in the Delta stable. And partly because having such cruel jibes thrown at him on a regular basis couldn't be doing Aiden's confidence any good.

'Are you coming to eat with us tonight, bella Melanie?'

Stefano sidled up behind her, grinning in a shamelessly flirtatious manner.

'Maybe, if you tell me who *us* are.'

'Me, Roberto, Frank ...' He went on to reel off several more names. It was the usual crowd, a mixture of engineers and mechanics who liked to eat together in a restaurant rather than alone in their rooms or in the motorhome.

'Doesn't Sally need us for any sponsor commitments tonight?'

He looked affronted. 'Would I be asking if she did?'

Mel nodded over to Aiden, who was still talking to the press. 'Have you asked your teammate?'

Stefano's dark eyes followed hers. 'You think he'd come? He seems to keep himself to himself. I got the impression he wasn't one for socialising.' Then he smirked. 'Unless of course it's with blondes who like to 'ave a few drinks.'

She couldn't defend Aiden against that one. He'd been stupid enough to put himself in that position. 'How do you know whether he wants to go out with us, if you don't ask?'

As the press conference came to an end she nodded over to where the drivers were making their way towards the door. 'Here comes Aiden now. Are you going to ask him?'

'I think he'd be more keen to come if you invited him,' the Italian drawled just as Aiden came into earshot.

'Invited me where?'

Mel felt herself flushing, which was more than just embarrassing. It was excruciating. She rarely blushed nowadays, not since she'd spent the last six years of her life working in a totally male-dominated environment. She thrived on the sexual innuendos, the ribbing and teasing, loving to give as good as she got.

Then again, it had been a long time since she'd been foolish enough to fancy any of the men she worked with.

'Stefano was saying that a group are heading into Kuala Lumpur this evening. Just a quick meal, nothing fancy.' There, she managed all that with barely a tremor.

Aiden nodded, not saying anything, his eyes flicking between her and Stefano.

'You should join us, man.' Mel tried not to jump as Stefano, who was almost a whole head shorter than Aiden, draped an arm around her shoulders. 'Wait till you see this one when she lets her hair down. She rocks.'

'Thanks,' she replied dryly, consoling herself with the thought that by now her face probably couldn't get any redder.

Aiden's eyes were watchful as they slid over her, no doubt taking in her flushed face and Stefano's rather familiar arm.

'Thanks for the offer but ...' He sighed, rubbing at the back of his neck. 'I think it's best if I get my head down after ... well, you know. After last week.'

There was a moment of heavy silence. Then Stefano slapped him on the back. 'No worries. Maybe next time. I'll see you in my rear-view mirror tomorrow, eh?'

He headed off down the corridor chuckling.

'He's a real comedian,' Aiden muttered, watching his teammate disappear round the corner before swinging his eyes back to her. 'Do you guys often go out?'

'Yes, I suppose we do, when we get the chance. Why, didn't you socialise with the Arrows team?'

They started walking back together towards the Delta motorhome. 'I guess they did.'

A telling answer. 'But you're not into going out with the team?'

His shoulders twitched slightly, half shrug, half, she suspected, *get me out of this conversation.* 'I don't think I'm a good team player.'

'Rubbish. Everybody is, if they want to be.'

Aiden slid Melanie a quick glance. He envied her relaxed friendliness around the team. She appeared to like them all and, if Stefano's arm around her was anything to go by, they liked her, too. In his previous teams he'd kept himself to himself but watching her he found he wanted the kind of easy relationship she had with the team. Damn it, he wanted it with her, too. *Especially* with her. But he wasn't used to sharing his feelings or emotions that way. He was used to looking out for himself, because nobody else had ever bothered to.

'I'd like to go out with you guys,' he admitted finally. 'Be part of a team. But not tonight.'

'I can understand that. After all, I'm the one who had a go at you after the last race.'

'You weren't the only one.'

'Oh dear, did Hugh—'

'Give me a stern telling off?' he interrupted flatly. 'Tell me I'd let both myself and the team down? Make me feel like a dumb schoolboy? Yes to all of those.'

'Ouch.'

'Yeah, though nothing I didn't deserve.'

His admission was rewarded with one of her smiles. Warm, open, friendly, it made him want to say to hell with making the right impression and go and join them. Join her.

But he'd already cocked-up the first race of the season. He couldn't afford to let anything mess up tomorrow. Anything at all.

They walked through the garage which still bustled with activity; many of the crew would work well into the night. As they emerged on the other side Aiden came to a rather abrupt stop, causing Melanie to bump into him. Just a slight nudge, but he felt the softness of her curves against his arm and down his side.

'Sorry.'

His stock reply when nudged by an attractive woman was something along the lines of *feel free to bump into me any time*. But though he opened his mouth, he couldn't say the words. They sounded too crass. Instead he gave her a slightly awkward smile. 'My fault. I wanted to avoid Carlos.'

He nodded in the direction of the Spanish driver, last year's world champion, who was striding through the paddock. A great driver, but an absolute prick in all other respects. Right now he was laughing with one of the heavily made-up sponsor girls as she held an umbrella over him to shade him from the sun. Though she was dressed in a demure sarong there was nothing demure about the way she pressed her body against his side.

Melanie's eyes flickered in their direction and he saw something flash across her face but before he had time to work out what it was it had gone, and she was staring back at him.

'Well, enjoy your evening,' he said.

'Thanks, I will.' She fiddled with the strap of the monster bag she took everywhere with her. 'Maybe you'll join us next time?'

'You bet.'

He found he meant it. More than that, he was really looking forward to it.

Chapter Six

Aiden finished the Malaysian Grand Prix in fourth place. It was respectable, gratifyingly one place better than his teammate, but a long way from jump up and down exciting. It was, however, a million times better than crashing out due to his own blundering incompetence.

There was a break before the next Grand Prix. Break was a loose term because even though they weren't on the road they were still working, getting the car ready for its next race. It entailed almost daily visits to leafy Surrey and the Delta HQ, though the sixty mile round trip commute from London was hardly a chore. Not in his Ferrari 599.

Today though, it felt pretty close to one. Not because his sleek grey Ferrari was any less responsive, but because of what was in store for him when he arrived. The more miles the supercar ate up, the more his insides gnawed and twisted. By the time he eased the purring metal machine into his parking space, his stomach had more knots than a stack of cheap timber.

There's nothing to worry about, he tried to reassure himself as he climbed out. It was just another interview. God knows, he'd done enough in his time.

Melanie, fresh-faced and wearing a pink blouse instead of the usual team white, greeted him in the reception area.

'Well, hello. Have you stood here all morning just waiting for me?'

She gave him one of her looks, the ones he was starting to enjoy. 'Sure I have. I've got nothing better to do with my day than hang out in the Delta reception area, waiting for my drivers to arrive.'

He grinned. 'That's good. And just a note for next time, if you could wait with a mug of tea, too, that'd be great.'

'You'll get your tea and I might even put it in a mug. After you've met with Mike Hayward.'

'Ah. So that's the bribe to make sure I don't duck out?' He ran a hand over his chin, wondering if perhaps he should have shaved. 'I'm not sure an hour of talking about my relationship with my father is worth a mug of tea.'

In fact he was bloody certain it wasn't. The damn stomach knots tightened still further and Aiden suddenly wanted nothing more than to turn around and walk out.

Melanie's hazel eyes softened and she reached out to touch him lightly on the arm, drawing him into a nearby meeting room. After closing the door behind her she turned to face him, all warmth and sweet concern. Bizarrely this time it was his chest that tightened, not his stomach, as if his heart was finding the space inside his ribs too small. Jesus, what was wrong with him? Why was her simple act of kindness making him feel so emotional?

'I know this is going to be hard for you,' she told him in a voice as soft as her eyes. 'But ever since it was announced you were joining Delta, Mike from *Motorsport* has been asking for an interview that explores your relationship with your father. Now, just because that's what he wants, it doesn't mean we have to give it to him. You've seen my briefing document?'

He nodded. He'd seen it. He just hadn't read it.

'Well, in there I give some suggestions about how you can deflect some of the questions he's going to ask if you think they're too personal, though I doubt you need my help on that score. But if you want my opinion, I believe if we get the whole relationship out in the open, if you talk candidly about what it was like growing up with such a superstar father, then the media interest in that angle will diminish. With a bit of luck they'll then get back to doing what they should be doing. Talking about you and your racing.'

'That would be nice.' Understatement of the year.

'So, are you ready to talk about Sebastian Foster, Aiden Foster's father?' The look she gave him was filled with such certainty, as if she absolutely knew he could do this. And maybe if his life had been the Swiss Family Robinson paradise they all imagined, he *could* have talked about it.

He exhaled deeply and began to pace the room, his stomach now tying knots within knots.

'Look, I understand how hard it is to talk about someone you loved and lost.' Melanie gave him a quick, wobbly smile. 'I lost my father, too.'

That snapped him out of his self-induced funk. 'Shit, I'm sorry. How?'

'Like yours, in a car accident.' Again she tried to smile but it was a sad version of her trademark high watt grin. 'Of course, my dad wasn't driving quite so fast, or on a racetrack. In fact he was coming home from a trip to the supermarket.'

Her voice had started to shake a little and Aiden suddenly wanted to tell her to stop. What she'd experienced was so much worse than anything he'd gone through. But before he could, she dropped another bombshell.

'My mother was in the car, too.'

He almost didn't dare ask the question. 'Did she ...?' his voice trailed off as he saw the answer in her eyes.

'Yes. They both died. I was eighteen at the time.'

His heart plummeted and he felt an almost desperate urge to comfort her. If he'd been Stefano, or Frank, hell anyone else with half-decent social skills, he'd have wrapped his arms around her. Instead he remained where he was feeling stiff, awkward and useless.

'All I'm trying to say,' she continued, her eyes welling, 'is I know how hard it is to talk about the death of a parent, so if you really don't want to do this—'

'I'll do it,' he cut in sharply, feeling like a blasted fake. Here she was, wearing her heart on her sleeve, crying over the death of her parents. People she clearly loved. And here he was, with a heart of stone, feeling only anger and bitterness towards his own father.

His harsh tone caused her to reel back a little and he swore under his breath.

'Sorry, I didn't mean to shout. I just ... I'm sorry you went through what you did. Really sorry. And in comparison, my story is ...' Feeble? Pathetic? Pitiful?

'What, Aiden?' She studied him with luminous brown eyes.

The truth stuck in his throat and he couldn't, wouldn't voice it. 'Very different,' he settled with, walking back towards the door. 'Come on, you'd better take me to this Mike fellow. And bring me that flipping cup of tea you promised.'

Here we go again, he thought as he trailed behind her neat figure. Once again he'd recount the story of how exciting it was to be the son of a racing car driver. Hell, if he told it often enough, maybe even he'd start to believe it.

Mel sat at the opposite end of the room from Mike and Aiden, ostensibly with her head down, trying to work. In reality she was listening and occasionally watching Aiden lie his way through the entire interview. And doing it with all the enthusiasm of a man walking into the dentist for a root canal filling.

'So, tell me about the time you first realised your father was a world-renowned racing car driver?' Mike asked.

Aiden smiled, the amenable smile that never really touched his eyes. 'Well, I guess I would be about five. I went to the race with my mother and we sat in these fantastic seats, right on the finishing line, opposite the pit lane. It was incredible. I remember hearing all these voices around me roar in excitement, cheering Sebastian Foster as he blazed through the chequered flag. I remember puffing out my chest and wanting to jump up and down shouting "that's my dad".'

Bullshit, she wanted to scream. Surely Mike could tell it was a lie? Surely he could see past the bland expression on Aiden's face and into the guarded eyes? Why was he lying? Why couldn't he just tell Mike the truth and be done with it? So what if he hadn't always seen eye to eye with his father. Name her a father and son who didn't have the occasional ding dong.

'Would you say you had a privileged upbringing?'

There it was again, the nonchalant shrug, though his tight jawline told her he was anything but relaxed.

'My father had plenty of money and a garage full of fast cars,' Aiden replied with that *shucks, wasn't my life wonderful* false smile on his face. 'What young boy wouldn't want that?'

Heaving out a sigh Mel began to write down the questions that Aiden had either lied through, or cleverly evaded answering.

'And was it your father who taught you to drive your first kart?'

A brief hesitation. 'You have to remember he spent a lot of time overseas, so the opportunity for him to actually teach me anything was fairly limited.'

Another evade.

'But what about when he wasn't racing?' Mike prompted. 'The weekends during the off season?'

Aiden shifted his stance, raising his arm casually across the back of the chair. 'Actually I went to boarding school, so I was only home during the holidays.'

Well, at least now she knew where his exemplary good manners came from, even if she hadn't learnt anything more about his relationship with his father.

Obviously realising his interviewee wasn't exactly playing ball, Mike tried another angle. 'Can you give us a sense of what Sebastian Foster was like as a dad?'

Aiden frowned, his face tightening. 'Look, Mike, I'm not sure what you want me to say? He died when I was ten and I don't have an awful lot of memories before that. I mean, how much can you remember of your first ten years? Most of the time I was away at school, or taking part in my own karting races.' As if aware he was becoming too tense, Aiden relaxed his face and smiled. 'Sebastian Foster was, and still is, a legend. What you saw in public was what I remember in private, too. I'm incredibly lucky to have had him as my father.'

'Do you think he would have been proud to see his son following in his footsteps?'

Mel cringed as Aiden briefly closed his eyes, as if the question was painful. When he opened them he shifted forward in his seat, resting his hands on his knees, his jaw muscle jumping. 'With respect, how the hell do I know?' Shaking his head, no doubt appalled at his brief slip into honesty, he sighed. 'I like to think he would have been pleased to see me take up racing, yes, but frankly until I win a Championship, there's not much to be proud of, is there?'

Mel couldn't take any more. She stood up and walked over to them. 'Sorry, Mike, but we're going to have to call it a day there. You know how it is. Aiden's next appointment is already champing at the bit, telling me we're late.'

Mike looked down at his watch. 'Well, sure, but I thought we had an hour?'

'Forty-five minutes was scheduled, and we're already at fifty minutes, so please, if you don't mind?'

'Actually, I had a few more questions.'

Mel glanced over to where Aiden was watching her, his expression a mixture of amusement and disbelief. Oh, and he might not want to show it but she was pretty certain there was a heavy dose of relief in there, too.

'Perhaps if you want to email the questions to me?' she suggested to Mike, trying her best to keep him sweet. 'We'll get you a reply as soon as the day quietens down.'

Looking slightly mollified, Mike put away his recorder and shuffled out of the room. Mel followed him, making sure he knew his way out. Then she went back to face Mr Evasive.

'My *next* appointment?' Aiden asked the moment she slipped back into the room. 'Don't tell me, it's with *Horse Weekly*.'

'Horse ... what?'

'You said he was champing at the bit?'

He was grinning widely at her now and it was hard not to respond. Hard to ignore the flutter of her heart. Taking her time, avoiding his eyes, she went to sit opposite him. 'Aiden, why did you lie to Mike?'

Instantly the grin disappeared.

'What do you mean?' He sat back, folding his arms across his chest in what she could see was an instinctively defensive gesture.

'Don't take me for a fool.'

For a long moment he said nothing. Then he rose to his feet, looking down at her from his six-foot frame. 'Look, are we done now?'

'No. We won't be done until you explain why you treated that interview as if it was a tedious chore you couldn't be bothered with, like sorting out the recycling.'

'Actually, I recycle as I go along. Don't most people?'

Mel had a reasonably long fuse, but it was just about to ignite. She leapt to her feet too, squaring up to him even though her eyes only made it to the top button of his black polo shirt. 'I thought we'd agreed you were going to be honest with Mike?'

His grey eyes flashed. 'Did you really want me to tell old Mikey boy that actually Sebastian Foster didn't give a damn about anybody but himself?' The veins stood out starkly on his neck as his face flushed with anger. 'Or how about that rather than being proud of me, he didn't even know I existed?'

Silence reverberated round the room. Mel didn't know where to put herself. What to do, what to say.

Then Aiden swore under his breath and went to sit down again, shoving his head into his hands. He looked so defeated, so utterly wretched, that instinct took over and she found herself putting her arms around his stiff, unyielding body. 'I'm so sorry.'

He raised his head and glanced at her with sombre grey eyes. 'Sorry for what? That my father was a jerk, or that you made me talk about the father that was a jerk?'

Oh God. Her heart began to swell in her chest, filling with feelings she didn't want. She needed Aiden to be the shallow, rich playboy she'd imagined. Not this vulnerable man sitting beside her now. 'I'm sorry for both.'

For a few moments he rubbed at his eyes with the heel of his hands, obviously trying to pull himself together. Then he let out a long, slow breath and sat back up. Immediately Mel snatched her arm away and stood out of touching range, afraid he might think she was coming on to him. Even more afraid he might be right.

His eyes told her he'd noted her quick slide away, but he made no comment. 'No need to apologise. I can't see how the first is your fault, and as for the second, you were only doing your job.'

'Perhaps, but if I'd known you carried all this ... anger inside you about him, I'd have never put you through that.'

He angled his head to look at her and all she could think was God, this man is absolutely, heart in the mouth, gorgeous.

'Strikes me that you kicked Mike out as soon as you realised.' He held his hand up to his ear in an exaggerated show of listening. 'I'm not sure I hear a load of other journalists clamouring to talk to me.'

Grateful for the dial down in emotional intensity, Mel smiled. 'Busted.' Then, because she had to ask. 'You could have told Mike what you just told me, you know. Nobody would think any less of you. In fact it might get some of the press off your back.'

'Do you really think anybody out there wants to hear that Sebastian Foster was anything other than a fabulous father?'

'From the sound of things, you don't owe him anything.'

His shoulders slumped as he let out another deep sigh. 'He was still my father.'

Mel's heart was now so swollen it started to ache. Finally she understood. How could the son, the pretender to the legend, knock his father off the pedestal the world had put him on?

Chapter Seven

It was an odd blip in the racing calendar to have three weeks between races but usually Aiden had no problems with it. The break gave the team a valuable chance to make the tweaks and adjustments that were so vital early on in the season. Since he'd made such a spectacular arse of himself in front of Melanie though, he was finding the lack of opportunity to focus on racing a real frustration. It meant he was focusing on other things instead. Like a petite, increasingly attractive looking press officer.

From across the Delta HQ dining area, he watched as Mel ... no, he couldn't call her Mel. Frank did, but then he'd known her for years. Sally did, too, but they were probably friends as well as work colleagues. It didn't give him the right to assume he had that ... connection with her.

His eyes followed *Melanie* as she laughed at something Stefano said to her and he felt a twinge of annoyance. Was his Italian teammate really that funny? He couldn't remember him ever saying anything even remotely amusing. Unless it was his usual pre-race announcement that he was going to wipe the floor with him. That cracked Aiden up every time.

The man on his left let out a loud series of coughs and Aiden reluctantly dragged his eyes away from Melanie and towards those of his race engineer. They were getting along better now. Or they would be, if Aiden didn't constantly wonder whether Frank was making father-son comparisons.

'What is it, Frank? Something go down the wrong way?'

The older man shook his head. 'I wanted to get your attention.'

Ah. 'And you thought you had to cough, rather than ... what? Just say my name?'

'I wasn't sure, if I spoke, you'd hear me.'

Aiden smiled. 'Very tactful. I suspect what you're trying to say is stop oggling my surrogate daughter.'

Frank wasn't an easy man to make smile. He took most things seriously, which Aiden could appreciate because he took his racing very seriously, too. Still, he managed a small smile for him now. 'You know, it's quite funny to see you watching her, because she's of the opinion that men don't look twice at her.'

'You're kidding me? Is that why she dresses how she does? To try and prove herself right?'

Frank seemed to take a sudden, compelling interest in the sandwich he was eating. 'I'm not sure I'm qualified to comment on that.'

'So, what's the deal with you and Mel ... Melanie then, Frank? How long have you known her?'

Frank raised his head again, clearly relieved to not be discussing women's clothing. 'I remember her first day at Delta. She was ... what, twenty-four? She'd been working for a motor magazine since leaving university and this was her first job in motorsport. Her father was an absolute petrol head apparently so I suppose that's where her interest in the sport sprang from.' He shook his head and actually grinned. 'She came across as this really tough cookie. Like she knew exactly what she was doing, even though she'd never done the role before. She didn't let anybody boss her around.' That pronouncement made him chuckle. 'Still doesn't.'

Because he was interested, Aiden gave up the pretence of eating and pushed his plate to one side. 'It must have been tough for her, having her parents die in a car crash.'

The older man raised his eyebrows, clearly surprised Aiden knew a private piece of information about *his* girl. 'Yes. Obviously I wasn't there at the time. When she joined Delta she was still getting over it and it took her a long while before she opened up to me.' His expression clearly said *so it's a flaming mystery why she's told you*. 'When she did, I got a sense of how hard it must have been for her. Friends went home from university during the holidays. Mel had no home to go to.'

Aiden's mind flashed back to his days at boarding school. Perhaps he and Mel – oops Melanie – were kindred spirits in a sense. Growing up he'd had a bed in a dorm at boarding school and a bed in a soulless mansion for the occasional holidays. Never anything he'd referred to as home.

Once again Frank cleared his throat.

About to make a joke about the man having a sore throat, Aiden saw the seriousness of his expression and shut up.

'I'm only saying this to help you understand something. Mel dated a driver when she first joined Delta. He broke her heart.' Though Frank's eyes were old, the look he shot Aiden was vibrant, intense and full of meaning. 'If you do the same to her, I'll flatten you.'

Aiden had thirty odd years and many more kilos of muscle on Frank but he didn't laugh out loud. He took the warning with the respect it deserved. 'I would never hurt her, Frank. I know I have a poor reputation when it comes to women, most of it deserved, but I only tangle with those who know the score.'

Briefly Aiden thought of Devon and winced. She'd known it, but for a while she'd chosen not to remember it. 'Mel is ... great. I really like her. Luckily for all of us though, she's not the type I go for, so relax. She's quite safe.' Bugger, he'd lapsed on her name again, but that was only because Frank called her Mel. It was no big deal.

'Hey, what are you two cooking up over here? That's quite a serious conversation you've been having.'

Melanie settled her tray down on the space opposite, making them both jump. Her eyes slid from Frank to Aiden and back again. 'And now you both look like two boys caught with their hand in the cookie jar. What have you been discussing?'

Her hazel eyes sparkled with amusement and though he'd promised Frank that Melanie was quite safe from him it didn't mean he could stop noticing.

Hastily he turned back to his race engineer. 'Sorry, I've got to dash. I'll leave Frank to explain our conversation.' Shooting him a silent apology, he got to his feet.

He was two steps away when she called him back. 'Hey, wait. Are you coming to the sponsor ball in Grosvenor House tonight?' When he hesitated, she waggled her finger at him. 'No, don't you dare pull out on me, Sally will go mad. Stefano has already given us some feeble excuse about a family do in Italy. These guys pay a fortune to put their name on our cars. We've got to have one of our drivers there.'

A frown line peeped its way through her wavy fringe and she looked so worried that had he not had every intention of going anyway, he would have cancelled all other plans in a flash. With a dramatic flourish he waved his arm and bowed. 'Cinderella, have no fear, Prince Charming shall go to the ball.'

He walked away to the sound of her laughter. Somewhere deep inside it tugged at him and as his step became lighter, a smile slipped across his face.

Mel was still laughing when she turned back to Frank.

The same Frank who was looking at her with an extremely concerned look on his face. 'Hey, what's up? Does this have anything to do with the heavy conversation you were having with Aiden?'

Frank grunted. 'Sort of.'

'But what ... hey wait.' Slowly it started to dawn on her. 'You were talking about me, weren't you?' Beginning to feel hot and cold all over, Mel prodded at the pasta on her plate. 'Please don't tell me you were giving him the heavy father treatment.'

'I just made it clear what would happen to him if he hurt you.'

Embarrassment vied with exasperation. In an effort to control her answer she drew in a long breath, letting it out so fast her fringe flapped in the breeze. 'For goodness sake, Frank. I've already told you I'm not his type.'

'Yes, that's what he said, too.'

She'd known there wasn't a cat in hells chance she would be, but her heart still plunged in disappointment.

'Still, if he's as smart as I think he is, he'll soon wake up to the fact that you've got far more to offer than all those fancy bimbos put together.'

Oh, Frank. She might have lost her parents but in loyal, big-hearted Frank, together with his sweet wife, Nancy, she'd found some amazing substitutes. Reaching across the table, she squeezed his hand. 'Thank you.'

Needing a moment to gather herself, she sipped at her orange juice. 'Do I dare ask what you've threatened to do if he hurts me?'

'Flatten him.'

She hiccupped out a laugh. 'Okay, that would work, though I can't quite picture how you're going to catch him first?'

'Enough of the cheek.' But he was starting to laugh himself now, a rumble in his large chest. 'You know what, Aiden didn't rib me like that. He treated me with the respect my more mature years should deserve.'

'Ah, but Aiden doesn't know you like I do. He thinks you're scary, when actually I know you're a pussy cat.'

'Or maybe the boy's more cunning than I thought. Maybe he knows in order to get to you, he has to get me on side first.'

'Oh, please.' She could just imagine Aiden, who'd probably never had to chase a girl in his life, bothering to sidle up to Frank just to get to plain old her. Who, if she was honest, he wouldn't even need to chase. If he crooked his finger she was rather afraid she'd lope after him like an overly keen Labrador.

'Are you and Aiden getting on any better now?' she asked, keen to move on from the depressing image she'd just created.

'I think so. We did have a bit of a chat about the fact that I was also race engineer for his father.'

'You were?' Mel's eyes almost bulged out of their sockets.

'I was.'

'Blimey, I didn't realise. How did he take that?'

'Let me see.' Frank finished his sandwich and wiped his mouth with a paper serviette. 'The boy is continuously compared, unfavourably, to his father. Now he finds his race engineer, the one man he really needs to trust in order to win a championship, was also race engineer for his father.' Frank sighed. 'Honestly, considering all that, he took it pretty well.'

'Outwardly.' Mel recalled Aiden's face as he'd admitted how he hadn't got on with his father. Hard enough to spend your life constantly wondering if you're as good as a parent you idolised, but if you didn't even *like* them? 'Inwardly, he's probably still reeling from it.'

Frank nodded. 'That's what I guessed, too. I told him he needs to enjoy himself more behind the wheel and the rest will come. Whether he believes me or not, I don't know. I certainly believe he has it in him.'

Mel stood, walked round the table and hugged the man she now thought of as Dad number two. 'And I believe with you as his race engineer, he's got it in him, too.'

'Get away with you,' Frank said gruffly, looking decidedly flustered. 'You know I'm not good with all this mushy stuff.' He pulled away, but not before he'd squeezed her right back, letting her know exactly what her words had meant to him. 'Now, about tonight. Nancy wants you to come round to ours and change so she can do your hair, or your nails or whatever else you women get up to before a fancy do.'

'She's coming too, I hope?'

'You bet. Went out last week and bought another new dress. I told her, nobody's going to remember the last one she wore, but apparently I'm a dumb male who doesn't know anything.'

For once in her life, Mel kept quiet. She'd be wearing the same boring black dress she always wore. It was easier that way and besides, the dress was comfortable. She'd gone past the age when she was prepared to suffer for fashion. There was nobody who cared what she looked like.

An image of Aiden looking drop dead gorgeous in a dark tuxedo swam through her mind and she laughed at herself. Sure, she could try and gift wrap the parcel but when the snazzy wrapping was removed, the contents remained the same.

Chapter Eight

Aiden couldn't drag his eyes away from Melanie. Or more precisely, from the body she'd been hiding beneath tidy, functional clothes. The woman had curves. Incredible round, in and out curves that a man would have to be blind or dead not to appreciate. Unfortunately he hadn't yet had a chance to see them, sorry her, close up. Since his arrival at the bash, the launch of some new fangled watch he was now wearing on his wrist – and apparently had to continue to wear even though he actually preferred his Rolex – their paths hadn't crossed. But now the pictures had been taken, the hands shaken and the polite conversation over dinner accomplished.

Smiling his apologies to the women either side of him at the table, he headed across the room towards her.

'Well, hello,' he drawled as he came up behind her, smiling to himself as she visibly jumped. 'Who are you, and what have you done with our press officer, Melanie Hunt?'

A rare blush crept up her slender neck. 'Very funny.' Her eyes scanned down her vivid purple dress and she grimaced. 'Before you say anything, it wasn't my choice. I got ... sidearmed, I think is the right word for it, into wearing it.'

That explained it. 'Let me guess, your choice was a neat black dress that not only covered your knees but possessed a neckline even your granny would have thought too staid?'

The noise she let out sounded like a laugh she'd tried to suppress but had snuck out anyway. 'It might have been.'

'Well, whoever browbeat you into wearing it deserves a medal. You look ... stunning.' And she really did. With her hair pinned loosely up on her head, a touch of make-up highlighting the depth of her eyes, diamond earrings dangling from her ears and the silk strappy dress draped around her spectacular curves, she looked a million dollars. Light years away from the fresh-faced press officer he thought he knew.

'Actually it was Frank's wife, Nancy, who made me wear this,' Mel admitted, clearly oblivious to the fact that he was standing there with his tongue, at least metaphorically, hanging out. 'She swears she bought it for herself and then realised it was a size too small. Personally, I don't believe a word of it. I think she bought it for me. She's always going on about the fact that I need to make the most of my figure and—' Grinding to a halt, she raised her eyes to the ceiling. 'Ouch, that was too much information. It's not as if I have a great figure either, just that she thinks I could make more of what I've got.' The sides of her lips curved up in an embarrassed grin. 'And why am I talking to you about all this?'

Aiden laughed, enjoying watching her talk. Enjoying listening to her talk, too, even if it was about women's clothing. 'If you want my personal opinion, I'm on Nancy's side. A woman's figure should always be enhanced.'

His comment received a sharp jab in the ribs. 'I knew you'd see it that way.'

'Err, excuse me, what other way is there? Why would you *not* want to show off what you've got?'

'Because it sends a certain ...' her voice trailed off and she shook her head, probably realising that trying to explain this to him was a lost cause. 'It sends a signal, all right? One that says "hey, look at me, I'm a woman. Come and flirt with me, play with me a while and then dump me for a far more attractive model."' Her eyes widened in horror and she slapped a hand over her mouth. 'God, I shouldn't be saying this to you. I've had way too much champagne. Promise me you'll forget I said any of that.'

As her blurted admission went a long way towards explaining why she dressed as she did – in disguise to protect herself from getting hurt again – he couldn't see how he was supposed to forget it. And what the blazes was he supposed to say now, anyway?

He cleared his throat, which instantly made matters worse because now she was looking at him, *expecting* him to say something profound. 'I ... um ... Frank told me that some bastard broke your heart.'

His stomach dropped as her face crumpled before him. 'He did?' The words came out as a high-pitched shriek. 'Well, that's just ... that's great. My humiliation is now complete.'

'Hey, he didn't give me any details.' Aiden was desperate to reassure her. 'He was only, you know, warning me off.'

Another noise came out of her throat, not quite the shriek of before. More a strangled cry. 'Oh God, I was wrong. The humiliation just keeps on coming.' Her eyes darted over his shoulder, then down to the floor and finally over to the bar. Anywhere, it seemed, but at him.

He clasped her arm and made her look at him. 'Why is that humiliating for you? I'm the one who was being warned off.'

'And you really need the warning, don't you?' She actually looked like she was going to cry. 'Someone like you is really going to want to get together with someone like me.'

Because he definitely couldn't handle tears he focused on her dismissive tone and the derision in her eyes. 'What do you mean, *someone like me*?'

Taking a tissue out of the slim black bag she had on her

shoulder, a far cry from her usual rucksack, she dabbed at her eyes. 'You know perfectly well what I mean.'

'I do?'

'Yes. You know the type you go for.' Reaching up she tugged hard on a wisp of her trailing hair, almost making him wince. 'Blonde, not brown.' She nodded down to her perfectly proportioned breasts. 'Large, not average.' When her hand went to point at her short but nicely shaped legs, he'd had enough.

'Okay, I get the picture,' he cut in, feeling more than a little insulted. 'What you're saying is that I go for dumb blondes with big boobs.'

'Are you going to tell me I'm wrong?'

And okay, now he was put on the spot and having to think back through the women he'd dated over the last few years maybe she had a point. 'It's not a requirement that they're dumb,' he countered sulkily.

For a split second she just gaped at him. Then her mouth tilted upwards and she started to laugh. And laugh. And he, watching her face light up and her eyes shine, found he was laughing with her.

Mel couldn't stop giggling. Some of it was down to inebriation, some to relief that they'd managed to move beyond the discussion about her pathetic love life and the bizarre fact that Frank had felt the need to warn Aiden to keep away from her. Most of her lightheadedness though came from watching Aiden let go and laugh. Really, really laugh. She didn't think there was a more beautiful sight in this world.

'I'm not sure how that conversation got so out of hand,' he said finally, his eyes still dancing. 'I only wanted to compliment you on how great you look.'

Simple words, but from his tongue they had the capacity to make her heart skip a beat. Time to remind herself he was only being charming, a product of those ingrained manners of his. This wasn't the start of a flirtatious dance that would lead them into bed.

The thought sent heat shooting through her blood. Staring down at her feet she took a few deep breaths and tried to school her face into a more chaste expression. 'In that case what I should have done is reply to your kind compliment with a simple, "why thank you."' Smiling sweetly she dipped her head, as she was sure they would have done in Austen's day. 'Are you having a pleasant evening?'

He gave her a dazzling smile. 'Thank you, I am. Miss Hunt, will you do me the honour of allowing me this dance?'

Before she could stammer out a reply he was propelling her onto the dance floor. As he settled his arm casually around her waist, drawing her towards him when she would have left more space, she realised she'd never been this close to him. It made her giddy. The dancing might be gentle and sedate but the firm feel of his body against hers and the scent of his darkly masculine aftershave put her in a tailspin. She wasn't a great dancer, lacking confidence, but he seemed to have enough for both of them.

In her high heels she came up to his shoulder and if she tilted her head slightly, she could see his profile. Straight nose, high cheekbones and firm, freshly shaven jawline. The hand she rested on his shoulder was only inches away from touching the dark hair that fell over his collar. In fact if she nudged her head a little, and stood on tiptoes, she could probably run her lips across his jawline ...

'Mel.' She gave a guilty start as he dipped his head down

to look at her. 'Is it okay if I call you Mel? I've noticed sometimes you're Melanie, other times Mel. I'm not sure what the criteria is, but I'd like to call you Mel.'

The sound of her nickname on his lips sent a shiver down her spine. It sounded dangerously intimate, implying a familiarity she wasn't sure she could handle. 'There aren't many people who get away with calling me Mel. Only people I'm really close to.'

Was it her imagination or did his grey eyes just cool a little? 'Fine. I'll stick to Melanie. I was just being lazy.' They danced in silence for a few minutes until Aiden's arm tightened slightly on her waist and he pulled her more snugly against his lean frame. 'What would you say if I told you I want to be one of those people who's allowed to call you Mel.' His voice lowered an octave and the husky tone sent further ripples through her already aroused body. 'I want to get closer to you.'

She fought to keep from floating into perilous territory. 'I'd remind you that I'm not your type.'

Warm breath fanned the sensitive lobe of her ear, his lips a whisper soft touch against her skin. 'I'm not so sure about that.'

He's playing with you, she reminded herself, fighting the rush of desire. Flirting is what he does. 'Well, you're definitely not my type,' she countered, easing herself away from the heady feel of his hard body.

'Oh?' His expression tightened and something flickered in his eyes that she couldn't read.

'Physically you're not bad,' she conceded. 'But I prefer my men with a little more emotional maturity.' She smiled to take the edge off her words.

'Is that your polite way of saying you want more from a man than hot sex?' When she nodded, he sighed and ran a hand slowly down her back. 'That's a damn shame, because from how you're making me feel right now, I reckon the sex between us could be *really* hot.'

Oh boy. She swallowed, trying to work some saliva back into her mouth. 'Is that the magic Aiden Foster chat-up line? The one you use with all those big boobed blondes we talked about?'

The hand now resting on her lower back stilled and he exhaled sharply. 'You're determined to typecast me as a playboy, aren't you?'

'I rather think you've managed that all by yourself.'

Briefly his jaw tightened but then he laughed softly. 'Fair enough.' Pulling away he clasped her hand in his and led her away from the floor towards a secluded corner where he tilted her chin, his thumb gently caressing her jaw. His eyes insistently searching out hers. 'I like your style, Ms Hunt, and right now I have this overwhelming need to kiss you. I can't work out if that's what you want, too, but as Frank will flatten me if he catches me even trying …' Expelling a deep breath, he shoved his hands into his trouser pockets. 'Perhaps we should change the subject.'

Mel's heart thumped, rattling against her ribs. 'I'd be lying if I said I didn't want that, too,' she whispered. 'It's not a good idea though, for so many reasons,' she forced herself to add, 'so, yes, please, let's talk about something else.'

When he said nothing, just continued to stare at her with hot, needy eyes, Mel blurted. 'How do you feel about working with Frank, now you know he was also race engineer for your father?'

She might as well have thrown a bucket of ice cold water over him. In a flash the sexy heat in his eyes vanished, replaced by irritation. 'That's certainly one way to kill the mood, Melanie.'

His deliberate use of her full name jarred, feeling cold and formal when what she wanted was to return to warm and intimate. But that was too dangerous. 'Mood killing was the general idea, though I'm interested in your answer nonetheless. A truthful one, that is.'

He gave her a sardonic smile. 'I'm very happy to be working with Frank. If he was good enough for my father, then he's certainly good enough for me, don't you think?'

She'd attacked him where it hurt, and felt a surge of shame. 'I shouldn't have asked that. It was a low blow. I just ... I knew that was one sure way to distract you from what we'd been discussing.'

'It seems you were right.' He smiled again though now his grey eyes were horribly flat. 'It's been a blast, dear Melanie, but all good things must come to an end. I guess I should earn my salary and do some mingling. I'll catch you later.'

Mel huffed out a breath as she watched him being swallowed up by the crowd. Woman after woman slid over to him, taking his hand, whispering in his ear. Mel tried not to be hurt by the way he smiled back at them, occasionally laughed, always so attentive.

Perhaps he *was* doing his job, but it looked awfully similar to how he'd just flirted with her.

She was prevented from making any more painful comparisons when the phone in her small clutch bag began to ring. Frowning she peered at the screen, not recognising the number. 'Hello, Melanie Hunt.'

A few minutes later she was pushing her way through the throng surrounding Aiden and tugging at his arm. 'I've got the head of St Michael's Boarding School on the phone. Apparently they've been trying to reach you all evening.'

He looked startled. 'Me?'

'That's what they said. It's about one of their students and they insist they need to speak to you.' When he continued to gape at her, she pushed the phone into his hand. 'They say it's urgent.'

Giving her a *I haven't a clue what's going on* shrug, he made his apologies to the crowd surrounding him and strode out into the lobby.

For a split second Mel dithered about whether to follow him or not but as he had her phone she thought she should. By the time she caught up with him he was pacing up and down in a quiet corner. She didn't want to eavesdrop but she couldn't help hearing his side of the conversation.

'Why aren't you phoning his mother?'

'I'm in London, for God's sake. What on earth do you expect me to do?'

Finally, in a resigned voice. 'Put him on the phone.'

Mel's heart shot into her mouth. Did Aiden have a son he hadn't told anybody about? And if he did, why had he looked so nonplussed when she'd told him who was on the phone?

'What do you think you're playing at, Tom? Your mother will have a fit when she hears you've tried to run away from school.'

Mel chewed her lip, wishing she hadn't followed Aiden out. Wishing she hadn't heard any of this very private conversation. It was none of her business if he had a secret son. None at all.

As Aiden dropped onto a nearby chair muttering, 'It's school, Tom. It's not meant to be fun,' Mel spun round and hastily made her way back into the ballroom.

Chapter Nine

Aiden stood at the bar, eyeing up the impressive selection of drinks and realising he couldn't have any of them. Not entirely true, as he was allowed to go wild and have a water, or indeed any soft beverage. What he really wanted, scratch that, what he really *needed*, was a long beer followed by a whisky chaser, a combination the team nutritionist would flip at. Technically he could have an alcoholic drink – they weren't travelling to Shanghai for another couple of days – but things had changed dramatically since his father's era, when drivers often got smashed the night before a race. Nowadays the sport was almost as much about fitness as it was about racing and teams paid people good money to lecture their drivers about regulating carb intake, maintaining hydration and limiting alcohol consumption to such a puny amount it was hardly worth bothering with. The next drop of alcohol he would allow to pass his lips was champagne when he stood on the podium. Note to self. He'd said when and not if.

'Aiden?'

He knew, from the way his pulse began to race, that Mel … he kicked himself. M.e.l.a.n.i.e – apparently he wasn't in that close inner circle of friends allowed to use the shortened form, probably because he wasn't *emotionally mature* enough.

Melanie was now standing next to him, her breast brushing lightly against his arm. He might have told Frank she wasn't his type, but truth was he didn't have a type, just a rule not to get involved with women who might get hurt. Melanie, with her warm heart and previous track record of heartbreak, fell firmly in that category. So he needed to stop looking at her and wanting to kiss her.

He slid her phone out of his jacket pocket and handed it back to her. 'Thanks.'

'No problem.' She glanced down at the phone and then back up at him, eyeing him cautiously. 'Is everything okay?'

'Fine, thanks.' He could tell she was curious about the phone call but she already knew too much about him. He didn't feel like adding to it. Besides, hopefully, that was the end of things. He'd done his duty, read Tom the riot act. His mother could sort the boy out next time.

His curt reply had brought a frown to her pretty features. She wasn't beautiful, even with the make-up and the fancy dress, but by God she was lovely. Better than beautiful, because he'd often found beauty associated with coldness. Melanie ... damn it to hell, Mel – he was going to think of her as Mel, even if he couldn't call her that. Mel wasn't a bit cold. If he was being fanciful, he'd say she was toasted marshmallows over an open fire. Cosy evenings cuddled up under a soft blanket.

'I don't know why you've got the hump with me,' she told him crossly, which certainly put a halt to his wistful warm thoughts. 'I only changed our conversation because you asked me to.'

'True, though a different topic would have been appreciated.' For a moment he considered her, wondering how she'd appreciate having one of her buttons deliberately pressed. 'How about why you go round dressed like a nun to avoid any intimacy because you assume all men are like the sod who hurt you?'

Her mouth opened, then closed. When it opened again, her face had gone scarlet. 'I don't dress like a nun.'

'No?' Deliberately he ran his eyes down her body, over the delicious bumps of her breasts, the neat indentation of her waist, the full curve of her hips. 'Tonight, you're definitely not a nun, but all the other days?' He shook his head, exasperated at her. 'How can a smart, intelligent, incredibly attractive woman like you let a stupid racing car driver make you feel less about yourself?'

'I … sorry, can you repeat that?' She looked part flabbergasted, part amused, still a tiny bit irritated.

'What, the fact that you're not dressed like a nun tonight, but—'

'No, no, the other bits. The smart, etc, etc. I definitely need to hear that again.'

He laughed, relaxing shoulders he hadn't realised were so tense. 'I'll repeat them, if you promise to answer my question.'

She glanced down at her empty glass and handed it to him. 'In which case, I'll need another drink.'

Aiden sorted her out with another glass of champagne and himself with a lacklustre sparkling water and slice of lime. Boy did *he* know how to party. After neatly sidestepping a few of the watch company directors with promises that he'd catch them later, he found a quiet table.

'Melanie Hunt, you're a smart, intelligent, very … sorry, incredibly attractive woman,' he told her, looking her straight in the eye, which was easy to do because he meant it.

Her eyes went a little glazed and her smile was as soft and sweet as he'd ever seen from her. 'And you're a generous flirt, Aiden Foster, but thank you.'

He held her gaze. 'I meant every word. Now, tell me about this git who broke your heart.'

She let out a short laugh at his abrupt change of subject. 'There's not much to tell,' she replied, taking a few gulps of the champagne he'd just bought her. 'Carlos and I dated for a year—'

'Carlos Ferrer?' he interrupted. 'Otherwise known as the Spanish sleazeball?'

Mel choked out a laugh at Aiden's shocked expression. 'Okay, so maybe I should have had a bit more sense than to fall for him, but I was young and naïve and he was handsome and dashing.'

'And a total scumbag.' Aiden shook his head, as if he was having trouble believing what he'd heard. 'Hell, Melanie, I thought you had better taste than that.'

'This coming from the man who fell into bed with a supposed journalist called Devon?'

She half expected him to go frosty on her again but he surprised her by roaring with laughter, touching her glass in a salute. 'Touché.'

Heat washed through her as she stared at his mouth and the sensuous curve of his lips. And the dazzling grey of his eyes. Grabbing at her glass she swigged back another gulp. If she carried on like this, she was going to get drunk. Factor in the way Aiden was gazing at her, as if she was a double helping of his favourite dessert, and she'd lose control of her senses, including the part of her brain which told her to stop.

She pushed the glass away.

Aiden watched, though he didn't remark on her action. 'So how did things with you and the sleazeball come to an end?'

'Through my press contacts I heard he'd been spotted taking three women back to his hotel room after a night on the town.' For the first time, recounting the tale didn't make her heart ache. She still felt sick at the thought of how stupid she'd been, but her heart was definitely whole again, beating solidly in her chest.

Until Aiden searched out her eyes that is, when it started to flip and turn over. 'We're not all like that,' he told her quietly.

'Maybe not, but I don't think I'm prepared to take the risk a second time,' she answered, just as quietly.

His expression was one of pure disbelief. 'You're talking to a man who takes risks for a living. If I can do that with my life, surely you can be brave enough to take a risk with your love life?'

'What are you trying to say?'

'I'm saying you should let your guard down and live a little. You don't have to involve your heart. Think of sex as a form of recreation. It's exercise, a stress buster and a feel good factor all wrapped up in one immensely satisfying package.'

She grabbed for the glass she'd pushed away. 'And who's going to supply that, err ... package?'

The mouth she'd wanted to kiss since she'd first clapped her eyes on him curved upwards and his eyes glittered. 'Me.'

Her head knew his proposal was far too dangerous to contemplate. Heck, she already had a crush on the man and she was even starting to like him, despite all his baggage. There was no way she'd be able to disengage her heart.

But that same head was feeling pretty fuzzy from champagne. As for her body – that was primed and ready to do whatever Aiden wanted.

'It's a very tempting offer,' she admitted, her voice rattling in her throat.

His eyes shimmered. 'Why don't you think about it?' he said finally, slowly rising to his feet, his lean tuxedo clad body towering over her. 'I'm going to call it a night.'

'I think I'm ready to go to bed, too.' He raised an eyebrow and she started to giggle, realising what she'd said. 'To sleep,' she added quickly.

'Shame.' Quickly his eyes scanned the room. 'Look, to avoid any rumours, why don't you go up first? I'll hang on a few more minutes and press a few more hands.'

She hadn't even considered, for one moment, how it might look if they both left the function room and rode up in the hotel lift together. Maybe even got out on the same floor, because she guessed Delta had a block booking. Instead she'd been thinking, *what if he pins me to the wall of the lift and kisses me? What will I do then?*

Now she wouldn't find out.

Feeling shamefully disappointed she weaved her way into the lift. Back in her room, away from Aiden's intoxicating presence, she found she wasn't quite as drunk as she'd thought. She'd even begun to meticulously remove her make-up when she heard a tap on the door.

'Mel?'

As her hand froze, her heart leapt. Automatically she scrutinised her face in the mirror. Could she do this? Open the door, when she had a pretty good idea what would follow if she did?

Of course he might just be checking she'd got back to her room safely.

Hastily – she didn't want to look like a total freak – she removed the rest of her make-up before walking to the door. Rubbing one hand over her chest, trying to calm the furious beating, she turned the handle with the other.

Aiden was leant against the doorframe, bow tie undone,

shirt open at the neck, jacket carelessly tossed over his shoulder. He looked every inch the poster boy, even down to his smoky grey eyes and dark hair flopping over his forehead.

He cleared his throat. 'I came to ... I just wanted to check ...' He swore. 'Damn it, can I come in?'

Without hesitation she flung the door open.

Heat blazed from his eyes and Aiden did exactly what she knew he'd do. He pounced.

In a heartbeat he was covering her mouth with his and kissing her. A long, drugging, toe-curling kiss that was never going to be enough, for either of them. In a well-practiced move he pinned her against the wall, his hand reaching behind to peel down her dress. With her breasts exposed, he let out a deep, satisfied groan and buried his face in them, kissing and licking until she was wild with lust.

'God, Mel.' He pushed his hips hard against her, grinding his arousal against her stomach. 'I want you,' he told her thickly.

Mel couldn't speak so she let her hands talk for her, reaching between them to touch him, running her hands up and down his fly. Pulling down his zipper.

'If you don't want me inside you in the next few seconds, you've got to tell me.' His voice sounded as undone as she felt and the knowledge that *she* was doing that to him, aroused her even further. Somewhere in the back of her mind she knew she should say no, but the only sound to come out of her mouth was a moan.

Aiden took it for the go-ahead it was.

There was the sound of foil rustling and moments later he was crashing into her, thrusting deeply, pushing her so high up the wall her feet were left dangling. 'Christ ...' he let out a deep, satisfied groan that shot straight to her core.

'Shit, Mel, that feels so bloody good.' A string of earthy profanities left his mouth as he pounded into her.

The pleasure built so fast and hot that Mel couldn't hang on, couldn't stop herself. Her body seemed to have a life of its own and, moaning and grinding against him, she exploded.

Seconds later he jerked against her, groaning out his pleasure. As the shudders died and her body sagged against him, she burst into tears.

Chapter Ten

Aiden had experienced more than his fair share of sexual encounters. Usually, if all went according to plan, he left the woman smiling, sometimes gasping for more. But *crying*?

'Shit, Mel, what is it? What's wrong?'

Her head was buried against his neck and he was still supporting her body with legs that were starting to buckle. Slowly, carefully, he slid her down so her feet were resting on the floor. Then he took her head in his hands and forced her to look at him.

'Was I too rough? I don't know what came over me. One minute I was looking at you, the next I couldn't wait to get inside you.' Gently he traced a thumb down her cheek, wiping away the trail of tears. 'Finesse went out of the window. I'm so damn sorry.' He'd never felt like a greater jackass in his life.

'No, I'm okay,' she gulped, standing back and hitching her dress back over her perfect breasts.

'So this is your usual reaction to stupendous sex, is it? Tears?'

She sniffed, giving him a watery smile. 'I've never had stupendous sex before, so I'm not entirely sure if this is usual or not.'

He didn't know whether to laugh or cry with her. After zipping himself up he took her hand and pulled her towards the bed, sitting down next to her. 'Come on, Mel. Sorry, Melanie. Tell me what's wrong. Much as my ego would love it, I know damn well those aren't tears of joy because of the great sex you've just had.'

'I guess you should call me Mel, now we've had sex.'

He cursed softly. 'I repeat. Tell me what's wrong.'

Hazel eyes that swum with tears finally found his. 'I ... oh God.' She started to cry all over again.

He held her close, rubbing his hand up and down her arm, trying to soothe when actually he had no idea how to do that. 'It's okay,' he murmured. 'It's okay.'

Finally she stopped crying, shaking her head at him as she pulled away. 'No, it's not okay. It's a long way from okay. I'm so stupid. I've just had sex with you. Now I'll want to have sex with you again. Shit, shit, shit.'

Bewildered, he stared at her. 'How on earth can the thought of repeating that again, and please God, again and again after that, be anything other than bloody wonderful?'

'Because you're you, damn it.'

She stood and walked to the bathroom to blow her nose. He was left reeling, feeling as if he'd driven into a wall at a hundred miles an hour.

'What's wrong with me?' he was forced to ask when she reappeared, her cheeks no longer wet but her nose slightly red and her hair, thanks to his rough handling, lying in a mess of brown curls around her face. Bedraggled, yet utterly charming.

'You slept with the bunny boiler, just because she was there. That's what's wrong.'

'I told you, that was a mistake.'

'And this isn't?' Her voice had risen so much she was almost screaming at him.

'No,' he replied firmly, shaking his head to add further emphasis. 'We've got a connection. You can't deny that. You're the only woman I've ever really talked to. The only one I've told about my father.'

She sighed and perched onto the bed, making sure she left a great gap between them. 'Well, I'm pleased for you, because when you've finished with the counselling, and the bonus sex, you'll be in a better place.' Her lips curved into a sad smile. 'I, on the other hand, will be back where I was after Carlos left me. Nursing another broken heart and needing counselling myself.'

'It doesn't have to end that way,' he countered, narrowing the gap between them by gripping onto her hand. 'It doesn't have to end.'

He didn't know who was the more shocked by his statement, him or her. Could he actually manage a real relationship? One that involved more than parties and lots of sex?

'Tell me, Aiden, what's your longest relationship been?'

The fact that he had to think, and trawl through too many faces while he did the thinking, shamed him. 'Two months. It doesn't mean I'm incapable though,' he added firmly. 'I just haven't found the right woman yet.'

'Do you really think there's the remotest chance I might be the *right* woman?' she asked incredulously. While he was working out his answer – yes, possibly, I don't know but I'd like to find out – she stalked towards the mirror. 'God, I look like a woman who's just ... who's ...'

'Been thoroughly pleasured,' he replied softly, coming up behind her and wrapping his arms around her. 'Against the wall, I might add. You look rumpled and incredibly sexy and I find myself wanting you all over again.'

Her eyes met his in the mirror and she started to laugh and shake her head at the same time. 'You're not going to make this easy for me, are you?'

He turned her towards him and stared deeply into her watery eyes. 'Come on, Mel. Let's just see where this takes us, eh?'

When she said nothing, just bowed her head and buried

it in his shirt, he sighed. 'You know after talking to Frank, I reckon you and I have more in common than you think.'

'I bet. I can often be found squeezing into a fast car and screaming round a racetrack.' Her words were muffled against his chest. 'And afterwards, when I climb out, all these men chase after me, dressed in only a G-string, thrusting their phone numbers into my hand.'

He bent to kiss the top of her head. 'Very funny. I meant that after your parents died, you must have gone through a terrible time. Frank told me how you would stay at university during the holidays because you had no home to go to.'

'Frank talks too much.' Her head rose from its resting place on his shirt front. 'How does that make us similar?'

Instantly Aiden wished he'd kept his mouth shut. How could he admit to this lovely, stable, secure, *together* woman how sad and pathetically lonely he'd once been? To distract her, he started pulling the pins out from her hair so it fell over her shoulders. It didn't tumble, or cascade, like it did on the shampoo adverts. Instead it straggled wonkily around her face.

'What are you doing?' She grabbed at his hand, pulling it away. 'That move might work with your usual women, but it doesn't work with me and especially not with my hair.' She huffed and started to pat the unruly strands down. 'God, I bet I resemble a raccoon after it's pushed its paw in an electric socket.'

He smiled, helping to rearrange her hair into some semblance of order. 'Actually, you look pretty damn adorable.'

Mel distanced herself from Aiden's twinkling grey eyes and enticing body and went to sit back on the bed. The man was an absolute master of dodging the hard question, but she was pretty certain that before he'd messed up her hair he'd been about to tell her something important. 'Why do you think you and I are so similar then?'

He gave her a slight, *oh we're sticking with this conversation are we*, smile and leant back against the wall, arms casually crossed over his chest. 'I just meant that with being away at boarding school so much of the time, I also have some experience of missing a home life.'

Suddenly his answers to her next questions took on a huge importance. It was a real test of his claim that he wanted a relationship and not just a sexual romp. Would he tell her the truth, or evade again, as he just had? 'Is that the boarding school you went to, the one on the phone? Is that why they wanted to talk to you?'

'Oh, no.' He slipped one hand casually into his pocket. 'That was just some family matter.'

Okay, so he wasn't going to tell her about his son. Perhaps she could understand that was too private. 'At least you had a home to go back to in the holidays, didn't you?'

'Of course.'

His cool, flip tone was starting to grate. 'You say you didn't have much of a relationship with you father but how about your mother. Did she make a fuss of you?'

His eyes flickered, but whatever emotion lay in there, he clearly wasn't going to reveal. Instead he pulled her to her feet and began to kiss her. Gently this time, his lips soft against hers, as if determined to show her there was another side to him. 'I can think of far better things to do than talk about my childhood.'

Mel knew she should tell him he'd had his chance and he'd blown it. How could she though, when her body was under such a delicious onslaught? So she threaded her hands through his luxuriously thick hair and melted under his caress.

She'd worry about everything tomorrow. Tonight was for living.

The following morning Mel woke to find she was alone in the bed. Beside her, in place of Aiden, was an indentation in the pillow, a lingering smell of aftershave and a hastily scribbled note. *Duty calls. Gone to the gym. See you in Shanghai! A xx*

Disappointment crashed through her and she fell back against the pillows. *Come on Mel, let's just see where this takes us* ... clearly the only place this was taking her was another notch on his flipping bedpost.

What the blazes had she done? Aside from drinking too much and behaving totally irrationally, that is. It didn't matter that she'd already decided it could only ever be a one-night stand. The fact that he'd already beaten her to that decision, snuck off without even having the decency to look her in the eye and tell her that, made her so flaming angry. Then again, she'd known who he was and had sex with him anyway, so perhaps the anger should be directed at herself.

A tear crept down her face and she swiped at it. If only anger was the only emotion she was experiencing. If only she didn't feel so hurt, so betrayed. So utterly disappointed that he hadn't hung around to say goodbye.

Or to ask for a repeat performance.

The phone by the side of her bed sprang into life and she grabbed at it, welcoming the distraction.

'Melanie Hunt.'

'Sally O'Neil. Remember me? We used to be friends,

as well as work colleagues. That was before you spent most of last night canoodling with Aiden Foster and then disappeared without a trace. Only a few moments before Aiden himself, I might add.'

Mel sighed, staring up at the ceiling. 'Do you believe in coincidences?'

'Nope.'

'Then I guess you'd better come to my room for a full breakdown.'

'Whoopee!'

Sally must have had a room down the same corridor because Mel barely had time to shrug on a robe before Sally was hammering on her door.

'Is that Sluts R Us? Open up!'

Hell's bells. Mel flung the door open and dragged her friend inside. 'Don't go yelling that in the corridor,' she hissed under her breath.

Sally just laughed. 'Relax, nobody's around and even if they were, they would hardly believe I was talking to you.' Holding onto both her arms, Sally studied her. 'Yes, you definitely had sex last night. From the looks of it, fabulous, earth shattering sex.'

'Okay, okay.' Mel wriggled out of her friend's grasp and headed for the coffee machine. 'If you want me to talk about this, first I need caffeine.'

'Wow, he didn't let you sleep at all, did he?'

'I ... we ...' She slid onto the nearest chair. 'No, we didn't get much sleep, and I'm really out of practice with all of this. The sex, the sleepless night *and* the talking about it afterwards.'

'Well, welcome back to the land of the living. Don't worry, it's like riding a bike.' She giggled at her innuendo. 'You never forget how to do it.'

Mel ignored her friend and took a slug of coffee. 'There are some parts I want to forget.'

'Come on, not every sexual encounter ends in heartbreak, you know. Loads of people manage to have a good, healthy sex life without ever involving their emotions.' She squeezed her hand. 'How have you left things?'

Mel handed Sally the note. 'I woke up to this. Obviously the whole thing was a huge mistake. I guess we'll have to talk about it after the race.'

'*After* the race? Aren't you flying out on Wednesday?'

'I am, but Aiden needs to focus and I don't want whatever happened between us to be a distraction. With failing to finish in the first race and only a fourth place last time, he needs to get his head in the right place. Frankly, if he's going to stand a chance of winning the championship he really, really needs to start winning.'

As her words finally ran out, Mel became aware her cheeks were stinging with warmth and her chest rising and falling. She glanced quickly over at Sally only to find her staring back, wide-eyed. Obviously her rather passionate outburst had just given away far more than she'd wanted to.

For while it was perfectly true that loads of people managed to have sex without involving their hearts, Mel wasn't one of them.

Chapter Eleven

The Shanghai International Circuit. Fifty-six laps over 5.4 kilometres, it had a long back straight descending into one of the trickiest corner combinations on the racing calendar. It was a track Aiden had won on twice before. If he was to have a shot at the title this year, he had to win this weekend.

For once everything seemed to be running smoothly. During the practice sessions they'd found the right set-up for the car with frightening ease. He felt happy on the harder tyre now and in qualifying yesterday, he'd not just achieved pole. He'd done it with relative ease.

If the car drove like that again this afternoon Aiden knew he'd win, no question.

As the chauffeur driving him to the track threaded his way through the chaotic traffic, Aiden glanced out of the window. He had a soft spot for Shanghai. He loved the way it mixed Western sophistication with oriental tradition; ultra-modern skyscrapers rubbing shoulders with art deco buildings and Buddhist temples. The skyline was even more incredible at night, dominated by the Oriental Pearl Tower, an amazing structure that always reminded Aiden of an upended pair of cartoon dumbbells.

Would he be celebrating in this cool, sophisticated city later today? If he wasn't it would be down to bad luck. Or bad driving.

The thought stuck in his mind as he jumped out of the car and headed towards the Delta motorhome for the pre-race briefing. He was so focused he nearly collided with the person coming down the stairs.

'Sorry, I ... oh, Aiden.'

Mel almost tumbled into his arms. He clasped a hand on each of her shoulders to steady her, keeping them there far longer than necessary. 'Well, well. A gorgeous woman throws herself at me. My day's just perked up.'

She squirmed out of his grasp. 'You're on pole for the first time this season. I hope ... I *believe*, your day will get a lot perkier than this.'

'I hope it does, too,' he told her, holding her eyes, letting her know he wasn't just talking about winning the race. He was thinking about how he was going to celebrate.

They'd not had a chance to talk properly since he'd reluctantly left her bed a week ago. He'd sent her a few flirty texts but her responses had been those of his press officer, not his lover. He was left with the distinct impression she wasn't as keen to repeat their encounter as he was.

He'd see about that. After he'd won.

Clearly finding the heat in his eyes too hot for comfort, Mel's gaze settled on his throat rather than his face. 'Well, umm, good luck.'

She tried to brush past him but he struck out an arm and held her back. 'Where's my good luck kiss?'

She shot him a look of disbelief. 'How about you win because you're a kick ass driver and not because some silly press officer gave you a kiss?'

He tugged harder on her arm, pulling her even closer, uncaring of who might be watching. 'How about I win because I'm a kick ass driver lucky enough to be kissed by his sexy press officer just before the race?'

Her hazel eyes softened and he knew he had her. At least for now. Gently he pressed his lips to hers, feeling the burn all the way to his groin. Groaning he angled his head, deepening the contact, knowing full well he shouldn't, but needing to feel her melt against him. Her breathy sounds of pleasure fuelled his desire, and also his hope.

Unwillingly he pulled back. 'There's no way I can lose now.'

Her answering laugh was husky, the soft sound curling round his insides. When he finally made it to the briefing room, a wide smile had bloomed across his face.

'Well, it's good to see you happy for once,' one of the engineers declared, regarding him quizzically.

Aiden glanced around the room, taking in the assembled core team. They hadn't bonded yet, though maybe today would kick start that process. He needed it to, because he couldn't win the championship without them.

'I'm happy because this weekend we've put together a car faster than any of the others on the grid.' Deliberately he let his eyes rest on each man in the room. 'You've all done your job. Now it's up to me to go out and do mine.' Finally he cast Frank a small smile. 'But first I'm going to get my orders from the boss.'

There was a smattering of laughter. Then it was down to business.

Several hours later Aiden was battling in the rain behind the front running cars from Arrows and Viper. Everything had been fine until he'd been unlucky enough to pit just before the damn safety car came out. Since then he'd been threading his way back up to the front. He had twenty laps to go and he was determined to get there.

'The Viper behind you is on a different strategy. You're not racing him,' Frank confirmed in his earpiece, which was a blessed relief. He only had to focus on the men ahead.

'Box the next lap,' Frank instructed a lap later.

Aiden happily slipped into the pit lane, as instructed. It was the last stop. A fresh set of tyres and eighteen laps to win the Chinese Grand Prix.

For a few seconds there was a blur of frantic activity. The pit crew undid the wheel nuts, jacked the car up, took the wheels off, placed new wheels on, wiped his visor, tightened the nuts, removed the fuel hose. It was precision timing, teamwork. The result of practice, practice, practice.

'Go, go, go.' Frank's voice boomed in his ear and Aiden got the message. He zipped smartly out of the pit lane, making it out just in time to maintain his third place position.

After that he forgot about the oppressive heat in the cockpit. Forgot, too, about the ache in his pelvis from the seat that might be molded to fit his backside, but was designed with his safety and not his comfort in mind. He focused on nothing but the track ahead. Within five laps he'd overtaken the Arrow. Only Carlos in the Viper to beat now.

He felt the tingle of anticipation down his spine as he closed in. This was why he loved his job. The thrill of wheel to wheel racing. Pitting his skill against an opponent, knowing he'd have only the smallest window of opportunity to pass. If he got it wrong, if he braked a split second too early or late, a collision would send him hurtling off the track. If he got it right, victory was his. And how satisfying if it came from overtaking Mel's ex.

The tingle became a throb and his heart lurched. Making use of the slipstream provided by the Viper, Aiden pulled out and floored the throttle. His car surged past.

His hands twitched on the wheel, wanting to punch the air, but he knew he still had a job to do.

'Three more laps, Aiden. Just three more.' Frank was

obviously thinking what he was thinking. Don't cock this up.

He didn't.

Three laps later the blur of the white and black chequered flag flashed before his eyes as he crossed the finish line. Flinging out his arm, he acknowledged the crowd as he completed his slowing down lap then swerved towards the run off area. There he performed a cheeky donut, spinning the car round and round, grinning manically as the smell of burning rubber flew up his nostrils.

'You beauty,' Frank bellowed in his ear. 'You bloody beauty.'

Aiden laughed, feeling the usual wave of euphoria that came with winning. This time though, it was tempered with relief. He hoped he'd just proved to his new Delta team exactly what he was capable of. Now all he had to do was repeat this victory again. And again and again, throughout the season.

First though, he'd savour this moment. Gleefully he drove his car into the coveted number one position in parc ferme, snapping open his seat belt and pulling off the steering wheel before hauling himself out. He was met with a sea of flags – Chinese flags and Union Jacks – and jubilant fans. Feeling light-headed with the twin emotions of joy and relief he moved to the fence to hug the team, his eyes searching for the one face he really wanted to see.

When they found her his heart almost skipped a beat. Her eyes shone, a wide smile split her face and she looked exactly how he felt. Bemused and utterly, utterly delighted.

Flinging his arms around her he squeezed her tight and as emotion clawed at his throat he worried that if he tried to talk, he'd cry.

'Is this a good time to get a post-race quote from you?' she asked, smiling and crying at the same time, which had to be one of those multitasking things women could manage and men couldn't.

Before he had a chance to embarrass himself with a reply he was herded off for the weigh in. After that, and having shoved all the required sponsor paraphernalia onto the parts of his body for which it was intended – cap on head, watch on wrist – he bounded up the stairs to take his place on the podium.

First place. He'd forgotten how good it felt.

Mel sat at the back of the garage by the TV screens and tried to gather her wits enough to produce a post-race press release. She knew there were tears running down her cheeks but she couldn't seem to stop them.

'Are you okay?'

Frank stared at her in bewilderment and she laughed. 'Yes, I'm fine. I think the emotion of the occasion just got to me. You know, seeing one of our drivers come in first.'

'Is that so?' He passed her a tissue from the pack she'd been using. 'So had it been Stefano on top of that podium instead of Aiden, you'd still be crying?'

After a quick wipe of her cheeks she smiled ruefully. 'Okay. You always were smarter than you look. I'm *especially* pleased for Aiden because I know how hard it's been for him coming to race for his father's old team.'

'Nancy and I saw the pair of you having a long talk at the ball last Saturday.'

Mel's heart gave a loud thump but she was saved a reply as the turgid chords of 'God Save the Queen' blasted through the speakers outside.

Automatically she turned towards the TV monitors.

Aiden stood on the coveted number one podium spot, joy sparkling in his eyes and across his beautiful face. How could he possibly fancy her? Yet she knew it had been her face his eyes had sought when he'd climbed out of the car. Her body he'd wrapped his arms around so tightly she'd not been able to breathe.

Following the podium interviews there was the press conference, and then more interviews. Mel oversaw them all, trying to remain professional which wasn't always easy when Aiden kept shooting her secret smiles.

'You realise it's been a couple of hours since I dragged this sweaty body out of the cockpit, don't you?' he grumbled as she shooed him towards yet another interview. 'It's a good job it isn't smellavision.'

'They aren't interested in how you look or smell. Just what you say.'

'And how about you? Are you interested in how I look and smell?'

It was one of several loaded questions he'd whispered in her ear during the last half an hour, all of which she'd responded to as his press officer. 'I'm interested in you telling the world what a great driver you are, and how fantastic the Delta team are to work with.'

He halted, frowning down at her. 'Hey, what's up? I know we haven't had a chance to catch up properly since last weekend, but …' He exhaled, rubbing a hand through his damp, tousled hair. 'First you seem reluctant to give me a good luck kiss. Now you seem reluctant to even talk to me. Are you going off me already?'

The line – it had to be one, surely – was delivered with just the right amount of vulnerability to make her heart flip. 'Please, let's not talk about this now.'

He shifted his eyes towards where the television crews

were setting up, cameras poised, microphones at the ready. 'When then, Mel?'

'Later.'

He glanced down at his watch. 'Give me a chance to get the media off my back, thank the crew and take a shower. Meet me at my hotel room in, say, two hours?'

She swallowed. 'Fine.'

With a nod he walked towards the waiting press. Mel hung back, her heart feeling suddenly very heavy. She had two hours to stew over what on earth she was going to say.

Chapter Twelve

When Mel walked towards Aiden's room two hours later she was no nearer to knowing how she was going to handle her silly crush – please God that was all it was – for the flavour of the day racing driver.

Outside his door she fiddled with her fringe, which absolutely refused to stay flat despite the ironing she'd just given it, and sucked in a deep breath. The wire from her bra, the lacy number she'd donned half an hour ago in a rush of guilt, shame and longing, cut into her chest and she surreptitiously tugged it down before knocking.

Aiden, so unbelievably sexy in a casual T-shirt and faded jeans, answered the door with a mobile phone glued to his ear and a fierce scowl on his face.

'You're flaming joking,' he yelled into the mouthpiece. 'What the hell am I going to do with a kid? I'm a bloody racing car driver. We're on the move eight months of the year and, in case you didn't know, this season has only just fucking started.'

She winced as he began to stalk up and down the room. Because his face looked so angry, her eyes strayed down to his feet. His narrow, naked feet. Was there something seriously wrong with her because she found even his feet incredibly sexy?

'Look, I apologise for swearing, but this is one hell of a bombshell you're dropping on me.' He sounded more agitated than angry now. 'I can hardly turn round to the FIA and say sorry, can we only race from Silverstone for the rest of this year, because I've got this kid to look after.'

She watched dumbfounded as Aiden thumped his

forehead with his free hand and slumped to the floor. How could he be so dismissive, so uncaring, of his own son? Especially after all the hints he'd made about his own father's treatment of him.

'Sure, by all means phone back later,' Aiden replied, a weary edge to his voice that matched his hunched shoulders, 'but don't expect my answer to change.' With that he ended the call and dropped the phone to the floor.

Mel cleared her throat. 'Is everything okay?'

And, yes, considering what she'd just heard on the phone, it was probably a stupid thing to say.

From his position on the floor, leaning against the wall, he gave her a tight smile. 'Just swell, babe, thanks for asking. Everything's absolutely fine and dandy.'

She could see he was suffering so she cut him some slack. 'Is there anything I can do?'

'Well, you could shag me. That would sure help take my mind off things for a while.'

She flinched. Slack be damned, she wasn't putting up with that. 'Jesus, Aiden, do you have to be such a prick?' Rigidly she turned her back on him and was halfway towards the door when he called her back.

'Don't go.' Her hand hovered over the door handle. 'Please.'

The desperation in his voice caught at her. When she glanced back at him she knew she couldn't walk away. He looked more than distressed, he looked miserable. This was meant to be his day, his moment. Instead it looked like his world had come crashing around his ears.

'I won't go,' she promised, taking a step towards him, 'as long as you tell me what the heck is going on.'

'Fair enough. Do you want a drink?' He let out a strained laugh as he wearily struggled to his feet. 'There's probably some champagne around here somewhere.'

She shook her head. 'No drink. Just an explanation.'

He faced her, hands on hips, his face strained. 'Tell me, Mel, if you hadn't walked in on all this shit ... would we now be stripping our clothes off and kissing each other senseless? Or were you going to turn me down?'

Oh God. Mel found she couldn't look into those direct grey eyes so she focused on the painting just above his shoulder. A few coloured boxes and what appeared to be an accidental splash of paint smeared over them. Very tasteful.

'Mel? Answer the flaming question.' He exhaled loudly. 'Please.'

Slowly her eyes connected with his. 'I can't answer it,' she told him truthfully, 'because I really don't know.'

There was the briefest flash of disappointment before he hid it behind his usual charming mask. 'At least it wasn't a no then, huh?'

'Does it really matter to you?'

He let out a short laugh. 'Does it matter whether the woman I'm crazy about wants to sleep with me?' Shaking his head, he moved over to the small settee and sat down, crossing one long leg over the other. 'What do you think?'

His tense face and bleak eyes told her it probably did matter to him. At least for now. And the way she was keeping her distance, pulling away when he clearly needed her, was hurting him. Adding to his misery on an evening when he should be celebrating.

Letting out a soft sigh she did what she'd really wanted to do all along. She marched over to him, wrapped her arms around him and kissed him.

He returned her kiss hungrily, voraciously. As his tongue began to do wicked things in her mouth, his hands found their way under her blouse, a rough warmth trailing across her suddenly sensitised skin. Whatever her answer might have been before she'd knocked on his door, now it was a resounding yes. She pushed herself more fully against him, making it absolutely clear what she wanted.

Taking her cue he eased up her bra – the lacy one, thank God for lust and vanity – and was starting to create exquisite torture with his tongue when he suddenly pulled back.

'Sorry.' His breath came out in pants as he rested his forehead against hers. 'After last time I told myself if I ever got another chance with you I'd slow things down.' He heaved in two long, deep breaths. 'It's harder than I thought.'

'I don't need it to be slow,' she reassured, allowing her fingers to take the fascinating journey across the planes of his high cheeks and then over the stubble at his jaw. 'In fact I'm a bit of a fan of fast and furious. But maybe we should talk first.' She planted a kiss on his beautiful soft lips. 'You were going to tell me about the phone call.'

'I know.' His mouth eased its way over hers. 'And I will.' He nibbled on her bottom lip. 'But please, can I just forget about that for a while longer? Celebrate my victory by peeling off this sexy bra and worshipping your fabulous body?'

'I don't have a—'

'You do.'

He silenced her with another deep, long kiss. While his mouth was causing havoc, his hands patiently and methodically removed her clothes. As a racing driver he was used to focusing on the task in hand; an attribute that clearly spilled into his love life, too. Emptying her mind of all her niggling doubts Mel clutched at his T-shirt, dragged it over his head and joined in.

When their clothes were strewn haphazardly over the floor,

Aiden picked Mel up and carried her to his bed. He *was* going to do this properly. By nature he was fast, but by God, he could be slow and careful and ... tender. Yes, he could do all that, if he put his mind to it. So once he'd yanked off the bedspread and laid her on the crisp white sheets, he knelt beside her and began to kiss every inch of her smooth, pale skin. The freckles above her breast. The soft curve of her stomach and down to the inside of her thigh.

The trouble was, she kept moaning. Quiet, delicious sighs of pleasure that tore at his supposed control.

'Oooh, Aiden, yes, just there.' Another gurgle in the back of her throat.

'You're not helping,' he muttered, raising his head fractionally only to find her flushed face beaming down at him.

'Oh?'

'You know perfectly well.' He slid off the bed and grabbed a condom from his wallet. He might as well put it on, even though he was going to torment her just a little longer.

Determinedly he settled his mouth over her breasts and began to lick at the proud nipples, every part of him aching as he studied the glistening peaks.

'Ahh, to hell with it.' With a grunt he lowered his body over hers and entered her in one long, powerful motion.

'Is this the slower version?' she gasped, then sighed as he tortured them both with long, deep thrusts.

'Are you complaining?'

Her lips curved. 'Certainly not ... I, ahh, yes, more of that.'

He stopped any further conversation by kissing her.

When he came back to earth, Aiden found Mel leaning on

her side, one hand propping up her head, watching him. He thought he could guess the first words to come out of her mouth, and he didn't think they were going to be, 'please can we do that again?'

'Now it's time to talk.'

He gave himself ten out of ten for his mind reading ability. Sadly it meant his abilities as a lover had to be questioned if all she wanted to do now was talk about that blasted phone call.

He tried for distraction. Reaching out a hand, he settled it over a luscious breast, smiling as it fit perfectly into the cup he'd made.

She laid her hand over his and gently took it away. 'Come on, Aiden. A deal is a deal.'

With a sigh of resignation, he flopped back against the pillow. 'It's actually not that interesting. Not half as interesting as discussing, I don't know, your top ten sexual positions.'

'Aiden.' It wasn't just frustration he could hear in her tone. There was also finality. If he didn't talk, she'd walk.

'That was St Michael's Boarding School on the phone,' he replied flatly.

'Oh no, has your son run away again?'

He shot to a sitting position. 'My *son*?'

Her hazel eyes blinked up at him. 'I overheard you talking to them last time. I didn't mean to, but it was my phone so—'

'You seriously think I have a son?' he interrupted.

'Well, yes.'

'Wow.' He scratched at his head, his mind spinning. 'That says a great deal about what you think of me, huh?'

'Who's Tom then?'

He laughed bitterly at the way she avoided his question.

'Tom is my ten-year-old half-brother who's now run away from school twice since he started boarding. They've tried to contact our mother. Apparently they can't get hold of her. After her, I'm the next of kin.' He pinched the bridge of his nose, trying to ward off the pounding headache he knew he'd get the more he talked about this crap. 'As the school are not surprisingly a) cross and b) worried they want to send him home.'

For a few seconds there was nothing but silence. 'Have I got this right. Your mother has disappeared without letting your brother or the school know where she is?'

Her surprise was endearing. She'd clearly never met a family like the Fosters. 'Yes.'

Mel pushed herself up into a sitting position. 'I'm really struggling to understand this. What sort of mother *abandons* her son?'

Sweet, naïve little Mel. 'The sort that doesn't give a flying fig for anyone but herself.'

'What about Tom's father?'

'From what I can remember he handed over a wedge of cash a few months after Tom was born and relinquished all responsibility for him.'

'Poor boy.'

The sympathy in her voice pricked at him. 'Yes, it sucks for Tom, but what the hell am I meant to do? I can't possibly look after him.'

'So what will happen?'

Aiden shrugged, fighting off the awful sense of déjà vu. 'He'll have to stay at the school.'

'And that's working so well for him at the moment, isn't it?' Her breasts bounced distractingly, drawing his eyes until she tugged at the duvet to cover herself. 'Just like it worked so well for you.'

'What's the alternative?' he asked defensively, though he knew damn well what it was.

'Tom could always—'

'No.' Aiden thrust his legs out of the bed and groped for his jeans. This wasn't a conversation he was comfortable having naked. 'For the next few months I'm focusing on winning a title. I can't do that if I'm trailing a kid round with me, one I barely know and who doesn't know me.'

It was a while before she spoke again. When she did her quiet words were uttered with enough scorn to chill his bones. 'So let me get this straight. Tom's father abandoned him at birth, his mother has effectively abandoned him at boarding school and now his *brother* is giving up on him, too. Wow, that's going to make him feel really special.'

Aiden's head began to pound, exactly as he'd predicted. 'We Fosters don't specialise in happy families,' he replied bitterly, stalking over to his holdall to find some painkillers.

'Is this some sort of perverse payback then? You had a miserable childhood so now you're going to make your brother have one, too?'

He snapped his head back round to her. 'It's not like that.' Hell, his head was going to burst.

'What is it like then, Aiden? How can you possibly explain why you're not going to do your utmost to look after your clearly very unhappy kid brother?'

Her eyes flashed furiously and he had a sudden image of her as a mother, defending her child. All he could think was lucky kid.

After a few thwarted attempts to find the damn painkillers he gave up and sagged onto the floor. 'Please, can we stop the shouting for a moment? I can't think straight right now. My head feels as if it's about to explode.'

She must have seen the pain etched across his face

because she immediately leapt out of bed, reached for her handbag and found him some tablets. For a few blessed seconds he enjoyed the sight of her naked body – apparently even a pounding head couldn't stop *that* pleasure – until she disappeared into the bathroom. When she returned, glass of water in hand, she had the hotel robe wrapped tightly around her.

Dutifully he swallowed the tablets. A few seconds later he was groaning in pleasure as she knelt behind him and began to massage his shoulders.

'It's not quite the end to the day you'd imagined, is it?'

Her lips brushed the top of his head and his heart did some sort of weird somersault in his chest. 'No, but if you carry on doing that, it'll end on a real high.'

'How's the head now?' she asked after a while.

He felt ready to slide to the floor and ooze through the floorboards. 'Better, thanks. I think I'm still dehydrated from the race, and the combination of that plus the phone call ...'

Her magic fingers stopped and she shuffled round to face him. 'I know it's none of my business, and I'm sorry if you think I'm being hard on you, but you need to think of what all this must feel like to that poor boy. Your brother.'

'Half-brother.'

'He's still family.'

Aiden let out a deep sigh, knowing exactly how Tom must feel. Like nobody loved him. 'I can imagine what he's feeling and believe me, I sympathise with him, but ... hell, Mel, I'm not part of his life. I never have been. I only saw the kid once, just after he was born. A few months later I left home for good. Without looking back, I might add.' He could thank his father for something. His death had left an insurance payout on Aiden's eighteenth birthday.

He'd finally been free to do what he wanted. Live where he wanted.

'He's your *brother*, Aiden.'

'No, he's not. He's a boy who shares some of my DNA, that's all.'

'My God, I can't believe I'm hearing this.' Shaking her head, Mel rose to her feet and started hunting around for her clothes.

Aiden watched with a sinking feeling in his gut. The look of disgust on her face, combined with the fact that she was getting dressed, had to signal a shitty end to his day. Unless he could somehow magic an explanation that would enable her to see his point of view.

Lurching to his feet he stooped to pick up the bra she'd been looking for and clutched it tightly in his hand. 'Mel, please, just listen to me. I'm being selfish here, I know, but God, I really feel this could be my year for winning the championship. I've wanted this so much, for so long, and now I'm finally driving a car that's capable of it. Plus I've got the backing of a team who've done it before. If I could win it, just once, it would mean ...' he trailed off, unable to say the words out loud. The chance to come out from under his father's shadow. Vindication to his supporters and his sponsors that he had what it took to be a winner. Most important of all, proof to himself. 'It would mean everything to me.'

'I see.'

She looked ... resigned. No, it was worse than that. She looked disappointed and he had a horrid feeling that disappointment was directed at him.

'Do you really?' he asked, his voice raw with desperation. 'I can't afford any distractions this year. I'm sorry, but I just can't.'

Wordlessly she shrugged off her robe, shimmied into her knickers and then into her trousers. He didn't even see her button up her blouse over her naked breasts – he was still holding onto her bra – because he was too focused on her face. Tears crept over her cheeks and she looked so damned upset it made his heart ache.

When at last she was dressed she gazed up at him with luminous hazel eyes. 'And what about me, Aiden? Am I a distraction, too? Or don't I even rate that high a priority?'

What? 'Jesus, Mel, of course you're not a distraction. You're far more important than that. You're a friend, a lover, someone who makes me laugh. Keeps me sane.' She wasn't listening to him. She was walking away towards the door. 'Please, don't do this. Don't walk out on me.' His voice was shaking and he couldn't seem to control it.

With her hand on the doorknob she stopped to look at him, tears now streaming freely down her face. 'I think it's best this way. You need to focus on racing and I could do without another broken heart.' She nodded, once. 'I'll see you in Bahrain.'

Then she was gone.

Aiden staggered to the bed, feeling as if something large and very heavy had burrowed its way into his chest. He flopped onto his back, eyes staring blindly at the ceiling, desperately trying to work out how a day that had held so much promise, and delivered such jubilation, had ended so spectacularly badly. He'd won the Chinese Grand Prix, for God's sake. So why was he now in his hotel room, his heart crushed, feeling so utterly alone?

He glanced down to find his hand still clenching her lacy bra. With a cry of despair he threw it across the room.

Sod it. He didn't need a woman to make his world feel right. He just needed a series of wins.

Chapter Thirteen

The Bahrain Grand Prix came and went, with Aiden picking up fourth place and twelve very precious points, putting him in third position on the leader board behind Carlos and Stefano. Mel kept out of his way as much as she could, making sure there was always someone else with her, be it Sally, or another member of the team, when she needed to speak to him. The resignation in his eyes told her he knew exactly what she was doing. Though walking away was the hardest thing she'd ever done in her life, she was consoled by the thought that the alternative, spending more time with him, falling head over heels in love with him, would be harder still.

It helped when she told herself he was a selfish bastard. Tom might have turned out not to be his son, but Aiden had to have a heart of stone to turn his back on his young sibling.

It didn't help when her heart reminded her Aiden hadn't had an easy childhood himself. From the tiny morsels of information he'd deigned to let slip she could understand why being dragged back into a family life he thought he'd escaped from would be hard. Of course looking after a kid brother would also be a distraction to Aiden's obsession with winning the World Championship. Something that apparently meant everything to him.

At least she knew where she stood.

Now they were in Barcelona, preparing for the Spanish Grand Prix. May was a fabulous time of year to be in Spain and Barcelona always lifted her spirits. How many other cities could boast such amazing Gaudi-inspired architecture yet also provide a waterfront and beach to rival many holiday hotspots?

Today though she was at the Circuit de Catalunya where the motorhomes were arriving and the paddock was alive with teams setting up for the next four days.

Mel was on her way to check out the Delta media centre when she caught sight of Aiden striding across the paddock, a mobile planted against his ear.

'Are you really trying to tell me you can't control a ten-year-old?' he shouted into the phone.

Unsure whether she should walk away or stop to help, Mel stood rooted to the spot, watching as Aiden struggled to control his temper.

'Let me talk to him,' he snapped. 'No, not later, now. I want to talk to him now.'

There was a few minutes of silence where Aiden paced up and down, running his hands through his hair and over his face. He must have sensed her looking because his eyes suddenly found hers and for what seemed like an eternity he stared. Then he pointedly turned his back on her. 'Hey, buddy, what's going on? I thought you promised last week to stop doing this.'

Mel's heart stuttered. Though she barely heard Aiden's softly spoken words, she knew he must be talking to the brother he apparently hadn't disowned, after all. By the sound of things, even though he hadn't gone to see him, he had at least begun a phone dialogue. Not that it mattered to her, of course.

Except she found it did.

Realising she was intruding on a private conversation, Mel scurried over to the Delta motorhome and found a quiet room to bury herself in the ever increasing mountain of interview requests.

Ten minutes later the door was flung open and a pair of turbulent grey eyes flicked round the room.

'Is everything okay?'

Aiden nodded pointedly at the empty room. 'Are you sure you want to talk to me on your own like this? Not afraid I might jump you?'

Wow, she'd never seen him so wound up. 'I'm pretty certain you can manage to control yourself around me.'

'Don't be too sure,' he muttered darkly.

Her heart stuttered and she tried to look away from the heat in his eyes but as he strode purposefully towards her, she found she couldn't.

'Right now, I'm finding it pretty damn hard to control this desire to kiss you until you can't remember your own name.'

His hands captured her face and those burning eyes, like pieces of hot charcoal, zeroed in on her mouth. Instantly her pulse began a crazy dance. Just as her body swayed involuntarily towards him though, he let out a muted curse and took a step back.

'There's enough chaos in my life at the moment. Much as I'd love to, it's probably not a good idea to add to it.'

Disappointment ricocheted through her, even though she knew he'd made the right call, for both their sakes. 'What's happened?' He started to shrug off her question, giving her one of his deliberately vague, *it's not important* looks, and she exploded. 'Don't you dare fob me off! I'm not stupid. I know that was your brother on the phone.'

Still he remained mute, staring guardedly back at her, and she actually found herself stamping her foot.

'For God's sake, how can you possibly claim you want a relationship when you won't even *talk* to me?'

'I was under the impression a relationship with you was off the table.'

'It is.' So why did telling him that feel like she was throwing away the best thing that had happened to her in a long, long time? 'It doesn't mean we can't be friends though. I want to be your friend, Aiden.'

Briefly his eyes closed. When they opened again, he let out a deep, heartfelt sigh. 'Well, as it happens, I could do with a friend right now, so thanks.' Nodding over to her table, he asked. 'Do you mind if I join you for a minute?'

'Of course.' Hastily she scrambled together the mess of notes she'd spread liberally over the surface.

When he'd sat down Aiden picked up one of her pens, running it through his fingers. 'The phone call you overheard was from the school, letting me know Tom ran away again this morning. They found him, thank God, but it's now the third time he's done that.' When he finally raised his eyes to hers he looked so sombre her heart ached for him. 'Next time they might not find him.'

She reached out and placed her hand over his. 'I'm sorry.'

Slowly he twisted his palm and for a heart stopping moment their hands entwined, his long fingered and tanned, hers smaller and paler. Abruptly he let go and picked up that stupid pen again.

Hurt, she snatched her hand back and stuffed it onto her lap. She could still feel the lingering warmth from his fingers.

'I got through to Tom and asked him what he wanted to do,' Aiden continued in a flat voice, lazily twirling the pen through his fingers as if Tom's answer had been of no consequence to him. 'He said he wanted to stay with me.' His eyes flickered towards her, a wry smile on his lips. 'Live at school, or live in a motorhome travelling across Europe from Grand Prix to Grand Prix. It wasn't much of a contest.'

'Maybe the choice was live with a group of children and teachers he didn't know, or live with his brother.'

'Whom he also doesn't know,' Aiden cut in quickly. 'I don't think you realise, Tom sees me as only one step removed from evil. Boarding school is evil. His mother, who abandoned him to boarding school, is also evil. As I abandoned him ten years ago, when he was only a few months old, he's reserving judgment on the evil part. At least until he gets to know me.'

'And will he have that chance?'

Disgust flashed across his face. 'What? You think ... you're actually still wondering if I'm going to let him come and stay with me, even though I told you he's run away from school *three times*?'

'You were adamant you didn't want any distractions this season,' she reminded him.

'I don't,' he replied sharply. 'But I can't see how wondering whether he's run away again, and whether they'll find him this time, is going to be any less distracting than having him where I know he's safe.'

'So he's going to come and live with you?'

Aiden took in a deep breath. 'Yeah. It looks like he is. At least until his mother finally turns up and takes him home.'

Mel suddenly felt an almost overwhelming urge to burst into tears. She was happy for Tom, whose life was probably about to take a giant turn for the better. She was happy too, for herself because Aiden had just confirmed what she'd suspected all along. He wasn't cold or unfeeling. He was a decent man, trying to do the right thing in an impossibly difficult situation.

Swallowing down the lump in her throat she smiled. 'It's a good thing you're doing, Aiden. The right thing.'

'But several weeks too late, eh?'

'You had your reasons.'

Aiden didn't need to look into Mel's eyes to know exactly what she thought of his reasons. His *selfish* reasons. Reasons that had cost him the chance to sleep with this woman who made him want ... he didn't know what, exactly. Just that it was a damn sight more than the *let's be friends* fob off she was offering. He knew, just *knew*, that if he'd gone to kiss her earlier, she'd have let him. More than that, she'd have well enjoyed it.

'How can I help?'

The kindness in her pretty brown eyes made his chest hurt.

'Well, luckily, I've got the motorhome with me, so he has a place to sleep. Plus I've told the school they need to sort out a tutor, so that should take care of his education.' The pen started to shake in his hands and instantly he let go, clattering it onto the table. Christ, he was all over the place.

'What about the times he's not with his tutor?'

Exactly. It was the part that brought him out in a cold sweat. 'I guess that will be down to me.'

'And how do you feel about that?'

'Fine.' He barely choked the word out.

She gave him a severe look. 'Friends don't fob each other off.'

He laughed, though there wasn't much humour in it. 'You want the truth? I'm bloody terrified. I don't know the first thing about looking after a kid. I might have been one once, but I'm damned if I can remember what a ten-year-old boy wants any more.'

'I wasn't even one once, so I'm not sure I can help there.'

'Maybe, but at least you've got the genes for this sort of thing.'

A sort of strangled noise came out of her throat. 'Oh my God, you think because I've got two x chromosomes I've automatically got some sort of mother instinct, don't you?'

He fidgeted slightly. 'Well, the thought had crossed my mind,' he admitted sheepishly. 'I'm going to need a back up, someone who won't mind stepping in and looking after the kid when I can't.'

'No problem.'

She said it with such certainty, as if it was an easy thing to commit to spending some of her free time with a boy she didn't know. The half-brother of a man she didn't want to get to know any further.

'But I want to make it clear I'm offering because I'm your friend. Not because I have a surfeit of x chromosomes.'

He tried to laugh but he was too emotional and it came out more as an explosive hiccup. 'Thank you. It means a lot to me, that you're willing to help out.' His voice came out all croaky and he took a moment to remind himself she was doing this for Tom. Not for him.

'I'm here for you,' she told him softly. 'Whatever you need, just ask.'

'What if I told you what I need is for us to be more than friends?'

Immediately her lids shut over her eyes and she stared down at the table. 'Please don't say that.'

'I thought you were all about telling the truth to each other?'

She rose abruptly, scraping her chair along the floor. 'For how long would it be the truth, Aiden? One week? One month?'

'Shit, not this again,' he muttered which was, of course, the last thing he should have said.

'Oh, I'm sorry, am I boring you with my determination

not to get involved with a man who specialises in breaking hearts? Who flits from one woman to another without batting an eyelid?'

'Now wait a minute.' He stood too, muttering an expletive when the door opened and a few team members wandered in. 'That's not fair,' he told her in a low voice. 'I haven't broken any hearts. The women I date know exactly what the score is.'

'And so do I, Aiden. Which is why it's a thanks, but no thanks.'

She turned and walked away, leaving him staring after her, shaking his head. The media had him down as some sort of playboy. An expert at charming women. They didn't have a bloody clue. Truth was, he'd never understood the opposite sex. Not when he was a boy, and certainly not now he was a man.

His phone beeped and he glanced down at the message. Tom and his tutor, a Helen Watson, were arriving on a flight tomorrow.

No backing out now. From tomorrow he'd have a ten-year-old staying with him. Still, it didn't need to be as daunting as it sounded. Considering his chance of getting lucky with Mel was now at less than zero, having his brother around might be more fun than he thought.

Chapter Fourteen

The first thing Aiden did the following morning was search out Mel. He found her in the Delta hospitality suite going through Stefano's media programme for the day. At least that's what he hoped they were doing. As he walked over she let out a laugh, or was it more of a giggle, and touched the Italian's arm. Instinctively Aiden's fist clenched and his stride lengthened.

'Have you got a minute?' he demanded gracelessly, his voice far more harsh than it should have been considering a) she was doing nothing wrong and b) he wanted a favour.

She gave him a long, considered look. 'I might have, once I've finished talking to Stefano.'

That put him neatly, and deservedly, he guessed, in his place. 'Thanks, I'll ... umm.' He nodded over to an adjacent table. 'I'll be over there.'

And so he sat, Mr Smooth, except that when it came to Mel he turned into a nervous, thumb twiddling, awkward sounding stranger. One who wished the slick Italian would stop making her laugh and go and do something useful. Like sort out the suspension issue they were both having.

In the end watching proved too painful. With a hiss of frustration Aiden leapt to his feet and wandered over to the bar area. He really didn't need this – he was feeling twitchy enough about the day already.

'What can I get you, sir?' The young girl behind the bar cocked him a flirtatious smile.

'Aiden, please.' He cast his eyes over the array of drinks behind her. 'Have you anything the nutritionist would approve of?'

'I can do you a smoothie,' she gushed. 'Banana and strawberry?'

'Great, thanks.'

She held his eyes for a few long seconds and Aiden translated her look as meaning she would be happy to do him, full stop. For a split second his eyes roamed over her trim, curvy body and he considered the instant gratification. Then he glanced sideways and caught Mel's eye.

Deliberately he stepped away from the bar, indicating where he was sitting. 'Could you bring it over when it's ready?'

Mel's eyes were still on him as he returned to his seat. He wanted to stride back over and tell her to stop expecting him to let her down. He was tired of women who wanted him because he was a racing driver. *She* was what he wanted. A woman with a warm heart who knew more of the real him than anyone else, and liked him anyway.

But she didn't trust him. Considering his track record, she probably had a point.

'Your minute starts now.' Mel slid onto the seat opposite him, her expression decidedly cool.

It wasn't the ideal start. 'Sorry if I was rude.'

'*If* you were rude?'

'Okay, okay. Sorry I *was* rude. I don't like seeing Stefano smarm up to you.'

She bristled. 'For goodness sake, Aiden, we were just talking.'

'I know.'

The girl from the bar placed the smoothie down in front of him. He gave her a brief, distracted smile and she left looking disappointed.

Opposite him Mel let out a sharp sigh. 'What's got into you this morning?'

Oh boy, he'd really cocked up this conversation. He stared directly into her cool hazel eyes and told her the truth. 'I'm nervous about meeting my brother. My little, ten-year-old brother.'

Some of the frost left her eyes. 'When is he due to arrive?'

He glanced down at his watch. 'In about an hour. I'm just about to go to the airport to meet him. The school sent over a photo so I should be able to recognise him.' He was aware he was babbling and couldn't stop. 'Of course I might get it wrong and end up accosting someone else's boy, which could mean I miss the race as I'll be had up for child molesting—'

'Do you want me to come with you?'

He did a double-take. 'Wow. That's not what I was going to ask, but if you can, then great. Fantastic. Yes, please. It might prevent my imprisonment.'

Her lips curved upwards in the beginnings of a smile. 'What were you going to ask then?'

'Would you mind coming over later to have dinner with us?'

'I can do that too, if you think it will help. But maybe you both need to spend a little time together to get used to each other before more strangers are added to the mix.'

'Or maybe the addition of someone else will help diffuse a potentially excruciatingly painful situation.' He exhaled a shaky breath, feeling utterly ridiculous. 'I'm so bloody nervous my hands are trembling.'

Mel stared down at Aiden's tanned, long fingered hands and then back up at his embarrassed, frustrated, strikingly handsome face. This man raced wheel to wheel at blisteringly high speed. He possessed nerves of steel. It didn't seem possible he was nervous at meeting a child, yet she could see he was because for once he wasn't hiding what he was feeling.

Reaching across the table she wrapped her hands over his. 'I suspect Tom will be even more nervous.'

He let out a sharp laugh. 'Somehow I doubt that.' Slowly he turned their hands round so he was clasping hers. 'Can we get this over and done with now? Please?'

The vulnerability in his voice touched somewhere deep in her heart. Though she knew it was right not to carry on sleeping with him, especially now he had the complication of his brother on the scene, it didn't stop this fierce, gnawing urge to hold onto him and never let him go.

'That's him,' Aiden told her quietly.

Mel turned her head to where he was pointing at a tousle-haired young boy with a thin, serious looking face walking next to … her heart sank into her loafers. His tutor wasn't the dumpy, middle-aged woman she'd imagined but a striking looking blonde dressed in tight fitting jeans, cowboy boots and a snug brown leather jacket. Great. As if there weren't enough fabulous looking women swarming around the race meetings as it was.

Casting a sideways glance at Aiden she saw his eyes weren't focused on the woman, but on the boy. She wondered if he saw a brother, or if he was just looking at a potential nuisance. A burden.

The two brothers walked towards each other, each eyeing the other warily. Mel guessed it would have been too much to hope that they'd share a hug. Aiden was too tense and Tom far too guarded and mistrustful.

'Good to see you, kid.' Aiden reached to shake Tom's hand but the young boy kept it tightly fisted at his side.

With a sigh Aiden moved his attention to the woman. 'I take it you're Helen?'

Predictably, Helen greeted Aiden with a lot more warmth than his brother had. In fact she positively gushed. 'It's wonderful to meet you, Mr Foster. I'm such a fan. I hope that, between lessons, Tom and I can manage to catch your races.'

'Racing sucks.' Having uttered his view, Tom jutted out his chin, daring his brother to disagree.

When Aiden didn't reply, just stared impassively back, Mel hunched down to Tom's level. 'Hi, I'm Mel, a friend of your brother's. I work for Delta and I'm partly responsible for their public image so I'm interested to know, why does racing suck?'

Momentarily his eyes lifted from their study of the floor. 'It's boring. A load of cars going round and round a track over and over and ...' he yawned for effect '... over again.'

Mel fought to suppress a giggle. Sure he was sullen – after what he'd been through who could blame him? At least he had some fight in him. 'Well, I guess we need to see if we can change your mind.'

He shrugged his slim shoulders and his eyes flashed with something that looked like a dare. 'You can try.'

She stifled another laugh. He certainly had his older brother's competitive spirit.

Helen's oh so sweet voice interrupted them. 'Mr Foster, would you mind terribly taking my case? I hate to ask, but I find it so hard to manoeuvre it. The wheels seem to have a mind of their own.'

'No problem.' Swiftly Aiden grabbed the handle of the errant case. 'And please, call me Aiden.'

Helen's soft, breathy laugh caused Mel's eyes to roll in their sockets, but then she couldn't hear any more because the pair of them were striding off towards the car park, leaving her with Tom. He raised his shoulders in another shrug but he wasn't as good as Aiden at hiding his feelings. Mel knew he felt slighted that his brother had waltzed off with his tutor.

He wasn't the only one.

'I guess we'd better catch up,' she announced, fixing a smile on her face.

Tom clutched at his case, manfully dragging it along the airport concourse, even though it was nearly the same size as he was. And not much smaller than the apparently *impossible to manoeuvre* case Aiden was carrying for the attractive tutor.

When they arrived at Aiden's gleaming black Range Rover Mel found herself shunted into the back seat with Tom. In front of her Aiden and Helen talked non-stop, the discussion moving quickly off Tom's tutoring and onto racing. Or more precisely, how *awesome* she thought it must be to drive such powerful cars.

Mel turned to Tom, who was staring out of the window. 'I know you find it boring, but do you follow the racing at all?'

'Mum does.'

Well, she'd neatly walked into that one. 'Do you watch it with her?'

'She never watches the race, not really. She's more into the drivers.'

Mel smiled. 'I guess she watches Aiden, huh?'

Tom gave her a scathing look. 'Nah, of course not. She doesn't fancy him, does she?'

Puzzled, Mel tried again. 'So your mum doesn't follow Aiden then?'

'Not specially. She's more keen on the other guy. Stefano.'

Tom's words echoed round the suddenly silent car. Mel looked up to find Aiden's eyes on her, watching in his rear-view mirror.

'I guess there's no accounting for taste,' he remarked lightly.

Helen laughed and the conversation in the front half of the car moved on. The back half remained quiet, Tom staring at the marina as they flashed past and Mel wondering how on earth a mother could be so dismissive of both her sons.

Aiden parked up outside the Hotel Arts, its iconic fish sculpture shimmering in the morning sun. Such a contrast to the gloomy atmosphere in the back of the car. 'Mel, you stay here with Tom while I check Helen in.'

While she sat there, open-mouthed, he calmly climbed out of the car and walked round to the boot to grab Helen's case. Mel thrust her door open and stormed up to him. 'I agreed to help you out,' she hissed under her breath, 'but that does not mean you get to treat me like your personal skivvy.'

He looked totally bewildered. 'What?'

Checking Tom and Helen were out of earshot, she laid into him. 'Helen's the one on your payroll, not me. And damn it, Tom's your brother, so why since he's arrived have you focused your entire attention on the tutor and ignored him?' She had to choke back the words *and me*.

'Shit, is that how it looked?' Visibly upset, he thrust a hand through his hair. 'I'm sorry. I was just trying to make sure Helen felt settled, because I really, really need her to stay.'

It didn't alter the fact that as soon as a pretty face had come along, he'd dropped her like a ton of bricks. 'Fine, but it's Tom you should be apologising to.'

Feeling slighted, let down and pretty damn angry with him, she climbed stiffly back into the car.

As Mel ducked back into the Range Rover, Aiden let out a deep sigh. It seemed he was becoming a master at pissing Mel off. But give him a break, Tom had barely even acknowledged him at the airport. He'd expected a bit of awkwardness, maybe even hostility, but the little guy had totally shunned him, refusing to shake his hand, periodically shooting him mutinous glares. It had been enough to panic Aiden into turning all his attention to the tutor. Keeping Helen happy was now a major priority. If she upped and left, he was buggered. Thank God she was a total petrol head. Even if Tom drove her mad, the lure of watching the races might just keep her with them.

He checked Helen in at the reception desk, listening to her with only half an ear. She wasn't bad looking but yet again he was being flirted with because of what he did, not who he was.

When the paperwork was done he passed her a sheet of paper with all his contact details, a paddock pass and the key to the car he'd hired for her, asking her to be at his motorhome by eight tomorrow morning.

Then he headed back to make peace with Mel and his brother.

'So, Tom, have you ever been to Spain?' he asked as he climbed back into the driver's seat.

'Dunno.'

'Hot country with beaches and paella.'

His attempt at a joke was met with a stony silence.

It was on the tip of his tongue to ask him if he ever smiled, but he recalled himself at that age and shut his mouth. Being a kid wasn't always as fun as it was cracked up to be.

'Have you ever been to a race meeting like this one?' he asked instead.

'Yeah, I guess.'

He caught Mel's eye in his mirror and knew exactly what she was thinking. 'It's a shame your mum didn't tell me. We could have met up. I could have shown you round the paddock.'

Tom scowled and continued to stare out of the window, his lips locked firmly together.

Fabulous. Now nobody was talking to him. Clearly his magic touch worked with both pretty thirty year olds and stroppy ten year olds.

As the silence stretched beyond comfortable and into bleak, he turned on the radio.

When they arrived at the paddock Mel couldn't seem to get out of the car fast enough, pleading a meeting. Yeah, right.

So now there were two.

Aiden drove the short distance to his motorhome and killed the engine. 'Welcome to your home for the next few weeks. Until your mum comes back.'

Tom eyed him belligerently. 'She's your mum, too.'

'Yes, she is. I'm just out of the habit of thinking that way.'

'What makes you think she's gonna come back?' His voice grew quieter, more scared child than cocky boy. Before Aiden had a chance to reply Tom had grabbed at the door handle and shot out of the car.

Aiden followed slowly behind, wondering what on earth he should do now. His instinct was to wrap his arms around the sad looking boy, but on the evidence of the last hour, that gesture would be rejected out of hand. So how was he meant to get through to him?

Feeling useless, Aiden unlocked the motorhome and indicated to Tom to go first. 'After you.'

Tom heaved his short legs up the high steps and immediately went to sit down. There was no excitement about looking round the fancy hi tech motorhome. No looking for where he was going to sleep.

With a resigned sigh Aiden went to the fridge. 'Do you want a drink? Juice, Coke?'

Tom shook his head, hair falling in unruly locks over his eyes. Heaven only knew the last time he'd had a hair cut.

Helping himself to a juice, Aiden sat down opposite him. 'Kid, I know this stinks.'

'I'm not a kid.'

He nodded. 'Fair enough. But in my eyes you're still a child who deserves a mother better than the one you've been given.'

'Don't you say anything bad about her,' Tom roared, clambering to his feet and giving Aiden a hefty shove for someone so slight. 'She's okay.'

Aiden grasped Tom's hands, holding him off, appalled that he'd let his own experience colour his judgment. 'Hey, buddy, I'm sorry. I should know better than to shout my mouth off like that. I'm glad she's been a good mother to you. I am.'

Slightly mollified, Tom climbed back onto the sofa. 'I wish she was here,' he said quietly, his eyes fixed on his shoes which dangled a few feet off the floor.

Aiden's heart went out to him. How could his mother just disappear without a word? 'Any idea where she went?' he asked carefully.

'Dunno. She had this new boyfriend. Maybe she went off with him.'

Oh God, it was like déjà vu. 'Has she done this before? Gone off with a new man and not let you know where she's gone?'

Tom kept his eyes on his feet. 'Yeah, but before there was always Jane.'

'Jane?'

'A woman who looked after me. Took me to school and stuff. Until I started boarding.'

'Right.' It was beginning to make sense. His mother hadn't changed one iota, shoving Tom off to boarding school so her son wouldn't cramp her style. 'I take it you don't like boarding.'

'What do you think?'

Okay, time to change the subject. 'Why don't I show you your room and then we'll go to the paddock and you can meet the crew.'

The pale, scared looking boy who was trying so damn hard to act cool finally glanced up at him. 'Can I see the car?'

It was the first glimmer of interest Tom had shown. Relieved, Aiden grinned. 'Sure you can. You can even sit in it, if you want.'

Tom shrugged. 'Sure.' But the gleam in his eyes gave him away.

Chapter Fifteen

Later that evening Mel knocked on the door of Aiden's motorhome. She wasn't completely sure why she was here. It was clear the brothers had a lot of bonding to do and she and Aiden hadn't exactly parted on the best of terms earlier. He'd texted to remind her of her promise though, and here she was.

As the door swung open she was hit with a sharp and pretty spectacular reminder of why she found any request from Aiden impossible to resist. Dressed in ripped, faded jeans that sat low on his hips, a white sponsor polo shirt and sexy bare feet he personified everything that was irresistible about the male form. *Only a few hours ago he treated you like a lackey.*

'Hey there,' he greeted her with his genuine, mega watt, dancing grey eyes smile.

Damn the man. She'd put up with just about anything from him as long as he continued to smile at her.

'Thanks so much for coming.' He reached down for her hand and gently pulled her up the steps. 'Are we still friends?'

Her pulse tripped. 'Yes.'

'Good.' He bent forward, his mouth hovering tantalisingly near hers. Her mind screamed pull back – friends don't kiss, not the type his eyes told her he wanted to deliver. But her heart, her instinct, every cell in her body moved towards him.

He planted the softest of kisses on her highly sensitised lips before smiling and taking a step back. 'I've cheated and got the catering guys to bring food over. It's warming in the oven, so ready whenever you are.'

'Where's Tom?'

'Why, afraid I've ditched him already?'

She held his mocking gaze and returned it with one of her own. 'Well, I know how you hate distractions.'

'Touché.' He sighed and walked over to the gleaming kitchen area, taking a bottle of wine out of the fridge. 'Tom's in his room so before he comes out can I please ask that we not fight over that again? I know I'm a selfish bastard.'

'No, not selfish. You want to win the title. I can understand that.'

'Can you?' he asked quietly, putting the bottle aside so he could give her his full attention. 'Can you really understand quite how much I want to win it?'

There was an intense, almost desperate edge to his voice and it made her realise how little she really knew him. 'No, I guess I can't. Why don't you help me understand?'

'I ... I'm not sure if I can. I want to, you have to know that, but—'

'I'm hungry.' Tom slunk into the living area, glancing from Aiden to Mel and back to Aiden.

Aiden drew in a deep breath. Frustration at the interruption or relief he'd been let off the hook?

'Okay then, let's eat.' He picked up the bottle again. 'White wine okay for you?'

Mel knew she'd be the only one drinking, but a quick glance at the stony look on Tom's face told her alcohol would be very helpful.

'What do you think of your living quarters, Tom?' she asked in an attempt to break the stiff silence as they started to eat.

'It's okay.'

'*Okay*?' Her eyes swept round the living-area-come-kitchen, taking in the shiny chrome surfaces, walnut

131

cupboard doors, soft cream leather sofas and over-the-top media system. 'It's not like any caravan I've ever stayed in, that's for sure.'

'*Caravan*?' It was Aiden's turn to look horrified. 'This is a state-of-the-art, top of the range motorhome.' He nudged Tom's elbow. 'Tell Mel about your en suite bathroom.'

Tom didn't raise his eyes from his plate. 'I've got my own sink.'

'Mate, you've got more than that. You've got a shower with hydro massage jets, mood lighting and a touch-screen music system.'

Aiden's attempt at cajoling any further response from Tom fell flat and the older brother looked ready to tear his hair out. The younger one looked like he wanted to be anywhere but here. Except maybe back at boarding school.

'Are you starting your lessons with Helen tomorrow?' Mel tried a different topic.

'I suppose.' Tom shovelled another forkful into his mouth. At least he had an appetite.

'Maybe after your lessons we can show you round the garages. You can meet some of the crew who work on the cars.'

'Did that today.'

With a jerky motion, Aiden pushed his plate aside. 'Right, that's it. I've had enough.'

Finally Tom's head snapped up.

'You'll treat Mel with the respect she deserves. That means looking at her when you're talking to her.'

Tom's face set into stubborn lines. 'You can't tell me what to do. You're not Mum. You're just my stupid half-brother.'

Aiden sprang to his feet and began to clear away his and Mel's plates with tight, controlled movements. 'Right now, buddy, I'm your brother, your father and your mother all rolled into one. While you're living with me, you play by my rules. Otherwise you go straight back to boarding school.'

'So? That's probably better than hanging around a boring racetrack all day.'

Mel watched as the two brother's squared up to each other. Tom might be half Aiden's height but he didn't look ready to give in.

'Fine, in the morning I'll phone the school,' Aiden replied with an icy calm. 'With luck you'll be back there by tomorrow night.'

Tom visibly gulped. Then he shoved away his plate and scrambled to his feet. 'See if I care. I hate you. I hate being here. I want to go home.' With that he darted across the motorhome and back into his room. There was a loud slam as the door closed.

'Bloody perfect,' Aiden muttered, swearing softly and clattering the plates into the dishwasher. When he'd finished he placed his hands either side of the sink and stared rigidly out of the window.

Mel's heart went out to him. After giving him a minute to calm down she joined him, awkwardly patting his arm though what she really wanted to do was hug him. Then nestle into his arms and hug him some more.

His eyes flicked over to her. 'That went well, don't you think? At least now I get to pack him off with a clear conscience, eh? After all, it's what he wants.'

She placed her hand over his, squeezing gently. 'What about you, Aiden? What do *you* want?'

Heat swirled in the eyes that stared down at her. 'You,' he told her hoarsely. 'What I want right now, is you.'

Suddenly his mouth was on hers and he was kissing her hungrily, so different to the soft kiss when she'd arrived. This was a kiss that meant business. A kiss designed to make her want to tear her clothes off; tear his off, too. And it was working. She moaned as his hands pushed their way underneath her shirt, warm and rough as they slid over her fevered skin.

'God, Mel, you have no idea what you do to me,' he muttered thickly.

She could feel his hard, heavy arousal against her stomach and pushed against him. 'I think I do.'

He choked out a laugh as he drew back. 'Yeah, maybe you do.' With a gentle tug of her hair he brought her face up to his. 'I want you to stay.'

Heat pulsed through her blood as her heart flip flopped. 'I can't. You know that.'

'Why not?'

She nodded towards the room where Tom had fled. 'Haven't you got something more important to do right now?'

'And if Tom wasn't here?' he asked darkly.

She extracted herself from the drugging warmth of his arms. 'We've been through this. Please, don't ask me that.'

'Why the hell not? I want you, Mel. I'm crazy about you. I know you feel something for me, too, only you're too flaming scared to admit it.'

Mel bit her lip and turned away. 'Yes I'm scared, and I'm right to be. Getting your heart stomped on isn't something you forget in a hurry.' Ignoring her racing pulse she went to pick up the handbag she'd left by the sofa, knowing she had to leave before this all spiraled out of control again. 'I wish I could be more like you and enjoy a relationship based solely on sex, but I can't.'

Aiden's heart sunk as he watched Mel walk stiffly towards the door. He wanted to argue, to drag her back, to spend the rest of the evening proving that though sex *was* key to a relationship, there was more than sex between them.

But Tom was in his room, probably fighting his tears, definitely wishing his older brother all kinds of painful death.

Cursing the timing of it all he followed Mel to the door and put an arm around her waist. 'You and me are about more than just sex,' he whispered in her ear. 'And I'm not going to keep taking no for an answer.'

She pushed open the door and hared down the steps without a backward glance.

Aiden let out all his frustration in one deep, angst-filled sigh. Then he turned and knocked on the door to Tom's room.

'Go away.'

He pushed open the door. 'Nope.'

Tom lifted his head off the bed and glared at him. He was trying so hard to be tough, to act like he didn't care. Something shifted in Aiden's chest as he realised that had been him at ten, too. Put a brave face on, kid the rest of the world that you're fine. Hide your feelings so nobody knows how much it hurts that they don't give a damn about you.

Carefully he perched on the end of the bed. 'Here's the thing, Tom. You're stuck with me. I'm your brother. I'll always be your brother. I'm sorry I wasn't around for you before. Maybe when you're older you'll understand why I had to go when I got the chance. But from now on, I'm not going anywhere. When your mother comes back, you'll still have me, whether you like it or not.'

Tom blinked. 'Does that mean I'm not going back to that school?' The relief on his face would have been comical had it not been so sad.

'That's right. I spent most of my childhood in a school

like that so believe me, I understand why you don't want to go there.'

'I didn't say that.' Then, as if he realised there was a chance Aiden could change his mind, Tom added hastily. 'But if you're making me stay here instead, I guess I can put up with that.'

Aiden smiled and automatically went to rough Tom's hair. God it was soft. He spent so much time trying to act tough, Aiden had forgotten how much of a child he still was. 'Right then, time for bed. Lessons begin at eight a.m.'

'Can't I watch you practice?'

He knew Tom was only asking because the alternative was schoolwork, but he felt a twinge of victory nonetheless. 'Sorry, no, not tomorrow. If you're good, and don't drive Helen away, then I'll see if I can find someone willing to sit with you so you can watch the qualifying and the race.'

'Mel said she would.'

He cocked an eyebrow. He was pretty certain Mel hadn't said that. Even more certain that after this evening, and his apparent inability to stop pushing her for more than she wanted to give, she wouldn't be rushing to do any more favours.

'She said she wanted to get me to change my mind about the racing,' Tom protested.

'We'll see. But first you've got to work hard tomorrow.'

Tom spent the next day with his tutor while Aiden went through two practice sessions and a lengthy debrief. As the meeting wound down Aiden found his thoughts turning to Tom, wondering if he was concentrating on what Helen was saying rather than on her breasts. He couldn't remember what age breasts became interesting but he had a feeling it wasn't too far away for Tom.

'You're looking a bit more comfortable out there,' Frank remarked when the others had left. 'Getting used to the car?'

'The car and the people.' He smiled awkwardly at his engineer. 'It's the fifth race of the season, probably about time I started to feel settled.' And he would be, if he could stop dwelling on the thought that twenty odd years ago Frank must have had similar discussions with his father. Not that he'd ever have had to reassure Seb Foster of his driving ability.

'Like I told you before, learn to relax, to rely on your instincts, and you'll win more.' Frank looked at Aiden long and hard. 'You know, despite what you think, you don't have anything to prove to the guys here. They respect you for the driver you already are.'

Aiden tried to smile but his mouth felt too tight. 'I appreciate the sentiment, but I guess there is still one person I have to prove myself to.' He stood and walked towards the door. 'And that's me.'

And probably you, too, he thought grimly as he escaped towards his motorhome. *And let's not forget the rest of the Delta hierarchy, or the hundreds of reporters ready to shoot him down if he failed again this year.*

But failure wasn't an option.

Chapter Sixteen

Mel was huddled in the pit garage with a motley collection of mechanics, engineers, physios and anyone else who'd managed to jam themselves into the relatively small space. They were watching the qualifying on the giant TV screens. Tom had pushed himself to the front, his eyes fixed on the timing screen. When the final times came in, there was muted applause.

'I suppose third isn't bad.'

'No, it isn't.' Stefano had taken second spot though, and Carlos had zipped into pole, looking a bit too quick for her liking. 'Anyway, I thought racing was boring?' she reminded Tom, giving him a nudge in the ribs.

Two hours of trying and she finally pulled a smile out of him. 'I guess it's more fun watching it here.'

'Especially when you've someone as smart as me telling you what's happening, eh?' she teased.

At which point he rolled his eyes, though not before giving her another cheeky smile. It bore an uncanny resemblance to his brother's smile. Both were capable of totally bewitching the lucky recipient.

'Can we go and find Aiden now?'

'He'll be busy with the press conference for a bit. You can watch it on the TV while I get on with my work.'

She sat next to Tom and listened with half an ear as she drafted out a press release. As usual there was a lot of discussion about tyre degradation and how it might effect the race tomorrow. Not surprising then that Tom started to fidget.

'Will he be finished soon?'

'You're not interested in tyres then?'

'Not much.'

'I'm sure it won't be long now.' Obviously not convinced, Tom jumped off the chair and started to wander around the garage, giving Mel palpitations. It wasn't how most people would think of a garage – it was more spotless operating theatre than dirty grease pit – but it did house some very expensive and potentially dangerous machinery. 'Please come and sit down, Tom. You shouldn't even be in here, never mind walking around.'

'What's this?' He prodded at some black shapeless objects sitting on trolleys.

'Tyre warmers. Now please come back here.'

'Why do they need them?'

For hours Mel had wanted Tom to show some enthusiasm for the sport, but why did he have to pick now, when she needed to finish this release and get it distributed to the print journalists? 'Because the warmer a tyre is, the more grip it has. These are like electric blankets for the tyres.'

The next time she looked up he was meandering off towards the spare wheel guns. Mel leapt up, ready to go and grab him, but was beaten to it by one of the mechanics.

'You need to keep that lad away from this stuff,' he yelled at her, shooing a disgruntled Tom away.

Easy for you to say, she wanted to shout back. How was she supposed to do her job and babysit? It looked like help was on it's way though because finally there was Aiden, striding into the garage, chatting to the crew. She waved, catching his eye.

'Tom wanted to see you,' she remarked when he made his way over.

'What? Oh, right.' Distractedly Aiden glanced down at Tom. 'Having fun?'

Tom sneered, clearly as fed up as she was. 'No. I'm bored.'

Aiden's breath came out in a hiss. 'Hey, come on. I've got work to do here, buddy. Today's session didn't go so well and I need to debrief with the guys. Then we've got to work out a race strategy for tomorrow.' Grey eyes full of tension and frustration caught hers, pleading with her. 'Maybe Mel can take you out somewhere?'

'Now wait a minute ...' She bit down on her protest, knowing she had promised to help out. 'Sure. He can help me finish the press release. Then maybe we can wander round the paddock for a bit.'

'I'm bored of the paddock. I want to go out.'

Mel could sympathise. She had a bit of cabin fever herself, but she also had a press release to distribute, a bunch of calls to catch up on and several journalists to see.

'Mel, do me a favour and take Tom out? Show him some of Barcelona?' Aiden unzipped the top half of his overalls and shrugged out of the arms, leaving it hanging round his waist. The white vest he wore outlined the fine muscles of his chest. 'You can take my car.'

'Well, no, actually, I can't.' A statement accurate in more ways than she was prepared to admit. 'I've got a job to do too, you know,' she reminded him, though it wasn't hard to guess whose was the most important.

'Come on, give me a break. Surely Sally can help out and besides, what the hell else am I supposed to do with him?' His breath came out in a rush of exasperation. 'Shit, this is exactly why I didn't want him here. I told you how difficult it would be.'

'Maybe you shouldn't have given Helen the afternoon off.'

He shot her a dark look. 'She wanted to watch from the stands. I told you before. I need to keep her happy.'

'Could you take Tom to your meeting?' she tried to placate. 'He might find it interesting.'

'You're kidding, right? He's ten. He's not going to want to listen to a group of men dissecting reams of telemetry readings. I find it boring enough and ...'

Mel tuned out, suddenly aware that Tom was no longer by her side. 'Aiden, can you see Tom?'

Instantly his eyes darted round the garage. 'Guys, have you got Tom with you?' he shouted over at the mechanics, but they shook their heads. 'Shit.' He bounded into the pit lane and she could hear his increasingly frantic cries of 'Tom!' but there was no answer.

When he came back his face was deathly pale. 'He's not here.'

Her stomach lurched. 'He must have heard us arguing and run off.'

'Yeah. No doubt at the point I said I didn't want him here. Jesus, I'm a moron.' Aiden pulled at his hair, his eyes filled with self-disgust. 'Please, Mel, we have to find him.'

'We will.' She squeezed his arm, as much to reassure herself as him. 'I'll alert security to put a message over the loud speaker. You go and check the motorhome. He might have gone back there.'

'Sure. That's exactly where a boy who knows he's not wanted would go.' But he nodded and set off through the back of the garage at a gallop.

Aiden spent fifteen long, painful minutes pacing uselessly near the motorhome before he received a call from Mel telling him a member of the security team had located Tom and they'd be with him in a few minutes. When he caught sight of Tom's mop-head, sandwiched between Mel and the burly security guy, his relief was so overwhelming for a moment he couldn't breathe. Charging up to him he wrapped his arms around Tom's slender body and squeezed tightly.

'Don't you ever, ever disappear on me again,' he told him shakily when he finally felt able to let him go.

'Why? You don't want me here.'

'That's absolutely not true.' Still crouching he grabbed the boy's shoulders. 'I do want you here. I'm really sorry about what you heard but it was said in the heat of the moment. I was cross at coming third on the grid when the car's better than that.' He tapped Tom's chin, forcing him to meet his eyes. 'You're my brother, Tom. Now I've met you, I definitely want you here with me. If you want to stay.'

Tom's eyes filled and he turned his head, rubbing at them. 'Mum doesn't want me.'

Behind Tom, Mel's face paled, mirroring what he was thinking, though her thoughts were probably a more PG version of his *bloody bitch*.

The security guard nodded sympathetically and walked away.

'I'm sure that's not true,' he reassured Tom. 'Though right now she certainly doesn't deserve you.'

He risked another hug and this time Tom accepted the embrace, even putting his thin arms around Aiden's neck. The gesture was oh so brief, but the touch went straight to his heart.

As he pushed open the door to the motorhome Aiden found his hands still trembling from the adrenaline rush. 'Go on in and grab yourself a drink, Tom. I'll be there in a minute. I just want to talk to Mel.'

Tom scampered up the steep steps and Aiden turned to face the woman who was fast becoming his anchor. 'Thank you,' he told her quietly, sincerely, pulling her gently towards him.

She shook her head, resisting him. 'No, all of this was my fault. If I hadn't argued with you, if I'd just agreed to look after Tom like I'd promised, none of this would have happened.'

'You don't really believe that, do you? I'm the one responsible for him. I'm the one who should be looking after him, not you.' He tugged her hand again and this time she fell against him. Unable to resist he flung his arms around her and held her tight, burying his face in her wavy hair. Jesus, he was shaking again. Mel must have felt it because she began to stroke her hand up and down his back in a soothing gesture. Selfishly he took the comfort even though his mind was screaming that this was the wrong way round. He wanted to be her hero, her protector. Instead he was trembling like a newborn kitten against a strong, confident woman.

When he broke away he had tears in his eyes. Mortified, he turned his head, blinking for all he was worth. 'Sorry,' he muttered, not daring to look at her.

'What for? Hugging me or showing a human reaction?'

Squeezing the telltale moisture out from his eyes with the base of his palms he let out a short laugh. 'I'm not sorry for hugging you, that's for certain. But I hadn't intended to blubber all over you, too.'

'Look at me, Aiden.' When he dared to glance at her he saw she too had tears falling down her cheeks. 'You're not the only one blubbing like a baby here.'

Gently he wiped at them with his thumb. 'Yeah, but it looks a lot better on you.'

Her lips curved and she started to laugh. 'We're a right pair, aren't we? Do you mind if I go in and speak to Tom? I've got an apology to make to him, too.'

'Be my guest. You're welcome here anytime.' Hell, she

was too irresistible standing there with her glistening eyes and her sweet, pretty face. He bent to kiss her. 'Day or night.'

Immediately she stiffened and he cursed softly. 'Sorry. I know I shouldn't push, but it's so damn hard for me to look at you and not want you.'

Her eyes fell to her vast handbag and she plunged a hand inside. 'It's hard for me to look at you, too,' she said finally, clutching at a pack of tissues. 'But, please, can we stick to friends, like we agreed? I'm not saying I don't want more, but—'

'You don't trust me,' he cut in flatly.

She gave him a sad smile. 'Well, you don't have much difficulty attracting members of the opposite sex, and you do seem to enjoy their company.'

'I prefer yours.'

'That wasn't how it felt yesterday when you allowed Helen to monopolise your attention.'

'I told you, I was trying to make her feel at home. I wasn't ... I'm not in any way attracted to her. I'm attracted to you.' Hell, he was far more than just attracted. He was starting to become obsessed.

She smiled, the wide, warm version that wrinkled her cute nose and gave his heart a mini cardiovascular work out. 'I'm attracted to you, too, Aiden Foster.'

With that she turned and climbed up the steps to the motorhome. He followed behind, ogling her bum and grinning like an idiot.

Tom was stretched out across the sofa, channel hopping. His muddy shoes were all over the soft cream leather and Aiden tried not to wince. He was a bloke, and blokes didn't worry about shoes on furniture.

'Hey, Tom, do you mind if I disturb you for a minute?' Mel asked, siting down near his feet.

Guiltily Tom shoved his feet off the sofa. 'Sure.'

'I wanted to apologise for what you heard earlier.'

Tom's eyes remained fixed on the television screen.

Exasperated, Aiden grabbed the remote off him and turned it to mute. 'Manners in front of the lady, buddy.'

For a few seconds Tom glared at him, but Aiden didn't back down. He had a lot of sympathy for the kid, but he needed discipline almost as much as he needed love.

Finally Tom shifted his attention to Mel. ''S'okay. I get how you didn't want to take me out.'

Mel looked horrified. 'No you're wrong. It wasn't that I didn't want to take you out. I had a lot of work to finish and ...' She stared down at her fingers, twiddling them restlessly and looking distinctly uncomfortable. 'The main problem was Aiden offering to lend me his car.'

Aiden gaped at her. 'What, the Range Rover's not good enough for you? It's only a rental. I can swop it for something faster if you want, hot shot. I just figured I needed something with a bit of room.'

'No, the car's fine. At least it would be.' She swallowed and let out a brittle laugh. 'If I could drive.'

Stunned, Aiden didn't know what to say, though his brother had no such problem. 'But you're a grown-up,' Tom argued. 'All grown-ups drive.'

'Driving isn't something that comes automatically when you turn eighteen, you know. You have to have lessons. Pass a test.'

Aiden was still struggling to understand. 'Seriously, Mel, you spend your life around cars and yet you've never bothered to learn to drive?'

'I didn't say I haven't bothered,' she replied stiffly. 'It's just that after my parents' died, I lost interest.'

Shame punched at his gut. 'Sorry, I forgot. They died in

a car crash, didn't they? God, I'm such a cretin. No wonder you didn't want to learn.'

'I didn't for a few years, no. Then I realised how stupid it was not to try, so I had a lesson, but ...' She looked from brother to brother, giving them each an embarrassed smile. 'Well, to be perfectly honest, I was useless. I was so tense and my leg shook so much I couldn't even move the car. I'm fine when someone else is driving, but when I got behind the wheel myself, my brain froze.' She squeezed Tom's arm. 'So *that's* the main reason why I told Aiden I couldn't take you out. Not because I didn't want to, but because I couldn't.'

Tom snuck a sideways glance at Aiden. 'Maybe my brother could teach you.'

Was Tom deliberately trying to put him and Mel together? If he was, Aiden was very happy to oblige. 'Sure.'

Clearly Mel wasn't quite so happy about the prospect, at least not if her choked laughter was anything to go by. 'I'm pretty certain I don't need to learn how to corner a car at a hundred miles an hour. Or to drive two inches away from the wheel of the car next to me. Thank you, but no. Definitely, no.'

'Hey, hang on a minute, I don't drive like that on the road. I'm actually very circumspect.' When there were speed cameras around, anyway. He was starting to warm to the idea of teaching Mel. The pair of them in a closed environment, the doors locked. 'Why not give me a go? I'm pretty cheap.'

She gave him one of her *I can't believe you just said that* stares.

'Okay, that came out wrong. I'll only charge in kind.' He received a glower this time. 'Okay, you get me for free.' He could see she still wasn't sold. 'Come on, an hour in a car with a famous racing driver. How can you resist?'

'What about me,' Tom piped up. 'It was my idea. I want to be there, too.'

Umm. The picture Aiden had of a grateful Mel smothering him with kisses was starting to look a little shaky. Still, it was worth a try. 'Okay,' he told his brother. 'It's a deal. Let's shake on it.' They gave each other a solemn, manly handshake.

'Hey, wait a minute, I haven't agreed to this,' Mel protested. 'In fact, I'm not at all sure about it.'

Aiden nodded pointedly over at his now grinning brother. 'You're not going to let young Tom down, are you? We won't go on the road, obviously. We'll find some private ground and see if we can get you to actually move the car.'

Mel's narrow eyed glare told him he was little more than scum for using a child so mercilessly. Trying not to laugh, Aiden shrugged back, silently replying that *a guy's got to do what a guy's got to do.*

'Fine,' she declared coolly. 'One hour in the Delta car park when we get home. The very end of the car park, which nobody ever uses. And no sniggering, no laughing, no teasing, no rolled eyes and absolutely no getting cross with me when I can't do what you tell me.'

'That's one heck of a lot of no's.' Laughter bubbled in his chest and it took all his self-control to retain a reasonably straight face.

Mel pursed her lips and put her hands on her hips. 'Do we have an agreement?'

'Well, umm, I'm not sure we can promise *all* those things.'

'Specially the bit about not sniggering,' Tom added. ''Cos you are a grown-up so you should be able to drive.'

Aiden had now resorted to biting his cheek to stop the laughter from erupting. 'I can promise not to shout at you.'

'You'd better keep to it,' she muttered threateningly

but then her sense of humour won the battle against her embarrassment and she started to giggle, setting them all off.

As his eyes rested on Mel, then on Tom, Aiden felt a rush of warmth. There was something so right about the three of them teasing each other, sharing a laugh. It was what he imagined real families did.

The moment was interrupted by the beep of Mel's phone. 'Frank says you've got five minutes to get your sweaty backside over to the team room for the debrief,' she read from the screen.

Aiden snorted. 'No way did he say that.'

'Okay, he might have put it more politely, but the sentiment's the same.'

And so was the issue. He still had Tom to look after. 'Buddy, I'm afraid you need to come with me. If it gets too boring we'll see if we can find a games console from somewhere.'

Mel dropped her handbag to the floor. 'I can hang here with Tom for a bit. I've got calls to make, but I can do them from here just as easy as the media centre and Sally can help with the press release. I'll drop him round on the way to my meetings.'

And suddenly the situation was resolved. Aiden realised if he'd approached it in a more civilised fashion in the first place, Tom would never have disappeared.

But then he'd never have got a hug from Mel. Or secured a chance of teaching her to drive. And Tom might never have taken that small step in starting to bond with him.

Whoever had made up that cloud and silver lining expression knew a thing about life.

Chapter Seventeen

The Spanish sun beat down on the tarmac as Aiden sat on the grid, body pumped full of adrenaline, waiting for the lights to signal the start of the race. If he got off to a flyer, he could get past Stefano on his inside and be right up the back of Ferrer, aka Mel's cheating sleazeball ex. The guy had secured two firsts and two seconds in the first four races. Not bad for a car that wasn't supposed to be as good as the one Aiden was driving. And a damn sight better than Aiden's collection of first, fourth, fourth and crashing dismal failure.

The red lights on the gantry went out one by one and Aiden's hands automatically tightened on the wheel. He was going to stop that bastard's run of luck, and where better to do it than on the Spaniard's home turf.

They were off.

The launch control pack stormed into action and Aiden flew off the grid. From the sluggish start both Carlos and Stefano made, Aiden had to guess they were running heavier with fuel. Either that or they were daydreaming. Whatever the reason, he flew past both of them and was heading into the first tight right-hand bend when he felt a sickening shunt.

'Contact from behind,' he shouted into the radio, not easy to do whilst plunging round a steep corner and praying to every God he knew that his car was still intact. If that Spanish git had ...

'No visible damage from here,' Frank's deep, calm voice broke through his ear piece. Aiden heard the hidden message. Relax. Just race.

And he did.

* * *

Mel was with a small crowd in the pit garage, watching the race on the TV screens. She'd rather have watched in the stands but here she was closer to the action if anything happened. To the side of her were men hunched over rows of monitors, each relaying the key information the drivers needed; telemetry, track positions, a weather map. Beside her were Sally and an utterly engrossed ten-year-old. The headset he wore was too big and kept slipping over his ears, but it didn't seem to bother him as he remained glued to the action on the screen.

It was a gripping race. Aiden and Carlos, the two main contenders, were both on different strategies making it hard to work out who was actually winning. Tom kept asking, but it was too close to call.

'He's not going to win, is he?' Tom said quietly on the sixtieth lap, so quietly she almost didn't hear him.

'I'm not so sure. Remember Aiden was on a two stop, so he might be behind now but he's got fresher tyres. There are six more laps to go. He could catch up.'

Tom nodded but kept his thoughts to himself. Mel guessed it was too soon to expect him to leap up and down and yell his brother on. Still, it wasn't going to stop her.

'Keep your bottom firmly on that seat,' Sally hissed from her other side when Mel made a movement to stand on the next lap. 'It's too early to start gigging. You'll embarrass me, Tom and yourself.' She jerked her head self-consciously at the ever growing crowd behind them.

'I don't care. Aiden's edging closer. You can see it, feel it. He's got the smell of victory in his nostrils and he's hunting Carlos down.'

'Umm.' Sally considered her carefully. 'I don't believe I've ever seen you so interested in the outcome of a race.'

Mel fidgeted on her seat. 'Of course I'm interested. It's about time we had another Delta victory.'

Her statement was met with a chorus of cheers from those watching behind them. Sally eased off her earphones and whispered. 'Don't get me wrong, I'm gunning for Aiden, too. Just not as much as you seem to be.' With a smug smile, she turned her attention back to the screen.

The final laps were unbearably tense. Aiden was still in second place behind Carlos, itching to get past but with time running out. As he went nose to tail with the Viper, Mel leapt out of seat. 'Come on, Aiden!'

The gathered crowd whooped as Aiden applied his DRS, drew alongside Carlos and zipped ahead into the corner. Mel started to scream and when she glanced down at Tom his eyes were bulging and his face was one giant grin.

With only one lap to go, the race was as good as over and the garage buzzed with the anticipation of a Delta victory. When Aiden finally took the chequered flag Mel was pretty certain hers weren't the only eyes that were suddenly moist.

Mel tugged off Tom's earphones. 'Come with me. We'll go to the pit lane so we can greet Aiden when he gets out of his car.'

By the time they reached the closed off area where the drivers would park it was already lined with photographers. Mel pushed her and Tom through, anxious for Tom to get a chance to see his brother as he climbed out of his car in the number one spot. Okay, anxious for *her* to see him, too. The more she pushed Tom though, the more he dug in his heels.

'Hey, don't you want to see Aiden get out of the car?'

'Nah.' Eyes down, he kicked at the track.

'Why on earth not?' Hadn't he just been roaring him on, only a few minutes ago?

'He won the race. Big deal.'

The words were uttered so dismissively, Mel didn't know what was real any more; the boy who'd cheered with delight when his brother had won, or this one, who seemingly couldn't care less. She watched as he took a furtive peek through the crowds. 'What's wrong? Are you worried Aiden won't notice you?'

'Nah.' Again he hung his head, scuffing the front of his shoe along the track. 'I've seen this part on the telly. The drivers go and thank the garage people, don't they? Sometimes they hug them with their helmets still on. It's stupid.'

Mel had a feeling Tom didn't really think it was stupid. In fact she thought Tom wanted his brother to acknowledge him so badly that the opposite, being ignored, was too horrid to contemplate. Well, she couldn't guarantee Aiden would see Tom amongst the crowds, but she was absolutely certain he'd be looking for him.

'Stupid or not, I want to see Aiden, so you're just going to have to stand with me.'

A few moments later Tom had no choice because Frank caught sight of them and herded them towards the front of the fencing.

The Delta car growled its way through the pits and parked with its nose cone in the number one spot. The cheers that erupted from the crowd were almost as deafening as the roar from the cars. Mel's heart jumped into her throat as Aiden climbed out of the cockpit and punched the air. As he walked to where the Delta team were gathered he undid his neck support and dragged off his helmet.

He looked gorgeous. It didn't matter that he was dripping with sweat. Or that his hair was plastered across his face and sticking up at odd angles. His smile was all anybody saw. A grin a mile wide stretched across his face and shone from his eyes.

Her hormones sighed and she knew that despite her vow not to sleep with him again, she was falling for him.

Aiden halted, helmet in hand, his eyes searching. As they met hers, her heart somersaulted. Still grinning he made a beeline towards her and in the next instant they were hugging, laughing, and she was pressed against him, inhaling the scent of man and engine. When he pulled away he looked down and found Tom. Reaching over the fencing he grabbed his brother under the arms and yanked him up, causing Tom to squeal and Aiden to laugh even harder.

'Watching racing is still boring, eh, little brother?'

Mel knew what a brutal sport it was, how much it took out of the human body, but nobody would have guessed that as Aiden lifted Tom even higher, leaving his feet dangling.

'I suppose it beats doing lessons,' Tom mumbled, though his beaming face totally ruined the *not bothered* image.

When Aiden finally took his rightful place on the podium, Mel felt ready to burst with joy for him.

It was a good day.

The team gathered in the Delta motorhome later that evening to celebrate Aiden's win and his teammate's third place. Unlike his last victory, tonight there was no surprise call from school to ruin the mood. It was low key, because this was only a step towards the goal, but Aiden had never felt happier.

Banging a spoon against a glass, he called for silence.

'Yes, I know, you don't want to listen to me waffling on when you could be drinking,' he began, eyeing up the room. 'But teammates have a duty to listen to me for a few minutes.'

'We have to listen to you all the time,' one of the engineers shouted, adding in a good mimic of Aiden's voice.

'The balance isn't right, why can't you get more pace out of the car, sort out the understeer?'

The room erupted in laughter.

'Okay, okay. I'll admit I can be a bit picky at times ...' perhaps a slight understatement '... but just look what we managed to achieve today. It brings us up to second place in both the drivers' and constructors' championship.' A huge, drunken cheer filled the room and Aiden raised his glass. 'Here's to Delta and continued progress towards our end goals.'

There was a lot of clicking of glasses and roars of agreement. 'Your dad would have been proud of you,' yelled one of the older mechanics from the back of the room.

Immediately there was an embarrassed hush. Aiden knew the guy meant well, but he also knew two victories weren't enough to quash all the doubts.

'Thanks for the sentiment, but all I've done today is win a race. Something I've done before, in common with many other drivers. What my father did was win race, after race, after race. Consistently. For five seasons. A feat I've never achieved.' He hoped to God there was no bitterness in his voice.

'A feat you've not achieved *yet*,' Frank countered.

The statement was met with shouts of agreement and immediately everyone started to talk again. Aiden tipped his race engineer a nod of thanks before slipping quietly out of the room, out of the motorhome and into the warm Spanish evening. Craving air and solitude he walked round to the back before slumping onto the tarmac. With his back resting against the cold metal of the motorhome, he shut his eyes. He was absolutely knackered.

'I thought I'd find you here.'

His lids pinged open to find Mel staring at him, sweet

concern in her hazel eyes. She looked fresh and so very pretty in a pair of slim jeans and a soft pink blouse.

'Sorry.' He huffed out a breath. 'I just needed a few minutes. I'll be back.' He angled his head. 'Is Tom okay?'

'Yes, he's fine. He's sharing schoolboy jokes with Frank, though I'm surprised Frank can remember any.' She smiled and eased onto the ground beside him. 'Are you okay?'

'Of course I am. I won today, didn't I?'

'Don't lie to me. Please.'

'Okay, truth is I *was* very okay, right up until that remark about my dad.' Sighing deeply he leant forward, resting his head in his hands. 'I'm not sure I can admit to this. Even in my head the words sound stupid.'

'It's only me.'

He stared at her. 'There is nothing, absolutely nothing, *only* about you.'

She swallowed and gave him one of her cute, bashful smiles. 'Thank you. Now tell me the stupid words.'

He let them blurt out in a rush. 'I can't shake this feeling that my father deliberately raced out of his skin just so he could leave me with a giant albatross of a legacy around my bloody neck.' A burden of expectations he could never hope to meet.

Mel didn't laugh, something she had every right to do because even he could see his paranoia rating was off the scale. Instead she reached out and held his hand. 'I think he probably raced out of skin so he could win. Isn't that all you drivers want to do?'

He gave her a wry smile. 'Is that your way of telling me to buck up and get my life into perspective?'

'It's my way of saying forget about him. Stop looking back at what he did, and start looking forward at what you're going to do. At what you're capable of doing.'

He tightened his hand on hers, feeling her warmth and strength. How could he tell her that looking forward wasn't necessarily going to help him, either? He really didn't know what he *could* do and that scared him just as much as what his father *had* done.

'I know I'm capable of kissing you,' he whispered finally. 'Of making love to you until you cry out my name and beg me for more.'

She tensed immediately, as she always did when he pushed her. Damn near every other woman on the planet would have melted in his arms at those words but not Mel. Oh no, she drew up the blinds and banged the ruddy door shut.

'Looks like I overstepped the mark again, huh?' Wearily he climbed to his feet and held out his hand. 'Come on. Let's go back in. I've got a victory to celebrate.'

She allowed him to lift her to her feet. 'I know you're capable of making me want you,' she whispered. 'But I'm not capable of making love, without falling in love.'

He lifted her hand to his mouth, planting a soft kiss on her palm. 'Would falling in love with me be so very terrible?'

Her beautiful eyes flickered. 'No,' she admitted. 'It would be wonderfully easy. But the part where we break up? That would be an absolute killer and I'm not prepared to go through it again.'

Before he had a chance to argue that he wasn't bloody Carlos, that there was no reason why they should break up, she was walking back inside. He waited a few minutes before following her, debating which victory party he preferred. The last one, where he'd actually got to make love to Mel – before she'd then walked out on him, telling him they were over. Or this one, where he'd end up sleeping alone but his brother would be in the next room. And Mel was at least still talking to him.

Chapter Eighteen

It was two weeks before the next race, though practically, with all the travelling, it only meant a week and a bit at home.

Despite the sponsor activities Aiden was earmarked to attend, and the meetings he had scheduled, he still had enough free time to squeeze in Mel's driving lesson. Lucky her.

'You know, we really don't have to do this now,' Mel protested when he caught up with her in the Delta headquarters reception area. 'I'm sure you've got far more important things to do and so do I, come to think of it.'

The corners of his mouth lifted and he gave her a knowing smile. 'You wouldn't be trying to put this off, would you?'

'No,' she replied, avoiding his eyes and crossing her fingers. 'I just don't want to put you to any trouble. Besides, a Ferrari is hardly a suitable car for a novice to learn in.'

He held the door open for her and she squinted in the afternoon sunshine. Next to her he slipped on a pair of ultra cool sunglasses. 'I don't have the Ferrari with me today.'

Sure enough, as they headed to where he usually parked she saw a dark grey saloon car. Not just any saloon, mind you. 'You really think that an M3, the car of boy racers, is a *suitable* car?'

He slid her his easy smile. 'Compared to the Ferrari, sweet Mel, this one is a carthorse. Besides, it's a sponsor car so if you smash it up, I don't care.'

Warily she eyed up the dark torture machine. In the back she noticed a little face peeking out from the window, waving at her. 'I see Tom's come with you. Any news on where your mother is?'

'Nope. I only have a home number for her and she's not picking up. I've left loads of messages and so have the school.' His expression tightened. 'The housekeeper did finally call me and say she'd been informed my mother was going on holiday for a while. I can only assume she's dumped Tom into boarding school so she can swan off with her new man.'

'Ouch.' Mel stared back at the smiling boy in the car. Despite his mother's callous actions, Tom seemed to be a lot happier now. 'Are you sure he needs to watch me? There must be plenty of other things he'd rather be doing.'

Aiden bent his head and surprised her by kissing her on the nose. The sparkle in his grey eyes, combined with a waft of his fresh aftershave, sent her heart spiralling. 'Tom's come along because a) he's finished all the work Helen set him and she's left for the day, b) he's got a bee in his bonnet about learning to drive and he figures he might learn something and c) ...' he flashed a grin '... well, c) he thought it might be funny.'

'I didn't think you'd ever get to c),' she mumbled, avoiding his eyes and staring instead at the v of smooth, tanned skin revealed by his navy polo shirt.

'What do you mean?'

'You say a) and b) a lot, but you don't usually have a c). I'm kind of wishing you didn't have one this time, too.' She hated to admit it, but she was scared. Waking up at dawn in a cold sweat and not being able to go back to sleep again, scared. She feared not being able to do what most adults seemed to manage without even thinking. Most of all, she feared looking ridiculous in front of Aiden.

'Hey, come on.' He cupped her face with his long, warm

fingers. 'You've got the look of a woman on her way to the gallows. This isn't meant to be torture.'

'I think I'd prefer to be whipped.'

His face cracked into a huge grin. 'Hey, I'm more than happy to tie you up and whip you instead. Of course I'd need you naked first.' He glanced back at the car. 'And we'll probably need to lose the kid.'

A laugh bubbled out of her and she shoved at his chest. 'Fine. I'll stick to the stupid driving instead.'

'Shame.' For a few moments he simply stood there, gazing at her, his eyes smiling.

Uncomfortable with the way his scrutiny made her feel – warm, needy and wanting – she hastily looked away. Equally fast his hand was back on her chin, forcing her eyes upwards.

'Are you thinking of your parents?' he asked softly.

'No,' she admitted. 'Though I'm sure their death has something to do with me feeling nervous in a car.'

'Well, then, we need to stop you being so tense. The way I see it I'm going to focus on a) getting you to relax, b) lifting your clutch leg smoothly and c) ...' He grinned down at her. 'Let's try c) making sure you're still talking to me at the end of this.'

With a casual authority she could only wonder at, he drove the car to the deserted end of the car park before climbing out and holding the driver's door open for her. Reluctantly she walked round the bonnet and slipped inside.

'Are you sure you want to sit in the back there, Tom?' She turned to face the small figure on the back seat. 'It might get pretty hairy.'

'I'm good. Aiden's already warned me the car will jump when you don't bring the clutch up properly.'

Beside her Aiden started to laugh, then tried to cover it up with a cough. 'Sorry. I just figured it was a chance for him to learn—'

'How not to do it,' she interrupted. 'Great. Thanks.' Gritting her teeth she adjusted the seat for her far shorter legs.

His hand reached across and pressed lightly on her left leg. 'Comfortable?'

As warmth radiated across her thigh she swallowed, trying to calm her fluttering heart. 'Yes, thanks. Are you?'

His soft chuckle sent shivers down her spine. 'Oh yes.'

'Are you really going to keep your hand there?'

'Yes. At the moment when you get behind the wheel, you're too tense to operate the clutch correctly. True?'

She nodded.

'I've been reading up on this and what we need to do is scramble those negative thoughts and get you to associate sitting behind the wheel with something pleasurable.'

'Like having your hand on my thigh?' she asked dryly.

She couldn't see his face, but she knew from his voice that he was smiling. 'Exactly. I know at least one of us is getting some pleasure out of this.'

She hiccupped out a laugh. He was flirting with her, but she knew it was at least partly his way of trying to distract her. And it was working.

Aiden turned round to Tom. 'Have you buckled up? We're in for a bumpy ride.'

Tom giggled, and despite her mind being over stuffed with nerves Mel noticed the camaraderie between the brothers. The bonding that had begun in Spain seemed to have deepened.

Aiden gently squeezed her thigh, making her jump. 'You know the basics of how to drive. All I want you to do now is turn on the engine, put her into first and move us to the other side of the parking lot.'

'Is that all?' Her fingers trembled as she turned on the engine. When it all but growled back at her she clutched at the steering wheel as if it was a life raft.

His big warm hand moved from her thigh to cover her hands. 'I'm here. Nothing bad is going to happen. Relax.'

Nodding she shoved her left foot down on the clutch and pushed the gear into first.

'Now gently press your other foot on the accelerator.'

The engine roared into life and Aiden let out a noise that sounded very much like a muffled laugh. 'I think you missed the part where I said gently.'

'That was flipping gentle.'

On the back seat, Tom sniggered.

'If you say so, but I want you to ease the throttle back a little.' When Aiden heard the revs go down, he nodded. 'Good. Now listen to the engine noise as you carefully raise your left foot. When it gets to the bite, you'll ease forward.'

The car jumped and stalled.

Tom snorted with laughter. 'There goes the kangaroo!'

Feeling stupid and incapable she huffed out a breath. 'Millions, no, probably billions of people in the world can drive. Why can't I?'

'You can,' Aiden replied firmly. 'It's only your head that's stopping you. Now we're going to do it again only this time I'm going to keep my hand on your leg as you push down the clutch.'

As his warm hand wrapped deliciously around her thigh she stifled a groan. At this rate she was going to have trouble remembering her name, never mind what she was meant to be doing with the pedals.

*　*　*

Aiden felt the heat of Mel's thigh burning his hand. He could feel the tension there, too but he could also feel the smoothness of her skin; the soft curve of her leg. He shifted in his seat, trying to get his libido in check.

She looked at him questioningly and he shrugged, his eyes facing forward. 'Come on then, Miss Kangaroo,' he drawled, trying to get back to the friends only platform she was so damn obsessed about. 'Let's see if you can make it round the car park without jumping.'

Gently he kneaded the muscles beneath his fingers, trying to relax her leg. To relax her.

'Maybe I should just forget this and try an automatic,' she grumbled when once again the car shuddered to a halt.

'Give in?' He looked at her in mock horror. 'Please don't swear in front of young Tom.'

Tom laughed. 'Yeah, you can't give in, Mel. If my brother can drive, anyone can.'

Slowly the tension eased from her face and she smiled over her shoulder at Tom. 'You know what, you're right.' Gripping the wheel she took in a deep breath. 'Come on you bugger. I can do this.'

Her pretty, sexy face looked so determined it was all he could do to stop laughing. 'I hope the bugger refers to the car and not to me.'

She shot him a look that suggested the term encompassed both. Then she turned on the engine and tried again.

It wasn't the smoothest of starts but the smile on her face when she made it all the way round without stalling shot straight to his heart.

He persuaded her to do it again, and then again, moving up the gears until they were up to the dizzy heights of third. When she finally pulled to a stop, grinning widely, her eyes sparkling with delight, he felt a crazy sense of pride.

'I did it.'

'You certainly did.' He moved his hand from her thigh to her face, wanting to kiss her, to wrap his arms around her, but they weren't alone. And she wasn't interested.

Biting back his frustration, he dropped his hand back to his lap.

'Can I have a go now?' Tom asked.

Aiden turned to find a pair of serious grey eyes staring at him. Eyes, he suspected, that were remarkably similar to his own. 'Has Mum ever taken you karting?' And why wasn't he surprised when Tom gave a slight shake of the head? 'We'll have to fix that. It's how most drivers start racing.'

'Is that how you did?'

The can of worms he'd part opened started to wriggle. 'Yes.'

'Did Mum take you?'

Aiden watched as Mel's eyes swung between the pair of them. She hadn't missed the wistful note in Tom's voice any more than he had.

'No. She didn't take me, either.'

'Did your dad?'

He tried to relax his hands, unclenching the fingers one by one. 'No, my father never took me karting.'

Surprised flickered across Tom's face. 'He was a famous racing driver, wasn't he? Why didn't he take you karting?'

Leave it to a kid to ask the obvious. Silence hung in the air as both Mel and Tom watched him, waiting for his answer. 'Because he died when I was young.' Tom wouldn't know that ten was pretty ancient in the karting world.

'That sucks. Still, at least you had a dad for a bit. I don't have one.'

The worms were now wriggling out of the damn can. 'Dad's aren't always as great as they're cracked up to be.

Sometimes not having one is better than having one who takes no notice of you.'

He was aware of Mel turning her head sharply to look at him but he ignored her, keeping his attention on his brother. The same brother who was clearly about to open his big mouth and ask another dynamite question. 'So, why don't we see if we can sort you out some karting lessons?' he said quickly, cutting him off. 'It won't be today but we can book some in, eh?'

Tom beamed and Aiden breathed a sigh of relief before firmly putting the lid back on the worm can.

Chapter Nineteen

Monte Carlo. Home to the most glamorous and famous race of the season. The circuit swept through the streets of Monaco, past the dazzling white luxury yachts on the harbour front and blasting through the famous tunnel. It had a narrow track and tight, tight corners – including a ridiculously slow hairpin – which made overtaking well near impossible.

To win at Monaco required precision driving, technical excellence, balls of steel – and usually first position on the grid.

Aiden didn't need the media's reminder of that as they fired question after question at him after the Friday practice. Nor did he need their reminder that this was the same track where Seb Foster had ploughed his car into a concrete wall and died.

'The last Foster to race around the Monaco track in Delta colours failed to make it home. Will that prey on your mind at all during the race?'

'It was nearly twenty years ago,' he replied mildly. 'A totally different age.'

'But still, he was your father. Were you watching at the time?'

Jeéz, did he really have to put up with this crap? The other drivers were asked about their cars and thoughts on the race to come. He was asked about a race his father had twenty years ago. 'I was ten. Can you remember what you were doing when you were that age?'

'No, probably not, but we're talking about a major occasion in *your* life. Watching your father crash.'

Aiden fought against the impulse to growl. 'I'm not here to talk about the past. I'm here to talk about me and the race I have coming up. Surely that's more relevant?'

'How is the car handling round the Monaco circuit? As well as it did in Spain?'

Finally, a decent question. Gratefully Aiden latched onto it.

He discussed tyres and downforce for the next five minutes before making his excuses and escaping through the garage and into the Delta motorhome. All the time he was aware of Mel on his heels, head down as she ended a call on her phone.

'Hey.'

At the sound of his voice, she glanced up. 'Hey, yourself.'

She was in her PR uniform again, as he liked to call the bland trousers and shirt ensemble. It wasn't exactly eye-catching, at least not until she smiled. She did more than catch his eye though; she made his heart ache. Why the hell was that? Was it simply because he knew she was out of reach?

'Well done for neatly deflecting the father question.'

'The neat deflection is my specialty.'

'Yes, so it is. Some day I'm going to sit you down and force you to give me an honest answer to all the questions I have.'

He waggled his eyebrows suggestively. 'Now that sounds interesting. How are you going to force me, exactly?' She gave him a disapproving look, which only goaded him further. 'I have a few ideas of what you could do that might make me more inclined to talk.'

'You can put those ideas back in the box,' she retorted primly but then frowned and moved closer. 'I'm glad I caught up with you, because I wanted to talk about Helen.'

'Helen? As in Tom's tutor, Helen?'

'Yes. Helen as in Tom's sometime tutor.' She hesitated, her eyes darting round to check nobody else could hear them. 'Have you spoken to Tom about her lately?'

'No, I guess I haven't.' His spine tensed as he clicked into defensive mode. 'Should I have done?'

'He's under your care and she's supposed to be teaching him, so yes, it would be a good idea to find out what he thinks of her.'

She's just looking out for Tom, he told himself, not having a dig. 'The way I see it, I employed a professional so he's in good hands. I shouldn't have to keep checking up on her.' Okay, maybe he should have, but he didn't like being told he should have.

'Did you employ a professional? Or did you just pick the one with the prettiest face?'

Stung, he let out a sharp laugh. 'That's really what you think? That I chose Helen because I thought I could get a real bang for my buck? Pun intended.'

Mel knew from the way Aiden was shaking his head, his laugh going nowhere near his eyes, that she'd hurt him. What she'd said had been bitchy, but it irritated her to see what Helen was getting away with. And, yes, she'd still have been annoyed if Helen had been pig ugly. Just not *this* annoyed.

'Of course I don't think you chose her just because you wanted to sleep with her. God knows, you don't have to go seeking women out. They come to you readily enough, wouldn't you agree?'

Hands on hips, he glared at her. 'How am I supposed to respond to that? Agree with you and I sound like an arrogant prick. Disagree with you and you become even more irate with me.'

'I'm not irate with you. I'm …' she searched in her mind for the right words '… I'm disappointed. I've seen Helen wandering around the paddock when I know perfectly well she should be with Tom. I think you should ask him how he feels it's going, that's all.'

'Thanks,' he replied flatly. 'Any other parenting tips you'd like to pass on?'

She'd handled it all wrong, she knew that. But heavens above, he didn't have to be so prickly. 'No, that's all for now. I take it there's still no news on the whereabouts of your mother?'

'Correct. Don't worry, I'm sure she'll turn up before the end of term. And before I've made a total hash of his education.'

As Mel opened her mouth to give him a sharp retort, Frank's voice boomed down at them from the upper deck. 'Aiden, we're up here waiting for you.'

With a curt nod of his head, Aiden turned his back on her and climbed up the stairs, two at a time.

Though Monaco was a gorgeous place to stay, the race itself was one to forget. Aiden had a poor qualifying and ended up fifth on the grid and, predictably enough, fifth in the race. Behind his third placed teammate. Well behind Carlos, who was now comfortably leading the championship.

Tom, who sat between Mel and Helen in the garage as they watched, was quiet throughout.

'That was pretty boring.'

They were the first words he'd uttered all race.

'Well, you can't expect Aiden to win every time.' Helen followed her trite statement with one of her tinkling laughs that got right on Mel's nerves.

'I don't,' Tom returned sullenly. 'But there was no overtaking or crashing. It was dull.'

'Watching drivers crash isn't fun,' Helen scolded.

'I guess it is when you're ten,' Mel cut in, now thoroughly fed up with the woman. All race she'd twittered on about Aiden this, Aiden that. She wished she'd just hurry up and launch herself at him. It was clearly what she wanted to do.

'Well, I'm off to do a bit of shopping.' Her glance dismissed Tom and settled on Mel. 'I presume it's okay if Tom stays with you?'

She waltzed out before Mel even had a chance to reply.

Tom watched her go. 'I don't like her.'

He said it with such finality Mel had to stop herself from giggling. 'You're not supposed to like your teachers.'

'I guess.'

Because she was a nosey cow, Mel couldn't let it slide. 'Why don't you like her?'

'All she ever wants to talk about is my brother. Where he is, what he's doing. Even whether he has any girlfriends,' he spat out disgustedly.

'Have you told Aiden this?'

'Nah. He'd just tell me to stop moaning.' He sat up straight and pulled a face. '*We're lucky to have her, kiddo,*' he parroted. '*Be nice to her, otherwise you'll have to go back to boarding school.*' His eyes arrowed in on hers. 'Is that true?'

Tricky waters. 'I'm sure there are other tutors who would be very happy to do what Helen's doing,' she told him honestly. 'But it would be a hassle to find another one, and there's no guarantee they would be any better.' At his crestfallen look she roughed his hair. 'Come on young man. Look on the bright side, having lessons next to a Grand

Prix circuit, even with Helen, has to be better than being at school.'

A glimmer of a smile. 'Suppose so.'

Later that evening a few of them went out for a drink on Aiden's boat. Of course he had to have a fifty foot motor yacht moored in the Monte Carlo harbour. Which racing driver *didn't*?

Their small group included two of the single engineers who weren't in a hurry to rush home, Frank and Nancy and Tom. Oh, and Helen, of course, who trailed after Aiden like an overexcited teenager.

'Now the race is over,' Frank was saying to Aiden as they settled onto the plush leather cushions on the top deck. 'Do you mind if I ask a personal question?'

Aiden sat back on the seat, an arm casually draped across the back. 'Sure, go ahead,' he replied easily, taking a sip of his ever present water.

Mel found she couldn't take her eyes off him. Surrounded by the trappings of his wealth he looked incredibly handsome in a pale blue shirt and casual jeans. So far beyond the reach of someone ordinary like her. He might claim to want her but it was hard to see how that could be anything other than a whim. A taste for something different.

'Do you ever think about your father when you race here?'

Aiden flinched, obviously not expecting Frank to ask that question.

Immediately Frank held up his hand. 'Sorry if that's too personal a question. It's just that I think about him every time I come here.'

With slow, controlled movements Aiden took another sip

of his water. 'I think perhaps you had a closer relationship with him than I did,' he said finally. 'The first few times I raced here, the image of his crash did cross my mind, but not now. Now the only times I think of him are when you guys remind me.'

'That's not exactly true, is it,' Frank replied quietly.

An awkward silence fell between them and Nancy tugged at Frank's arm. 'Now's not the time for this,' she hissed, glaring at her husband. 'Not in front of an audience.'

Frank nodded. 'Yet again, my wife is right. Sorry.' Slowly he stood up. 'I'm going to grab myself another beer. Anyone else want anything?'

As others stood, the awkward moment was successfully navigated and Helen took the opportunity to sidle next to Aiden. It left Mel trying to entertain Tom while also trying not to notice how close Helen was sitting to Aiden. She was practically on his lap. Not that Aiden seemed to be pushing her away, though to be fair he didn't appear to be encouraging her, either. He was leaning forward, arms resting on his thighs, and from the occasional word she overheard she guessed they were talking racing.

It was another hour before Aiden finally noticed how tired his brother was. 'Sorry to break up the party, guys, but this little lad here needs to get to bed.'

Tom started to protest but Aiden grabbed him, swinging him up and over his shoulder. 'Yes you do, buddy.'

'Can't we sleep on the boat?' he moaned from his upside down position.

'I told you earlier, we'll do it another day when the harbour isn't so busy. Sleeping here tonight would be like camping in the middle of Piccadilly Circus at rush hour.'

As Aiden and a wriggling Tom clambered off the boat, Frank and Nancy caught up with her. 'If looks could kill,'

Nancy whispered, 'young Helen would be lying ten foot under by now.'

'Oh God, was I that obvious?'

Frank chortled. 'Only to us.'

Mel huffed out an evening's worth of suppressed irritation. 'I can't stand women who make such an obvious play for a man.'

'Any man, or just this one?' Though Frank's voice was teasing, his eyes were serious.

'Any man,' she replied, firmly crossing her fingers. Possibly, probably, definitely, she was lying.

Nancy smiled, squeezing her arm. 'You know we love you like a daughter, don't you?'

The softly spoken words caught at her throat. 'I'm lucky enough to know that, yes.'

'So if you ever need to talk to us about what's in your heart, you know we're always there for you.'

Mel bit at her lip, willing the tears in her eyes not to spill over. 'I do, and thank you.'

Gently Nancy patted her cheek, her eyes kind and full of understanding. 'You know if a woman's going to lose her heart to a man she needs to make sure he's somebody special.' Her gaze fell on Frank, and then over to where Aiden was walking with Tom still hanging over his shoulder, laughing his head off. 'I don't know Aiden as well as Frank does but I can tell you this. He's not another Carlos.'

Mel's heart jumped. 'How can you be sure?'

'Carlos is selfish. He treats women, and people in general, like objects, there to entertain him while the mood strikes. He would never have risked his shot at a World Championship to help look after his brother.'

'No, he wouldn't,' Mel admitted, watching Helen laugh

at something Aiden said. 'Just because Aiden is a kinder man though, it doesn't make him a more reliable one.'

Nancy smiled. 'True. It doesn't automatically make him unreliable, either.'

It was only a short walk back to the hotel where they were all staying. As they waited for the lift Mel saw plenty of people do a double-take at Aiden as they crossed the lobby. Also plenty of women flashing him a seductive smile – and receiving a charming one back.

She knew he was only living up to his image, his brand, yet still it hurt. Aiden might not be as callous as Carlos but there would always be women surrounding him, tempting him.

Tom, who was now just about standing upright, nudged her leg and raised sleepy eyes up at her. 'Are you gonna come and say goodnight?'

Why did she find it impossible to refuse those grey eyes? 'Sure.'

As Aiden opened the door to his suite, Mel's jaw dropped. 'I definitely haven't got a view like this one.'

His eyes glittered. *You could have*, they seemed to be saying, before he nodded back at the stunning view from the floor to ceiling windows. 'I figured it's quieter, safer and more comfortable for us to stay here and look out on the marina than to try and sleep in it. At least during a Grand Prix.' Turning back to Tom, he ruffled his hair. 'Change, teeth and bed. You've got five minutes. Ready, get set. Go.'

Tom legged it into the swanky slate grey bathroom, leaving Aiden and Mel alone for the first time since their altercation about Helen on Friday.

'I see you've got the bedtime routine down to a fine art,' she remarked when she couldn't stand the silence any longer.

173

'At least I'm getting something right.'

So, he was still cross with her. 'You're getting a lot of things right,' she told him honestly. 'He's almost chatty now and he certainly smiles a lot more. That's all down to you.'

Aiden slumped onto the sofa. 'I'd like to think so, though when you've been through something really bad, the alternative can seem fun for a while. I'm just not sure how sustainable it is in the long run.'

'You're thinking of keeping Tom with you even when his mother comes home?'

He glanced up at her and gave her a tight smile. 'Yeah, and I can see from your face exactly what you think of that idea.' She wanted to protest, but he cut her short. 'No, don't worry, you're right. I'm being stupid thinking this could work. He needs stability. A home and a school, not a motorhome and tutor. It's just if she forces him back to boarding school.' He rubbed at his face in a weary gesture. 'I know why he hates that. I hated that.'

'Tom does need a proper education,' she answered carefully. It was the only thing that concerned her about how Tom was currently living. Sure mixing with people his own age was important, but not as much as being around somebody who loved him. The pair of them might not realise it yet, but that was something Tom now had.

Aiden glanced at her imploringly. 'Please let's not have another argument about Helen. Right now, we need her.'

'So I understand. Apparently she's the only person capable of tutoring Tom. If he's not nice to her, he has to go back to school.'

Grey eyes narrowed. 'What do you mean by that?'

'That's what you've told Tom, isn't it? Yet by all accounts he doesn't like Helen much and she spends all her time asking him about you.'

Aiden's body language was becoming more and more rigid and Mel knew they were heading for another argument but she couldn't stop. This was too important.

'Doesn't it worry you that Tom's tutor is more interested in you, than him?'

'It would worry me more if it was the other way round.'

Mel shook her head at him. 'Why do you always try to turn everything into a joke? This is serious.'

'The tutor's got the hots for me, so what.' He shot to his feet and stalked towards her, his body fizzing with suppressed anger. 'You know what all this is, Mel? You're jealous, pure and simple. You don't want to sleep with me, but you can't stand watching somebody else try.'

'Oh, please, spare me the egotistical rant. You're responsible for a young boy now. It's time you grew up.' Frustrated, fed up with him and damn it, angry herself now, she turned away and marched towards the door, wrenching it open. She was almost through it before she remembered why she'd come. 'Please tell Tom I'm sorry, but I had to take an important phone call.'

As she shut the door behind her, tears streamed down her face. To hell with Aiden Foster. He was an arrogant git and she wasn't falling in love with him. She wasn't.

Chapter Twenty

The following week they were in Montreal, home to the Circuit Gilles Villeneuve, built on a man-made island in the middle of the St Lawrence River. Aiden had just finished his first practice session and was waiting patiently for the briefing room to clear so he could have a word with Frank. There were a few conversations left hanging since Monte Carlo and this was one of them. Later he'd tackle the one with Mel. Since she'd left his hotel room in Monte Carlo angry and upset, the only contact he'd had with her had been a few cursory emails reminding him of his media duties. Looking back on it, he knew he'd handled the issue of Helen badly but, by God, he hated being told he was wrong.

When the last of the engineers left the room, Frank closed the door quietly, but firmly, behind him.

'So.' Frank looked as uneasy as he felt.

'So.'

A glimmer of a smile crossed the older man's face and he went to sit back down. 'I'm better at discussing aerodynamics and race strategy than emotions and feelings.'

'Ditto.'

Frank nodded. 'Usually I'd stick with what I know, but I happen to believe it's actually the emotional stuff that's holding you back.'

'My father,' he said heavily, grabbing himself a drink from the fridge so he wouldn't have to look at Frank.

'It's hard for any son to follow a famous father.' Frank paused. 'Even harder when there doesn't appear to have been any love lost between them.'

'I didn't say that,' he replied defensively, taking a seat opposite.

'You didn't have to. When you're forced to talk about him, the light goes out of your eyes. Heck, I'm not a shrink, but it seems to me there's a lot of unresolved stuff going on in your head where he's concerned. You think about him far more than you should and it's not healthy.'

Aiden's fingers tightened on the water bottle. 'You want to criticise my performance, go ahead. That's your prerogative. Just keep my personal life out of it.'

'I will, if you do.'

'Bloody hell, Frank. What on earth do you expect me to do? Perform some sort of voodoo ritual before I race, to expurgate the spirits of the dead?'

'How about talk to someone about what's going on in your head?' Frank replied calmly.

'Are you telling me I'm some sort of nutter?'

Frank let out an exasperated snort. 'Now you're overreacting.'

Aiden tensed, ready to stand up and walk out. He was fed up with people telling him how he should feel about his father, or what he should do with those damn feelings. For the millionth time he wished he'd had a normal, boring father who'd worked in an office and read him stories when he came home.

But then you'd never have been a racing driver.

'Have you ever told anyone what it was like growing up with Seb Foster as a father?' Frank asked quietly. 'I mean the truth, not the Disney version you spout out at regular intervals.'

Aiden drew in a deep breath and let it out slowly, fighting for calm. When he glanced over at Frank all he could see in the guy's eyes was concern.

'Mel knows some of it,' he admitted, then raised his eyes to the ceiling. 'Shit, this is ridiculous. It wasn't even that bad. It's not like he beat me up or anything. I've got nothing to complain about.'

'Why don't you let Mel be the judge of that? Talk to her, Aiden. Talk to somebody. Then you might find you can let it all go.'

Aiden gave him a small smile. 'You know for a race engineer, you're not a bad psychiatrist.'

'I'm not a good one either, so let's move onto something we're both more comfortable discussing. Tomorrow's practice session.'

When Aiden finally made it out of the briefing room and into the hotel shower he was still thinking about what Frank had said. Was it possible that just talking to someone would help him drive better? Sure he understood that in cases like sudden bereavement or abuse, talking helped but he'd had neither of those things. Wouldn't admitting how he felt only shame him in Mel's eyes? Poor old Aiden, left at boarding school because his parents didn't want him.

It sounded so flipping pathetic.

Quickly he towelled off and slipped on a T-shirt and jeans. Tom was in the adjacent room, working with Helen. Maybe he'd take a peek at how the guy was doing. Reassure himself he was getting that education Mel was so obsessed about.

He felt a bit foolish knocking on the door, so he knocked and entered at the same time. Both their heads swung up and both of them smiled. Tom's was one of pure relief. He obviously thought he was going to be let off the rest of the afternoon. Helen's was … yes, okay, he knew what her smile was saying. Fancying him didn't make her a bad tutor though, did it? He liked to think it just meant she had good taste.

'How's it going?' he asked, ruffling Tom's hair. They still hadn't managed to get the guy a cut, something he needed to rectify.

'Fine.' The reply wasn't filled with enthusiasm but then Aiden hadn't enthused over his studies, either.

'We've been focusing on English this afternoon,' Helen told him, giving him another coy smile. 'Tom's writing an essay on what he wants to be when he's older.'

His interest piqued, Aiden pulled the paper towards him, expecting to see an essay about becoming a racing driver. 'A car mechanic?' he blurted, surprised by the dent to his ego. 'You're kidding, right?'

'What's wrong with being a mechanic?' Tom replied belligerently. 'They do all the important stuff, like put the tyres on. All the driver does is go round and round a track. There aren't even any obstacles. He's got an easy job.'

'No obstacles apart from the twenty odd other drivers on the track,' Aiden muttered. Still, the little guy had a point. Driving was pretty easy. It was winning that was the hard part.

'Can I finish now?'

Aiden looked at his watch and then at Helen. 'Has he worked hard enough?'

She smiled smoothly. 'He certainly has.'

'Okay then, buddy, looks like school is out.'

Tom let out a shriek and threw his pen on the desk. 'Can we go to the track? Hang round the garage?'

'Watch all those greasy mechanics, eh?'

'You mean monkeys,' Tom replied gleefully, scuttling round the room searching for his jumper and his shoes. 'Greasy monkeys.'

Hiding a smile, Aiden turned to Helen. 'How are you going to spend the afternoon? Presumably not watching greasy monkeys. I understand Montreal has some decent shops. And there's always Crescent Street. They close it to traffic for the Grand Prix. It's got one hell of a party atmosphere.'

'Umm, maybe. But it's not much fun on my own.'

That was no doubt his cue to invite her to join them. Aiden regarded her dispassionately. She was beautiful and smart, but bland. Soulless. If he was a man who ran the local garage rather than a millionaire driver, she'd no doubt cut him dead. 'Well, whatever you do, enjoy.'

If she was disappointed she hid it well, giving him a polite smile before sauntering out of the room.

'I'm glad she's not coming with us.' Having located his shoes Tom sat on the bed, trying to squeeze them on without undoing them first.

Aiden sat next to him and calmly undid the laces. 'Don't you get on with her then?' Mel's words echoed back at him, making him feel guilty that he hadn't asked Tom that question sooner.

'She's okay.'

'Is she a good teacher? Do you think you're learning much?'

He shrugged his slim shoulders. 'I suppose.'

'Are all ten year olds this hard to talk to, or is it just you?' Aiden muttered, lacing up the final trainer. He looked Tom directly in the eye. 'Mel's a bit concerned that Helen's not doing a good job.'

A whole gamut of emotions crossed his brother's face; surprise, glee and finally, fear. Then he quickly looked away and bounced off the bed. 'She's fine.'

Aiden took hold of Tom's arm and forced him to look

at him. 'Do you mean that, or are you saying it because you think the alternative is going back to boarding school?'

When his cheeks flushed and he continued to stare determinedly at the floor, Aiden sighed. 'I think I get the picture.'

Again Tom didn't say anything but he did finally look at him; two stubborn grey eyes and a mop of brown hair. Aiden felt an unexpected squeeze on his heart. 'Okay, we'll talk about this again some other time, but you need to know this. I won't make you go back to boarding school. If Helen's no good, we'll find someone else who is. Even if it means we go through thirty tutors before you're happy with one, we'll do that rather than send you back to that school. Got it?'

Tom began to smile but as fast as it arrived, it vanished. 'Will I have to go back there when Mum comes back?' He hung his head. 'If she ever comes back.'

Aiden's heart stuttered and he grasped Tom by the shoulders. 'Where you go to school will be her decision, not mine, but of course she'll come back.'

'When then?'

Oh boy, the kid's sad eyes expression was like a punch to the stomach. 'Shit, Tom, I don't know. Maybe not for another month or so, till the end of term.'

The sad eyes widened. 'You said sh—'

'I know what I said,' Aiden cut in quickly. 'A word I shouldn't have. For Go—goodness sake, don't repeat it when we're with anyone else.'

'Mel would tell you off.' The haunted look disappeared and Tom grinned. 'She tells the men in the garage off when they swear in front of me.'

'I bet she does.' He had a sudden vision of Mel holding

Tom's hand, berating anyone who let him down. He loved that she was fiercely loyal. Not afraid to stick up for those she cared for.

He just hoped he was on that selective list.

It was Sunday, race day. Mel had been rushed off her feet ever since landing in Montreal. Journalist after journalist had begged for interviews, presumably because, after a shaky start, Delta were climbing up both the constructors' and drivers' championships. Carlos might be dominating the leader board but his Viper teammate had suffered two recent DNF's (Did Not Finish) leaving Stefano and Aiden second and third respectively. Delta had also just done a deal with a new sponsor which meant press releases and further commitments to cram into the drivers' already overloaded schedules.

Sitting in the team room she stared again at her most recent email, from a film producer no less. She had a feeling this would be one too many commitments for Aiden. There was no way she was going to discuss it with him today though. He had enough to worry about.

She wished she'd kept her big mouth shut about Helen and not launched into him like a banshee back in Monte Carlo. Considering the pressure he was under to perform both on and off the track he was doing a pretty great job with Tom. All her outburst had done was cause an uneasy rift between them.

With a sigh she turned off the laptop and as it slowly shut down she sat back, stretching out her neck.

'Working too hard?'

She spun round to find Aiden in the team room doorway. Tom, his ever present sidekick, standing next to him.

'Hi, there.'

Aiden's eyes narrowed slightly as he scrutinised her face. 'You're looking tired. You need to slow down a bit.'

Embarrassed, and more than a bit miffed at the tired reference, Mel ducked her head and made a big play of tucking the laptop into her bag. 'I'm fine. At least most of my work's already done for today.'

When she risked looking up again he was smiling, his eyes still on her face. 'Racing isn't work. It's fun.' Slowly, as if working something out in his mind, he turned to Tom. 'Go and grab me a bottle of water from the bar downstairs please, mate?' Tom dutifully dashed off and Aiden took two long, purposeful strides towards her before perching on the edge of the table she'd been using. 'Are you okay?'

Dressed in Delta T-shirt and an old pair of jeans, he smelt of a recent shower. Mel had to steel herself not to fling her arms round him. How long had it been since he'd held her? Clearly not long enough, because she could remember it all too vividly.

'I told you, I'm fine,' she replied lightly, easing away from the table and standing up. 'Or I would be if you didn't keep telling me I look knackered.'

He laughed softly. 'Why is it when I comment you look tired you're offended but when I say you look beautiful, you don't believe me?'

'Because the former is an accurate observation while the latter is flattery, intended to soften me up.' She smiled to show him there were no hard feelings.

'Wow, are you really that cynical? Or is it just me you choose not to believe?'

The edge to his tone left Mel uncertain how to reply. She thought he did mean every word he said to her – at the time. He'd also mean it when he said those words to the next woman he took a fancy to. And the one after that. It wasn't even that he was cold or calculating, simply that he liked women. And they liked him.

'Okay, I get the message.' He spoke testily into the silence. 'I just came to apologise for the other night in Monte Carlo, when you tried to tell me how Tom felt about Helen.'

'And you accused me of being jealous. Yes, I remember.'

'I thought you would,' he replied dryly, shoving a hand into his jeans pocket. 'I was out of order. You were concerned about Tom's welfare, rightly as it turns out, and I should have listened like a grown-up. Not retaliated like a ten-year-old.'

It was impossible for her to stay angry with him. 'You're forgiven.'

Their eyes locked and slowly his grey eyes darkened. He never tried to hide his desire for her and it terrified her, because she knew if he wanted to push it, she'd tumble into his arms in a flash.

'Mel.' Her name was a husky whisper on his tongue, making her insides unravel. When he moved to stand in front of her, not touching but close enough that she could feel his heat, those same insides nearly fell to the floor. 'God, Mel.'

He raised his hand to her cheek just as Tom burst into the room. 'Water delivery!'

With a wry grin Aiden dropped his arm and took a small step back, accepting the cold drink. 'Cheers, mate.'

'Have you asked her?'

Aiden unscrewed the cap off the bottle and took a sip. 'Not yet. Maybe you should.'

'Ask me what?'

Tom squared his shoulders. 'Can I watch the race with you today?'

Aiden gave his brother a none-too-subtle kick.

'Please?'

Mel had as much trouble turning down the younger brother as she did the older one. 'Sure you can.'

Tom sidled closer and said in a loud whisper. 'And can we not tell Helen?'

'Ah.'

They exchanged knowing looks.

'I think we can manage that, too.' Instinctively she bent to give him a quick hug.

When she glanced back up she found Aiden watching them with a curiously intent look on his face.

'Right then.' He seemed to say it as much to himself as her and Tom. 'If you two guys are okay, I'd better go and suit up. Catch you later.'

Before she had a chance to wish him luck he was out of the door and running down the stairs.

The race was hard fought. Carlos started in pole and remained out of reach throughout. His calamitous Viper teammate managed to clip another driver, sending them both spinning off the circuit and back to the garage. It left Aiden and Stefano duelling for second place. There were hairy moments, one in particular when he heard Frank's sharp intake of breath over the radio, but Aiden's luck held and he ended ahead of his teammate in second place.

Predictably Stefano wasn't best pleased. 'That was some wild driving out there, man,' he remonstrated as they waited to go on the podium. 'You nearly had us both crashing out.'

Aiden simply smiled. 'A miss is as good as a mile, my friend.'

After the unavoidable press calls, Frank caught up with him in the garage. 'Good race.'

Aiden considered the widening points gap between himself and Carlos. The near-miss he'd had with Stefano. 'Just not good enough.'

Frank inclined his head in that considered way he had when he had something important to say. 'Both the car and the driver are capable of better.'

The words hung around Aiden's head as he showered. Stayed with him as he ate that evening. And were still there as he lay awake in bed that night.

Chapter Twenty-One

Silverstone, home to the British Grand Prix. Aiden had a love hate relationship with the place. He loved winning in front of his home crowd. He hated performing poorly in front of his home crowd, something he seemed to have done too often in recent years. In fact, he'd only ever won once at Silverstone. Of course his father had won there more years than Aiden could count on one hand.

As he sat in the local barber's next to Tom though, the latter making faces at him in the mirror, his father seemed like a distant memory.

'What would you like, sir?'

Aiden glanced over to Tom who shrugged. 'I don't even want a stupid hair cut.'

'Says the boy with the tangled mop on his head.' He gave his own rather-too-long hair a harsh scrutiny. 'Give us both a four round the sides and a good hack off the top.' He slid Tom a sideways glance. 'Just make sure mine looks better than his at the end.'

Tom hooted with laughter. 'My hair's going to look way better than yours.' Then he leant across and whispered. 'Does that mean we're having the same cut?'

Aiden formed a fist with his hand and nodded at Tom to do the same so they could fist bump. 'It's a Foster special.' As Tom grinned and bumped his fist back, Aiden marvelled again at how close he felt to the boy. They carried the same surname, thanks to his mother not marrying again (though it wasn't for want of trying) but they didn't have the same similarities in their DNA that full brothers had. It didn't matter. He felt closer to Tom than he'd ever done to anyone else.

Except maybe Mel.

An hour later he left Tom and Helen hard at work in his motorhome and made his way to the Delta 'brand centre', as the marketing team had now decided the giant corporate motorhome would be called. Just as he reached the entrance he was accosted from behind.

'Have you got a minute?' Mel asked, a little breathless.

He'd have liked to think the catch in her voice was down to seeing him, but he knew damn well it had more to do with her dash across the paddock.

'For you, I can always manage a minute. In fact, I can give you hours. Days in fact, though we'd have to wait until after the season.' He grinned but received only a small smile in return. Had his brother been with him she'd have no doubt managed something a lot wider and warmer. With Tom she was cheerful and relaxed. With him she was polite and formal.

He hated it.

'Could you be serious for just one minute. Please?'

He frowned at the anxious note in her voice. 'What's up?'

Quickly she scanned the busy paddock behind them. 'I need to talk to you somewhere private.'

Usually he'd make a joke about getting her on her own but he had the feeling if he tried that now, she'd clock him one. 'Team room?'

She nodded briskly. 'Yes. Let's head there.' Wearing her standard sensible flatties she bustled past him and shot straight up the stairs.

'Hey, where's the fire?' When she didn't glance back, his anxiety level notched a little higher.

When she firmly and deliberately shut the door to the team room behind them, it reached alarm level.

'Okay, now I'm really scared.' He meant it as a joke although his heart was thumping in his chest.

'Why? Because you're shut inside a closed room with me?' Her half smile did nothing to allay his fears. Not while the sheet of paper she carried shook in her trembling hands.

'I love being in a closed room with you, though I'd prefer it if you weren't looking terrified.'

'I'm not, at least not of you, more your reaction to what I have to tell you.' Her eyes glanced down at the paper and then back at him. 'I like the haircut.'

'Thanks, but I've a feeling you're only saying that to put off telling me about what's in your hand.'

'Guilty.'

His thumping heart now plummeted. 'Hell, what do the flaming press want from me now? Have they latched on to Tom? I've seen the way they watch us but I had hoped they'd give the kid some privacy. I mean, it's hardly news, my brother watching me race.' He tailed off as he saw her swallow and bite her lip.

'Please sit down.'

'Seriously?' Shaking his head he perched on the nearest chair, resting his elbows on the table. 'Better spit it out quickly, the apprehension isn't good for my blood pressure.'

She slid onto the sofa opposite him, her hazel eyes looking directly into his. 'They're going to make a film of your father, timed for release on the twentieth anniversary of his death.'

Aiden heaved in a long, deep breath and exhaled very slowly. Remaining calm and unruffled was his racing trademark. 'I'm sure it will make great viewing.'

'Umm, well, here's the part you might not be so happy about. Your mother has apparently agreed to provide some family photos and video for inclusion in the film.'

He snorted. 'Well, I wish her luck finding any of that. The family part, anyway.' Then Mel's words finally started to sink in. 'Hang on, when did she agree to do this?'

'According to the producer, last week.'

'*Last week?*' Calm and unruffled flew out of the window. 'She's managed to find the time to contact the flaming producer but can't be bothered to contact her own *son?*'

As Aiden's eyes blazed with fury Mel instinctively recoiled. 'I can only go by what I've been told.' *Please don't blame the messenger.*

His mouth tightened. 'Can you get her phone number from this producer guy?'

'Yes. I knew you'd ask for it, so I've done it already.' Silently she slid the sheet of paper she'd been holding across the table to him.

'Thanks.' His eyes swirled with emotions she could only guess at. 'Is that what this was about? My press officer obtaining contact details for my wayward mother. Or was there something else?'

With the anger still pulsing off him in waves, Mel wanted to duck out now and have the conversation another time. But that would be cowardice. 'The producer contacted me because he wants you to be in the film. Well, actually, I suppose we should call it a documentary.'

'What, exactly, does he want me to do in this film, slash, documentary?' The words were uttered slowly and precisely. 'Drive fast round a track to prove I've got some of my father's genes?'

Aiden could be warm and funny, or coldly sarcastic. It looked like today she was going to get the least likable side of him. 'He wants you to recount memories from your childhood.'

'Does he now.' He steepled his hands together, as if contemplating the idea. Mel thought he'd prefer to walk through a snake infested jungle in his bare feet. 'What do *you* want me to do?'

Ah. This was where Mel the press officer differed from Mel the friend. 'As Seb Foster drove for Delta, and the documentary is a celebration of his racing achievements, we'd like you to take part in the film. It will give us some control while also helping your profile and that of the company.'

'I guess that depends on what I say.'

'Well, there is that.'

Instantly he lurched to his feet. 'I'll think about it.' With that he snatched at the paper with his mother's number on it and thrust open the door.

As it shut behind him, Mel let out a deep sigh and sat back against the sofa. Bugger, bugger, bugger.

Her afternoon continued to go downhill when she bumped into Devon, the blonde so called journalist of *Just for Ladies* magazine fame, at a press conference.

'It's Devon, isn't it?' she enquired coolly.

The half-woman-half-girl smiled back. 'Ooh, yes, well done. I know we've met, but I'm sorry I can't remember your name.'

That put her neatly in her place. 'I'm Melanie Hunt. Press officer for Stefano and Aiden.'

Devon visibly perked at the sound of the second name. 'Yes, yes, I remember. We met at Aiden's place. It was the morning after he and I ... well, you know.'

She giggled, making Mel want to respond by saying *shagging Aiden Foster isn't that special. I've done it myself.* Only, of course, that would be a lie, because sex with Aiden had been incredibly special. At least it had been to her. 'So you're still researching your article then?' she asked instead.

'Umm, yes. I've been a bit sidetracked with a few fashion pieces but now my editor wants me to focus on this one. It would be really helpful if I could interview Aiden again because the last few times we met …' she let out a coy little smile '… we really didn't do that much talking.'

Mel was loathe to let this man trap loose on Aiden again, but as that was for non-professional reasons she had to suck it up. 'I'll see what I can do. Give me your card and I'll give you a call when he's got some time in his schedule.'

As she wedged Devon's card into her handbag, Mel reflected that some days she hated her job.

'How the hell could you abandon your son like that?' Aiden hissed into the phone at his mother. He wanted to yell but he was in his motorhome and Tom was only a closed door and a hunk of fibreglass away. Nevertheless, it was the longest sentence he'd spoken to her in nearly ten years. He'd left home only a few months after Tom had been born. Since then he'd contacted her once, when he'd gained his racing license. Following her complete disinterest, he hadn't bothered to phone her since.

'I didn't abandon Tom,' she replied bad-temperedly. 'He was at boarding school.'

'A place he loves so much he tried to run away three times. Not that you'd know,' he added, his temper flaring, 'because you didn't bother to leave any contact details.'

'There's no need to raise your voice with me, Aiden. It's not like I knew this was going to happen. I left him in good hands.'

'You left him in a place he hates and *haven't contacted him since*.' He uttered the last few words slowly and clearly. 'Didn't it occur to you to let the school know where you were in case he was taken ill? Or, here's a novelty, perhaps even to call your son to talk to him now and again? Or were you too *busy*?' He couldn't resist emphasising the last word.

'You can stop the snotty attitude. I'm still your mother and I won't tolerate you speaking to me like that.'

'You were never my mother,' he told her flatly. 'Not in the usual sense of the word.'

'How can you say that? If it hadn't been for me ensuring you made it to all those damn kart races, you wouldn't be the driver you are now.'

'Yes, I owe a whole heap to all those nannies you employed.' He paused for a moment, trying to get a lid on his fast unravelling temper. 'So when are you coming back?'

'Well ... as long as Tom's with you, there's no rush is there? Bradley wants to sail round a few more islands before we head back.'

Bradley was lover number what? Five? Ten? He'd lost count and interest after two. 'Any chance of this one proposing?'

'Perhaps.' He heard her light, insincere laugh. 'Who knows?'

Depressingly, it all made perfect sense. Just as she'd done to him after his father had died, she was now doing to Tom. Chasing after every rich, eligible man she met and totally ignoring her child.

He ended the call with a curt 'call me when you return home' and went to find Tom. No longer doing his schoolwork, he'd shifted to the sofa to watch television and was giving a running commentary on everything he was seeing to ... Mel?

'Helen had to go and do something,' Mel informed him hastily, before he had a chance to say anything. 'I agreed to sit with Tom for a bit. I didn't realise you were here.'

'Only place I was guaranteed some privacy.' He indicated the sheet of paper she'd given him, with his mother's number on it.

'Oh.' Immediately her eyes filled with sympathy. 'How did it go?'

He glanced at Tom who was giggling at some inane cartoon. To any observer he was a chilled, happy ten-year-old. With a reluctant sigh Aiden switched the set off.

'Hey, I was watching that.'

'And you can continue to watch it in a minute, but first I've got something to tell you.' He eased next to him on the sofa. 'It's about your mother.'

Immediately Mel shot to her feet. 'I think I'd better go.'

'No. Stay.' He was surprised how needy his reply was. 'Please?' She sat back down and Tom turned to him with large, watchful eyes. 'I've just spoken to her and she's fine. Very fine, in fact. She's sailing round the Caribbean with some guy called Bradley.'

'She wants to marry him.' He kicked at the sofa with his foot. 'She's always wanting to get married.'

Aiden almost smiled. 'Yeah, she is. Picking up men doesn't seem to be a problem. It's keeping them that's proving more difficult.'

Tom sniggered which Aiden reckoned was worth the admonishing glance Mel directed at him.

'Anyway, I just wanted to let you know that your mum's okay and she'll be back as soon as she's finished her little island hopping jaunt.'

The smile slipped from Tom's face and Aiden couldn't read what he was thinking.

'Is there anything you want to ask?'

'Can I turn the telly back on now?'

With a sigh Aiden stood and switched the set back on. It

looked like he and his brother had one thing in common, at least. An intense dislike of voicing their feelings.

As Tom settled back down in front of the big screen, Aiden followed Mel outside.

'She'll be back in a *little while*?' Mel repeated incredulously the moment they were out of earshot. 'I don't understand how she can not want to rush right over here and see him.' Then she shuddered, her face an expression of pure disgust. 'Forget that. I can't begin to comprehend how she could have left him in the first place.'

'I can.'

She had a world of questions in her eyes but he wasn't prepared to answer them. Tom was only a thin wall away and besides, Aiden was a coward when it came to this stuff. He knew his evasiveness would lead to her imagining the worst, and that if she ever did hear the truth she'd eye him pitifully and wonder why he'd made such a colossal deal of it all.

He *could* man up in one area, though. 'Look, I'm sorry for my earlier rant. It's not your fault they want to make a film of the great Seb Foster. I needed to let off steam and you were unlucky enough to be in the firing line.'

'I understand.'

'And thank you for getting my mother's number. You went out of your way and at the time it didn't look like I appreciated it, but I did. Really.'

'No problem.'

Her smile was soft, her eyes kind and the desire to kiss her pulsed through every cell in his body. *But she didn't want that from him.* He cleared his throat. 'While I'm on a roll with the thank-yous. Thank you for sitting with Tom. Did Helen say where she was going? How long she'd be?'

Mel's gaze skimmed past him and over his left shoulder. 'Umm, no.'

'I take it this isn't the first time this has happened?'

'No, not the first.'

Something he should have known. 'Okay, I'll have a word. If my mother comes back when she claims she will, we won't need Helen for much longer, anyway.' Because Tom would go back home. God, he felt choked at the thought. Visions of saying goodbye to the little tike swam through his mind and Aiden felt so unsteady he had to plonk himself down on the step.

Mel hunched in front of him. 'Are you okay?'

'Yeah, yeah. I'm fine.' To prove his point he forced himself back on his feet, though to be on the safe side he leant against the side of the motorhome. 'I just hadn't quite twigged that my mother coming back meant Tom leaving.' He shrugged awkwardly. 'Stupid, eh? I've got quite attached to the little guy.'

Mel's smile looked as wobbly as he felt. 'So have I.'

Because she looked upset. And because he ached to do it anyway, Aiden took the two steps needed to bring himself right up against her. Then he placed his arms around her shoulders and hugged her. It was a gesture of comfort. Of friendship.

Of course his body didn't realise that. The instant it had a soft, pliant Mel within its grasp, it acted on instinct. Immediately she went rigid in his arms and took a giant step back.

Frustration bubbled inside him, along with a desire to punch something hard. As the only available surface was his hugely expensive motorhome, he slammed a hand through his hair instead. 'Right. Well. I'll see you later.'

Swearing under his breath he stomped back inside. This flaming friends lark was going to be the death of him.

Chapter Twenty-Two

The Silverstone meeting in late June was one of the busiest in Mel's diary. There was something about a British racing team and a British driver at a British Grand Prix that conjured up a media frenzy. It was heightened further during practice when it became clear Aiden had the fastest car. It reached fever pitch when Aiden qualified on pole.

On race morning the sun decided to make an appearance which had both her and Sally sighing with relief. A soggy Silverstone was a miserable one. By contrast Silverstone in the sun was sparkle and champagne, celebrities in white trousers and sexy shades meandering down the pit lane, laughing fans sitting on the grass banks, waving their flags.

Dashing between appointments Mel caught sight of a familiar figure chatting to some of the Delta engineers outside the garage. He flashed a beautiful smile, white teeth against a swarthy complexion, and for a brief moment Mel stopped to admire. Carlos Ferrer was still an incredibly handsome guy.

As if sensing her he looked up and caught her eye. Waving farewell to the engineers he trotted over.

'Ah, *mi hermosa*, Melanie.' He bent to kiss her hand. 'You get prettier every day.'

A few years ago her breath would have caught at his words. Now she knew them for what they were. Charming and frivolous. Not, under any circumstances, to be taken seriously.

'Hello, Carlos. What are you up to? Trying to prise information from the competition?'

He laughed, the movement causing dark hair to flop onto his forehead. 'Why, no. Just catching up with old friends. So how are you, my sweet Melanie?'

'Good, thank you.'

'Broken any hearts lately?'

'Isn't that your domain?'

He pretended to flinch. 'You wound me. How is that new driver of yours coming along? He's trying his best to beat me, but he lacks the killer instinct, yes?'

Without being consciously aware of it, her back straightened and her chin jutted. 'He's on pole today and he's already beaten you twice this year.'

Dark eyebrows snapped over similarly dark eyes. 'Ah, you defend him. Like a mother defending her child. Or perhaps a woman defending her lover?'

'We're not lovers.' She prayed her cheeks weren't going red. 'I defend him because he's part of the Delta team now.'

He gave her a sly smile. 'Your eyes tell me otherwise. Now I will enjoy beating him even more.'

'Why? You're the one who decided you didn't want me any more.' Okay, that sounded just a teeny bit bitter.

He looked askance. 'Not true. I always wanted you.'

'It's just that you wanted other women, too.'

His shoulders gave a laconic shrug. 'I was young and easily swayed. Now I'm older and more, how you say, selective.' Gently he brushed her cheek. 'If I were to date you now I would be more appreciative of what I had and less easily distracted by other ... temptations.'

He gave her his most disarming smile. Once it had sent flutters through her heart. Now it just made her smile back. Carlos had hurt her once, but he'd been a valuable lesson in life and she was happy to forgive and forget.

She watched him wander back to the Viper garage before turning and making her way towards the Delta one. That was when she noticed a tall, dark haired driver staring in Carlos's direction, a scowl marring his exceptionally handsome face. Well, good. It gave her ego a much needed massage to see Aiden brooding over the sight of her with another man for a change. Never mind that Carlos had never once, in the whole year they'd gone out, made her want him as much as Aiden had done last night when he'd hugged her. That Aiden had felt it too, had been obvious. What was becoming less and less obvious was why she kept denying herself.

Sunday afternoon, forty laps into the British Grand Prix, and Aiden did the unthinkable. He drove into the wrong blasted garage from the pit lane. The look of astonishment on the faces of his old pit crew team galvanised him into action and he jerked past them and into the right garage. On the way out, still cursing his stupidity, he compounded his error by speeding down the bloody pit lane, earning a drive through penalty. By this stage there weren't sufficient swear words in the world to do his self-loathing justice. A split second's loss of concentration and the lead he'd carefully and, damn it, skillfully amassed had been wiped away. By the time he re-entered the race he was languishing in fifth.

He made up a couple of places but his pole position, and almost certain first, ended in a dismal third. The deafening silence as he walked past the team afterwards told him everything. And, joy of joy, because he'd managed to scrape a podium place, he had to go through the torture of the televised post race interviews.

Mel met him in the podium anteroom but he couldn't bear to look at her as she handed him the sponsor gear he was contracted to wear for the cameras.

It wasn't long before he was asked the predictable question.

'What happened?'

'Isn't that rather obvious? I drove into the wrong garage and later speeded out of the right one.'

'Do you think that lapse cost you the race?'

He fought to keep his expression bland. 'I went into the pit lane leading by three seconds, timed to come out before the Viper. By the time I'd completed the drive though penalty I came out behind him and had to spend several tortuous laps trying to overtake. What do you think?'

'Going into the wrong garage isn't something that happens very often, is it? I can't recall your father ever missing his. Can you?'

Inwardly he lobbed a few burning arrows at the reporter. Outwardly a muscle in his jaw twitched slightly. 'I can't recall ninety-nine point nine per cent of drivers missing their garage,' he responded flatly. 'I mucked up. I want to take this opportunity to thank the team for all their hard work and to apologise. The car was capable of first and I'm sorry I didn't deliver on that. Hopefully I'll get the chance to make amends in the next race.'

Now please stop asking me questions and let me go and crawl under a stone. Thankfully the first half of his wish was granted but before he could find a large enough stone, Aiden had to endure listening to a beaming and gracious Carlos Ferrer being congratulated on winning another Grand Prix.

Aiden clenched his fists, nails digging into his palms. It couldn't have happened to a nicer man.

Over the last hour Mel had died a million deaths for Aiden. She'd started the moment he'd shot into the wrong garage and continued all the way through the excruciating interview he'd given to the waiting media. They'd met up briefly after the press conference, when he'd responded to her questions with a remoteness that had made her heart ache.

'What do you want me to put in the press release?' she'd asked.

'I ballsed up.'

'I might have to phrase it a little more politely.'

'That is the polite version.'

She'd bit her tongue and changed tactics. 'Would you like me to look after Tom for a bit?'

'Yes, please.'

His eyes, his face, his whole body language had been so lifeless she'd decided not to push any further.

When she'd finished her duties Mel texted Aiden to tell him she was taking Tom back to her hotel. That morning the place had swarmed with Delta team members but now it had all the buzz of a stadium the day after a sell out concert. With no victory to celebrate – Stefano had come in fourth – the team had departed to spend a rare Sunday evening at home.

Tom clambered onto her bed, shoes still on, and began flicking through the TV channels. He looked painfully sad.

Slipping off her own shoes she went to join him, sitting cross-legged next to him. 'Are you upset about the race?'

'A bit. He should have won.'

Mel silently thanked God Aiden wasn't here. He wouldn't dispute the truth of Tom's remark, but he would be hurt by the accusatory tone.

'He knows he should, Tom,' she pointed out. 'He didn't do it on purpose. I suspect he's got a lot on his mind.'

Guilt washed through her as she recalled their conversation earlier in the year. Since he'd told her he didn't want any distractions she'd done nothing but ram them down his throat. Sleeping with him, pushing for him to look after Tom, asking him to do interviews about his father.

'What else is making you sad?' she asked Tom gently, preferring to focus on him than her own shame. 'Are you worried about what will happen when your mum comes home?'

With a violent jerk of his hand he threw the remote across the room where it clattered against the wall. 'No.' His voice throbbed with hostility. ''Course not.' Bounding off the bed he headed for the door. 'I'm going to find my brother.'

Before he had a chance to turn the handle there was a knock on the other side. 'What's going on in there? Tom, Mel, open up.'

The moment Tom opened it wide enough to squeeze through he flung himself at Aiden's legs, clutching at them like he'd no intention of letting him go.

'Hey, buddy.' Aiden shot Mel a confused glance before bending to pick Tom up and carry him to the bed. 'Why all the yelling?'

'You mucked up the race,' Tom wailed.

Aiden's face crumpled, his expression so agonised Mel had to turn away. 'I know I did. I'm sorry.'

'You were winning.'

Mel couldn't stand to hear any more. 'Your brother doesn't need you to tell him all this, Tom. He needs sympathy, not a lecture.'

'What I need,' Aiden countered tightly, 'is for everyone to shut the fuck up about the damn race.'

Tom's eyes grew stalks. 'You just said f—'

'I know what I said. And if you repeat it in front of your mother, she'll crucify us both.'

'I don't want to go back with her,' he blurted.

Aiden stared at him. 'You don't?'

Tom gave a wild shake of his head. 'I want to stay with you.'

'Is that what all the shouting was about?'

Miserably, Tom nodded.

'Okay then.' Looking like a man struggling to think clearly, Aiden rubbed a hand over his face. 'Well, first you need to apologise to Mel for shouting. And did I hear you throw something?'

Tom slid a quick, sheepish grin towards Mel. 'The remote kind of slipped out of my hand.'

'And the apology?'

'Sorry for shouting,' he mumbled quickly, eyes fixed on the floor.

'Is that it? And it's Mel you should be directing this to, not the flipping carpet.'

Tom huffed and turned a conciliatory face towards her. 'Sorry. I was rude and I won't do it again.'

Mel tried to keep a straight face. 'You're forgiven.'

'Right then.' Shoving his hands in his jeans pockets, Aiden blew out a long breath. 'We'll talk about your mother when we've all had a chance to calm down. I'm not up to that conversation right now.'

''Kay.' Tom sniffed. 'But don't make me go home—'

'Buddy,' Aiden interrupted heavily. 'I won't make you do anything you don't want to. I promise.'

Mollified, Tom climbed off the bed to find the remote.

Aiden finally looked in her direction. 'Thanks for bringing Tom back here.' He smiled grimly. 'I guess it didn't take a genius to work out I needed the space.'

'Did it help?'

'Not much.' As Tom settled himself back on the bed, Aiden picked up a chair and sat down next to her. 'I'm very aware we're intruding on your Sunday evening. We'll be out of your hair in a minute.'

She tried not to stare at his tanned forearms as they rested on his thighs. 'You're only intruding on an evening where I sit alone in a hotel room because I can't be bothered to check out and get a train home.'

A flash of understanding crossed his face. 'It's times like this you really miss your parents, huh?'

'Yes.' The familiar ache was there in her heart. No longer severe enough to hurt, it was still a clear reminder of what she'd lost. 'After the other races there's always a crowd who choose to spend Sunday evening chilling together rather than joining the mass struggle to get home. But after Silverstone, everyone scarpers back to their families.'

'Well, Tom and I are staying put. I'm taking him karting tomorrow, so no point going home. Why don't you come to the motorhome and do that chill and meal thing with us?' He gave her a painfully honest smile. 'Truth is, I could really do with the company.'

Her heart shifted. 'Are you cooking?'

'What's the answer that would make you say yes?'

'"Mel, I promise not to cook. We'll get a takeaway pizza."'

Deadpan, he recited. 'Mel, I promise not to cook. We'll get a takeaway pizza.'

Feeling ten times lighter than she had a few minutes ago, Mel scrambled off the bed. 'Sold. Give me a minute to change and I'll come over with you.'

Aiden rose from the chair and shifted into the space she'd vacated on the bed, next to Tom. 'There's no rush. Take all the time you need.' He pushed his arms behind his head, sprawled his legs out in front of him and joined his brother in watching the TV.

They looked far more like brothers now they had the same haircut. Perhaps because the shorter style also emphasised their striking grey eyes. As she watched Aiden's features relax for the first time that day Mel had a feeling if she took too long, he'd soon be asleep.

Chapter Twenty-Three

Aiden tried to enjoy his Sunday evening, and mostly he succeeded. Coming third wasn't a total disaster, he kept reminding himself. Sure the gap between him and Carlos was wider now but they weren't even halfway through the season yet. There was time to catch the smarmy bastard.

Plus it was hard to keep kicking himself about losing a race when his brother was reciting an endless stream of schoolboy gags, one or two of which Aiden had actually managed to laugh at. If he was honest though, it was Mel who gave him the biggest lift. Listening to her lilting voice as she encouraged Tom to regale more of his jokes. Smiling with her when Tom, inevitably, forgot the punchline. Laughing at her when she finally gave in to the giggles. Yes, having Mel around was the best antidote to a dismal race he'd ever come across.

Which was why, once he'd shuffled Tom off to bed, Aiden desperately didn't want the evening to end.

'Another drink?' If she accepted, he was guaranteed at least another half hour of her company.

'Are you going to join me?'

He debated for a moment. So far he'd stuck to the rules and the only alcohol he'd drunk was winners' champagne, so his bloodstream wasn't exactly overburdened with the stuff. Plus the next race was two weeks away and he could really murder a beer. 'Yes.' He fiddled about in the kitchen area, prizing the lid off a lager bottle, retrieving a bottle of wine from the fridge, before joining her on the sofa.

'Have you thought what you're going to do about Tom when your mother comes back?'

Midway through filling her glass, his hand stilled. 'No,' he replied rather abruptly. After the crappy day he'd just had the last thing he wanted to do was think about even more crap.

'Fine.' Her single word response was filled with exasperation. 'As it's clear you don't want to talk I'll leave the wine, thanks, and go back to the hotel.'

'Now wait a minute.' He grabbed hold of her arm, just in case she had any ideas of making a break for it. 'Of course I want to talk to you. I can think of plenty of other things I'd like to do with you too, but I guess they aren't on the agenda, so talking is good. Just not about Tom. Not at the moment. Please?' Even to his own ears his voice sounded whiney. More than a plea, closer to a beg.

'What are we allowed to talk about then, Aiden? Because I know you won't want to talk about the race, Tom's off the agenda and heaven forbid I ask you anything about your past. So, what's left?'

He had a feeling he was being very skilfully manipulated. 'There are lots of areas,' he countered defensively. 'How about we talk about you? I'd really love to know what it was like to be Melanie Hunt growing up.'

'It's not a story that will thrill you.'

'Don't you worry, I've got other ideas how we can achieve that.' He smiled when she flushed, knowing it proved he still had the ability to affect her. The day she stopped reacting to him was the day he'd blown any further chance with her.

'I was a much adored only child,' she began, ignoring his remark. 'My parents wanted a sibling for me, but it never happened.'

'I suspect they were pretty happy with what they had.'

'Yes.' She smiled wryly at him. 'God, that sounds so arrogant, but I knew they were happy because they showed

206

me. They doted on me. I wasn't spoilt with material things. I was spoilt with love.'

'In my case it was the other way around.' He'd meant the words to stay in his head but she glanced sharply at him so he must have uttered them out loud.

'What—'

'We're talking about you,' he cut in firmly.

'Fine, though it's your turn next.'

Not if I can help it. This time he made sure the words stayed in his mind.

'There isn't much more to say,' Mel continued. 'Mum was a schoolteacher, which was really cool because she kept similar hours to me so I didn't have to be shunted off to childminders or spend hours home alone. She was also French so I grew up bilingual.'

She smiled at a distant memory, her pretty eyes growing soft and dreamy. 'We'd have these great holidays in France with my grandparents where the locals would assume I was this English schoolgirl and occasionally make snide remarks behind my back. You should have seen their faces when I rattled off a sarcastic comeback in perfect French.'

'I can imagine.' He could also picture Mel as a schoolgirl, hair in wayward pigtails and a short skirt showing off her perfectly formed legs. 'What about your dad?'

'He was a teacher too, but at university where he lectured on English. I inherited my love of words and writing from him, which is why I went on to study journalism. He was also a major racing enthusiast, which is no doubt why I ended up in the sport.' Once more she smiled fondly at the memories. 'I repeat, we're talking major here. He went to as many race meetings as he could and those he couldn't he watched religiously on the television. When I became old enough to take an interest, he'd take me to meetings, too.

Mum would hit the shops while Dad and I hit the circuit. Watching races together became our thing for many years.' As she'd talked her eyes had filled with tears and now they spilt down her face.

'Hell, I didn't want to make you sad, Mel. You don't have to talk about this.'

She brushed at her damp cheeks. 'I'm fine, really. In a funny way I'm actually enjoying this. It's been a long time since I talked about them and it's lovely to relive the memories.'

'Even though they're making you cry.'

'Yes.' She wrestled a tissue out of her handbag and blew her nose. 'I don't often get the chance to indulge in looking back. Sometimes I do when I'm by myself, but it's not the same.' She glanced up at him with watery eyes. 'It's lovely to share them with someone else for a little while.'

It gradually dawned on him quite how tough her life had been following their deaths. 'Do you have any grandparents, cousins, aunts and uncles nearby?'

'Mum had a brother who lives in Scotland, but we were never close. Dad was an only child. I have grandparents in Provence whom I try and see once a year.'

'So who was there to support you after your parents died?' When she didn't immediately reply, he felt a rush of anger on her behalf for the injustice of it all. 'Heck, Mel, you were eighteen and effectively all alone in the world?'

'No, it wasn't that bad. Friends rallied round and my grandparents came over for a few weeks and helped me with the funeral arrangements. Then I went back to university and tried to carry on as normal.'

'Jesus.' He shook his head and drained back his beer. 'I'm in awe of how you handled it all. By rights you should be angry and bitter at how they were taken away from you, and yet you're the most grounded, warm, real person I've ever met. They'd be so proud of you.' Her eyes rounded in shock and he had to laugh. 'What, you really don't know how incredible you are?'

Stunned, Mel stared at Aiden. She knew he could fake words, but it wasn't possible to fake the look in his eyes. This gorgeous man, one of an elite bunch who risked death on a racetrack most weekends, surviving through sheer grit, determination and mind boggling skill, thought *she* was incredible?

'I'm not,' she told him honestly. 'I just choose to be grateful for the time I had with them, rather than bitter at what I'd lost. Many children weren't as lucky as me.' Pointedly she looked at him. 'From the few details you've shared, I sense you weren't. I was on my own from the age of eighteen. When did you feel on your own, Aiden?'

Immediately his lean frame tensed, quickly followed by the other familiar gestures. The awkward shifting. The avoidance of her eyes. A minute ago she'd bared her soul for him yet he looked ready to bolt. Which was why it was such a shock when he finally spoke.

'I've felt on my own for as long as I can remember.' He scratched his head, as if he couldn't believe what he'd said.

'Will you tell me about it?'

Wordlessly he rose and got himself another beer. It was as if he couldn't talk about this without anaesthetising himself first.

'What do you want to know?'

'Let's start with your father. When did you realise he was a famous racing car driver?'

Aiden lay his head against the back of the sofa and stared up at the ceiling. 'I don't know. It was sort of a gradual thing. He wasn't home much, though neither was my mother for that matter. I didn't question it because that was how things were. The house was filled with trophies and racing paraphernalia and there was always some car race on the TV. I can remember the nanny telling me that my dad was driving one of the cars and I wasn't shocked, so on some level I must have known. Certainly by the time I was old enough to go to school I knew my dad was a World Champion driver.' He turned and gave her a slight smile. 'It gave me bragging rights.'

'Did they take you to watch him when you were older?'

He snorted. 'Hardly.'

'What, you never saw your father race?'

'I saw him at Silverstone once. I bunked off school, caught two buses and then snuck in with a large party. There were all these people sitting on seats, enjoying a great view and then there was me, getting the occasional glimpse of fast metal through the wire fencing. I remember thinking if I told them I was Seb Foster's son, they wouldn't believe me.'

'*I* can't believe he didn't take his own son to his races.'

Aiden shrugged. 'You have to understand I wasn't planned, wasn't wanted. Occasionally I served a purpose, when the great Seb Foster needed the image of the warm, family man, or when he wanted to show-off to his son about his latest victory, but mostly I was a nuisance. I'll always be grateful they allowed me to go karting though. I guess my father's ego demanded his son would be a driver, too.'

'Did he at least watch some of your races?'

'No, never.'

A haunted look settled over his face and Mel suddenly had a clear view of a little boy, desperate for some attention from the man he idolised. 'Where was your mother in all this?'

'Following my father round like a lost puppy. She knew

he held all the cards. He was the man with the talent, the money and the fame. I think she was very aware her glamorous life could be over in a flash if he ditched her, so she tried to ingratiate herself with him at every opportunity.'

Mel felt a brief twinge of sympathy for the lady. It wasn't hard to imagine how insecure she'd felt with everyone wanting a piece of her husband.

'And after he died?'

'She put all her efforts into finding the next rich man to replace him. Dragging a kid around with her was hardly going to help, so she made sure I was hidden away at boarding school for as many weeks of the year as she could manage.'

The bitter edge to his tone made her wince. 'You still carry a lot of hurt around inside you. I can't imagine that's very healthy.'

He gave her a rather flat smile. 'Thanks for the psychoanalysis.'

'I don't mean to belittle how you feel.' She wished she knew how to tread through this emotional minefield without risking an explosion. 'But dwelling on the past isn't doing you any good. You need to move forward.'

'And stop feeling sorry for myself, huh? We're not all as perfect as you, Mel. Some of us find it harder to put the shit behind us.'

He'd had a tough day, but still. She didn't need to sit here and take this. Quickly she drank the last of her wine. 'It's time I was going.'

'Why? If it's because of that last remark, I'm sorry. It was graceless.' He drew a hand down his face and she thought how drained he looked. How sad. 'Truth is I admire the hell out of you, Mel. I wish I had half your strength.'

He wished he had *her* strength? 'It's easy to be strong

when your memories are good ones.' Rising to her feet she bent to kiss his cheek. 'I'm leaving now because it's late and we both need to get to bed.'

The harsh lines of his face finally unbent and he smiled. 'Excellent. Finally we're in agreement.'

'Different beds,' she corrected. 'As in you in yours and me in mine.'

For a few heart beats he didn't reply. Just gazed fiercely up at her, letting her know that wasn't what he had in mind. 'Let me kiss you,' he said finally. 'Then, if you still want to go, I'll let you.'

'Aiden, please, no—'

'Just one kiss,' he interrupted. 'You don't even need to think of it as a kiss. You could consider it a humanitarian gesture. Your way of ensuring this Delta driver ends the day on a positive.'

His grin was completely disarming, leaving her with no real choice, or so she told herself.

'Mel?'

He stood, tilting his film star handsome face towards her and aligning his sensual lips with hers.

'Just one kiss,' she whispered.

There was no chance to stress the point any further because already he was swooping, claiming her mouth as greedily as his hands claimed her body. As she was drawn closer into the circle of his arms his tongue plundered her mouth. Delving, tasting. Driving her crazy.

And that was before his hands shot under her shirt and inside her bra. Before he started to tease her breasts with his clever fingers.

'God, Mel, I can't get enough of you. I'll never be able to get enough of you.'

'I bet you say that to all the girls.' Unbidden an image of

Devon with her busty body draped around him raced into her mind. 'Did you say it to Devon?'

He pulled back, his face dazed, his lips slightly swollen. 'What? Who?'

'Devon. The journalist you slept with not that long ago.'

'I know who Devon is. What I don't know is why we're talking about her.'

'She was asking after you today. She's still sniffing round.' God, why was she saying this now? Why was she saying it at all? She sounded so jealous.

'Mel, if you're going to have me sleeping with every woman who comes sniffing round, as you so elegantly put it, I'm going to be bloody knackered.'

Suddenly Mel didn't want to be in his arms. She tried to push away but he caught her, holding her still.

'Hey, come on, that's a joke. Of course I'm not interested in her, or anyone else for that matter. It's you I want.'

He looked so earnest and so utterly frustrated with her. Mel wished she could smooth the frown lines from his forehead and kiss the tightness from his mouth but the image of Devon wouldn't budge from her mind. Nor would the casual way he'd slept with the journalist and then discarded her. 'I'm sorry. I want to go now.'

He let out a loud expletive. 'For Christsake, Mel. I'm not sure how much longer I can do this friends only lark. You're driving me crazy.'

She regarded him sadly. 'If it helps, I'm doing the same to myself, too. But one thing I've learnt since losing my parents is that I have to look out for myself.' Reaching up, she planted a light kiss on his lips. 'Goodnight, Aiden.'

Quietly she slipped out of the door and into a rare English balmy evening. Neither that, nor the thought of a few days off work, managed to lift her spirits.

Chapter Twenty-Four

The following morning not even Tom's unbridled excitement over his first go-karting lesson could disperse the giant cloud that had settled over Aiden's head. He wouldn't have minded so much if the cause had been yesterday's pitiful race, or because he was languishing third on the Championship leader board. But no, his dark mood was to do with a woman.

Why had he spilled his guts to Mel last night? He wanted her to see him as a cool, fearless racing driver but now he'd blown it. Even sweet, empathetic Mel had ended the evening telling him to pull himself together. Just before she'd walked away when he'd told her how much he wanted her.

Even he'd got the message now.

He forced his mind away from the crap of yesterday and back onto the track. This was Tom's first karting lesson and he wasn't going to let anything spoil it for the guy. As his kart flashed by Aiden put his fingers in his mouth and whistled. Briefly Tom raised his hand, then slapped it quickly back on the wheel as the kart veered sharply to the right.

After that, Aiden made do with simply watching, though he couldn't help pumping his fist as the little tearaway only went and finished the final race in first.

Something Aiden had only managed twice all season.

'Hey there champ.' He bent to high-five the beaming red cheeked, sweaty haired boy dressed in Delta overalls and clutching the replica helmet Aiden had bought him.

'Not bad for your first outing. How did you find it? Are you going to be a kart racer?'

'It was awesome.' The thrill in Tom's voice matched the excitement in his eyes. 'I went nearly fifty miles an hour and I only crashed once.'

Ruffling his hair, Aiden let out a slow whistle. 'And you won your last race. Sounds like you nailed it. We'll have to make sure we put you down for some more lessons once the racing season's finished.'

Tom's face crumpled and he stared down at his feet. 'Mum won't take me.'

'She won't need to. I will.'

His face shot up again. 'Really?'

The expression on his face, as if he was afraid to hope, forced Aiden to have to swallow several times before he could speak. 'Really,' he confirmed. 'From now on, I'm part of your life. I'm sorry I haven't been around for the first ten years, but you can rely on me being around for the rest of it.'

What Tom must have gone through ... heck, it wasn't hard to imagine, because Aiden had lived through it himself. All the more damning then that he'd taken the selfish route and stayed away. Even when he'd heard Tom had run away from school and his mother was nowhere to be found, Aiden's instinctive response had been to ignore the situation rather than accept his responsibility. So not just selfish; gutless, too. No wonder Mel had been disgusted with him.

He glanced down to find Tom smiling up at him, his small hands gripping tightly to the helmet and his eyes filled with something that looked like adoration.

Emotion filled his chest, making it feel as if everything inside was too tight; his heart too large. Needing the connection, he flung an arm around Tom's slim shoulders and drew him close to his side.

Together they wandered back through the now deserted

paddock. Or should he say almost deserted because there was a blonde figure zeroing in on them. One sporting a bouncy ponytail and rather large, equally bouncy, breasts. His heart sank.

'I was hoping I'd catch you. The guys at the Delta garage said you hadn't left yet.' Devon peered down at Tom. 'And this must be your gorgeous little brother.'

Aiden had to admire the way Tom coolly nodded back. He didn't think his ten-year-old self would have been quite so laid-back in front of a dazzling blonde.

'What did you need me for?' He found it hard to look at her without feeling a prickle of shame.

'I was talking to your press officer, Melanie, I think her name is, about doing that interview we didn't actually ever get round to. She said you'd be happy to spare me some time?'

Did she now? So when Mel had told him Devon was still sniffing around, she'd meant *so why don't you go after her*, rather than *I'm jealous, please don't sleep with her again*.

Disappointment crashed through him, but he fixed a smile on his face. 'When did you have in mind?'

'Mel mentioned you might be at the Pirelli bash tonight? If you are, I can get a press pass and maybe see you there?'

Well, well, anyone would think Mel was trying to pair him and Devon up again. 'Sure. I'll catch you later.'

With a tinkling laugh and eyes full of promises, she went on her way.

Tom let out a snort. 'She fancies you.'

Aiden burst out laughing. 'Umm, yes, she probably does. That's the thing with being a racing driver. The girls come chasing after you.'

'If they're like her, I don't want to be a driver.'

'What, you didn't think she was pretty?'

'Nah. She's plastic and laughs like a girl.'

'Maybe because she is a girl, buddy.'

'Mel's a girl, but she's got a proper laugh.'

Aiden couldn't fault the boy's perception. He far preferred Mel's laugh, too, but Mel only wanted him as a friend and he was getting mightily pissed off with being parcelled into that category. Maybe it was time he did as she wanted and took up with a more willing woman.

Mel sat with Sally in her hotel room, watching the latter get ready for the party being held in the plush stateroom downstairs. As the invitation had come from the company who supplied the tyres, all the teams had been invited and strongly advised to attend. She could barely contain her beating heart.

'I see you've decided to really push the boat out with your dress tonight,' Sally remarked as she wriggled into a bright pink number.

Mel glanced down at the plain black dress that perfectly summed up her mood. 'The last time I wore something fancy it got me into trouble. Tonight I'm playing safe.'

Sally tutted. 'You must be the only single female alive today who's actively trying to put Aiden Foster off.'

Mel tried to smile. 'Okay, when you put it like that it makes me sound like an arrogant nutcase.'

'Nutcase, yes, but arrogant?'

'Arrogant to believe he actually needs putting off.' Though when she remembered the way he'd looked the other night and his husky words *it's you I want*, perhaps she wasn't being arrogant.

'I've seen the way he watches you. You're far from arrogant, though you are stark raving bonkers.'

Silently, Mel agreed. Pushing Aiden away was making

her so miserable she had to wonder if she was doing the right thing.

Her misery rating rose even higher when they entered the stateroom and she spotted Aiden surrounded, predictably, by an adoring female fan base. Wearing a sharp dark navy suit, open neck crisp white shirt and killer smile he exuded sophistication. Handsome, smooth as melted chocolate, he held the gathered crowd in the palm of his strong, steady hand.

'You really don't want to sleep with that man again, given half a chance?' Sally whispered in her ear. 'I would, if he showed me the slightest bit of interest.'

'No, you wouldn't. You've got a gorgeous husband at home.'

Sally sighed dramatically. 'Oh, so I have. It looks like Aiden's all yours then.'

At that moment Devon wandered into view. Squeezed into a slinky silver number that made her look like a mermaid with legs, she made quite an entrance. Certainly enough to make Aiden notice, if the crooked, *pleased to see you* smile he threw in Devon's direction was anything to go by.

'Clearly he's not mine,' Mel muttered, abruptly turning away so she wouldn't have to witness Devon sliding up to him and taking his arm. Probably kissing his tanned, freshly shaved cheek. 'Have we got a guest list somewhere?' she snapped. 'It's time we networked.'

As the evening wore on, Mel's eyes wouldn't stop scanning the room. Each time they landed on Aiden, Devon was by his side and her heart sank a little further towards her feet. Clearly her misery was showing because at one point Nancy put an arm around her and gave her a knowing smile. 'What you see isn't always the truth, Mel.'

'He looks happy enough to have her plastered against him.'

Nancy shook her head. 'He's doing what he's paid to do, being charming, though if you keep making it clear you're not interested he will go elsewhere, my dear.' She gave Mel's arm a quick squeeze. 'Perhaps you need to think about what you really want, before the choice is taken away from you.'

The words were kindly meant but they only added to her misery. As Nancy left to speak to other guests Mel glanced down at her plain dress, feeling drab and ordinary. She didn't want to be in this glitzy party, making polite conversation to glamorous people, watching Aiden flirt his way through every beautiful woman in the room.

'Ah, Melanie.'

She turned round with a start to find Carlos smiling down at her. Handsome, happy to see her, Carlos. As a giant wave of emotion threatened to swamp her she flung her arms around his neck.

'Whoa.' Having caught her, Carlos inched back so he could study her. 'I'm not complaining about the greeting, my sweet, but what's wrong?'

'Nothing.' She wasn't sure whether it was her welling eyes, or the following sniff that gave her away.

'I may be a, how you say, dumb? Yes, dumb racing driver, but I know if a woman is upset.'

'That's probably because you have lots of experience in making them upset.'

He pretended to look hurt. 'Your words are a dagger through my big, soft heart.'

'What heart?' Though she couldn't stop a little giggle.

He swooped down for her hand, planting gentle kisses across her knuckles. 'For sure I have a heart, lovely Mel. You stole it a long time ago.'

Mel rolled her eyes, though she couldn't help but smile. With Aiden allowing Devon to monopolise him all evening, the attention, even from an outrageous flirt like Carlos, was a very welcome boost to her flagging ego.

Aiden had been keeping his eye on Mel all evening. Noticing the regular glances she'd shot in his direction he'd deliberately stayed close to Devon, his determination to make Mel jealous riding roughshod over his guilt at stringing the journalist along. He had no intention of taking the flirtation with Devon any further than this room but the small minded git in him wanted to prove that if Mel didn't want him, he could find someone else who did.

Of course Devon didn't actually want *him*, nor did any of the other women fawning over him tonight. Still, better to be wanted for being a racing driver than not to be wanted at all.

He tensed as, at the other end of the room, Carlos sidled next to Mel. Hell, she was flinging her arms around his neck. Laughing with him. And was he really *kissing her hands*?

'I'll be back in a minute,' he told Devon curtly.

Ignoring the people who tried to catch his attention, and the woman thrusting her breasts and a business card at him, he pushed his way towards the cosy couple.

Carlos's dark eyes watched him speculatively as he turned to face a startled looking Mel. 'Can I talk to you for a minute?'

'Well, I ...' She glanced from him, to Carlos, and back to him. Either she was embarrassed to be caught making goo goo eyes at his rival, or embarrassed because his curt request had been a shade away from downright rude. Aiden didn't care, as long as Carlos buggered off.

The Spaniard took a step back, though not before giving Mel a look loaded with promise. 'I shall get myself a drink, pretty one. I'll see you again soon. We have much to discuss.'

Carlos took his sweet time sauntering out of earshot, leaving Aiden almost vibrating with anger. 'So, you'll flirt with Carlos but not with me?'

Clearly agitated she bit into her plump bottom lip. 'Yes.'

'Why?'

'Because he no longer has the power to hurt me.'

'And I will?' Aiden couldn't believe they were on this topic again.

'You have the power to, yes.' Before he could ask what on earth she meant by that, she nodded over towards Devon. 'Anyway, you don't need me to flirt with. You seem to be doing a perfectly good job over there.'

'Thanks to you,' he countered, clutching at his glass of water when what he really wanted to do was put his hands on her. Her arm, her shoulders, the back of her neck so he could pull her mouth towards his and flaming *kiss* her.

'What do you mean, thanks to me?'

'Well, you did practically shove Devon at me, didn't you? Telling her I'd be happy to talk to her. Letting her know I'd be here.'

She blinked up at him, eyes flashing. 'I was just doing my job. Besides, I didn't volunteer any of that. She kept phoning, asking when she could see you. I suggested tonight because I thought it would be easier for you to get rid of her here. *If* that's what you wanted to do.'

Though he was slightly mollified by her response, the image of her laughing and cooing with Carlos wouldn't go away. It hurt that she let others get close but pushed him away. 'Yeah, well, Devon seems game to make a real night of it, if you know what I mean.'

She inhaled sharply. 'Why are you telling me this?'

'Because I don't want her, I want you.' Did he sound as desperate as he felt? 'I want you to care enough to get angry and bloody stop me.'

Emotion he couldn't define – confusion, disgust? – swirled in her eyes and she gave a sad shake of her head. 'Of course I care, you fool, but I can't stop you. This is you. This is what you do. It's why we would never work.'

He was too angry to continue the conversation, his heart too crushed. So instead of grabbing her by the shoulders and pleading with her to stop judging him, he turned on his heel and walked.

'Why do you do it?'

Her quiet question halted him in his tracks and he turned back towards her. 'Do what?'

'Sleep with women you don't care for?'

Momentarily he shut his eyes. When he opened them again she was still there, waiting for him to answer. 'Because she wants me,' he admitted, hating the way his voice sounded so raw, so damn vulnerable. 'I know it isn't me she wants, just the image of me, but hey, it's good to feel wanted.'

She looked puzzled. 'What about what you want?'

Aiden knew he shouldn't answer that, but it was as if Mel had opened the box on his innermost feelings and he couldn't shut the lid quickly enough. 'Sometimes, when it's dark and I'm feeling lonely, it's just good to feel another body next to mine. Arms around me. Holding me.'

Biting back the emotions that clawed at his throat, he fled across the room, down the corridor and out into the fresh night air. There he leant against the wall and took in several long, shaky breaths. Hell, even his hands were trembling, as if he'd had a blowout at two hundred miles an hour rather than simply making a fool of himself in front of Mel. Again. Why did he keep opening up to her, making himself so vulnerable? Now she knew one of his deepest fears. Loneliness.

As a kid he'd craved companionship and warmth. Just someone to give a damn about him. Now he was an adult, the cravings remained. Sure the women who threw themselves at him didn't really care, but that was the only type he'd come across. Until Mel.

So how gutting to find that the only real woman he'd ever met, and ever cared for, wasn't only unimpressed by his wealth and fame. She was unimpressed by him.

Chapter Twenty-Five

For several minutes Mel stared at the route Aiden had taken, struggling to make sense of what she'd just heard. Was he really trying to imply that he, hot shot racing driver whose looks, money and talent were the envy of every man in this room, was so desperate for company he simply went with what was on offer?

It was nearly impossible to believe, yet the gaunt look in his beautiful eyes when he'd spoken suggested he'd been brutally honest with her. And when she recalled his conversation about his childhood, how neither of his parents had shown him any attention, maybe she could see how it could be true.

Was it possible Aiden didn't realise he was worth so much more than he was telling himself?

'Ah, I have you to myself again.'

As Carlos drew alongside her, Mel was still reeling from the implications of her conversation with Aiden to pay him much attention. Aiden was going to sleep with Devon because she was available and he was lonely. Yet he wanted Mel to stop him.

'I think your feelings are no longer for this racing driver, but for another,' Carlos murmured, taking her hand and leading her towards a quiet corner. 'Perhaps the driver who was born with ... let me think about your English phrase. How about, born with the silver steering wheel in his arms, eh?'

'You might be right,' she admitted slowly, still staring at the door through which Aiden had long since disappeared.

'About the silver steering wheel, or the feelings?'

She let out a shaky breath and gave him a small smile. 'Both, but if you tell anyone about this, I'll chop off your balls and hang them in my car over the rear-view mirror.'

He winced dramatically. 'Your car? I thought you couldn't drive?'

'I still can't, but I'm having lessons again.' Thanks to Aiden, who with his gentle teasing and warm hand on her thigh, had somehow managed to rid her of her fear of sitting behind the wheel.

'You take a test?'

'Soon. Perhaps in a few weeks,' she answered distractedly, conscious that if Aiden came back into the room now and saw her talking with Carlos he'd be livid. Even though Carlos was only flirting with her because he didn't know how else to talk to women. And Aiden only wanted her because ...

It was the question she always stumbled over. Why *would* Aiden want her?

'Ah, I think I've been given the evil eye again.'

Mel followed the direction of Carlos's gaze and immediately her heart plummeted. There was Aiden, his face a mask of controlled anger, glaring at them both. He'd wanted her to care enough to stop him from sleeping with Devon, Mel thought miserably. Now it looked like she didn't even care enough to stop from going off with his rival.

'I'm sorry, Carlos, I have to go.'

She didn't wait for Carlos to reply. Maddeningly her progress towards Aiden was hampered by people wanting to talk to her and by the time she'd smiled and made her excuses, Devon was back at Aiden's side. Clutching his arm in a clear gesture of ownership.

Squaring her shoulders, Mel ignored the queasy feeling in the pit of her stomach and marched towards them.

'Hi there, Devon. Did you manage to get your interview?' she asked sweetly.

For a second Devon looked puzzled before clearly remembering what she should have been doing with Aiden. 'I did, thank you. Aiden's been very accommodating.'

Mel almost choked but Aiden remained rigid, his expression bearing no hint of his previous vulnerability. 'Well, I'm afraid his accommodating has come to an end. I'm here to take him away.'

'The only place I'm going is upstairs to my room,' Aiden replied coolly before tugging on Devon's arm and nodding in the direction of the exit. 'Shall we?'

Pain seared Mel's heart as Aiden turned his back on her and began to walk away. Devon, in her ridiculously high shoes, struggled after him.

'Aiden, wait.'

He stilled and turned towards her, his eyes sweeping the room. 'If you're looking for company, I see Carlos is still here. Enjoy the rest of your evening.'

She watched bleakly as they walked out together. Devon with her stupid bum, wriggling away in a dress that was two sizes too small. Aiden with his lean athletic body, stiffly setting the pace.

As Mel's heart slowly shrivelled in her chest she felt an arm around her shoulders. 'Oh my goodness. What's wrong my love?'

Sally looked worriedly into her eyes.

And Mel burst into tears.

Aiden couldn't hear a word Devon was saying to him. His mind was stuck on the image of Mel and Carlos together.

Again. After everything he'd said about wanting her to care about him, it looked like she really didn't give a toss.

Well, sod it. He was tired of going after a woman who clearly wasn't interested in him. It was time to spend the night with one who was. He didn't have his brother with him, cramping his style – Tom was hopefully fast asleep with the sitter back at his apartment – so Aiden had a night to do what he liked. To indulge in the carnal joys of the flesh.

Stepping into the lift, he pulled Devon towards him and kissed her. It wasn't a kiss of passion. Nor had it anything to do with liking or caring. Or wanting. Instead it was a statement of his intentions. A warning to give her the chance to back out. From the way she coiled herself around him like a python, he didn't think backing out was what she had in mind.

The lift opened at his floor and almost gratefully he pulled his mouth away. Taking her hand he marched them both up the corridor towards his room. She talked incessantly, interspersed with the occasional giggle though thankfully she didn't seem to need any reply from him. Just as well, because his mind was still downstairs.

Why the hell was he bringing Devon into his room when his heart was tied up with Mel?

But Mel didn't want him.

He came to a halt outside his door but the anticipation, the throb of desire, was missing. All he felt was self-disgust. Devon was looking up at him with big blue eyes and he knew, just knew, that if he slept with her tonight he wasn't only sending all the wrong signals again, he was demeaning her. Demeaning himself.

Carefully he opened the door and drew her in before

closing it behind them. 'Devon, I'm sorry but I don't think this is a good idea.'

Surprise, quickly followed by shock, flickered across her face. 'What do you mean?'

Shit. He wasn't used to bringing women to his room and then turning them down. 'I mean I'm not the type of guy someone like you deserves. You're worth more than a quick tumble between the sheets, and that's all it will ever be between us.'

'I see.' Her bottom lip wobbled slightly and her eyes told him she clearly didn't see. 'So is this not now, or not ever again?'

He exhaled and let go of her hand before walking slowly to the desk where he grabbed automatically at a bottle of water. 'Seriously, Devon, this is for your own good. Don't you want a man who'll actually take you on a date? Ring you up just so he can hear your voice? Buy you flowers for no other reason than he saw them and thought of you.' Jesus, where was all this coming from? Aiden couldn't remember ever doing any of it, so why did he suddenly have the urge to do it all? But not with Devon.

'Well, yes.'

She looked so stiff and awkward standing in the room, not knowing where to put herself, and Aiden cursed himself again for leading her on. He really was a bastard. 'Then you should see this as a lucky escape. Go and find yourself a man who'll do all that for you. Who'll treat you properly.'

Nodding once, Devon stalked to the door. As she opened it she gave him a final withering glance. 'You know what. You're right. You don't deserve me.' With a flick of her blonde hair, she was gone.

Aiden slumped onto the bed and hung his head in his hands. The bugger of it was, she was absolutely right.

And if he didn't deserve Devon, there wasn't a chance in hell he'd ever deserve Mel.

Mel didn't manage much sleep. Each time she shut her eyes her brain decided to torture her with images of Aiden and Devon together. Her blonde hair draping over his naked chest as she slid her tongue over his skin. Him smiling into her eyes as she moved lower ...

It explained why the reflection she stared at in the hotel mirror the next morning was far too pale. Why her eyes looked scarily bloodshot and weighed down by dark circles.

In an effort to perk herself up she showered and washed her hair, but the end result was still the same. She looked plain, washed out and every one of her thirty years.

Briskly she collected her belongings and set off down the corridor. Time to go back to her little house for a few days, away from anything that reminded her of Aiden Foster. Before the whole blessed Grand Prix circus started up again.

At the sight of the man waiting for the lift, she faltered. It looked like she wasn't going to get away from Aiden any time soon.

She debated turning round and waiting in her room until he left, but that seemed too cowardly. Besides, she wasn't the one who should be embarrassed.

'How was your evening?' she asked coolly as she drew up alongside him. He was wearing jeans and a plain dark T-shirt and though he still looked sexy, he clearly hadn't managed much sleep either. Of course in his case it wasn't because he'd been imagining people having sex, but because he'd flaming well been having it.

'I've had better evenings.' She didn't get a chance to ask him what he meant by that because he immediately came back at her. 'How about yours? Did you manage to catch up with your charming ex again?'

His grey eyes were like flint as they bore into hers. How could he care enough to be jealous, but not enough to stop sleeping with someone else? 'Carlos and I are just friends, Aiden. I've made that mistake once. I'm in no hurry to repeat it.'

'Friends?' His right eyebrow shot up. 'How can you be friends with someone who treated you like he did?'

'I've forgiven him,' she replied quietly, wondering how they'd got onto this topic. 'I realised he wasn't really to blame. It's not like he set out to hurt me. Just that he couldn't resist a prettier face.'

'*He wasn't to blame?*' Aiden raised his hands, as if he wanted to shake her, but then restlessly shoved them into his jeans pockets. 'It's about time you took a good look at yourself, Mel.' His eyes flicked over her shapeless jumper and standard chino trousers. 'Despite all the dowdy clothes you wear, designed to deliberately put us males off, you're an incredibly attractive woman. What Carlos did to you, cheating on you with other women, reflects badly on him. Not on you.' For a moment his eyes softened. 'You need to start believing in yourself again. Stop blaming yourself for not being pretty enough, or whatever crap you've got going in that head of yours, and start blaming Carlos for being a selfish prick.'

She stood, stupefied, and Aiden had to practically drag her into the lift when it arrived. While he fended off questions from the other lift goers with the casual grace he was renowned for, his words went over and over in her mind.

When the lift doors pinged open and they all strolled out into the lobby Mel clutched at Aiden's arm, holding him back. 'Is that really what you think I've been doing? Blaming myself?'

His expression told her he couldn't believe she was asking such a stupid question. 'Tell me, how did you dress before you met Carlos? Or while you were dating him, for that matter. Like this?' His hand waved pointedly at her baggy jumper.

'I don't remember what I wore.'

'Well, I bet it wasn't what you've got on now. Do you remember the night you put that sexy little purple dress on?' For a tantalisingly brief moment his face lit up with one of his brilliant smiles. 'Hell, you knocked me for six. That's the woman you really are. The one standing in front of me now is lovely, but her? She's smoking hot.'

Mel's heart flipped slowly in her chest and she found she couldn't speak, couldn't breathe. She liked the way she dressed now ... didn't she? It was easy. Comfortable. Following Carlos's betrayal it was how she'd wanted to be seen. Professional, one of the guys. A girl men would find easy to talk to and not feel threatened by, but not attracted to. She'd never thought of it as punishing herself though.

The sound of the lift doors opening again brought Mel out of her trance and she watched as Devon sauntered out. Looking every inch a woman, the blonde wafted by in killer heels, white skinny jeans and a tight pink T-shirt. Next to her Mel felt drab and sexless. As she drew closer to Aiden, Devon gave him a frosty stare before click clacking across the lobby, her pink floral bag bouncing off her hips with each stride.

Mel glanced up at Aiden's stony face. 'She looks upset with you.'

'She is. The evening didn't go as she'd planned.' He shook

his head, as if trying to get rid of an unpleasant mental image. 'I'm hoping it's just her pride I've hurt.'

Mel's mouth went suddenly dry. 'Why didn't it go as planned?'

He stared at her with stormy eyes. 'I might be a feckless sod, but it turns out even I can't sleep with one woman while my mind is obsessed with another.'

As Mel's mouth gaped open he turned on his heel and stalked towards the reception desk.

Chapter Twenty-Six

Two days after the fancy ball in the fancy hotel, Mel woke up back in her two up, two down terraced house. It was a mess but she didn't notice the clutter. Why would she, when messiness and her went together like, well Tom and Jerry. Fish and chips. And anyway, her mind was on more important things than the chaos of her home. It was fixated on the chaos in her heart.

She wished her parents were around to talk to. Her mother would have clucked and sympathised. Her father would have comforted and added much needed insight into the male psyche. Of course she had substitute parents in Frank and Nancy, but Nancy had already given her opinion on what she should do, *think about what you really want, before the choice is taken away from you*, and as for Frank ... he had a soft spot for Aiden that made his opinion too biased.

It was why she was now sitting in the kitchen with Sally, chewing over the events of yesterday.

'You need to stop being such a wus and start the relationship the pair of you so clearly want,' Sally told her baldly.

'But—'

'No. Don't you dare give me all that tosh and piffle about how you've been hurt before, blah, blah, blah. Do you honestly believe you're the only woman in the universe to be let down by a man? It happens. Newsflash, some men can turn out to be selfish, immature, fickle creatures out for only one thing. But equally some can be strong, steadfast and loving. Hey, sometimes the former can mature into the latter. You have to learn from past mistakes and trust your ability to pick the good from the bad.'

'I, umm. Tosh and piffle?' she asked on a small laugh.

Sally threw her hands up in the air. 'I give you the ultimate in life advice and that's the only thing you remember?'

They caught each other's eye and burst into merciless giggles. Eventually, wiping away tears of laughter, Mel sighed. 'I suppose that's what you managed to do, huh? Trust your instincts and pluck out that lovely hubby of yours.'

Sally's smile could only be called smug. 'Yes. He's not perfect, but my life is a lot happier with him in it.'

A simple phrase, but it caught Mel unawares and she felt her eyes start to well. 'Oh, shucks, how sweet. Carry on like that and you'll have me in tears.'

'Don't mock it until you've tried it.' When Mel would have defended herself, her friend gave her the stern eye. 'I know you think you tried it with Carlos, and maybe you did, but if you're really honest it was your pride and ego that took more of a bashing than your heart. If you'd truly loved Carlos you wouldn't be able to talk to him so easily now. It would still eat you up.'

Mel smiled, acknowledging her friend's logic. 'I don't suppose I can argue with that.'

'Yet you usually try.'

She rose from her seat and gave Sally a hug. 'Today I'll keep quiet. Besides, I've taken up far too much of your time. That husband of yours is probably cursing me.'

'He's watching football in his den with a beer and a bag of tortilla chips. I doubt he's remembered I'm not there.'

'But your life is still better with him in it, eh?'

'Yes, because at the end of the day I get to snuggle down next to him in bed and remind him of that fact.'

Mel had a brief mental image of her snuggling down next to Aiden. Was that what she really wanted? Even though she'd always feel like he was biding his time, waiting to move on? The ache in her heart seemed to provide the answer.

Aiden passed Tom the plate of pizza. Balancing the controller on his knee, Tom grabbed another slice, dropping at least two pieces of pepperoni onto the cream sofa as he shovelled the pizza into his mouth.

'Doesn't that fancy boarding school of yours teach you how to eat properly?'

Tom simply grinned, smearing tomato sauce further over his face as he wiped his mouth with the back of his hand. 'Nah. Told you the place was useless.'

Aiden was loathe to break the mood but he knew at some point he had to talk to Tom about school, his mother, and the future. These last two months had been special but there was only so long either of them could bury their heads in the sand.

'You know there's stuff we need to talk about,' he said, trying the cautious approach. 'Maybe not tonight, but soon.'

'What stuff?'

'Your schoolwork, for one. Your mates will probably be breaking up in a week or two but you've missed so much you're going to have to keep working. You know that, right?'

Tom licked at his fingers before wiping them on his jeans. 'Yeah, you told me. I get time off when you're off, but when you're working I have to work.'

It had been the bargain they'd struck recently, Aiden figuring having Helen tutor Tom only when they were on tour was the easiest, and least disruptive solution. Not only had it helped him and Tom bond, it had also meant Helen had no need to come to his apartment. He'd felt uncomfortable letting a woman who was so clearly out to snare him, into his private space. Odd, considering how easily he'd allowed Devon to do just that.

Perhaps he was a little more aware of how his actions looked to others now. To Tom, to his team.

To Mel.

'Okay then, good, I'm glad you understand. The summer holidays might be coming but you still need to knuckle down for a bit before your mum comes to pick you up.'

'Yeah, yeah.' Tom waggled the controller. 'Time for me to kick your ass now, brother.'

Aiden barked out a laugh. 'Aren't you the hard man, eh?' He surveyed the debris on the coffee table. The mountain of PlayStation games Aiden had bought to entertain Tom, all of which they'd played today. The three pizza boxes, still containing a few slices of congealed pizza. The almost demolished bowl of crisps. The full bowl of cherry tomatoes he'd snuck onto the table at the last minute but hadn't been touched.

His nutritionist would bust a blood vessel.

So, he suspected, would their mother.

'We need to clear up first, mate,' he told Tom, standing to pick up the boxes. 'And this is the very last game we're playing.'

He should have taken Tom out today, shown him some sights, given him some fresh air. Instead he'd let his bad mood from last night spill over into today and barely managed to get out of bed, never mind out of the apartment. In a fit of jealousy he'd nearly slept with Devon again. How shameful was that? Hell, he'd been a whisker away from proving to Mel he was everything she thought he was.

Tom elbowed him in the ribs. 'Aiden?'

Aware he'd been staring into space, Aiden shook himself. 'Sorry. I've been lousy company today. I'll make up for it tomorrow. See if we can go karting somewhere.'

'Cool.' Tom helped him carry the leftovers into the kitchen but when they settled back down on the sofa, he stared at him, a small frown on his face. 'Didn't you have a good time last night?'

Aiden blinked, surprised at Tom's perception. 'It was work really, but as work goes, it was fine.'

'Did you see that woman? The one with the plastic face who fancies you?'

Despite his lousy mood, Aiden found himself laughing. 'Devon was there, yes.'

'Was Mel there, too?'

'She was.'

'Which one do you like best?'

Aiden jerked upright. 'Whoa, where did that come from? I didn't say I liked Devon. If you remember, you said she liked me.'

'What about Mel. You like her, don't you?'

His heart thumped and as Aiden stared into his brother's solemn face he wondered if Tom knew what he was really asking. 'Of course I like Mel. She's a good friend, to both of us.'

Tom nodded, seemingly satisfied, then snatched up the controller. 'Time to play. Prepare to meet your doom, racing car driver.'

Aiden smiled and picked up his own controller though his mind wasn't on the game any more.

Chapter Twenty-Seven

Two weeks and one miserable race later they were in Hungary. Aiden stood with his race engineer in the Delta garage, staring at his car.

Frank sighed and put his hands on his hips, not a good sign. 'You're distracted.'

Aiden tried not to flinch at the disapproving tone. Though drivers were often considered the most important part of the team, Frank had this uncanny ability to make him feel like an errant schoolboy. 'It would appear I am.'

What else could he say? The paltry two points he'd picked up from ninth place in the last race spoke for themselves. His edge simply wasn't there. He knew it. Frank knew it. The whole bloody team knew it.

'I bet next you're going to tell me my father never let anything distract him from a race, huh?' The moment the words were out, he cringed. 'Forget I said that. It was churlish and stupid.'

'Probably true though,' Frank drawled. 'The guy was one selfish bastard most of the time.' Aiden's mouth dropped open in shock and Frank let slip an understanding smile. 'What, you thought I didn't know that? We race engineers tend to see through all the flash imagery and into the real person beneath. Seb Foster was selfish. It didn't always make him a nice man to work with, but it sure made him a brilliant driver.'

'I didn't want any distractions this year,' Aiden admitted. 'It seems circumstances have conspired against me.'

Frank smiled. 'Tom's a great kid. Looks a lot happier now than when he arrived.'

'Yes.' But could he hand on his heart put all his poor performance down to Tom? It was true he was worried about his mother coming back and dragging his brother away. It was also true that his thoughts were mainly dominated by a certain hazel eyed woman he couldn't shake out of his system.

'Well, you need to sort your head out, Aiden. We can tinker with the car and the strategy all we like, but at the end of the day if the man out on the track isn't giving his all, we might as well give up and go home.'

Trust Frank to lay it bluntly on the line. He couldn't even argue with him. The last dismal performance was solely on his head. As was the fact that he'd slipped to fourth in the championship. His only saving grace was that Carlos had suffered a DNF in the last race thanks to a tyre blow out, so the gap between them had stayed pretty much as it was.

Acknowledging Frank's words with a curt nod of his head, Aiden walked back out into the paddock and took in a few lungfuls of air. Nestled alongside fields and farmland the Hungarian Grand Prix had a real countryside feel to it. Well, at least there was a hint of fresh air mixed in with the usual car fuel and burning rubber.

Waving away the journos who dashed towards him, hoping for a quick quote, Aiden strode towards the Delta motorhome where he'd left Tom and Helen hard at work. Time to check up on the lad. As he entered his eyes automatically scanned for Mel, as they always did. He hadn't seen much of her at the last race. Oh, she'd been here and there, doing her job, but the opportunity to talk to her alone hadn't arisen, which he knew was a deliberate ploy on her part.

Pushing off his gloom, Aiden bounded up the stairs to

the meeting room where he found Tom sitting by himself, playing with an iPad.

'What's happening here?'

Tom gave a guilty start and shoved the iPad onto his lap. 'I finished the stuff she gave me.'

'Show me.'

With a huff of annoyance Tom rustled through the papers strewn across the table and found his workbook. Aiden flicked through it, noting the kid was about as scruffy as he'd been as a ten-year-old. 'When did you finish this?'

Tom gave a casual shrug of the shoulders. 'Dunno. A while ago.'

With a heavy heart Aiden sat down opposite him. 'Come on, buddy, this is serious. Helen's being paid to teach you. How often has she been doing this?'

Tom shifted edgily on the seat. 'Boarding school is shut for the holidays now, isn't it? I mean, you can't send me back?'

Aiden sighed, hating the fear that had crept into his brother's eyes. 'Yes, it's closed, though even if it wasn't I already told you I wouldn't make you go back there. Now dish the dirt.'

With a small nod, Tom leant forward. 'She's been leaving me loads. When we're at a racetrack, as soon as you go, she sets me some stuff to do and then disappears.'

Aiden thumped the table. 'Okay. That's it. When she comes back here, I'll fire her.' As Tom's eyes grew round, Aiden had to laugh. 'Don't get too excited, it's not the end of schoolwork. You still need a tutor. I'll get an agency to send someone else.' He winked. 'What about a guy this time, eh? Less trouble I think.'

Having attended Stefano's perky press conference, Mel

wandered back through the paddock. Stefano was currently one place ahead of Aiden in the championship and had just had a very quick first practice session. At least one of her drivers was happy. The other seemed very flat, as if the stuffing had been knocked out of him. She desperately wanted to check if he was okay, but her feelings were too muddled for such a personal conversation at the moment. Instead she'd stuck to business, satisfying neither of them.

Speak of the devil. Her eyes, apparently capable of hunting down Aiden's form from a ridiculously long distance, zeroed in on him as he stood deep in conversation on the steps of the Delta motorhome. Her spine automatically stiffened as she saw who he was talking to but as she continued to watch she noticed a distinct unease between the two figures. There were no smiles, just grim faces and tense conversation until Helen suddenly whipped round on her dainty heels and stormed off.

Unconsciously Mel stopped in her tracks. What was all that about?

Aiden chose that moment to look up and pin her with his clear grey eyes. Bugger. It was more than obvious she'd been nosing in on the pair of them.

She gave him an awkward wave. Now what was she meant to do? Walk by and pretend she wasn't interested? As if. Taking in a deep breath she walked straight towards him. 'Umm, what just happened there, with Helen?'

His gaze followed the tutor's retreating back. 'I fired her.'

'Oh?' She tried to retain at least a semblance of professionalism but her traitorous face split into a wide grin.

Aiden gave her a wry smile before shuffling her inside and leading them to a quiet table in the hospitality suite.

'I know, I know,' he said as he sat down next to her. 'You warned me all along. Seems as soon as my back was turned Helen was setting Tom work and then buggering off.' He let out a snort of disgust. 'I should have paid more attention. God knows what damage it's done to his schooling.'

Mel's glee dimmed a little. 'Hey, come on, don't beat yourself up. I'm sure she was doing a good job of actually teaching him.'

'Yeah, when she was there.' He thrust a hand through his hair in a familiar gesture. 'He's only ten, Mel. She shouldn't have been leaving him alone. Christ knows, I've been trying to make sure there's always someone with him.' In a weary gesture he pushed his head into his hands. 'Maybe I'm just kidding myself. Sure I've asked people to sit with him, but I've never bothered to check he's okay.' He looked up at her with slightly accusing eyes. 'I told you I'd be rubbish at this. I can barely look after myself, never mind a child.'

Though she wanted to be angry at the implication that this was her fault, all she felt was sympathy. He was beating himself up because he hadn't found the time between his endless press calls, team briefings and actual racing to keep tabs on the tutor.

'You're a great brother to Tom,' she told him honestly. 'The scared, sullen little boy who first arrived is a long, long way removed from the happy boy he is now. That's down to you.'

'And you.'

His eyes held hers and she found herself unable to swallow. 'Not really, but if I've helped at all, I'm glad.'

Silence pulsed between them. Although chatter floated across the sleek hospitality suite, Mel could hear the gentle exhale of Aiden's breath. Almost feel the steady beat of his heart. The words he'd uttered the other day buzzed through her mind. *I can't sleep with one woman while my mind is obsessed with another.*

'I like your skirt.' His statement took her unawares and she glanced down at the flirty summer print skirt she'd put on this morning. The one she'd bought two days after Aiden had told her she looked smoking hot in sexy clothes.

'Thank you.' She smiled self-consciously at him. 'Someone whose opinion is important to me told me it was time to express myself again.'

'Clever guy.'

'Umm. I'm not sure. I have a feeling his motives were on the selfish side.'

'Being a kind soul, it makes you happy just knowing you've made him happy though, doesn't it?' He gave her an impish grin. 'Did you only buy one?'

Slowly she shook her head. 'I bought a whole new wardrobe.'

He let out a long whistle. 'If the skirt is a sign of things to come, I'm looking forward to seeing the rest.' Lazily his eyes travelled up her legs. 'Do they come any shorter?'

Caught between embarrassment and amusement, she ended up laughing. 'Come on, this one is indecent enough.'

'Nah, indecent isn't the right word. Sexy works. So does pretty. If I were to be hyper critical though, it needs taking up another five inches.'

Mel waggled her finger at him, enjoying the banter. Enjoying the way his eyes travelled over the lines of her body with such frank appreciation.

Sally was right. Staying away from Aiden was cowardly and stupid in the extreme. She'd already gone and fallen in love with the man, so why keep holding back? He'd make no promises and when he'd had enough, he'd let her down as gently as he could. She'd hurt, but she'd get over it, as she had before. And the memories she'd take to her grave would fill several lifetimes.

Rising from the table she whispered into his ear. 'I tell you what. Invite me over to your motorhome for dinner tonight and I'll wind it up another five inches.'

As astonishment flooded his face, Mel grinned to herself. For the first time in years she let her hips sway a little as she walked away. Only a little, because God knows, she didn't want to come across as a hooker. Just a real woman again.

Chapter Twenty-Eight

Aiden dropped a knife for the second time in the space of as many minutes. Tom gave him a withering stare and grabbed the rest of the cutlery off him.

'Not much good at laying the table, are you? Didn't Mum teach you?'

'No,' he returned a touch sulkily. 'I was at boarding school, remember?' Not that he needed to be taught how to lay a ruddy table. It's just that his fingers seemed to have turned into big fat sausages, incapable of holding onto anything. If he didn't know better, he'd say he was nervous about having Mel over, but that wasn't possible. He wasn't even nervous at the start of a race, waiting for the red lights to go out, so he certainly couldn't be nervous about having a woman over to dinner. Besides, Tom was there as a chaperone.

His mind replayed the look in Mel's eyes as she'd promised to hitch up her skirt and the plate he'd picked up clattered to the floor.

Tom shot him a dirty look.

'Okay, okay. I'm heading for the shower. I'll leave you to finish setting the table. The guys from catering should be here to deliver the food any time now so listen out for them. You know what they look like, right?'

'Duh, yes. And I have to check through the window first to see if it's them before I open the door. I'm not stupid, you know.'

'We'll find out tomorrow when the new tutor arrives. He's called Stanley and he's a fifty-five-year-old bloke who's old school. Which means he's strict.' Tom's face paled a little and Aiden's lips twitched. 'Not so mouthy now, eh?'

'What do you mean by strict?' The tyke crossed his arms in a tough guy stance and Aiden had to work hard not to laugh.

'As long as you do as he says, you won't need to worry.'

'I always do as I'm told,' he grumbled, hunching his shoulders slightly as he turned his attention back to the table laying.

Aiden wasn't sure what caused it. Maybe the slight world weariness of his brother's stance, or the put upon expression on his face. Whatever it was, his heart experienced a sharp tug. Surprising the hell out of both of them, he bent to hug him. 'You're a good kid, Tom. I know that.'

Tom was quiet for a few seconds but then a mischievous twinkle entered his eyes. 'In that case I don't need a strict tutor, do I?'

Aiden chuckled. 'Being a good kid means I can trust you to behave when the tutor's trying to teach you.'

Tom gave the answer some thought, then with a satisfied nod of his head he returned to his table duties. Aiden finally went for his shower.

When he opened the motorhome door half an hour later, his jaw almost hit the floor.

'God help me.' His eyes greedily devoured the vision in front of him. 'How on earth am I meant to keep my hands off you tonight?'

His voice was that of a man whose balls had been grabbed and were slowly being squeezed. Mel's skirt, a different one than earlier but no less sexy, barely covered her thighs. Beneath it was a pair of short but eye catchingly slender legs. Lightly tanned, they were so shapely his hands itched to slide over them.

She gave him an uncertain smile, far too uncertain considering how amazing she looked. 'You don't have to keep your hands off me tonight. Not if you don't want to.'

Once more his mouth fell open. 'I definitely don't want to,' he managed to croak past the boulder in his throat. Then a frisson of panic shot through him as he considered she might misunderstand his meaning. 'To put it in a more positive way, I definitely want to put my hands all over you. Followed by various other parts of my anatomy.'

A delightful flush stole across her cheeks, making him realise once again that Mel was unlike any other woman he'd ever taken to bed. She wasn't being coy, simply genuinely shy when it came to flirting. 'As Tom's joining us for dinner, I think we should stop at hands.'

'How about we save the rest for later. When ten-year-old boys are fast asleep.' Feeling as if everything was suddenly right with the world, he gently tugged her inside.

The meal seemed to take forever. Aiden wolfed his portions down like a starved animal, barely tasting the food. Frustratingly Mel and Tom didn't seem to share his desire to get the whole eating bit over and done with. They chattered away as if they had all the time in the world. As if there was no urgency. As if dinner was the main part of the evening.

When the last mouthful of Tom's chocolate cheesecake disappeared into his mouth, Aiden's patience gave way.

'Time for bed,' he told Tom. He didn't need Mel's raised eyebrows to tell him his tone was too sharp.

'It's early yet,' Tom complained. Predictably.

'I said, bed.'

His voice was so harsh Tom flinched and Aiden

immediately felt like a total asshole. Letting out a slow breath he reassured himself Mel would wait for him. At least she might if he didn't continue to upset Tom. 'Sorry, I didn't mean to snap at you, buddy. It's just your new tutor will be here tomorrow morning so you need to have an early night. You'll want to make a good impression on him.'

'Him?' Mel's face telegraphed her surprise.

'Yeah. I figured having a man might be less trouble.'

'Oh.'

'Right, say goodnight to Mel.' He turned Tom's shoulders to face her.

'Night, Mel.'

'Sleep tight, Tom.' Her face did everything required of a smile – lips curved upwards, eyes crinkled at the edges, grooves sat prettily on her cheeks – but she seemed suddenly uncomfortable. As if she was remembering her promise and wondering whether she wanted to go through with it.

Or was he simply being paranoid?

'Come on, young man,' he told Tom briskly, guiding him towards his room. 'I'll hunt down your pj's while you clean your teeth.' At the threshold of Tom's room Aiden glanced back at Mel. 'Make yourself at home. I won't be a minute.' When she didn't respond, simply gazed at him with her large brown eyes, a sliver of worry wormed its way into his gut. 'You will still be here when I come back, won't you?'

'We need more toothpaste!' Tom's vociferous request put a halt to any reply Mel might have given.

As he rifled through the bathroom cabinets, Aiden briefly wondered how his life had come to this. Hunting down toothpaste when his instincts screamed at him to go and put his arms around the scared looking lady on the sofa before she had second thoughts.

* * *

Mel sucked in a deep breath and told herself to stop being so stupid. It wasn't as if she'd never slept with Aiden. She had, twice. So why was she feeling so nervous? Standing, she smoothed down her itsy bitsy skirt and acknowledged the reason. This time she'd come to him. It had been easy to flirt, to make promises when he'd been gazing at her with eyes that blazed with desire. Not so easy when she'd been talking to Tom, aware of Aiden getting more and more fidgety. He'd been like a man on the edge and his tenseness had rubbed off on her. What was he expecting from her now, apart from the obvious? How had his legion of other women seduced him?

The knots in her stomach tightened. She wasn't this confident, sexy woman she'd somehow conned him into expecting. She was the same one who'd burst into tears on him after they'd first made love.

Placing the used dishes into the dishwasher, Mel straightened her shoulders and marched towards the bedroom at the opposite end of the motorhome to Tom's. She could do this. She could be the type of girl Aiden was used to. It simply meant burying her nerves and dredging out some of the self-confidence she'd lost after the disaster of her relationship with Carlos.

By the time she heard Aiden firmly shut the door to Tom's room, Mel had managed to wriggle out of the majority of her clothes, leaving on just the matching bra and pants she'd bought in anticipation of exactly this moment. Drawing in another deep breath, she opened the door.

And did a double-take at the sight of Aiden, hunched over on the sofa, head in his hands.

'What's wrong?'

His head jerked up so quickly, it was almost comical. As an expression of utter delight shot across his face, she found herself laughing.

'You stayed,' he croaked, then wiped a hand across his eyes, as if he couldn't quite believe what he was seeing.

'Of course I stayed.' The idea that he'd, even for one second, considered she might not melted her heart and the last of her nerves shuffled away. Placing one hand on her hip she attempted a glamour model pose. 'Are you going to sit there all evening, or are you going to come here and help me out of these?'

Immediately he stood and three long strides later he was backing her into the bedroom, holding her face in his hands. 'Oh, it's the latter. Most definitely the latter.' He trailed hot, teasing kisses across her lips before dipping down to her neck where the feel of his warm breath made her shiver. 'Umm, your pulse is racing.'

'I know.'

Slowly he straightened and stared deep into her eyes. 'Nerves or desire?'

'A little of both,' she admitted, her breath catching in her throat.

He stooped to plant a gentle kiss on the hammering pulse at her neck. 'Why the nerves, Mel?'

Embarrassment shot through her. 'I've never tried to seduce a man before,' she mumbled against his shirt.

She felt his chest rumble with laughter. 'Well, I can confirm you're a flipping ace at it. I'd prove it by putting your hand on my crotch, but one touch from you right now and I might embarrass myself.'

She started to laugh though it quickly became a gasp as his hands began to roam restlessly over her body.

'Mel, Mel,' he groaned, pulling her even tighter towards him. 'I've dreamed of doing this again for so damn long.'

'Me, too,' she whispered. Then, as if a green GO light

had suddenly switched on in her head, hands that moments ago had trembled with nerves now reached out to attack his clothing.

He quickly got the message. In no time at all he was nudging her fully naked body onto the bed. Staring up at him through her now mussed hair Mel found he was still wearing a half unbuttoned shirt and unzipped trousers with no belt. He personified sex on legs, but there were too many clothes. 'I feel underdressed.'

Grinning wolfishly he yanked off his remaining clothes in quick succession. 'Not for this party, you're not.'

His beautiful body was comfortingly familiar, yet wickedly new. She wanted to feast her eyes on the planes of his taut, hard muscles but he had other plans. Bossily he pushed her flat onto her back and began to kiss every inch of her, murmuring words that were wildly flattering. As her skin glowed and her body began to throb her mind filled with only one thought. All these weeks she'd been missing out on *this*.

Dimly she became aware of him shifting, settling his body over hers. Then her mind emptied of everything and she was swept away on wave after wave of deep, bone melting pleasure.

'Are you going to stay with me tonight?' he asked a while later, raising up on his elbows to gaze at her. 'Make love again. Sleep with me. Wake up with me.'

'What about Tom?'

He looked puzzled. 'What about him?'

'I'm not sure I should be here when he wakes up.'

With one neat movement he rolled onto his back, taking her with him so she ended up snug against his side, her head nestled on his chest. 'Why on earth not?'

'He's ten, Aiden. What sort of message will it send him if he finds me here tomorrow morning, dressed in the same clothes?'

'You think he'll care what you're wearing? I can lend you a T-shirt if you're feeling that sensitive.' She elbowed him sharply in the ribs.

'Ouch. What was that for?'

'For being deliberately obtuse. You know what I'm getting at.'

She felt his chest deflate as the breath went out of his lungs. 'What I know is my brother, who must have seen so many men stroll through his mother's life he's lost count, won't bat an eyelid if he finds you at the breakfast table.' He bent to kiss the top of her head. 'In fact he'll be delighted to have someone other than his brother to talk to while he munches those sickly chocolate loops.'

Mel pulled a face. 'If that's what's on offer for breakfast, I'm not sure I want to stay anyway.'

'The idea is that you stay because you want to wake up next to me,' he replied dryly. 'Not because of the free breakfast.'

'Oh, sorry.' She paused. 'But just in case waking up with you isn't enough of a temptation, what could I expect on the food front?'

She squealed as he rolled them so she was beneath him again. 'You'll get me for breakfast,' he told her in a low, throaty voice. 'And if you're really lucky, I'll throw in a double helping.'

'Umm.' She pretended to think about it until he nestled himself firmly between her legs.

A long while later she peered up at him. 'So *that's* what I can expect for breakfast?'

'I might throw in a few variations, but, yes, that's the

general theme.' He darted her a sharp glance when she didn't respond. 'Well?'

'Well what?'

His eyes glittered. 'Are you staying?'

He looked tense, as if he wasn't completely sure of her answer, so she threw her arms around his neck and kissed his cheek. 'Crazy man. Of course I'm going to stay.'

His body relaxed against hers. 'Good.'

Wrapping her tightly in his arms he kissed her one more time and promptly fell asleep. Mel stayed awake a little while longer, listening to the steady beat of his heart, trying not to feel too at home in his arms.

Chapter Twenty-Nine

Aiden's body woke up before he did, clearly overjoyed to find itself nestled against soft, warm curves. With a grin of pure male satisfaction he eased himself onto his elbow so he could begin the mouthwatering task of kissing his way down her, beginning with her dainty collarbone. To date he hadn't considered that an erotic part of the female anatomy, but Mel was starting to redefine his concept of sexy.

He'd reached her stomach before she stirred. 'Is this breakfast?' she murmured, her voice husky with sleep.

'You bet.'

In the blink of an eye her body went from relaxed and fluid to uptight and rigid. 'What about Tom? Is he awake yet?'

With a small grunt Aiden stopped his exploration and lifted his head. 'Chill. If he's awake, he's watching TV. It's what he does in the morning.'

'But what if he comes in?'

'He won't.' Heck, it was no wonder parents claimed their sex life went downhill after having kids. 'I promise,' he continued more gently. 'It's our rule. He doesn't disturb me unless there's an emergency.' His fingers drifted downwards, towards her heat. 'Are you willing to risk there not being a fire or flood? Or one of those world famous destructive Hungarian tornados?'

Whether it was his words that convinced her or the trail of his fingers, he didn't know, but he managed to make her forget all about Tom for a while.

When they lay back, catching their breath, Aiden threaded his fingers through her small hand and raised it to his lips. 'I don't want this to be another one off,' he told her quietly. 'I know I suck at relationships. Thanks to my screwed up childhood I find it hard to let people in. But I want to try.' Reaching over, he planted a tender kiss on her lips. 'Please, Mel. Let me try.'

He watched in astonishment as tears filled her eyes before she hastily rubbed at them. 'Yes.'

A single word, barely a whisper, but it was all he needed to hear. 'Thank you.'

Heck, now his voice was sounding scratchy, too. It was definitely time to get up and dressed. He had a final practice session to get to. Before he could muster the strength to swing his legs out of bed though, there was something he needed to know. 'Am I allowed to ask, why the change of heart? I was beginning to think this,' he nodded at the sight of their naked bodies, 'you and me as lovers, might never happen again.'

She brushed at his hair with her fingers, then trailed them down his cheeks, her touch so soft he wanted to purr. For once in his life he felt ... cherished he supposed was the word. Plenty of women had laid their fingers on him, but their purpose had only been to arouse. Never to simply caress.

'Sally told me it was time to stop being such a coward.' Mel smiled as her fingers traced his lips. 'Actually her words were stop being such a *flaming* coward.'

'Remind me to send her some flowers.' He opened his mouth and sucked in her finger, making her giggle. Combine that with the light in her eyes and the flush on her cheeks, and his body started twitching again. 'I wish I could spend all day here with you,' he told her after finally releasing her captive finger. 'But I've got a car to throw around the track.'

She glanced across at the time on his alarm clock and

squealed, jumping out of bed. 'Help. I've got a meeting in under an hour and I've got to get back to the hotel to change first.' Haphazardly she began to throw on her clothes, swearing under her breath. 'Bugger, bugger.' Her fingers fumbled with the buttons on her blouse, making such a mess of it he was forced to abandon the warmth of the bed and go and help her. 'This is all your fault, distracting me with your body,' she muttered as he calmly finished doing them up.

'Hey, you distracted me first. You and that flirty short skirt.' He eyed it up as she zipped it into place. 'If you wear that for your meeting, you'll get whatever you want out of it.' While she dived into the bathroom, he shoved on his jeans and a T-shirt.

She emerged a few seconds later, her hair scrunched into a messy ponytail. Adorable was the word for her, he thought with a rush of tenderness. 'Can I give you a lift back to the hotel?'

'No, I'm fine.' She added a slight shake of her head and her ponytail started to unravel. 'There are always plenty of cabs outside. You stay here with Tom.'

He grabbed her arm as she was about to leave. 'Hey, wait a minute. What about my goodbye kiss?'

Raising her eyes to the ceiling, she gave him a peck on the lips. Not what he'd been after so he pulled her back and gave her a demonstration of what a goodbye kiss should involve. They were both flushed when they came up for air. 'When you get to the hotel, pack up and check out. I want you to stay here with me and Tom.' Her eyes bulged and as her mouth opened, no doubt to argue, he added his killer punchline. 'Please.'

He'd never seen anyone so flustered. 'Are you sure that's a good idea?'

'How can we be in a relationship if you're in a hotel and I'm here?'

'There's being in a relationship, and then there's moving in together,' she countered. 'Usually one comes quite a long way before the other.'

She had him there, though the thought of her actually moving in with him, into his home, didn't phase him. He could easily imagine Mel in his apartment. Messing up his drawers. Taking over his wardrobe. Filling his place with her clutter. And her laughter. 'How about, while we're on the road, you think of it as going on holiday with me?'

'Okay.' She wrinkled her nose. 'But if you ever do take me on holiday I want to go somewhere with more beaches than Hungary.'

He was still laughing when she closed the door behind her.

Even as he wandered with Tom over to the Delta motorhome – the boy had demanded a bacon sandwich from the *people who knew how to cook* – a grin remained plastered across Aiden's face. Hit by the smell of bacon as they entered the hospitality suite, his stomach leapt with joy, forgetting he was on a strict high carb, zero fat intake. Yet even as he meandered to the porridge station and ladled a few gelatinous spoonfuls into his bowl, his smile remained.

Mel tried her best to listen attentively to the journalist, but her eyes kept wandering to the bulging suitcase sitting in the corner of the meeting room. The case she would take over to Aiden's motorhome later today. Her heart gave a wild thump.

'... the film of Sebastian Foster's life?'

She blinked. 'Sorry, do you remind repeating the question?'

'I asked,' he replied slowly and with a fair amount of

poorly disguised irritation, 'if you can confirm whether Aiden will be taking part in the documentary film of his father's life?'

'I can confirm he's been asked and is considering the proposal. We need to determine whether it will fit with his schedule.' She made a mental note to chase Aiden up on that. It was bound to put him in a bad mood, so maybe she'd do it after they'd retired to his bedroom …

God, she'd be there tonight. Him and her, rolling about in that big bed of his.

The journalist gave her another piercing look and Mel pinched herself, hard. Time to stop thinking about Aiden and focus on the only long-term commitment she was ever likely to make. Her job.

Thirty minutes later, having pinned down some future interview dates for both Stefano and Aiden, Mel had just eased her visitor out of the door when her phone rang.

'It's security here. We've got a woman with us who claims she's Aiden's mother. As he's out on the track, can you talk to her?'

Mel's head fell back against the chair and she let out a quiet groan. Goody wasn't the phrase that came to mind. Still, she'd entertained the youngest Foster and slept with the oldest. Maybe she was due a grilling from Mrs Foster.

'No problem. If you can give her a pass and direct her here, I'll meet her at the entrance.'

The slender, elegant, dark haired lady who accosted Mel on the steps of the Delta motorhome five minutes later obviously didn't share her sons' charm. Only their grey eyes. 'Where's my son?' she demanded in a tone as cold as her face.

Mel held out her hand. 'Hello, you must be Caroline Foster? Pleased to meet you. I'm Melanie Hunt.'

The older lady ignored Mel's outstretched hand. 'I repeat. Where is my son?'

'Aiden's on the track.'

Caroline gave her a haughty glare. 'I'm talking about Tom. Where is he?'

Mel itched to ask her why the sudden concern, when for the last umpteen weeks she hadn't seemed to care. 'I'm guessing Tom's in Aiden's motorhome with his new tutor.'

'I want to see him.'

Mel stared back at her. How could this cold, hard bitch possibly be Aiden's mother? 'I'm sure you do, but I suggest we wait for Aiden to finish first.'

'Who are you to tell me I can't see my own son? Take me to him, now.'

'No.'

Caroline's mouth fell open and her body vibrated with such animosity Mel wondered if she was about to get slapped. But then the fight seemed to leave her and her shoulders slumped. 'I deserved that. I've been travelling a lot and I'm jet-lagged and bad-tempered. Would you mind, please, taking me to see Tom?'

Mel was torn. Though her instinct was to wait for Aiden, who she knew would want to talk to his mother first, what right did she have to stop her from seeing her son? 'Okay. If you'd like to follow me.'

Caroline seemed to take her literally – or maybe her high shoes prevented her keeping up. Either way she kept a few steps behind, thankfully preventing any conversation. At the motorhome, Mel hesitated. She wanted to warn Tom his mother was here but she couldn't think how to do it without asking the lady in question to wait round the corner. Something that might upset the tenuous truce they'd just formed. So, heart thumping, knowing she was about to rock the poor boy's world once more, she knocked on the door.

The look on Tom's face when he found his mother on the doorstep nearly broke Mel's heart. There was an instant burst of pleasure; a ten-year-old boy's natural love for his mother. It soon faded as anger filled his eyes and a scowl marred his face. 'Mum.'

'Hello, Tom.'

Mel waited for the hug, at the very least a peck on the cheek, but there was no movement from either of them. They simply stood, staring, the awkwardness so painful it made Mel's teeth ache.

Just then the bewildered looking tutor popped his head round the door. Grateful for the distraction, Mel climbed inside and made some stilted introductions, very conscious that Tom had moved to stand by her.

When silence descended once again Caroline gave her a very pointed look, clearly her cue to leave. But how could she with Tom almost glued to her hip, his eyes pleading with her to stay? Instead she walked into the kitchen area and began filling up the kettle.

'You look at home here,' Caroline remarked as Mel spooned coffee into three mugs.

'That's because she lives with us.'

Mel's hand jolted, spilling some of the coffee onto the worktop. It was a relief to hear Tom speak at last, but she could have done without him uttering those particular words. 'I don't. Not really.' Hastily she mopped up the spillage.

'Well, you stayed last night, and Aiden told me you're going to be staying with us whenever we're travelling.'

Oh God. There were so many grenades for Caroline to detonate in that one sentence. The fact that Mel was sleeping with Aiden. With the full knowledge of her impressionable young son. Who'd blithely assumed he was still going to be travelling with his brother after today.

'Well—'

About to pounce on heaven knew which target, Caroline's words were interrupted as the door flung open, announcing the arrival of Aiden. His eyes quickly scanned the room, taking in Tom with his hands on hips, her with a flushed *get me out of here* face and his mum poised to yell, very loudly. He dropped the bag he'd been carrying, which landed with a resounding thud, and let out a crude oath.

'Don't swear in front of Tom,' Caroline scolded.

'Good to see you, too, Mum. How many years has it been?'

'Ten.' There was no warmth in her expression, no hint that she was talking to her eldest son. 'Your choice, I might add.'

'You seriously think I had a choice?' With a dismissive shake of his head he strode over to where the tutor was currently trying to appear invisible. 'Sorry, Stanley. I didn't realise we were having a visitor today. Would you mind taking a break for half an hour?'

For a man in his fifties he could certainly turn on the pace, Mel thought, as the tutor darted out of the door. 'I should go, too.'

'No.' Aiden's grey eyes silently begged her. 'I'd like you to stay, please.'

'Why, she's not family.'

The glance Aiden gave his mother could have seared paint off wood. 'She's been more a part of this rag tag family over the last few months than you have.'

Caroline had no answer to that, except to go and sit on the far end of the sofa, eloquently indicating that she wasn't going anywhere, either. Needing something to do Mel went to finish off making the drinks, even though she doubted anyone wanted one. Clearly also needing something to do, Tom helped her carry them to the coffee table.

Aiden ran a hand over his sweat streaked face and sighed. 'You'd better say what you came to say, mother.'

'I've come to take Tom home.'

'No!' Tom jumped to his feet. 'I'm not going home. Not with you. This is my home now. You'd rather be on holiday with that man than with me.'

As his voice started to wobble he stormed off to his room, slamming the door shut with so much force the whole motorhome shook.

Mel's heart didn't know which son needed the most sympathy. The little boy whose world had been turned upside down for the second time in as many months, or the older brother who was left holding his head in his hands, trying to pick up the pieces. Still in his racing overalls, what Aiden clearly needed was a hot shower and some quiet time. Not an episode of unhappy families.

'I see you've successfully managed to turn him against me.'

Aiden darted his mother a withering look. 'Don't you think swanning off across the world without a word had rather more to do with that?'

'You're making such a big deal of it. Like any single mother, I needed a break. I left him in safe hands and now I'm back.'

'Well, while you've been away, having your break, Tom's been living with me. We've got into a routine, of sorts. You can't just come back and disrupt it all over again.'

'Tom needs to be with his mother.'

Aiden gaped incredulously. 'What Tom needs is

someone to take notice of him. To share his excitement when something good happens. To console him when the shit inevitably hits the fan.' He gave his mother a harsh, unwavering glare. 'He needs to know that someone out there gives a damn.'

'Are you saying I don't?'

'Well, do you? Because from my experience I find that hard to believe.'

'How dare you.' Her eyes blazed at him. 'You wouldn't be here today if I hadn't paid for all those lessons. Made sure you were taken to all those race meetings.'

'And how many races did you actually watch?' he asked tightly.

His mother flushed and Mel had to look away. This was beyond painful.

'I want joint custody of Tom, or whatever the hell the term is for an equal say in my brother's future,' Aiden continued with a controlled fury. 'I don't want him going back to that boarding school. I want to see him every school holiday and have him stay with me at weekends during the off season. I don't want him growing up thinking nobody gives a damn about him, because I do.'

'So do I.'

'Then start acting like you do. Stop chasing after every man who looks at you and start being a mother to your son.'

In one swift movement Caroline rose from the sofa and slapped Aiden round the face. Hard.

As the shock registered he blinked, then wearily shook his head. 'Get out of my trailer. Don't bother to come back until you're ready to listen.'

Caroline snatched up her handbag, shot a few mental daggers in Mel's direction and headed toward the door.

It thudded shut, the sound reverberating throughout the motorhome.

'I don't know what to say.'

Aiden gave her a wry smile and rubbed at his reddening cheek. 'Don't worry. She has that effect on most of us. I shouldn't have spoken to her like that, but by God she makes me steaming mad. I stood by and let her treat me like dirt, but I can't and I won't let her do the same to Tom.'

'Good.' Her love for him rose up inside her, making it hard for her to breathe. Feeling dangerously close to tears she wrapped her arms around his waist.

'You might not want to get too close,' he murmured against her hair, his arms settling lightly against her. 'I'm pretty whiffy.'

She inhaled a lungful of petrol, rubber and sweat. 'It's a good whiff. Maybe we should bottle it and have a Delta aftershave range.'

At his answering chuckle her heart sighed. All those weeks spent pushing him away, and she'd fallen for him anyway. 'Tom's lucky to have you sticking up for him, you know.'

'Lucky?' He let out a short laugh. 'I've ignored him for the last ten years. In fact if it wasn't for you, I'd still be ignoring him.' He kissed the top of her head. 'You make me a better man, Mel.'

Oh God. Tears filled her eyes and her arms tightened around him. 'You were always that man. He just needed a bit of encouragement to come out.'

She felt his body slump in her arms. 'Speaking of encouraging someone out.' He glanced at Tom's shut door. 'I'd better talk to Tom.'

Reluctantly she let him go. 'Good luck.'

She was nearly out of the door when he suddenly asked. 'Did you bring your case?'

'Yes.'

A satisfied smile burst across his face. 'This little showdown hasn't scared you off?'

'I'm made of stronger stuff than that. Besides, I love a good soap opera.'

'I prefer an action film myself.' He licked his lips and leered wickedly at her.

Shaking her head, she blew him a brief kiss before making a quick exit. It saddened her to know that the moment she left, the smile would slip off his face as he went to have that heart wrenching talk with his brother.

Chapter Thirty

Aiden had a mother to placate and a brother to cheer up. Oh, and a race to win. How ironic that he'd started this season saying he wanted no distractions. His head was spinning so much now he didn't even know which way to face.

One thing he did know; his mother could wait. Since their showdown two days ago she'd kept her distance, perhaps finally realising that turning up out of the blue and making demands had pissed off both her sons.

His race couldn't wait, though then again, neither could Tom. He'd withdrawn into his shell since his mother's arrival, not prepared to listen when he'd tried to talk to him. Aiden wasn't sure what more he could say to the little guy, but he had one more shot at catching him before he had to put his mind into race mode.

He gave the door to Tom's room a cursory knock before walking in without waiting for an answer. Predictably Tom had his nose in an electronic game.

'Are you going to watch the race?'

'Might.'

For two days he'd put up with this crap. Now he'd reached his limit. With a quick lunge he swiped the game out of Tom's hand.

'Hey. I was playing on that.'

'And now you're talking to me. I repeat. Are you watching the race?'

Tom shrugged, barely glancing in his direction. 'Mel said I could watch with her.'

Aiden already knew that. It was a good job at least one person was talking to him. 'Why are you giving me such a hard time?' he asked, lowering himself onto the bed. 'I've already told you I want you with me, but Mum wants you at home and though it might not seem like it now, that's the best place for you. Being on the road for most of the year isn't good for your education. It isn't good for you. Besides, mother's are better than brothers at some stuff.'

'Yeah?'

'Yes. They make you eat proper meals, not takeaways.' At least the housekeeper would, anyway. 'They can take you to see your mates, give you parties.' Or they employ a nanny to do that. 'They buy new shoes when yours don't fit any more and they drill hygiene and manners into you.' Though that was probably the nanny, too. He could have gone on, rattled out things like they hug you when you're down, listen to you, protect you, but what was the point? Their mother didn't have those in her job description. 'I'd love to have you with me, buddy, but that's not the best thing for you. You're better off at home,' he finished lamely.

Tom raised his eyes momentarily, his expression one of such disillusionment the kid could have kicked him in the balls and Aiden would have felt no less pain. This boy had started to open up to him. To look up to him, even. Now he was letting him down. 'I'm sorry, mate. You don't know how damn sorry I am.'

'Do I have to go back to boarding school?'

'No.' Aiden didn't care what his mother said. That was at least one point he wasn't going to fail Tom on.

For one long moment Tom simply stared at his racing car duvet cover. Then, without warning, he launched himself at Aiden, his arms clutching at his shoulders. 'I still get to see you though. Like you promised,' he mumbled into his neck.

'God, yes. Of course. I'm your brother, Tom. We're family. Never forget it.'

Tom sniffed, the sound echoing down Aiden's earhole. 'Okay then. You'd better win this race though, 'cos it might be the last one I see.'

Aiden swallowed down the lump in his throat. 'It won't be, I'll make sure of it,' he promised. 'But I'll try and win it for you anyway.'

Nobody was more surprised than him, when he did.

At parc ferme Mel hung back, watching as Aiden hoisted his brother in the air, their faces wearing almost identical grins.

'Do you really want to break that relationship up?' she asked the woman beside her.

Each time Mel had raised this subject, Caroline had gone on the attack. *He's my son. I know what's best for him.* Blah, blah. As if a woman who could abandon her son for several months really knew what was best for him. This time though, as she continued to stare at her sons, Caroline's reply was muted. 'No, I don't.'

Mel fought the impulse to punch the air. 'Good. Because the Tom I first met was a lot different to the one I can see now. You should see them together, Caroline. They joke about, banter, have fun like two brothers should. Aiden's a great role model for him.'

'Umm. And what about you and my eldest son? What are you to each other?'

Mel twisted her hands awkwardly. 'I like to think we're good friends.'

'Good friends who sleep together.'

'Look, Aiden's going to be on the podium in a minute. We need to move to get a good view.' Mel started to shuffle away, keeping her eye on Tom who was now watching the officials check over the cars.

'You are aware Aiden takes after his father, aren't you?'

'He certainly seems to have acquired his ability to drive a car very fast round a track.'

'I mean he's a ladies' man. Most racing car drivers are, I guess. Women throw themselves at them so much, I suppose it's hard for them to say no after a while.'

Mel halted and glared at the woman by her side. 'Why don't you just come out and say what you want to say. Then we can focus on what's important right now and celebrate your son's victory.'

'I'm only trying to give you some advice. Racing drivers find it impossible to stay faithful. You might think you've captured Aiden, but there'll be another buxom bimbo round the corner, waiting to grab him off you.'

'I resent your use of the word *another*,' Mel countered, 'though I don't doubt the accuracy of your sentiment.'

All through the presentation and interviews Mel tried to concentrate on Aiden's victory. Tried to watch him raise the trophy, spray the champagne, laugh and joke with the other drivers without Caroline's words drilling through her head.

Tried and failed.

Across the heads of the cheering crowds Aiden's eyes sought hers out, his smoky gaze sending her a clear message. For tonight at least, the only woman he was interested in, was her.

At last it was the two of them. Tom was asleep in the bedroom next door, the team had departed happy but exhausted to the hotel and after a lengthy discussion with Aiden, Caroline had gone back to England.

'So you've worked out an agreement with your mother that you're happy with?' Mel asked as she lay on his bed, watching him undress. Another of today's highlights.

'Yep. I'll drop him home tomorrow. After that she'll bring him to race weekends when she can during the season, and he gets to stay with me during school holidays and every other weekend out of season. And he won't be going back to boarding school. She was remarkably okay about it all in the end. I didn't even have to threaten legal action, though I'll keep that in my back pocket just in case her promises are all hot air.' He narrowed his eyes. 'I can't help thinking someone made her see sense, because I sure as hell wasn't getting anywhere.'

'All I did was point out how happy Tom was. I think her own conscience did the rest.'

Aiden and his lithe, naked body slipped into the bed beside her. 'Did I tell you you're the most incredible woman I've ever met?'

He planted a tender kiss on her lips and her eyes fluttered closed. 'Umm, you'll get bored of my incredibleness pretty soon.'

Suddenly the warmth of his lips left hers. When she opened her eyes, he was staring at her intensely. 'I'll never get bored of you, Mel. Never.'

Oh heavens, her heart was going to burst. Quickly she slid her arms around his neck and kissed him slowly, deeply and for a long, long time.

When they came up for air Aiden lay on his back and pulled her onto his chest. 'So what happens tomorrow?'

'We go home,' she replied quietly, already hating tomorrow night, when she'd have to sleep alone.

'Is that it? We don't see each other again until the next race?'

'Well, of course we will. You've got this meeting with the film producer that I'm going to be at. Then I need to talk to you about a magazine article and no doubt we'll bump into each other on site.'

'That's all work. What about the fun stuff? Do I get your company for that?'

His expression was so earnest Mel found it hard not to smile. 'Aiden, have you taken a good look at yourself in the mirror recently?'

'What?'

'Not only are you kind and funny, you're flipping gorgeous. Oh and pretty rich, too, so I hear. A woman would have to be mad not to want to see you every chance she could.'

'But do *you* want to see me?'

Was the guy serious? 'Of course I do. Where have all these insecurities come from?'

'Perhaps from the fact that for the last few months you've turned me down on a fairly frequent basis.'

Mel snuggled in, needing to feel skin against skin. Beating heart against beating heart. 'That was because I was a coward. Not because I didn't want a relationship with you.'

'You still think I'm going to hurt you?'

Tears stung at her eyelids and she had to bite on her lip to stop them from falling. 'I think neither of us knows what the future will bring, so we should just relax and enjoy life now.'

She felt his chest lower as he let out a deep breath. 'Okay. So when will I see you next?'

Mel had an important date on Thursday. It was one she was absolutely dreading but couldn't change, though maybe Aiden could help out before that. 'I could come to yours on Tuesday and Wednesday, if you like.'

'I like.'

She smiled. 'Okay then. But in return, I need you to do me a favour.'

'Anything.'

'Will you take me out driving again on Wednesday?'

He angled his head to look at her. 'Sure I can. Are you still keen to learn then?'

'Well, actually, I've been having lessons.'

'Really?'

'Yes, really.'

He rolled over so he was on top of her. 'Then I'd better see what they've been teaching you.' Hot kisses trailed across her forehead and down her nose. 'Check you've not got into any bad habits.'

'Like speeding, you mean?'

'Hey, nothing wrong with doing something fast.' She gasped as he eased himself back into her. 'Though slow and steady is highly rated, too.'

Monday came round far too quickly and before he knew it Aiden was dropping Tom off at his official home. The one he shared with his mum, rather than the trailer they'd both started calling home. Tom's figure looked far too small and forlorn as he stood on the doorstep of the palatial, six bedroomed neo Georgian house his mother had obviously deemed was the perfect size for her and her small son. In just under two weeks he'd see him in Spa for the Belgium Grand Prix. It helped ease the parting a little, though Aiden was nagged by the realisation that would only happen if their mother kept her promise.

'Here, remember to take this.' He shoved the mobile phone he'd bought two days ago into his brother's pocket. 'Text me, phone me, whenever you want. If you need to talk, to mouth off about something, even help with your homework. Whatever. I'm there for you.'

'What if I need money?'

Tom gave him a slightly wobbly version of his usual

beguiling grin and, God help him, Aiden almost cried. To prove to them both he was made of sterner stuff, he gave him a mock clip round the ear instead. 'Cheeky mite, aren't you?'

Tom screwed up his face. 'Isn't a mite a sort of little bug?'

'Yeah, and you're a little bug … ger.'

His brother dissolved into giggles and Aiden took the opportunity to give him a final hug before slipping into his car while he still felt emotionally capable. As Tom's figure grew smaller and smaller in his rear-view mirror, Aiden tightened his grip on the steering wheel and reminded himself Tom had a phone now. They could contact each other whenever they wanted, and without involving their mother.

Providing the little guy remembered the lecture about charging the damn thing up.

The rest of Aiden's day proved equally as draining. He felt pulled in so many directions, he thought he'd snap. Most of the afternoon he spent holed up in a team meeting, working on the Spa race strategy. Thanks to his win in Hungary he still had a shot at the title, so the heat was definitely on. That meant the meeting was even more intense than usual and it overran late into the evening, leaving Aiden with sponsor commitments and interviews that needed to be re-scheduled. Sally was juggling it all as best she could but something was going to have to give and his heavy heart knew who that something would have to be.

He'd begged Mel to come and stay with him – and now he was about to blow her out.

Feeling like a total schmuck he used the three free minutes he'd been granted to go for a pee (twenty seconds), grab a low carb, high protein snack from the canteen (thirty seconds) and find a vacant meeting room to phone Mel.

'I miss you,' he stated bluntly. Honestly.

He could hear the smile in her voice. 'You saw me this morning.'

'So? That was,' he checked his watch, 'fourteen hours ago.'

'Well, you'll see me tomorrow.'

'Ah. About that. Unless you can tell me how to squeeze forty hours into a day, I'm afraid the next two days are shot to pieces now.'

'Oh.' A small sound, but it echoed with the same disappointment he felt.

'Unless you fancy a trip to Paris? Apparently I've got to cram that in Wednesday night.'

'I've got an appointment first thing Thursday morning.'

Her voice sounded quiet and flat. Was she miffed with him, or the circumstances? 'This isn't me ducking out. I really want to see you and Thursday seems too damn far away, but it's the best I can do. Will you come and stay with me on Thursday? Allow me to take you out to dinner to make up for letting you down?'

'Don't be silly, you don't have to make up for anything. Though I might have to put chilli in Sally's coffee next time I see her.'

'Ouch, you press officers are evil. You didn't answer the question, though. Is Thursday night a date?' His heart seemed to come to a stop as he waited for her answer. Hell, he'd never felt this unsure over a woman. He was used to being chased, used to women falling over themselves to see him. Though he was very happy to be doing the chasing instead, this feeling of uncertainty was a real bitch. Was she into him as much as he was into her?

'Yes, Thursday is fine.'

'Fine?' He wished he could see her face, because right now he had no clue as to what she was feeling.

'Okay, sorry, it's better than fine. It sounds lovely.'

And she still sounded too quiet for his liking. 'I'm not playing fast and loose here, Mel. Everything I said about wanting to make this work between us. I meant every word.'

'Good. I believe you.'

'Then why do you sound so unsure?'

'I'm not. I'm just ...' Her sigh sliced through him. 'I'm disappointed.'

'In me?'

'Of course not. I was looking forward to seeing you, that's all.'

'I bloody hate phones,' he told her roughly. 'I ache to hold you, Mel. I want to look into your pretty eyes and tell you how much you mean to me.'

There was a small pause and when she answered her voice was softer, huskier. 'Could you do that on Thursday?'

'Yes. A million times, yes.' He glanced over to the glass door where he could see Frank frantically waving his arms, reminding him he'd used up more than his allocated three minutes. 'Sorry, Mel, I've got to go. Take care and I'll see you Thursday evening.'

Three bloody long nights away.

Chapter Thirty-One

Wednesday night, fifteen hours before her driving test, and Mel was a bundle of nervous energy. She really, really needed someone to talk to. It worried her that her first thought was to phone Aiden, but he was in the middle of some posh function and besides, she hated to come across as the needy girlfriend. Sally was out in Paris with Aiden, which left Nancy or Frank. Whoever was unlucky enough to pick up the phone.

'Mel, my darling, how are you holding up?' Nancy's voice sounded warm and motherly. Exactly what she needed.

'I'm shitting bricks, if you want the truth. Thank you for the good luck card. I'm going to need a lot of it.'

'Come now, you'll be absolutely fine. And afterwards you can let Aiden take you out to celebrate.'

Mel laughed. 'Good to see the Delta grapevine is alive and kicking. Sorry, I really should have told you myself.'

'Nonsense. I hope you're too busy enjoying yourself to call a couple of oldies like us.' She paused a moment and when she spoke again Mel could almost hear her smiling. 'If it helps at all, we're really pleased, for both of you. You make a wonderful couple.'

'Thank you. It's very early days but we'll see how it goes.'

'Has Aiden been giving you any tips on how to pass your test tomorrow?'

Mel toyed with the hem of her jumper. 'Ah, no. In fact he doesn't know I'm taking it.'

'You've not told him? Heavens above girl, why ever not?'

'Because.' Now she was going to sound really pathetic.

'He's got so much going on in his life and this isn't really that big a deal.'

'It's a huge deal.'

'To little old me, yes, but not to a man vying to be world champion who's currently away in Paris at yet another sponsor event.'

'I think he'd have wanted to know, Mel.'

'Maybe, but I don't want to be another item to cross off his to-do list.'

'If he's the man I think he is, he wouldn't see it that way. He'd be upset that he wasn't here to hold your hand.'

'Perhaps.'

'Well, good luck, my dear. I've got Frank standing next to me, he just wants to say a few words, too.'

Frank's gruff voice came on the phone. 'You don't need luck, Mel. You've always punched above your weight so don't let a silly test rattle you. If that man you're apparently seeing can overtake at two hundred miles per hour going into a sharp bend you can manage thirty miles an hour down the high street with your eyes closed. Though I'd very much recommend you keep them open.'

Mel was laughing when she ended the call. A few seconds later it vibrated with a text.

Thinking of you, A xx

As she stared at his words her heart performed a neat somersault. He didn't know about the test, yet still he'd bothered to find the time in his hectic evening to message her. Quickly she typed back. *Not as much as I'm thinking of you xxx*

She caught his reply as she climbed up the stairs.

Am I naked when you're thinking? You are xxxx

Laughing she bounced on the bed and typed back. *You're naked and in bed next to me. Night night xxxxx*

By the time she'd undressed and cleaned her teeth she'd had another message.

Until tomorrow night – remember where we left off. Night night 2 xxxxxx

An hour ago she'd worried she might not sleep but she went off like a light – with a smile on her face.

Aiden had taken to pacing the room and he never paced. He wasn't the type. He was a calm and relaxed type of guy. What did the press say? He had a laid-back demeanor. To be fair, that was true of most racing drivers. When you gambled with your life on the track most weeks it was hard to get keyed up about anything off it.

Well, it was now seven o'clock and Aiden was most definitely fidgety. Restless would describe it, too. Where the hell was she? He'd been home for two hours and twelve minutes, approximately, and despite Mel's assurance that she was on her way, she still hadn't arrived.

He grabbed at his phone, ready to call her for the third time, when his doorbell sounded.

About bloody time, too.

Flinging the door open, he bundled the waiting woman into his arms. 'God, I was beginning to think you weren't coming.'

She laughed, kissing him soundly on the lips. 'You promised me dinner. Why wouldn't I come?'

He gave her ponytail a quick yank, causing her to yelp. 'Is that all you've come for? Dinner?'

'Well, there was also the promise of finishing what we started last night.'

Her husky words shot straight through to his groin. 'You're in for a treat then, because I like to keep my promises.' Taking her overnight case he shoved it into the hallway before clutching at her hand and almost frog marching her through to his bedroom.

As he made quick work of removing her clothes she started to giggle. 'I guess you really did miss me.'

'Don't doubt it for a moment.'

She rubbed against him and he groaned, his fingers fumbling with zippers and belts as he made a total hash of undressing himself, displaying none of the finesse his image suggested. Finally he had Mel where he wanted her. Naked and beneath him. He thrust into her in one joyful movement and as she let out one of her ego inflating moans, he damn near came on the spot. Gritting his teeth he wrestled with his desire, determined not to go off like a horny teenager, but while he was trying to slow things down she was grasping hold of his buttocks and urging him on. One glance at her face, hazel eyes alive, an impish smile on her lips, and he was done for. He let himself go over the edge, giving in to the sheer pleasure of being inside this wonderful woman.

Thank God she came over with him.

'Shit. You've turned me into a seventeen-year-old again,' he panted as he rolled them both so she was snuggled up close to his side. 'My control's shot to pieces.'

She grinned up at him through a fuzz of wild hair. 'Maybe we should work on your stamina.'

He grabbed her arms and hauled her up to face him. 'I'll have you know there's nothing wrong with my twenty-eight-year-old stamina.'

She wriggled in his grasp, laughing as he gave her a mock glare. 'Okay, okay. How about you use some of that famed stamina to wine and dine me, then?'

'In or out?'

Her nose wrinkled as she considered his question. 'Isn't

that programme on tonight where they transform bodged DIY jobs?'

He was used to women who wanted to dress up and go out, see and be seen, so it took him a second to register her answer. 'I think my television only shows sport.'

'In that case you order the takeaway and I'll fix your television.'

Grabbing his jeans he reluctantly shrugged them on while sneaking a few looks in her direction. There was something pretty sexy about watching a woman dress, slipping on lacy underwear, or in Mel's case ... a pair of striped pyjama bottoms and vest top?

'Fantastic. Are we going to bed again?'

She froze, flushing as she stared down at her pj's. 'Sorry. That's really rude of me. I must have switched off for a moment and thought I was at home.' The happiness he'd seen in her face only moments ago drained away and she started to rummage through her overnight bag.

Aiden crossed over to her, pulling her into his arms. 'Hey, I wasn't complaining.'

Her eyes refused to meet his. 'Well, maybe you should. You invited me round for a date and somehow I ended up treating it as a pyjama party.' Finally she raised her head. 'I did bring a dress with me. I can wear that.'

'Mel, Mel, shh.' He kissed her forehead, her nose. Her soft lips. 'I love to see you in a dress, especially if it ends at the thigh, but I'm pretty partial to these, too.' He ran his hands over the jersey bottoms which clung very nicely to her curves. 'The fact is, you could wear a bin liner and I'd still find you incredibly attractive.'

She bit at that luscious bottom lip. 'God, you're so sweet to me. I must be the weirdest date you've ever had.'

Gently he caught at her chin, angling it upwards so she'd

have to look at him. 'The most refreshing, yes. The women I've dated have been more concerned with how they look, and where we're going, than being with me. I began to ask myself, do they want to be with Aiden Foster the guy, or Aiden Foster the racing driver? I think the answer was pretty obvious.' He dipped his head and kissed her. 'So now, do you want to put on a dress and go out with a racing driver, or sit on the sofa in your pj's and watch TV with me?'

She sighed against his chest. 'I choose TV and you.'

'Good.' He started to move away, then halted. 'Hang on, isn't that the wrong way round? Shouldn't I come first?'

She put her hands on her hips and pursed her lips. 'That depends. How well can you entertain me?'

The glint was back in her eyes and a smile back on her face. Aiden reckoned he could put up with coming second to the TV.

Her stomach full of a delicious Thai takeaway, Mel cuddled up against Aiden on his huge leather sofa. After witnessing her die a thousand deaths when she'd unthinkingly put her pj's on, he'd calmly proceeded to take off his jeans and replace them with tracksuit bottoms, joining her in slouch land. Except that his lower half was clad in designer sportswear that made him look like the athlete he was, while she was in comfy cottons that were really only designed for bed.

'So what about this driving then.' He lifted her hair and kissed the side of her neck. 'I seem to remember promising to take you out in a car again.'

Surprised, she raised her head off his chest. 'I thought you'd forgotten.'

'Of course not. I told you, my schedule got totally

screwed over the last two days, but I'm back on track now. I can take you out tomorrow afternoon, if you still fancy it?'

She found she couldn't look him in the eye. 'How about I take you out, instead?'

'Well, yes, that's what I mean. You do the driving. I'll do the sitting terrified in the passenger seat, ready to yank the handbrake on at any moment.'

'Actually, you don't need to be so terrified.' She swallowed, regretting now that she hadn't told him. 'I passed my test yesterday.'

He lurched into a sitting position. 'You what?'

'I passed my test, yesterday morning. First attempt,' she added with a touch of smug.

His face was a picture of utter bewilderment. 'That's fantastic, but why didn't you tell me?'

'I am telling you.'

'Don't be cute. I mean, why didn't you tell me earlier? You must have known for ages that this date was coming up.' There was a thread of annoyance in his voice.

Aware she was on slippery ground, she tried to play it down. 'It wasn't a big deal.'

He shifted so their bodies weren't touching any more. 'Prior to having a lesson with me you were terrified about sitting in the driver's seat.' His eyes slammed accusingly into hers. 'Now you tell me it wasn't a big deal that you had a driving test?'

'Of course it was a big deal to me, but I didn't think anyone else would be interested.'

His expression tightened. 'Did you tell Sally?'

Bugger. The longer this conversation was going on, the worse he was making her feel. And the less she could remember her reasons for keeping quiet. 'Yes, I did.'

'Nancy, Frank?'

Guilt lay heavy in her stomach. 'Yes.'

'I see.' There was a whoosh of air as Aiden launched himself off the sofa and stood rigidly before her, hands on hips. 'Tell me, what do you think's happening here, between you and me?'

'What do you mean?'

'I mean, are we in a relationship? Or are we just going to shag now and again?'

His words cut deep, as she knew he'd intended. 'I hope we're in a relationship.'

'Yeah, I hoped that, too. How can we be though, if you can't be bothered to tell me about any of the important stuff?'

He wasn't angry, she realised now, but hurt. 'I'm sorry. I was going to tell you when you took me driving, but that didn't happen.'

His body flinched, as if she'd struck him. 'It didn't happen because my schedule got screwed up. Not because I didn't want to.'

Fighting her tears, Mel reached out to take his hand. 'You were busy. I heard it in your voice. I didn't want to add to your burdens. Make you feel guilty for not taking me out.'

He tightened his hand around hers, pulling her up and towards him. 'Goddamnit, you're not a burden, Mel. You're a bloody joy. A highlight in my day.'

Her heart faltered and she had to squeeze her eyes to stop the tears from falling. 'Okay, so now I feel stupid.'

'Please, you've never treated me like a celebrity. Don't start now. Are you interested in whether I win a race or not?'

'Of course I am.'

'Then I'm interested in whether you have a driving test, though it's far more than that. I want to know where you are when you're not with me. If you're feeling happy or sad. Hell, even if you buy a new pair of shoes, I want you to tell me. Okay?'

Her heart lodged firmly in her throat and she threw her arms around him. But even as she toppled even deeper into love a small part of her mind insisted on picking up on their differences. He was winning races in an elite racing franchise. She was passing a driving test and buying shoes.

Chapter Thirty-Two

Aiden came first in Belgium and second in Monza, results which pulled him back into third on the leader board, only one point behind his teammate and still in touch with the championship leader, Carlos. He felt his life was turning a corner and was happier both on and off the track. Even his mother appeared to be keeping her end of the bargain, bringing Tom out to both races.

Singapore followed, one of the most gruelling races on the circuit, but a mechanical failure meant he failed to pick up any points. Undaunted he went on to get two wins in Korea and Japan. Now in India he'd just picked up a second place, taking him to second in the championship. Ahead of Stefano. Closing the gap on Carlos.

The run of success didn't escape the attention of his engineer who collared him in the Delta garage after the presentations.

'Is she the reason you're picking up points now?' Frank asked, nodding towards Mel who was deep in conversation with Stefano, no doubt trying to prize a quote out of him about how great it was to finish third.

'You're putting the rise up the leader board down to the press officer and not the expertise of the driver or the team?'

Frank gave him *the look*. 'You'd better not be playing games with her. She's not your usual type. She's special.'

'I know.' Did he really need to be told the obvious?

Frank gave him a long, searching look. 'You're happy.'

It wasn't a question, but Aiden answered anyway. 'Yes, I am.' And it scared the bejesus out him when he realised the happiness had little to do with his rise up the leadership board and everything to do with the woman they were discussing.

'It shows in your driving. You're more relaxed. I get the feeling you're not racing your father any more. Only racing the other drivers on the track.'

Aiden frowned. Was that true? Now he came to think about it, he hadn't thought of his father in a while.

Mel glanced over and caught his eye, her private smile, one lover to another, making him feel ten foot tall. No, he had far better things to think about now than his father.

'My warning still stands though,' Frank continued. 'Don't hurt her.'

Reluctantly Aiden swung his eyes back to his engineer. 'You really think I have any intention of doing that?'

Frank seemed to study him for a moment. 'No, I don't.' Then he did something pretty rare, in Aiden's experience. He grinned. 'Bugger me, you're really going to win that championship this year, aren't you?'

'Yes.' The certainty of his reply surprised him.

Frank nodded appreciatively before clapping him hard round the shoulders and going off to find someone else to psychoanalyse.

It left Aiden free to go and pester Mel who was now laughing with ... Carlos? When the heck had he snuck his way into their garage? Before the Spaniard had time to blink Aiden had managed to insert himself firmly by Mel's side, his arm thread possessively around her waist. He had half a mind to plant a smacker on her lips for good measure, but didn't want to alert any skulking media. Not that he gave a monkey's who knew, but Mel wanted to keep a low profile. *I spin the news. I don't want to become the news*, were her words.

Having sufficiently staked his claim on Mel, Aiden turned

to his rival. 'Come to gloat?' Carlos had come first to Aiden's second today, but it was the Spaniard's first podium place in three races.

'I've come to check on my sweet little Mel.'

Like a cat ready to pounce, Aiden felt himself tense. 'I agree Mel's sweet and slightly on the short side, but she's not yours.'

As they squared up to each other Mel cast an eye from one to the other and shook her head. 'Too much testosterone, boys.' Reaching up she gave Carlos a brief peck on the cheek. 'It's lovely to see you, but time you went back to your Viper teammates and left us alone so we can plot your downfall.'

Carlos laughed, a dazzle of white teeth against olive skin. 'Ah, but now Aiden is here I was wondering. How is the documentary going?'

Aiden froze. 'What documentary?'

'Word gets about. Your father was one of the greatest drivers that ever lived. I'm interested to hear how they plan on keeping his memory alive.'

'The documentary is nothing to do with us,' Mel cut in quietly.

'No? I understood Aiden was to contribute some touching memories of his times with the great man.'

Aiden stared coolly at his rival. 'I'm not sure how that's any of your business.' He and Mel had met with the producer a few weeks ago and though he wasn't sure about the touching part, they had persuaded him to be interviewed.

Carlos shrugged in that laconic southern European way. 'As a child I was a big fan. It must be a burden, living up to such a legend, no?'

Aiden smiled. 'How can being lucky enough to share some of Sebastian Foster's genes possibly be a burden?'

Carlos gave him a knowing smirk before blowing an extravagant kiss at Mel and strutting back to his own garage. He reminded Aiden of a peacock, minus the trailing feathers. Or the beak. Then again, his nose could qualify. 'Why do I get this urge to throttle that bastard?'

'Because he beat you today? Because he's trying to wind you up about your father?'

Aiden bent to give her a light kiss. 'No. Because he hurt you.'

'Then thank you, my brave knight, but that was a long time ago. I've moved on since then, in case you hadn't noticed.' She grinned up at him. 'It didn't work, did it?'

'What?'

'Carlos, trying to needle you about your father. It's no longer a sore point for you.'

As she was the second person to remark on that in the space of a few minutes he had to believe both Frank and Mel were right. He was no longer racing the ghost of his father. The only guy he was racing now was the one in front of him.

As that happened to be Carlos, so much the better.

He must have been too absorbed with his thoughts because Mel broke away to study him. 'Are you okay?'

'I will be, as soon as I can drag you away from here and get my hands on you.'

'Now that's the best offer I've had all day.'

He smiled down at her, kissing the tip of her nose. 'I should bloody hope so.'

The next race was Abu Dhabi. A day-night race on the Yas Marina Circuit. The track wrapped round a marina filled with super yachts and was straddled by the futuristic looking five star Yas hotel. A stunning setting during the day, it looked even more spectacular at night when it was all lit up.

Sadly Mel couldn't see any of it. She was sitting in the back of the garage with Sally, watching the race on the monitors. Sitting wasn't quite accurate. She was perched on the edge, teetering between standing and yelling and cowering and biting her fingernails.

'Are you actually watching this between your fingers?' Sally asked in disbelief. 'I thought that was a pose reserved for horror movies.'

'It feels like a horror movie.' God, did Aiden and Carlos have to drive so close to each other? 'Any minute now they're going to crash. I can feel it.'

'Don't you have any faith in your former or current lover?'

Mel couldn't answer that. She was too busy wincing as Aiden and Carlos again went wheel to wheel.

At the next corner they both held their breath. 'Is it my imagination, or is this more than a jostle for first and second place?' Sally remarked once the immediate danger had passed.

'What do you mean?'

'I mean, they're racing like a pair of duelling knights. You didn't give them both a lady's favour, did you? You know, like a scarf or a pair of knickers?'

'They've got more on their mind at the moment than my knickers.' Her hands clenched as Carlos took the next corner slightly too wide and Aiden swooped inside him. There was a split second of terror as the two cars came dangerously close but then Aiden was off and away. 'He's in the lead!' She clutched at Sally's sleeve. 'Two more laps to go. Oh God, I can't bear it.'

Her phone beeped and she glanced down at the text.

It was from Tom. *Go bro!*

For the races Tom hadn't been able to attend, he'd taken to texting her. Mel couldn't have explained to anyone how special it made her feel when he did.

I can't watch, she texted back.

Chicken. He's gonna win.

And he was. There was the streak of silver and red as Aiden's Delta came round the final bend, in first place. Eyes glued to the monitor, her heart thumping she watched as the man with the chequered flag got ready. Anxiously Mel moved to stand, to cheer him home, but suddenly his car started to slow.

What? Tom texted.

The garage was in uproar as they all watched first Carlos and then Stefano slip past Aiden to take first and second. He limped across the line in third.

Her phone beeped. *Man on TV says no fuel* ☹

A moment later. *I hate this sport.*

Mel collapsed back on the chair. Right now she hated it, too. Quickly she typed. *Wish you were here to cheer him up.*

You do it. He's happy when you're there.

'What's with all the texts?' Sally asked, leaning over. 'Not journos out for blood already, I hope?'

'No. Just a miserable ten-year-old.'

She nodded sympathetically. 'I expect the elder brother will be even more unhappy.'

Mel tried to put her professional head back on as she went to hunt down statements for the press from a very despondent garage team. How did they spin this one? It was hard to create an impression of absolute professionalism when your lead driver had just limped into third place on petrol fumes. It was also hard not to watch the images that flashed across the TV screens without her heart twisting.

Though Aiden's mask was firmly in place he walked as if every movement was painful.

By the time he was put in front of the cameras at the press conference, Mel's eyes stung with the effort of not crying.

'From certain first to a disappointing third. What went wrong?'

Aiden shrugged his shoulders, fooling nobody. 'I ran out of fuel. Just one of those things.'

'Whose fault was it?'

He glared at the questioner. 'We win as a team and we lose as a team. Today we didn't get that win, but we did get valuable points and we're still in with a shot of the championship.'

'But realistically, to do that you're going to have to win the next two races.'

'I was leading today going into the final bend. What makes you think I can't win the next two?'

The professional in her swelled with pride at how well he handled the questions but the lover knew it was all a performance. She ached to hug away the frustration and dejection lurking in the back of his eyes.

Finally the conference was over and the drivers and sports correspondents meandered out. Mel tried to catch Aiden but she was waylaid by journalists and by the time she'd prized her way out of the room, he'd vanished. Or had he? Was that the rumble of his voice in the adjoining room? Hand on the door handle, she was about to enter when she overheard Carlos.

'Embarrassing, I think, to run out of fuel. How would you put it? So near and yet, so far?'

'Did you have anything important to say to me, Carlos?'

'I was just wondering what was going on in your head today. You raced like a crazy person.'

'I raced like a man who's going to beat you.'

'Ah, but what do you want to win? The Championship, or the girl?'

Mel gasped. What on earth was Carlos playing at?

'Leave Mel out of this.'

'But why? She is something else we both want, no? I was thinking to myself. What if I say to Aiden, I'll give you the championship if you give me the girl? What would he do?'

Tell him to take a running jump. Mel willed the words out of Aiden's mouth, but they didn't come. 'You're full of shit, Carlos. You had your chance with Mel and you blew it. Besides, you'd no more deliberately throw a championship than I would. Now, if you've finished, I'm done.'

Mel heard footsteps coming towards the door and instinctively she turned and hurried back to the conference room. As their footsteps echoed down the stairwell she staggered onto one of the seats, hands trembling, her mind racing. Aiden hadn't answered Carlos's question. Of course it was a moot point – Carlos would never throw a race – but that didn't stop her desperately wishing Aiden had taken her ex by the scruff of the neck and told him he'd never give her up. Ever.

The swish of a door opening made her jerk her head round and there was Aiden, overalls undone to his waist, a white body vest hugging the hard lines of his chest.

'There you are. I've been looking all over for you.' He hunkered down beside her, looking concerned. 'Are you all right?'

'Yes.' It came out as a pathetic whisper so she tried again. 'Yes, I'm fine.'

She didn't look it, Aiden thought as he ran a hand across Mel's pale face. 'You look tired.'

'Me?' She captured his hand and held onto it. 'You're not looking too sprightly yourself.'

Because she was right, because he felt so mentally and physically drained he simply wanted to curl up in a ball and sleep, he slumped to the floor by her feet. 'I cocked up,' he admitted, forcing the words out. 'Frank told me to ease off to conserve fuel. Stressed that second was good enough.' He let out a short laugh, rubbing his free hand across his hot, sweaty face. 'I couldn't do it though. I wanted to beat that bastard so much I kept gunning for the overtake.'

Aiden could still see Carlos's face as he'd tried to wind him up for the second time in as many weeks. The jibe about his father had barely rattled him. The one about Mel had hit straight home. *I'll give you the championship. You give me the girl.* Hell, it wasn't as if Mel was his to give up. Aiden knew she was keeping a bit of herself back from him. Scared to commit, or not sure of her feelings? He wished he knew.

His own feelings weren't in doubt.

Talking to Carlos had made him realise he'd give up the championship tomorrow if it meant spending the rest of his life with Mel. A frightening admission from a guy who'd spent the last six years thinking about nothing else.

But was it greedy of him to want *both*?

'You can still beat him,' she told him, gently kissing his forehead.

'Yeah.' He raised himself higher so his mouth was more aligned with hers. He wanted a kiss that hit the spot. But as he zeroed in on her lips, her phone beeped and instead of focusing her attention on him, she was looking at her screen. 'What?' he asked, slightly irked.

Smiling, she showed him the phone. There was a text from Tom. *Have you cheered him up yet?*

A surprised laugh shot out of him. 'Does the him refer to me?'

'Of course. What shall I say?'

'Give it here.' He took the phone off her and started typing. *Not yet but I'll spend the rest of the evening trying, love Mel xx*

She rolled her eyes at what he'd written and tried to grab the phone back but Aiden quickly pressed send. 'You regularly text each other, huh?'

'Well, not regularly, but he has taken to texting when you're racing. I guess we watched a lot of your races together, so maybe he feels a connection.'

The knowledge that while he was out on the track the two people he loved most in the world were communicating caught at his heart. 'That's great,' he croaked.

'I really enjoy it. He's a lovely boy.' She smiled and bent to kiss him. 'Almost as lovely as his big brother.'

Her lips were soft and sweet but it didn't take long for Aiden to up the tempo to wild and hot. It was only when he jammed his elbow against the metal edge of the seat that he retained his senses enough to realise they were still in the press room. Reluctantly he shuffled to his feet, pulling her with him. 'Kissing you went a long way towards cheering me up, but if there's to be any further progress in that direction I'm going to need a hot shower and a big bed.' He stopped for a second to kiss her again. 'And you.'

Chapter Thirty-Three

In the penultimate race of the season Aiden did exactly what he needed to do. He came first. In a slice of karma that had him grinning in his cockpit when he'd heard it on the radio, Carlos hit pit trouble and only managed a meagre fourth place.

It meant the Constructors' Championship was now Delta's.

And the Drivers' Championship was still all to play for.

The statisticians had worked out all sorts of permutations that might give him the championship, but Aiden was only interested in one. If he won in Brazil, he'd win the title.

But Brazil was next week. Right now he was in a hotel suite, buttoning up his dress shirt, getting ready to smile for that very needy but also very important breed. The sponsors.

A muffled curse from his left had him shooting a glance in Mel's direction. She was on the phone and though he couldn't hear what was being said her face looked far from happy.

'Hey, what's up?'

'I'm stupid, that's what,' she snapped, throwing her phone onto the cushions. 'I work with the media all the flipping time, you'd think I'd have learnt how they work by now. One of the journalists from those damn gossip magazines has photos of us sharing what have been described as *intimate moments*.'

'I hope they took my good side.'

Her eyes flashed angrily. 'This isn't funny. I didn't mind the team knowing, but now everyone and his dog are going to know that we're ... that you and I are ...'

'Dating?' he supplied. 'But we are, aren't we? At least that's what I thought was going on.'

She gave a frustrated toss of her head. 'You don't get it, do you? Now I'm not just going to be asked for interviews about your racing, they're going to want to know our private life, too.'

He walked over and traced his thumb gently down her cheek. 'I know you wanted to keep us quiet but it was bound to come out sooner or later. And it's not as if you can't handle the press, is it? Besides, you must have had all this with the slippery Spaniard, surely?'

She didn't smile, just gave him a glum look that made him feel distinctly uneasy.

'I did have this with Carlos, yes, and it was awful but with you it'll be even worse. You're English, for heaven's sake. The tabloids here are renowned for prying into the lives of celebrities and you can't get much more celebrity than a millionaire racing driver who also happens to be the son of a national institution. God, they'll be all over us like a bad case of measles, hives and chickenpox all rolled into one.'

Fear pricked at the back of his neck. 'They'll only be interested for a short while. Then we'll be old news.'

'I don't want to be any sort of news.'

His heart stopped beating. 'What are you trying to tell me?' His hands flew to either side of her face, forcing her eyes upwards. 'Mel?'

'I'm not *trying* to tell you anything. I am telling you I don't want to be in the media spotlight. I work behind the scenes to help facilitate a story. I don't want to be the blasted story.'

Panic shot though him. 'What do you want me to say? I can't make any promises about this, you know that.'

She sighed, her warm breath tickling the open neck of his shirt. 'I know.'

He almost choked on his next words. 'Is this it, then? We're over?'

Her head jerked back. 'What?'

'Mel, are you telling me we're *finished*?'

Mel stared back at Aiden in shock. 'No, of course not, you ninny.'

Relief flooded his eyes and instantly his face relaxed. 'Well, thank God for that.' Shaking his head he began to laugh. 'Ninny? Seriously?'

'Okay then, of course not you nincompoop. I just wish ...' She let out a deep sigh. 'I just wish we didn't have the media on our back, that's all.'

She had been through all this with Carlos, and it had bloody hurt. The speculation over whether Carlos was seeing other women. The unflattering comparisons with previous lovers. A cold shiver ran through her.

'Are you cold?'

She shook her head, giving him a reassuring smile. It was time to start having more confidence in herself. Flipping heck, she was dating a wildly handsome racing driver. There had to be *something* attractive about her.

Aiden's hands slipped from her face and smoothed over the thin straps of her cocktail dress. 'Are you sure you're not cold? Because you could always put a jacket on over this. It would stop all those men ogling your breasts.'

She darted a look at her rather ample cleavage. 'Am I revealing too much?' Since going out with Aiden her wardrobe had spiced up considerably, but maybe this deep red number was a step too far.

'Too little.' Gently he pulled down both straps. 'Now that's better.'

As his mouth fastened greedily over one of her breasts, laughter spluttered out of her.

The moment they entered the room together, cameras flashed and microphones were thrust under their faces. Mel had half considered denying their relationship, but Aiden blew any chance of that by planting a seductive kiss on her neck. 'Here we go,' he whispered.

'How long have you two been an item?'

The forthright question threw her for a moment, even though she'd expected it. Immediately Aiden slipped an arm around her waist, drawing her even closer to his side. 'A while,' he replied evenly.

'Dating the press officer is a departure from your usual type, eh, Aiden?'

Coolly Aiden turned to the short twit of a man asking the question. 'If you're asking have I been out with a press officer before, then the answer is no, I haven't.' He turned to give Mel one of his poster boy smiles. 'Then again, no disrespect to any previous press officers, but I haven't had one as gorgeous as this one before, either.'

Mel started to smile but then the attention turned to her. 'You dated Carlos Ferrer a few years ago, I believe?'

She prided herself on being able to handle the media effortlessly, almost without drawing breath, but all she could manage was an indistinct 'yes.'

'How does it feel to have your former lover and current lover both in contention for the championship?'

Dear God, now they were making her sound like a racing groupie. 'I wish them both well.' She was too stiff and formal, the exact opposite of how she advised people to answer the media. 'Naturally I hope Aiden will win.'

'What about you, Aiden? Does it feel as if you're fighting Carlos for the title and the girl?'

Mel drew in a breath, ready to tell the dumb ass that these two men had far more important things on their mind than her, but Aiden was already answering.

'I'm fighting Carlos for the title,' he said mildly. 'Mel is not up for grabs. Now, if you'll excuse us.' Politely, gracefully, Aiden steered them away from the huddle and towards the bar where he took one look at her face and ordered a large wine. 'Here.' He nudged her, pushing the glass into her hands. 'You look like you need it.'

She clutched gratefully at it and took an inelegant slug. 'That was horrid.'

He quirked a brow. 'I thought you liked Sauvignon.'

'Very funny. If that's your attempt to try and improve my mood, you've got a way to go yet. Being at the wrong end of a group of journalists is very close to terrifying.'

'Yet it's a torture that you, my dear Mel, set me up for on a daily basis.'

The irony wasn't lost on her. 'Maybe I'll be a little more sympathetic to your gripes in the future.'

He reached up to wrap a lock of her hair around his fingers, tugging gently. 'Are you okay?'

His obvious concern moved her. 'I'm good, thank you.' Taking another sip of wine, she grew more bold. 'What did you mean by *Mel isn't up for grabs*?'

'Exactly that. Carlos can keep his slimy mitts off you.' He flashed her an intense grey look. 'You're already taken.'

The possessive tone of his voice sent the air rushing from her lungs. She reached across to touch his cheek, ready to tell him he was right. She was his for as long as he wanted her, but their moment alone was interrupted by three attractive, half naked, very giggly women.

One draped her arms around Aiden. 'We've come to drag you away,' she said in a sing-songy little girl voice. 'Time to pose for the photographs.'

With an exaggerated sigh Aiden slipped off the bar stool. 'It's a tough job,' he drawled, putting an arm around two of them. 'But I guess someone's got to do it.' Blowing Mel a kiss, he allowed himself to be pulled away.

That just about summed up their relationship, Mel muttered to herself as she knocked back some more wine. One minute she had the man's undivided attention, the next he was lured away by dazzling models and she was left ... alone.

She watched as he laughed and posed with the trio of beauties, but he didn't once glance back. Did he laugh like that with her? A shiver of panic worked up her spine but she forced it away. Of course he did. In fact he laughed a lot when they were together.

Still, the unease remained. Only once before had she felt this insecure. Not long afterwards, Carlos had casually ditched her for a more elegant model.

'Hey, why are you looking so miserable?'

'I'm not,' Mel protested, but Sally followed her line of sight and swore.

'Come on. Give the guy a break. I know he looks like he's enjoying himself, but actually he's working.'

'I know.' And she did. She also knew the Aiden smiling at the cameras wasn't the real Aiden. So why didn't it help?

Sally squeezed her hand. 'Don't you trust him?'

'Yes. No.' Mel huffed out a breath and tried to straighten out her thoughts. 'I trust him not to have an affair behind my back. He's too honest. But do I trust his feelings for me? Do I think I'm really it for him? No, I don't.'

'So what you're really saying is it's yourself you don't have faith in.'

'Come again?'

'You don't believe you're attractive enough, smart enough, captivating enough to make him fall in love with you.'

Mel raised her eyebrows. 'Wow, you're blunt.'

Sally merely shrugged. 'Tell me I'm wrong then.'

'I want to,' she admitted quietly. 'So much. I want to be the confident woman Aiden deserves, not the wallflower you've just described. But I can't tell you you're wrong. I just can't.'

Obviously sensing Mel was on the verge of tears, Sally threw an arm around her shoulder. 'Oh, Mel. What can I say to convince you that you've got all of those attributes, and more? Aiden's well and truly hooked.'

As if on cue, Aiden turned his head, sought her out and winked.

Immediately Mel felt Sally's elbow in her ribs. 'There you go. He's surrounded by lush, though it has to be said probably brainless, women, yet his eyes are searching for you.'

But for how long? Mel kept the words to herself. Sally, secure in herself, happily married to a man she went to school with, couldn't possibly understand her feeling of inadequacy.

Then again, as Aiden strode purposefully towards her, his startlingly handsome face fixed firmly on hers, sometimes neither did Mel.

Chapter Thirty-Four

It was the final race of the season. The Brazilian Interlagos circuit in Sao Paulo. A bumpy anti-clockwise track that didn't rate in anyone's top ten favourite, unless of course you were Brazilian. What the circuit lacked on the track though, it made up for in the carnival like atmosphere that surrounded it. Between the beating drums, frenetic whistling and exuberant dancing, it was sometimes hard to concentrate on the race itself.

And that was without all the stuff that had been going through Aiden's head these last few days.

He was in love with Mel. It was as simple and as unbelievably complex as that. Simple because he had no doubts whatsoever that he'd met his soul mate. The one woman capable of seeing through the crap that went with being Aiden Foster, into the man he was beneath. And liked him anyway. It didn't hurt that she was warm, clever, funny and unbelievably sexy. Or that she didn't have a clue what she did to a man.

The complexity came when he started to consider her feelings. She'd freaked out when the press had found out about them and though she hadn't referred to it since, he thought she was still freaking out. Did she like him enough to put up with all the baggage he came with? Bugger like, did she *love* him?

'Where's your head, son, because it sure as hell isn't where it should be?'

Aiden's aforementioned head shot up with a guilty start at Frank's words. He was in the team room, surrounded by men doing their utmost to work out the best way to secure him a victory in Sunday's race. At least they would be doing if their driver was paying attention. 'Sorry.'

'Are we going with grip or speed?'

'How about both for a change?' His lame joke was met with a bank of stony faces. Rightly so. This win wasn't just important to him. Scores of people who worked tirelessly behind the scenes were relying on him to bring the title home for the team. Winning the Constructors' Championship ensured them sponsorship but it was winning the Drivers' Championship that brought the glory.

'Let's go with speed,' he decided. It would make the thing bloody difficult to drive, but Sunday wasn't about gaining points. It was about winning the race.

At the end of the meeting Aiden made to get up but one glance at Frank's expression told him he wasn't finished with him. Heaving in a sigh he sat back down; the kid being made to stay behind after class.

'I'm sorry,' Aiden began when the others had filed out, but Frank waved his apology away.

'I'm a fan of this new, relaxed version of Aiden Foster. He's a far better driver. Just be careful you don't take it too far. Whatever else is on your mind, this weekend it needs to be shoved to one side. If we're going to win this damn race, we need some of the old Aiden back. The grit, determination and unwavering focus.'

'I know.' He'd started wanting no distractions, just a championship title. A brother and Mel later, he was on distraction overload but incredibly he was also only one race away from proving to the world he had what it took to be a champion. Just like his dad. 'You'll get him back,' he promised Frank.

He only hoped Mel would understand.

*　*　*

She stood in his suite, her eyes like those of a puppy who'd just been pushed out in the cold. 'You want me to stay in my own hotel room?'

'No,' he almost shouted, gritting his teeth against his frustration. 'Of course I don't *want* you to, but Frank thinks I'm not focused and I can't disagree with him.' He snatched at her arm when she moved to turn away. 'Just for the next two nights, Mel. That's all. Please. I need to get my head out of you for a few days and back into racing.' He laid a finger against her sweet lips. 'You're way too much of a distraction.'

'Okay. That's fine.' Her body language, as she moved to pick up the case she'd only just deposited, totally contradicted her statement.

'Is it really fine?'

'Of course. It'll be good to have a bed to myself for a few days. I might even get to see the duvet.'

Deliberately he took the case out of her hand and dropped it back on the floor. Then he took her in his arms, needing to feel her. Needing to know they were still okay. 'Don't get too used to it.' He eased back a smidgen so he could see her face. 'On Sunday night I want you back where you belong. With me.'

Mel remained quiet but the arms around his waist tightened and he had to assume she was hating this as much as he was.

'Hey, I nearly forgot, there is some good news. Tom's flying in Saturday morning. Of course the bad news is Mum's with him.'

She eyed him through her fringe. 'Surely that's good news. Even your Mum didn't feel she could put him on a long-haul flight to Brazil by himself.'

'Yeah, I guess there's that.'

'Or have you considered that maybe, just maybe, she wanted to see you win the Championship.'

He exhaled a half laugh. 'This is my mother we're talking about. Let's not get carried away.'

Carefully she extracted herself from his arms. 'Well, I'd better go and find my room. It's a good job these bookings are made months in advance or I'd be sleeping in the corridor.'

He cringed, feeling like a total bastard. 'It's just until Sunday, Mel. That's all.'

She gave him a slight smile and slipped out of the door.

As it banged shut he let out a strangled cry and thumped the back of the sofa. Goddamnit, why was nothing in life ever simple? He knew Mel wasn't fine about this, that she saw it as a rejection and every instinct in his body – and hell, yes, his heart, too – warned him to run after her and drag her back to his room.

But Frank's words ran through his brain like a grim warning. He wasn't going to win unless some of the blinkered, focused Aiden came back. For the next two days he had to shove himself into a racing cocoon and not burst out until he'd taken the chequered flag.

First, though, he had one important thing to do.

Mel hung her things in the wardrobe, stared for a moment at the pristine looking double bed, then flung herself onto it and burst into tears.

This was one of the most important times in Aiden's life, certainly the most important in his professional life, and yet he didn't want her near him. What message did that send her? She understood his need to focus on the job ahead but why did that automatically mean she had to be excluded? She didn't want to be a flipping distraction. She wanted to be his life and soul. The one person he couldn't do without.

She allowed herself a few more minutes of self-pity then sat up and wiped her eyes. Feeling sorry for herself served no purpose and anyway, she had a job to do.

She spent the next few hours down at the track. Between emails, phone calls and reviewing a magazine article the time sped by. It was with a jolt of surprise she realised she was due to see Aiden in an hour to go over the two appointments she'd scheduled for him after practice tomorrow. Maybe she couldn't sleep with him, but at least she could look forward to seeing him. It wasn't like they'd split up.

The time came and went though, and there was no sign of Aiden. Worry wormed its way into her stomach as she dug out her phone and called him.

'Aiden? Where are you?' The line was pretty poor and there seemed to be a lot of noise at his end so she raised her voice. 'We had a meeting booked to go through tomorrow's interviews.'

His voice was really unclear and the only words she heard for certain were *sorry* and *can't make it*. 'Well, if you want any background on them you know where to find me.'

She heard the sound of a honking horn and a man's voice speaking in fast Brazilian Portuguese. Then the line went dead. Wherever Aiden had disappeared to, she'd clearly slipped his mind.

Staring down at her phone she couldn't shake off a sense of impending inevitably. It seemed that all the despondent, negative thoughts she'd tried to push away were slowly coming true.

The next two days passed in a blur of frantic activity and

Mel hardly saw her sometime lover. She saw a fair bit of the racing driver, but other than fleeting conversations over press release quotes he spent the majority of his time either on the track, or in a huddle with the backroom team. Occasionally he'd glance her way and wave, or smile, but the distance he'd been determined to put between them was turning into a gulf.

'Have you and my brother had a bust up?' Tom asked over lunch in the cafeteria. Not an unreasonable question as Aiden was sat on the opposite side of the room to them, talking to Frank and Hugh, the team principal.

'Just because I'm not having lunch with him it doesn't mean to say we've split up. He's working.'

'He was working all those other times too, but you used to hang around, giggle, flutter your eyelashes. That kind of weird stuff.'

For the first time in days, Mel laughed. 'I'm saving it all for after the race on Sunday.'

Tom chewed on his sandwich for a moment. 'Is he going to win?'

'Now how on earth am I meant to know that? First he's got to get a good place on the grid this afternoon. Then,' she gave Tom's anxious looking face a gentle pat. 'Well, then I guess he needs us all to help cheer him home.' Her stomach cramped and she shoved aside her half eaten lunch, suddenly unable to face it. Maybe it was no wonder Aiden had withdrawn from her. Nerves were starting to affect them all, so what on earth must he be feeling?

The mood in the team wasn't helped when Aiden only managed third place on the grid in qualifying. A very ebullient Carlos was on pole and after the press conferences he made a point of seeking her out in the paddock, greeting her with a flirty kiss on the cheek.

Annoyed, she pulled away sharply. 'I know your game. You're just trying to wind Aiden up.'

'How can you say that, *mi encantadora*?'

'Because you've taken more notice of me since I started dating Aiden than you ever did during the months we were dating. What is it, poking him about his father didn't have the desired effect so now you're changing tactics?'

Carlos smiled, but his dark Spanish eyes weren't looking at her. They were fixed over her shoulder. Mel shifted round to see what was grabbing his attention and her heart sank. 'Well, it looks like you've achieved your aim,' she told him coldly.

From across the paddock the ferocity of Aiden's gaze seared right through her. Then he started stalking towards them, his half unzipped overalls flapping round his thighs, his face like a dark, heavy sky just before a storm.

'Time for a Ferrer special, I think,' Carlos whispered, chuckling when she frowned at him. 'A fast get away.'

'What did he want?' Aiden demanded, his hands clenched into fists.

'What do you think he wanted? To annoy you.'

'Well, he bloody succeeded. Sniffing round you like a dog in heat.'

'Does that make me a bitch then?'

He exhaled loudly, acknowledging her rebuke with a wry smile. 'No, sorry.'

It hurt to look at his tired, miserable looking face. He must be absolutely gutted that the man who stood between him and the title had just pinched pole on the grid. 'Ignore Carlos. He has no interest in me. All he wants is to beat you tomorrow.' She touched his arm, giving it a light squeeze. 'Please don't let him.'

'I've got no intention of letting him get anywhere near what's mine.'

She smiled at his grimly determined tone. 'The title's yours already, huh?'

'That's not what I meant.'

'Oh, Aiden.' Uncaring of his stupid rule about keeping out of his way, Mel threw her arms around him. 'I miss you.'

He wound his arms around her shoulders, ducked his head and kissed her, right there in the middle of the paddock, a place that swarmed with interested media. Uncaring she melted against him, pulling him further towards her, wishing she could crawl inside him and forget everything but him and her.

'Christ,' he muttered as he finally let her go, though he kept hold of her hands. 'I want to haul you back to my room so badly it hurts.'

'But you can't.' Though her body groaned with unfulfilled desire she forced herself to step back. 'If you give in now and lose tomorrow, you'll always wonder.'

Hungry eyes searched her face. 'Right now it feels worth it.' She gave a small shake of her head and he let go of her hands with a sad smile. 'Until tomorrow then.'

Aiden watched as Mel walked away, her curvy figure on show in the neat skirt she now wore in place of those unflattering trousers. He'd nearly blown a gasket when he'd seen Carlos with her. There was no way that man wasn't interested in her. It niggled that Carlos had been the one to break the relationship up, not Mel. Would she be tempted again, if the Spaniard asked?

He let out a frustrated breath. Why did being in love make him so damn unsure of everything? Wasn't it meant to be happy and joyous? Not leave him in a state of permanent emotional upheaval.

Feeling older than his years, Aiden trudged wearily back to the Delta motorhome. He had enough on his plate figuring out how to get from third to first in seventy-one laps tomorrow. Time to stop thinking about anything else.

The rest of the day was spent huddled in tense team meetings. The evening, and long into the night, he spent lying on his bed, staring at the ceiling, wishing for dawn to come. This was his moment, and he wasn't going to let a slippery Spanish lothario cock it up for him. Not the race.

And definitely not the girl.

The following afternoon, forty laps into the race of his life, Aiden felt good. Carlos was still ahead of him but Aiden had fought his way up to second place and his rival was still very much there to be beaten. Frank continually drip fed him information through his ear piece but Aiden was only half listening. He was in the zone, feeling the response of the car through his hands and the seat of his pants. The tension that had been building over the last few days and the nervous energy from the morning had vanished the moment he'd stepped into the car.

He was enjoying himself.

He wasn't thinking about living up to the legacy of his father or even winning the damn championship. His entire being was focused on one thing. Overtaking the man in front of him.

'Box this lap,' Frank's voice came into his ear, telling him to pit. Damn. He didn't want to go in, not feeling as he did. Clearly sensing the way Aiden's thoughts were going, Frank repeated his words. 'Box this lap.'

Reluctantly Aiden diverted into the pits. Following a quick, clean stop he was soon making his way back onto the track. 'We're now on strategy B,' Frank stated.

Aiden understood. They didn't believe Carlos was going to pit again. Aiden might have slipped further behind but now he was going to race the leader with fresh tyres. They'd calculated it would give him the edge when it came down to the final laps. He could only pray they were right.

Lap after lap whizzed by but after each one Aiden inched closer and closer to his target.

'Push, Aiden. Clean air in front. Go.'

It was the stuff of dreams. Driving his car on a knife-edge through the corners, knowing he had the speed in his tyres to take his rival down. On the penultimate lap he finally caught Carlos up and now he was right behind him, heart thumping wildly, hands steady on the wheel. His mind crystal clear.

The moment Carlos twitched, gave him the sniff of an opening, he'd have him.

And then it wasn't just a possibility, it was really happening. Carlos went wide, showing Aiden too much of the next corner. Heart in his mouth he chucked the car up the inside, breaking deep into the corner and coming out ahead.

But shit, he'd gone in too fast and now he was drifting wide and Carlos was looking to sneak up his inside.

Aiden put his foot to the floor and surged forward. Carlos, on older tyres, didn't have the grip and Aiden flew down the straight.

Bloody hell. He was going to win.

Down in the pit garage Mel held her breath, half crying, half laughing, as Aiden took the chequered flag. She was clutching Tom so fiercely she feared she might snap him, though if the beam on his face was anything to go by he didn't give two hoots about being squeezed.

'My brother won.' His voice was so excited he could barely speak. 'He's a champion.'

Mel could only nod, her throat so jammed full of emotion that even if she could find the words, she couldn't speak them.

She caught Caroline's look and even her eyes seemed to glisten. 'Well, that was rather tense.'

Mel choked out a laugh. 'An understatement if ever I heard one.'

'Nah, I knew he'd get past Carlos,' Tom announced, full of confidence now the race was over.

'Sure you did.' Mel grinned at him, knowing full well he'd been as anxious – no, terrified – as the rest of them that Aiden had run out of laps.

'Can we go and see him?' he asked, jumping up and down as more and more of the mechanics and engineers piled into the garage, cheering and slapping each other on the back.

Mel looked at Caroline, who stunned her by smiling broadly. 'Absolutely. Let's cheer him out of the car.'

Pushing past the assembled pit crew they rushed out to parc ferme just in time to see Aiden's gleaming red and silver car come to a stop in the prized number one slot.

Tears streaming down her face, her heart feeling far too large for her chest, Mel watched Aiden climb out of the cockpit and punch the air, his handsome face beaming with elation.

He'd finally proved to the world, and himself, what he was capable of and she couldn't feel happier for him.

Chapter Thirty-Five

There was one problem being a press officer for a winning driver who was also your lover. There was barely a chance to get close enough to yell congratulations, never mind anything more. Especially when he hadn't just won a race, but the championship.

While Mel was busy preparing press releases the race organisers were pushing Aiden here and there as if he was a doll they could do with as they wanted. Not that Aiden looked like he minded, she thought, glancing at the TV monitor in the garage. Happiness seemed to surge off him in waves. He was a man in his element, feeding off the adulation, his handsome face split by grin after grin.

A while later a loud eruption of cheers and claps heralded Aiden's arrival into the garage. Mel just about caught sight of him as he was mobbed by the pit crew. Tom was there too, proudly clinging to his brother's arm, smiling like a kid who'd been told it was going to be Christmas every day.

'He looks to be having the time of his life,' Caroline remarked as she watched her eldest son receive a series of hearty back slaps.

Mel gave her a sideways glance. 'It's something he's always dreamed of achieving. Why wouldn't he look pleased?'

'And you, Mel? Are you pleased for him?'

What a question. 'Of course I am.'

Caroline gave her a small, knowing smile. 'You do realise that from now until he retires his life is going to be pretty much always like this. Constant demands on his attention, most of which he'll be only too happy to give in to because racing is his life, just like it was for his father.'

'I'm perfectly aware of that.'

Caroline nodded, her eyes still trained on Aiden. 'I hadn't realised how alike they were, until now. Both with that absolute determination to succeed. The ability to focus on exactly what they want and sod anything else that gets in their way.'

'You make that sound like a bad thing.'

'For them no, but for the people who love them?' Her smile took on a bitter edge. 'Trust me, this life isn't only tough on a racing driver. It's tough on their partner, too.'

Mel wanted to tell her Aiden wasn't as callous as that, but after the last few days she wasn't sure she could.

As if sensing her confusion, Caroline patted her arm. 'I know you don't like me very much. That you think I abandoned my children and you're right, I did. But you don't have any idea yet how hard it is to maintain a relationship with a racing driver.'

'Aiden isn't the only driver I've dated,' she countered defensively.

'No, there was Carlos, wasn't there? And I don't think you need me to remind you what happened there. When you weren't with him, he found others who could be, didn't he?' Mel stiffened and tried to move away but Caroline's hand tightened on her arm. 'I'm not saying this to be cruel, Mel, but take my word for it, these drivers can't be tied down. Their first love will always be racing. Depending on where they are in the season, you'll come either a short or long way after that.' She let out a long, sad sigh. 'And you can kiss the relationship goodbye if you don't follow them round. You think I left Aiden with nannies and boarding school because I wanted to? No. But I was besotted with

Seb and trailing him round the globe was the only way I knew to cling onto him. Not that it did me much good. He managed to find his bits of totty anyway.'

Mel was surprised to see tears in Caroline's eyes. 'I'm sorry.'

'Not as sorry as I was.' Reaching into her handbag Caroline drew out a tissue and dabbed daintily at her eyes. 'I never recovered from losing him, you know. I know Aiden despises me for the way I continue to chase after men but Seb's death left such a huge hole in my life. I can't seem to stop trying to find something, someone to fill it. For a while I thought I'd found something with this latest, Bradley. It seems I was wrong. I'm resigned now to knowing nothing will ever come close to what I had with Seb.'

Mel's heart shuddered in sympathy. 'Why are you telling me this?'

'Because I wish someone had been kind enough to have this conversation with me, before I fell foolishly head over heels for Seb. Of course it's not necessarily the case of like father like son, but still. Don't say I didn't warn you.' She patted Mel's arm again. 'Now where do I find some champagne?'

The champagne was still flowing several hours later as the Delta crew and various invited sponsors partied in a private room in the hotel. Aiden still hadn't managed to really talk to her. The only connection they'd had since she'd kissed him after the race was a hasty congratulations at the press conference before he'd been pulled away to speak to someone clearly more important.

Biting on her cheek, Mel tried to shrug off her bad temper. She wasn't being fair. Many times he'd caught her eye and smiled, his eyes letting her know she wasn't forgotten.

'I suspect it's not easy being on the sidelines watching your man being monopolised.' Nancy drew alongside her and gave her a warm, understanding smile.

'He's hardly my man.'

'Why do you say that? I've seen how his eyes keep returning to you.'

'Yes, sorry. I'm just feeling a bit ...' abandoned, insecure? It all sounded so needy, so feeble. 'Frustrated,' she settled with.

'I can imagine.' She eyed her sympathetically. 'Delta are certainly milking their World Championship win, aren't they, though it's hard to blame them.'

'Especially as I'm the one responsible for some of it,' Mel agreed with a wry smile.

'It won't always be like this, you know.' She gave her a hug, enveloping her in kindness and compassion. 'Just hang on in there, my dear.'

Mel nodded but as Nancy moved away to find her husband, laughing with him as they linked arms, Mel's heart once again felt heavy. If only she hadn't felt so pushed away before today. If only she could stop feeling as if her relationship with Aiden was unravelling before her eyes and she was helpless to do anything but watch it happen.

'Champagne tastes like piss.' Tom pulled a face as he came to stand next to her.

'And you'd know that because?'

'Aiden let me have a swig from a bottle.'

'Okay, that's how you know what champagne tastes like. And the pee? When did you try that?'

'Duh. I haven't. I was just, you know.' He shrugged and glanced down at his feet.

'You were trying to be funny,' she supplied, feeling the squeeze of her heart at his endearing awkwardness. 'Emphasis on the word trying.'

'Hey, why are you all sarky? Haven't you given Aiden a big sloppy kiss yet? You know, when you get married you'll have to do that all the time.'

'Married?' she shrieked, so loud the man behind them gave her a startled glance. Mel held Tom's hand and pushed him to the edge of the room. 'Nobody said anything about marriage,' she muttered, darting furtive glances around her.

'But I thought ...'

'No. We're just dating, that's all. It doesn't automatically lead to marriage.'

'Don't you want to marry him then?'

Oh God, help her out of this mess. Distraction was the only answer. 'Tom, do me a favour and go and get me another glass of that piss, will you?'

Thankfully he had the attention span of a typical ten-year-old boy. Forgetting all about his unanswered question, he strutted off self-importantly to find another glass.

Mel felt as if her head was going to explode. First Aiden's distance, then Caroline's warning. Now she had Tom thinking they were getting married? Since when had this little fling become so complicated?

Of course the answer to that was easy. It had never been a little fling, at least not to her. How can you have a fling with a man you're in love with?

Her heart faltered and she gripped at the edge of the table. Oh God, what was she going to do? She didn't think she was strong enough to end it, but if she didn't, would she end up like Caroline? Forever in the shadows, chasing after a man who would never truly be hers?

Across the room Aiden caught her eye and gave her that rare, dazzling smile that was so much more than the flash he gave to the cameras. It carried desire, warmth, intimacy. She tried to smile back, but somehow her lips wouldn't work.

In an instant his face fell. Without even a glance at the people he was talking to, Aiden broke away from the group and started walking towards her.

Her heart thumped against her ribs and panic began to bubble up inside her. She couldn't deal with him now, not with her brain so frazzled. God knows what she'd come out with and one thing was certain. She did *not* want to ruin this moment for him.

Blindly she turned away and headed towards the ladies. Maybe there she could get her head together. But as she swerved round a table, her heels skidded on the floor and before she knew it she was lying in an undignified heap on the floor.

'Mel, are you okay?' Aiden's hands reached out to her, helping her up.

'I'm fine,' she muttered, mortified less about the fall and more about the fact that she hadn't escaped. 'Don't you dare say anything about women falling at your feet.'

Amused grey eyes twinkled back at her. 'You just stole my line.'

He was holding her hand with his elegant fingers, the warmth shooting shivers of awareness up her arm. She felt the desperate clutch of her heart and wondered again why she couldn't just be happy with what she had. Why she had to keep worrying about the future. But she'd lost people before, and it bloody hurt. Carlos's betrayal had taken years to get over and she'd never really loved him. The loss of her parents she was still coming to terms with, twelve years later.

'You need to let me go,' she whispered, looking down at their entwined hands.

His fingers tightened on hers. 'What do you mean? Look, if this is about today, I'm sorry I've not had a proper chance to catch up with you. It's been crazy, but I'll make it up to you. Later. In our room.'

She forced a smile, because tonight wasn't the time for a heavy discussion. 'I don't recall *us* having a room and anyway, there's nothing for you to make up. I'm fine, really, just a bit of a headache. Go and enjoy yourself.' Her hand trembled slightly as she traced the strong lines of his face. 'You're a champion, Aiden. I'm so proud of you. You deserve all this.' She waved towards the posters and banners proudly declaring his victory, the laughing crowds in Delta shirts and the gleaming trophy in pride of place in the centre of the room. 'You've worked so hard for it. I'm going back to my room now, but come and find me when you're ready.'

He looked unsure what to do, whether to believe her or not, but then someone called his name and a few scantily dressed women pulled him away. 'I'll see you later,' he mouthed before he disappeared into the crowd.

Mel walked slowly back to her room, her heart a lead weight in her chest. She really wasn't sure if she could do this any more. It was like trying to enjoy a book when you'd already seen the ending, and it wasn't a happy ever after.

The hours slipped by and Mel dozed in and out of sleep. When the clock by her bed read five a.m. and she was still on her own, she'd had enough. Maybe he was still partying. Or maybe he'd found his way to another room, and another woman.

No.

She sprung off the bed and started to throw on her clothes. Aiden might be a playboy, but she was pretty certain he cared enough to finish with her before he moved on. The thought had still crossed her mind though, reaffirming how unsure she was of their relationship. Hardly surprising when he hadn't even bothered to come and find her last night, even though he knew she'd been waiting for him.

Within half an hour she'd packed her bag and checked out. Within an hour she was at the airport, buying a ticket to Marseille. If she hadn't felt so utterly miserable, her predicament might be laughable. In the blink of an eye she'd gone from ecstatic, wildly cheering lover of World Champion racing driver Aiden Foster to … what?

Lonely thirty-something woman, crying her heart out on a plastic chair in a soulless airport lounge, on the way to see her grandparents.

Oh God, what was she doing?

Aiden was in pain. As he slowly lifted his cramped body from where it was lying, he rubbed at his eyes. Hell, his head hurt. It was as if an army of builders with pneumatic drills were digging away in his brain.

'And he finally rises from the dead.'

He snapped his head round to where the voice was coming from, and immediately regretted it when the room began to spin and the pounding in his head multiplied. 'Frank?'

'Sorry to disappoint, but yes.'

Aiden massaged his head, trying to remember what had happened last night. After winning the championship, that is. He hadn't forgotten that part. 'What am I doing with you? I should be with Mel.' With a loud curse he noticed the time on his watch – eight o'clock. 'Shit. Does she know where I am? I promised to go to her last night.'

'And I was supposed to know that how, exactly?' Frank shook his head. 'Better get yourself together and go and find her.'

Aiden struggled up from the couch, every part of him – from the thump of his head to the yelp from his cramped muscles – screaming out in pain. 'How did I end up here?'

Frank smiled sympathetically. 'A combination of dehydration, too much alcohol and raging exhaustion. I found you collapsed in the men's room, fast asleep, so I dragged your sorry ass up here. Nancy and I figured it was slightly more fitting for the World Champion to spend the night on our sofa than the floor of the gents.'

Aiden managed a weak smile, glancing over to the bed where Nancy was obviously still fast asleep. Like he wished he was. Only this time in Mel's arms and having downed a handful of painkillers, first. Why had he drunk so much? It wasn't as if he'd even enjoyed the evening, not after Mel had left, anyway. He could vividly remember the look on her face when she'd told him she had to go, as if her heart was breaking. Of course Mel being Mel, she'd then plastered on a smile for his benefit and told him to go and enjoy himself. She'd wait for him. Oh God, he had to go and find her.

After thanking Frank for his babysitting duties, Aiden hauled his body along the corridor to Mel's room, but there was no answer to his knock. Yanking out his phone, he dialled her number.

'Aiden?'

'Where the heck are you?'

He heard something that sounded like a sniff. 'The airport. I'm going away for a few days.'

'Jesus, Mel, why?' When she didn't immediately reply, he filled in for her. 'It's because I didn't make it back to yours last night, isn't it? I'm so damn sorry. I've just woken to find myself on Frank's couch. Turns out he found me crashed out in the gents and took me back to his room.'

There was more silence at the other end before finally he

heard her voice. 'It's not just that, no.' That noise again, more like a stifled sob this time. 'Please, Aiden, I've got to go.'

'No, don't you dare leave me. Wait there. I'm coming to get you.'

'My flight's about to leave. I'll see you when I get back. I can work remotely and Sally's going to cover any PR issues I can't handle—'

'As if I give a fuck about that right now.'

Another pause. More quiet sobs. 'Okay. Well, I'd better go. Don't worry about me.'

'*Don't worry?*' His voice sounded like he did. Completely unravelled. 'You're sitting alone in an airport, crying your damn eyes out and you tell me not to worry?' He exhaled a curse. 'Where are you going?'

'France, to see my grandparents. It's been a while since I've been and … well, I just needed to see them. I'm so sorry to leave you like this. Please forgive me.'

The dial tone rang loudly in his ears, bluntly letting him know she'd ended the call. The woman he loved was running away from him.

He staggered blindly back to his hotel room, trying to make sense of what the hell was happening. How had he gone from being on top of the world yesterday, to this feeling of utter desolation this morning?

In a daze he showered and put on some clean clothes. He also rang room service for some painkillers. When there was a knock on the door only two minutes later, he almost cried with relief.

Until he found his mother standing outside.

'How are you this morning?'

'My girlfriend's done a runner, my whole body aches and I've got the biggest humdinger of a hangover ever. Apart from that, I'm great, thanks.'

'Mel's *left* you?'

'Yep. I didn't make it back to her room last night, largely because I passed out, but apparently that's not the reason she's left. In which case I'm blowed if I know what the hell it is I'm supposed to have done.' He noticed her swallow and suddenly her eyes had difficulty holding his. 'What is it?' He grabbed her shoulders, pulling her inside. 'Do you know something I don't?'

She reached out to remove his hands and then coughed delicately. 'I think I might know what's wrong, yes.'

'What then?'

'This will take a while, so why don't we discuss it in my room? I've left Frank looking after Tom while Nancy's getting ready but I think they're rather anxious to go home.'

'Okay.' Grabbing his wallet he all but frogmarched his mother back to her room.

'Did you find her?' Frank asked as soon as he pushed the door open.

'Yes and no. She wasn't in her room, but when I tried her phone I did manage to speak to her for a few minutes before she had to get on her flight.'

'Her *what*?'

'She needed to see her grandparents, apparently.'

He must have looked as wrecked as he felt because instead of chewing his ear off about not hurting Mel, Frank gave his shoulders a sympathetic squeeze. 'I'm sorry. It will all sort itself out. I see you guys have things to talk about so I'll be on my way. See you around, champion.' With that he slapped him lightly on the back and made his way out.

'Hey, what's with all the long faces?' Tom piped up, glancing from him to his mother. 'Didn't you win some big trophy yesterday? Shouldn't you still be smiling?'

The emotion Aiden had been trying to hold back for the

last half an hour threatened to make a break for it and he almost choked on his next words. 'I don't feel much like smiling any more.'

Tom stared wide-eyed at him. 'Why?'

'Did you know Mel left?'

'Left? What you mean left, or left, left?'

'Left, left.'

Tom's face fell and his whole body seemed to slump. 'Oh crap, so *that's* who you were talking about just now. Where'd you say she went?'

'I don't know. Somewhere in France.'

'Did you have a fight?'

'No, we bloody didn't. I don't know why she's gone off.' Slowly he turned to his mother. 'But I'm hoping she does.'

Though his mother flinched at his accusatory tone, she held his gaze. 'I think I might have inadvertently scared her off.'

Aiden struggled to rein in his temper. 'What the blazes did you say to her?' he ground out.

She walked slowly over to the small armchair and sat down, taking so long over crossing her legs Aiden wanted to shake her. 'I know you hate me,' she said finally. 'And I deserve a lot of that hatred. I let you down as a child.' Her eyes flickered to Tom. 'Both of you. I was far too obsessed with trying to keep my husband, and later to find another one, than bringing either of you up. But you have no idea how hard it is to love a man in the spotlight. A glamorous man who has women throwing themselves at him, maneuvering in on him the moment he's alone. It can make a wife or lover so insecure.' She wrung her hands with quick, jerky movements. 'I know it's no excuse, but that's how I felt. It was why I always put your father first, Aiden.'

When she raised her eyes the sadness and remorse he

saw actually tugged at his heart a little. 'Seb was and will always be, my greatest love. I gave up everything to keep him, including the bond with my son. But in the end none of it worked. He still had his affairs, sometimes flaunting them in my face.'

She seemed to age before his eyes, anguish making her features sharper, harder. No longer the distant, coldly attractive woman who'd barely acknowledged him. All he saw now was a sad, middle-aged woman with a whole heap of regrets.

Slowly, oh so slowly, the years of hatred he'd felt towards her began to slip away. He wasn't sure they could ever be close but at least now he understood her a little. 'Is that what you told Mel?'

'Yes.' She gave him a wistful smile. 'I know you won't believe this, but I didn't mean to do any harm. I just didn't want her going into a relationship with you with her eyes shut.'

Aiden sank onto the sofa and raised his eyes to the ceiling, hoping he'd find some answers. Knowing he wouldn't. He was too exhausted to think straight, too hurt to feel any compassion for the woman staring sorrowfully at him now. 'Well you certainly opened her eyes. And it looks like she didn't like what she saw.'

'I'm sorry.'

'Yeah, so am I.' But what good was that going to do? 'I appreciate you telling me this, but can you leave now? I need to be alone.'

She rose and walked towards the door. He followed, aware of Tom watching them with round, solemn eyes.

'Do you want to travel back home with me,' Aiden asked him, 'or with your mother?'

'With you.'

Relieved, Aiden nodded. At least having the little guy around would take his mind off this aching loneliness.

On reaching the door, his mother sighed. 'Right then. I guess I'll say goodbye.' Tentatively she reached out an arm, about to … hug him? Kiss him? He was damned if he could remember a time she'd done either. As if realising, she took a sudden step back. 'I'm sorry I didn't see you race when you were younger, Aiden. I really enjoyed yesterday.' Her eyes looked directly into his. 'Is it allowed for me to say I'm very proud of you?'

Aiden dragged himself out of his misery for long enough to recognise that she was making a real effort. 'Thank you.'

When she'd left he stared blindly at the closed door. It had been a weekend of almost unthinkable outcomes. He'd won a World Championship, yet managed to lose the woman he loved. Given the choice, he'd reverse the order in a heartbeat.

To cap it all, he'd maybe, just maybe, for the first time in his life, started to connect with his mother.

Chapter Thirty-Six

Mel was all over the place. She'd arrived back from France to find her house was a mess. True, it had been a mess when she'd left it, but now she'd added more chaos by dumping her unpacking – over a week's worth of washing and other assorted travel essentials – onto her living room floor.

All that had little to do with her current state of mental turmoil though. It was the call from Sally a few moments ago that had triggered it.

'Expect Aiden round in the next hour,' she'd baldly announced only moments after Mel had opened up her case and turned it upside down.

As Mel had stuttered a few unintelligible words, Sally had continued in her no-nonsense fashion. 'The guy's been out of his mind with worry, wondering where you were. I couldn't bear to listen to the agony in his voice any longer so I told him you were back. Suck it up, my friend. The least you owe him is an explanation.'

It didn't help knowing Sally was right. What she'd done to Aiden had been unforgivable. To run off on the greatest weekend of his life – how could she? Which was why she was now sitting numbly on the floor, surrounded by crumpled, dirty clothes, and feeling like the biggest bitch to have ever lived. And she still didn't know what she was going to do. The few days in France had only made her more confused. What she'd longed for was her parents to talk her muddled emotions through with, but she didn't have them. As kind as her grandparents had been, and as lovely as Nancy and Frank were to her, she now knew it was up to her to work out what she wanted in life. And if she was brave enough to go for it.

Half-heartedly she grabbed at some clothes, pushing them back into the case. How could she imagine herself being brave after the cowardly way she'd run out on Aiden?

The deep rumble of a car engine outside catapulted her heart into her throat. Oh God, he was here already. Helplessly she stuffed a few bras into the case but within moments the doorbell was ringing, its incessant tone telling her the man who was pressing it was mightily pissed off. With a despairing sigh she kicked at the remaining clothes, trying to hide them underneath the table. Why did he have to be here *now*, when it wasn't just her place that was rumpled and dishevelled. It was her, too.

As the bell mercilessly continued to ring Mel zipped into the downstairs cloakroom and studied her face. Thank God for the hint of a tan which hid some of the dark circles, reminders of nights spent staring at the ceiling, not wanting to close her eyes because every time she had, she'd see Aiden's face. After pushing a few stray strands of hair into her ponytail she took a deep breath and walked to the door.

Her fingers trembled as she fumbled with the lock, prolonging the agony.

She heard Aiden's impatient voice on the other side. 'Mel, will you hurry up and open the blasted door?'

Finally the lock clicked and the door swung open. They stared at each other for several long, long moments and all Mel's worries about her own appearance dissolved at the sight of his. If she looked tired, he looked ravaged. She'd never seen him look so drawn. All the vitality had drained out of him, leaving a handsome but empty shell.

'Aiden.' His name came from deep within her heart and

she flung her arms around his neck, holding him, savouring him. God, what had she done to this wonderful man?

His body remained stiff beneath hers, his arms held rigidly by his side. Slowly she pulled away.

'You left me.' His tone accused yet his eyes were bleak. A deserted moor on a cold, grey morning.

'I know. I'm so, so sorry.' She could hardly breathe her chest felt so tight. Suddenly she didn't need her parents to tell her what to do. *She knew.* Aiden was nothing like his father, nothing like Carlos. Though every inch a man on the outside, inside a large slice of him was still a boy who simply needed someone to love him.

'Why, Mel? In God's name, why did you run away?'

She reached for his tightly clenched hand and drew him into the house. 'Come in, sit down. I'll make us a drink and we'll talk.'

It was only when he came to an abrupt halt in her living room, blinking several times, that Mel remembered the mess.

'Did they take much?'

She stared back, puzzled.

'The guys who ransacked your house.'

The small smile that accompanied his attempt at humour was so tight tears welled in her eyes. How much damage had she done to them both?

'They didn't take anything,' she told him, stepping over a toiletry bag. 'Probably couldn't find anything valuable amongst all this clutter.'

His lips twitched but it was all too fleeting. The next moment he was sitting on her sofa, looking grim and distant. So very, very distant.

Fear seeped chillingly through her bones as she went through the motions of making the drinks. Now she'd finally woken up to what she wanted, was it too late? Had her careless treatment of him done irreversible damage?

He took the proffered mug without speaking. A clear signal; it was her turn to talk.

Clutching at her coffee she sat down next to him on the sofa and tried to work out where to begin. 'I got scared, Aiden. I guess the fear had always been there, right from the start. You knew that.'

'I knew that for some crazy reason you assumed I was going to get bored with you and go off and sleep with any, hell, maybe all the women who gave me their phone numbers.' He rubbed at his forehead, as if this whole conversation was giving him a headache. 'But I thought you'd come to your senses.'

'I told myself to stop being a coward, yes.' She reached up to touch his face. 'I fell in love with you, Aiden. I couldn't keep away.'

Aiden stared into Mel's gorgeous hazel eyes and nearly lost himself. *She loved him*? Or was that in the past tense. I fell in love, she'd said. Not I am in love. 'You had no trouble keeping away last week,' he reminded her roughly. 'In fact if I recall correctly, you *ran* away.' God that had hurt. More than anything else that had ever happened to him.

Tears spilt onto her cheeks and she reached for his hands, gripping them tightly with her dainty pair. 'I shouldn't have done that. It was so wrong, but it had been building up inside me. The doubts and fears that I wasn't ...' she trailed off as her voice started to break. 'I'd started to not feel important,' she began again after taking a drink. 'You couldn't take me driving – I know, not your fault,' she added quickly, 'but it had been such a milestone for me. Then you told me you didn't want me to stay with you in Brazil.'

'Oh, Mel.' He shook his head. 'This is where I need to apologise. I should never have done that. God knows, I'd have slept one heck of a lot better if you had stayed. But when Frank told me I wasn't focused, I knew he was right. That's when I came up with the not so clever idea of keeping you out of sight for a bit. You know, out of sight, out of mind. Of course it didn't work that way because you were always in my head.'

He squeezed gently at her fingers and she gave him a weak smile.

'That's good to know and anyway I understood, sort of. It hurt, but I could see the reasoning. Then the night of your victory party you didn't even make it back to my room.'

He switched their hands around so he was clutching hers. 'I told you, it wasn't through choice. I crashed out in the toilets, for crying out loud. You think I *wanted* to be on Frank's sofa rather than in bed with you?'

'No, I don't, but you have to see how it felt to me. Like you didn't need me.'

He groaned and did what he'd wanted to do ever since he'd seen her gorgeous, tanned face in the doorway. He put his arms around her, hugging her to him. 'I'll always need you, Mel,' he told her hoarsely. 'Always.'

'I hope so.' She dipped her head and snuggled into his chest, which felt blissfully good. 'The worst part was the conversation with your mother the night you won.'

'Ahh. Yes, she told me about that. But heck, Mel, you of all people should know I'm nothing like my bloody father.'

Her arms wrapped round his waist. 'I do know. It's just that when you were standing there next to your gleaming trophy, wearing your gleaming smile, not to mention your gleaming good looks, and surrounded by all that adulation, I forgot for a little while.'

He let out a snort of laughter, but quickly sobered up when he worked out what she was trying to say. 'You do know none of that is important, don't you? In a few years time I'll retire and the only people who'll be interested in me will be my wife, hopefully, and my children, hopefully again.'

Her body stilled beside him. 'So you plan on getting married then?'

Now or never. He plunged in. 'Yes. I've even got a ring. One I bought in San Paulo.'

Her head shot up. 'You bought one in San Paulo?'

'Yes.' His voice wasn't steady enough for his liking so he swallowed and started again. 'I was planning on using it to bribe a lady to marry me, but then she ran away.'

It felt as if his whole body was on a knife-edge. A nudge in one direction, ecstasy. A nudge the other way, grief and despair. Basically a lifetime of what he'd experienced last week.

'What ... what if she's decided not to run any more?' Mel asked huskily.

Bang went his heart. 'Then I'd drop down on one knee.' Gently he eased her away so he could kneel on the floor. He had to push a bra, crumpled T-shirt and pair of pants out of the way to do it, but even that made his heart sing. 'After that I'd tell her I love her. I'd stress to her that she is the most important thing ever to happen to me. That if I had to choose between her and winning the World Championship, I'd choose her every time. Then I'd ask her if she'd do me the honour of becoming my wife.'

Mel tried to blink back her tears but they were flowing too fast so she gave up. 'If it wasn't for the fact that you're kneeling amongst all my dirty clothes, I'd say that was the most romantic proposal I'd ever heard, and that the lady in question would be an absolute fool if she didn't throw her arms around you and kiss you till you fell over.' She moved forward, then stopped and grinned. 'After she'd said yes, of course.'

Then they were hugging and kissing and crying. Well, Mel was crying, she wasn't sure whether the wet on Aiden's cheeks was her tears or his but it didn't matter. He wanted to marry her.

'So let me get this straight,' she asked when they had to break away to breathe. 'Even when you were telling me I couldn't stay with you because you had to focus on winning, you were planning on proposing?'

'Yes. It's why I blew you out on our meeting. I thought I'd be able to dash out, buy a ring and come back in time, but choosing the flaming thing was harder than I thought.'

Her heart was going to explode, she thought dreamily. She'd been thinking the worst, that he was pulling away, but actually he'd been on a mission to bring them closer together. 'Do I get to see the item that caused you so much angst?'

Suddenly he was pulling her onto her feet. 'Have you got any clean clothes left?'

'I, umm, I don't know. Why?'

'Never mind. For what I've got in mind, you won't need any.'

With that he lifted her into his arms and started to stride towards the front door. 'Hey, wait up, where are you taking me?'

'To see the ring. I didn't bring it with me because ... well, I think you can guess.' He hadn't been sure of his reception. Her heart lurched and she clutched him tighter. 'So in order for you to see it, you'll have to come to my place.'

Within minutes they were zooming down the motorway. The only time Aiden let go of her hand was to phone Tom. 'Buddy, tell Mum I'm on my way back. I've got Mel with me. She wants to see her ring.'

Over the speaker Mel heard a loud whoop.

A second later she received a text from Tom. *Does this make you my big sister?*

Mel clutched the phone to her, laughing and crying at the same time. It seemed that overnight she'd found herself a new family.

'What's so funny?' Aiden demanded.

'I've never had a baby brother to torment before. I'm just thinking about all the things I can get up to.'

'You can forget about him for a while. I want you focusing on all the things you can get up to with me. At least for the first few decades.'

They shared a smile. And Aiden put his foot down hard on the accelerator.

Epilogue

There had been a time when staying in a hotel suite had been an oasis of calm for him. A place to escape from the press, the autograph hunters. The women. Now his room was positively teeming with people. But as Aiden surveyed the chaos around him, trying to summon up some irritation, all his mouth seemed to want to do was grin.

'I look bloody stupid.'

He turned to find his brother, now a gangly twelve, surveying himself in the mirror. 'Language, Tom. Especially in front of the ladies.'

Tom snorted. 'I don't see no ladies.'

'You don't see *any* ladies.'

His eyes gleamed. 'Exactly!'

Chuckling, Aiden shook his head. 'Funny boy.' As Tom wrestled with his tie, Aiden felt a twinge of sympathy for him. No twelve-year-old wants to wear a suit. 'You look smart, not stupid,' he remarked, grabbing hold of the tie. 'At least you would be if you ever learnt to dress properly.'

'I don't see why I have to wear a dumb suit.'

'Because everyone else will be smart. Because you're nearly a man now, not a kid. Because you're about to walk down a red carpet and attend a film premiere.'

'It's the cinema. Nobody wears a suit to the stupid cinema.'

'Well, they will tonight.'

Aiden fixed his brother's tie, smoothing down his collar. 'There you go. All set. Now all we have to do is wait for the women.'

Tom let out a dramatic sigh. 'That will take for-ev-er,' he announced slowly, making Aiden laugh again.

'Congratulations. You've already learnt a very important lesson when it comes to the fairer sex.'

'Hey.' Mel drifted in from the bedroom in a waft of something uniquely feminine. 'I'm ready on time.' She did a little twirl, the soft pink of her dress fluttering around her legs. 'What do you think?'

Before Aiden had a chance to speak, Tom gave his informed opinion. 'You look like Barbie.'

Mel narrowed her eyes at her brother-in-law, and Aiden was forced to stifle a grin. 'Tom, lesson number two. Always tell a lady she looks lovely. Always, no exception.'

'Even when she looks crap?'

Aiden winced. 'Yeah. Even if she's not looking her best, even if she thinks she looks bad.' Hastily he sidled up to his wife – God, it still killed him to think of Mel that way. 'But in this case it's easy to follow the rule because your sister-in-law looks absolutely stunning.' Aiden planted a kiss on her pink lips and whispered into her ear. 'It looks gorgeous on, but it'll be even more gorgeous when it's on our bedroom floor.'

She rolled her eyes at his admittedly rather clichéd line but before she could give him a hard time for it there was a sudden wail from a tiny, but very tough, pair of lungs. They both sighed.

'Grandma, sort Lizzie out will you?' Aiden bellowed.

Caroline poked her head around the bedroom door, mascara in hand, eyes looking daggers at him. 'I've told you before, I'm not Grandma. I'm Caro.'

Two years ago that would have been the start of an argument. Now mother and son shared an amused glance. It wasn't all plain sailing between them, but they were getting there.

Mel darted him a sly look. 'Stop palming your daughter off on your mother. You know it's you she wants.'

Aiden didn't bother to dispute the statement. It seemed his beautiful, incredibly precious little daughter had already wrapped him so far round her little finger he was a slave to her every need. He couldn't feed her, only Mel had the necessary equipment for that, but anything else he was game for. Reaching into her travel cot, his heart swelled as her chubby arms shot up and her pink cheeks creased in a smile. After shuffling her expertly against his shoulder, her favourite position, he ambled back to the other room where Tom was fidgeting around in his case.

'I can take my iPad, right, for when it gets boring?'

'Why is it going to be boring? It's a film about a famous racing driver, Tom. My father.'

'Duh, I know that, but are there guns? Robberies, shooting? Car chases round streets rather than a boring track?'

Aiden raised his eyes to the ceiling. 'I'm in it. Will that make it more interesting?'

'Depends what you're doing.'

For a moment Aiden was distracted by his wriggling daughter. Unable to resist, he rested his mouth on the dark fluff that constituted her hair. What was it about the smell of her that made him want to keep on kissing her tufty head?

'Are you racing in the film?'

Tom's prompt reminded him he hadn't answered his question. 'No, I'm talking.'

With a dramatic flourish, Tom pulled out his iPad. 'I'm definitely gonna need this then.'

They sat near the front row, holding hands, which made Mel smile. Aiden was an old-fashioned boy at heart, something she hadn't realised during their brief, slightly frantic courtship the season he'd won his first championship. It had been a whirlwind, in every sense, with Aiden so adamant he wanted a ring on her finger before she changed her mind – as if – that they'd been married within two weeks of their engagement. They hadn't spent a night apart since. It was hard to believe that once she'd doubted his love for her so much she'd run away. Now he seemed determined to show her that love every day. A private smile, a tender kiss, a caress when she least expected it. A grasp of her hand, as he was doing now.

'Bloody hell,' he muttered as across the screen flickered an old piece of cine footage showing Sebastian Foster standing by a kart track, hat and sunglasses on, watching a kart race. 'Seems he did watch me, after all.'

Hearing the rough emotion in his voice she reached to kiss his cheek, knowing how much it meant to him that his father had shown at least some interest, however small, in his son's early racing career.

'My part is coming up now,' he whispered.

Mel fixed her eyes back onto the screen. She didn't know what Aiden was about to say. When he'd asked her advice on it, she'd told him to be honest. Afterwards, when she'd asked him how it had gone, he'd given her his secret smile and told her she'd have to wait and see.

Suddenly his image filled the screen, and Mel felt a flush of pride. Her husband. More than handsome, he was dazzling.

When he started to talk about his childhood, she automatically tightened her grip on his hand. The camera picked up his clear grey eyes, unblinking when he admitted he hadn't actually seen much of his father. Heartbreakingly honest when he discussed how difficult he'd found it racing under his shadow.

'I used to envy my father his championship titles, and worry I'd never be as good,' his giant screen image confessed. 'And I won't be. I'll never emulate his incredible run of five titles, but now I realise racing's not my life. It's my job. An incredible one, yes, one I'm privileged to have, but there are more important things in the world, at least to me. I have a beautiful wife. A precious family. Anything I achieve after that is just icing on the cake.'

Tears flooded Mel's eyes and after giving his hand a massive squeeze, she rummaged for a tissue.

'Does that include me?' a small voice hissed from the other side of Aiden.

Aiden winked at Mel before turning to face his brother. 'Does what include you?'

'The precious family bit.'

'You spend at least half the year with me. What do you think?'

Tom gave his brother a satisfied nod. A moment later she heard his voice again, this time a bit louder. 'Where's the popcorn?'

Thank you

Thank you so much for taking the time to read *Before You*. The hero of this book, Aiden Foster, gets a thrill out of driving fast round a track. Me, I prefer a gentler pace. In fact I get a thrill simply from hearing that someone has enjoyed my book. I'm not alone in that. Authors love feedback — it can inspire, motivate, help us improve. So if you feel inclined to leave a review on Amazon, Goodreads or any of the retail sites, that would be really helpful.

Kathryn x

About the Author

Kathryn was born in Wallingford, England but has spent most of her life living in a village near Windsor. After studying pharmacy in Brighton she began her working life as a retail pharmacist. She quickly realised that trying to decipher doctors' handwriting wasn't for her and left to join the pharmaceutical industry where she spent twenty happy years working in medical communications. In 2011, backed by her family, she left the world of pharmaceutical science to begin life as a self-employed writer, juggling the two disciplines of medical writing and romance. Some days a racing heart is a medical condition, others it's the reaction to a hunky hero ...

With two teenage boys and a husband who asks every Valentine's Day whether he has to bother buying a card again this year (yes, he does) the romance in her life is all in her head. Then again, her husband's unstinting support of her career change goes to prove that love isn't always about hearts and flowers – and heroes can come in many disguises.

Before You is Kathryn's fourth novel with Choc Lit. Her other books include: *Too Charming*, *Do Opposites Attract?* and *Search for the Truth*.

For more information on Kathryn visit:
www.kathrynfreeman.com
www.twitter.com/KathrynFreeman1
www.facebook.com/kathrynfreeman

More Choc Lit

Too Charming

Does a girl ever really learn from her mistakes?

Detective Sergeant Megan Taylor thinks so. She once lost her heart to a man who was too charming and she isn't about to make the same mistake again – especially not with sexy defence lawyer, Scott Armstrong. Aside from being far too sure of himself for his own good, Scott's major flaw is that he defends the very people that she works so hard to imprison.

But when Scott wants something he goes for it. And he wants Megan. One day she'll see him not as a lawyer, but as a man ... and that's when she'll fall for him.

Yet just as Scott seems to be making inroads, a case presents itself that's far too close to home, throwing his life into chaos.

As Megan helps him pick up the pieces, can he persuade her that he isn't the careless charmer she thinks he is? Isn't a man innocent until proven guilty?

Search for the Truth

Sometimes the truth hurts …

When journalist Tess Johnson takes a job at Helix pharmaceuticals, she has a very specific motive. Tess has reason to believe the company are knowingly producing a potentially harmful drug and, if her suspicions are confirmed, she will stop at nothing to make sure the truth comes out.

Jim Knight is the president of research and development at Helix and is a force to be reckoned with. After a disastrous office affair he's determined that nothing else will distract him from his vision for the company. Failure is simply not an option.

As Tess and Jim start working together, both have their reasons for wanting to ignore the sexual chemistry that fires between them. But chemistry, like most things in the world of science, isn't always easy to control.

A Second Christmas Wish

Do you believe in Father Christmas?

For Melissa, Christmas has always been overrated. From her cold, distant parents to her manipulative ex-husband, Lawrence, she's never experienced the warmth and contentment of the festive season with a big, happy family sitting around the table.

And Melissa has learned to live with it, but it breaks her heart that her seven-year-old son, William, has had to live with it too. Whilst most little boys wait with excitement for the big day, William finds it difficult to believe that Father Christmas even exists.

But then Daniel McCormick comes into their lives. And with his help, Melissa and William might just be able to find their festive spirit, and finally have a Christmas where all of their wishes come true …

Available as an eBook on all platforms and will be available as a paperback from November 2017. Visit www.choc-lit.com for details.

Introducing Choc Lit